BLACK WINGS OF CTHULHU 2

Black Wings of Cthulhu 2

EIGHTEEN NEW TALES OF LOVECRAFTIAN HORROR

EDITED BY S. T. JOSHI

TITAN BOOKS

Black Wings of Cthulhu 2
Print edition ISBN: 9780857687845
E-book edition ISBN: 9780857687852

Published by Titan Books
A division of Titan Publishing Group Ltd
144 Southwark St, London SE1 0UP

First edition: February 2014
1 3 5 7 9 10 8 6 4 2

What did you think of this book? We love to hear from our readers.
Please email us at: readerfeedback@titanemail.com,
or write to us at the above address.

To receive advance information, news, competitions, and exclusive
offers online, please sign up for the Titan newsletter on our website:
www.titanbooks.com

WWW.TITANBOOKS.COM

CONTENTS

Introduction

S. T. JOSHI

HAT DEFINES A "LOVECRAFTIAN" STORY? THIS SEEMINGLY simple question is in fact full of ambiguities, perplexities, and paradoxes, for the term could encompass everything from the most slavish of pastiches that seek (usually unsuccessfully) to mimic Lovecraft's dense and flamboyant prose and mechanically replicate his gods, characters, and places, to tales that allusively draw upon Lovecraft's core themes and imagery, to parodies ranging from the affectionate (Fritz Leiber's "To Arkham and the Stars") to the faintly malicious (Arthur C. Clarke's "At the Mountains of Murkiness"). My goal in the *Black Wings* series has been to avoid the first at all costs and to foster the second and, to a lesser degree, the third. The days when August Derleth or Brian Lumley could invent a new god or "forbidden book" and therefore declare themselves as working "in the Lovecraft tradition" are long over. What is now needed is a more searching, penetrating infusion of Lovecraftian elements that can work seamlessly with the author's own style and outlook.

That being said, it becomes vital for both writers and readers to understand the essence of the Lovecraftian universe, and the literary tools he used to convey his aesthetic and philosophical principles. One of the great triumphs of modern Lovecraft scholarship has been to demonstrate that Lovecraft was an intensely serious writer who, as his letters and essays suggest, continually grappled with the central questions of philosophy and sought to suggest answers to them by means of horror fiction. What is our place in the cosmos? Does a god or gods exist? What is the ultimate fate of the human species? These and other "big" questions are perennially addressed in Lovecraft's fiction, and in a manner that conveys his "cosmic" sensibility—a sensibility that keenly etches humankind's transience and fragility in a boundless universe that lacks a guiding purpose or direction. At the same time, Lovecraft's intense devotion to his native soil made him something of a regionalist who vivified the history and topography of Providence, Rhode Island, and all of New England, establishing a foundation of unassailable reality from which his cosmic speculations could take wing.

How contemporary writers have adapted these and other central ideas and motifs into their own work is well demonstrated by the tales in this volume. Cosmic indifferentism is at the heart of Melanie Tem's "Dahlias," which does not require explicit horror, or the supernatural, to convey its effects. The uniquely topographical, even archaeological horror that we find in such a tale as *At the Mountains of Madness* is powerfully demonstrated in Richard Gavin's "The Abject" and Donald Tyson's "The Skinless Face." Tom Fletcher in some sense draws upon the claustrophobic horror that Lovecraft created in "The Dreams in the Witch House" in his unnerving tale, "View." Nicholas Royle's "The Other Man" is a searching and terrifying meditation on the theme of identity, a theme is that found in such of Lovecraft's tales as "The Outsider" and "The Shadow out of Time."

Alien incursion is at the heart of many Lovecraft tales, and

John Langan ("Bloom") and Jonathan Thomas ("The King of Cat Swamp") ring very different but equally engaging changes on this complex theme. Thomas's story is a clear nod, both in setting and in character, to Lovecraft's "The Call of Cthulhu," as are, in a very different manner, Jason C. Eckhardt's "And the Sea Gave Up the Dead" and Brian Evenson's "The Wilcox Remainder"; Caitlín R. Kiernan's "Houndwife" is a tip of the hat to "The Hound," and Nick Mamatas's "Dead Media" plays a riff on "The Whisperer in Darkness." But in all these cases, subtle character development of a sort that Lovecraft generally did not favour raises these tales far above the level of pastiche. A rent in the very fabric of the universe is at the heart of Darrell Schweitzer's inextricable fusion of fantasy and horror, "The Clockwork King, the Queen of Glass, and the Man with the Hundred Knives," while Steve Rasnic Tem's "Waiting at the Crossroads Motel" fuses setting and character in a tale whose cosmic backdrop is thoroughly Lovecraftian.

One of the most interesting developments in recent years—perhaps inspired by the mountains of information on Lovecraft's daily life and character that have emerged through the publication of his letters—is the degree to which Lovecraft himself has become a character, even an icon, in fiction. In very different ways, John Shirley's "When Death Wakes Me to Myself" and Rick Dakan's "Correlated Discontents" draws upon Lovecraft's own personal idiosyncrasies to convey terror and weirdness. The proliferation of Lovecraft's work in the media—especially film and television—is at the heart of Don Webb's "Casting Call" and Chet Williamson's "Appointed," tales that skirt the borderland of parody while remaining chillingly terrifying. Jason V Brock takes on Lovecraft's voluminous letter-writing directly with an epistolary tale that suggests far more than it tells.

The fact that writers of such different stripes have chosen

to work, however tangentially, in the Lovecraftian idiom is a testament to the vibrancy and eternal relevance of his central themes and concerns. As he memorably wrote, "We live on a placid island of ignorance in the midst of black seas of infinity, and it was not meant that we should voyage far." But it is the very purpose of the writer of fiction to venture, in imagination, beyond that placid island, and very often the result is a harrowing sense of our appalling isolation in the cosmic drift. Lovecraft himself spent a lifetime seeking to probe beyond the limitations of the human senses toward the vast cosmos-at-large, and it is evident that a growing cadre of writers are eager to follow him.

S. T. Joshi

When Death Wakes Me to Myself

JOHN SHIRLEY

John Shirley is the author of numerous novels, collections of stories—including the Bram Stoker Award-winning "Black Butterflies"—and scripts. His screenplays include The Crow. His newest novels are Demons (Del Rey, 2007), Black Glass (Elder Signs Press, 2008), Bleak History (Simon & Schuster, 2009), Bioshock: Rapture (Tor, 2011), and Everything Is Broken (Prime Books, 2011).

"SOMEONE'S BROKEN INTO THE HOUSE, DOCTOR."
Fyodor saw no fear in Leah's gray eyes. But he'd never seen her afraid, and she'd worked closely with him in psychiatrics for almost eight years—ever since he'd finished his internship. She brushed auburn hair from her pale forehead, adjusted her glasses, and went on, "The window latch is broken in your office—and I think I heard someone moving around down in the basement."

"Did you call the police?" Fyodor asked, glancing toward the basement door. His mouth felt dry.

They stood in the front hallway of the old house, by the open arch to the waiting room. "I did. I was about to call you, when you walked in."

They didn't speak for a long moment, both of them listening for the burglar. Wintry morning light angled through the bay windows of the waiting room, casting intricate shadows from the lace curtains across the braided rug. A dog barked down the street; a foghorn hooted. Just the sounds of Providence, Rhode Island...

Then a peal of happy laughter rippled up through the hardwood floorboards. It cut short so abruptly he wondered if he'd really understood the sound. "That sound like laughter to you?"

"Yes." She glanced at the window. "The police are in no hurry..."

"You should wait out front, Leah." He was thinking he should try to see to it that whoever this was, they weren't setting a fire, vandalizing, doing serious damage to the house. He was negotiating to buy it, planning to expand it into a suite of offices with various health services—especially bad timing for vandalism. It was a big house, built in 1825, most of it not in use at the moment. The ground-floor den was ideal for receiving patients; the front living room had been converted into a waiting room.

Fyodor took a step through the archway, into the hall—and then the basement door burst open. A slender young man stood there, a few paces away, holding a bottle in his hand, toothy grin fading. "Oh! I seem to have lost all track of time. How indiscreet of me," said the young man, in an accent that sounded Deep South. He wore a neat dark suit with a rather antiquated blazer, thin blue tie, starched white shirt, silver cufflinks, polished black shoes. His fingernails were immaculately manicured, his straight black hair neatly combed back. Fyodor noted all this with a professional detachment, but also a little surprise—he'd expected the burglar to be scruffier, more like the sullen young men he sometimes counseled at Juvenile Detention. The young man's dark brown eyes met his—the gaze was frank, the smile seemed genuine. Still, the strict neatness might place him in a recognizable spectrum of personality disorders.

"You seem lost," Fyodor said—gesturing, with his hand at his side, for Leah to go outside. Foolish protective instinct— she was athletic, probably more formidable in a fight than he was. "In fact, young man, you seem to have lost your way right through one of our windows…"

"Ah, yes." His mouth twitched. "But look what I found for you, Dr. Cheski!" He raised the dusty bottle in his hand. It was an old, unlabeled wine bottle. "I never used to drink. I wanted to take it up, starting with something old and fine. I want a new life. I desire to do things differently. Live! I bet you didn't know there was any wine down there."

Fyodor blinked. "Um… in fact…" In fact he didn't think there *was* any wine in the basement.

A siren wailed, grew louder—and cut short. Radio voices echoed, heavy boot-steps came up the walk, and the young man, sighing, put the bottle on the floor and walked past Fyodor to open the front door. He waved genially at the policemen.

"Gentlemen," said the young man, "I believe you are here for me. I'm told that my name is Roman Carl Boxer."

ARRYING THE DUSTY WINE BOTTLE, FYODOR DESCENDED the basement steps, wondering if this Roman Carl Boxer could have been a patient, someone he'd consulted on, at some point. The face wasn't familiar, but perhaps he'd been disheveled and heavily acned before. *I'm told that my name is Roman Carl Boxer.* Interesting way to put it.

The basement was a box of cracked concrete, smelling of mildew; a little water had leaked into a farther corner. A naked light bulb glowed in the cobwebbed ceiling, bright enough to throw stark shadows from what looked like rodent droppings, off to his left. To the right were his crates of old files, recently stored here—they seemed undisturbed. He saw no wine bottles. He could smell dirt and damp concrete. A few scuffs marked the dust coating the floor.

Fyodor started to turn back—it was not a pleasant place to be—but he decided to look more closely at the files. There was confidential patient information in those crates. If this kid had gotten into them...

He crossed to the files, confirmed they seemed undisturbed— then saw the hole in the floor, in the farther corner. A small shiny crowbar, the price sticker still on it, lay close beside the hole. His view of it had been blocked by the crates.

He crouched by the hole—almost two feet square—and saw that a trapdoor of concrete and wood had been removed to lean against the wall. He could make out a number of dark bottles, down inside it, in wooden slots. Wine bottles.

One slot was empty. The bottle he'd brought with him fit precisely in that slot.

WEEK LATER.

"Deal's done," Fyodor said, with some excitement, as he came into the waiting room. He took off his damp coat, hanging it up, sniffling, his nose stinging from the cold, wet wind. "I own the building! Me and the bank do, anyway."

"That's great!" Leah said, the corners of her eyes crinkling with a prim smile. She was hanging a picture on the waiting room wall. It was a print of a Turner seascape: vague, harmless proto-Impressionism in gold and umber and subtle blues; a choice that suggested sophistication, and soothing to psychiatric patients. Still, some psychiatric patients were capable of feeling threatened by anything.

Leah stepped back from the painting, and nodded.

Fyodor thought it was hanging just slightly crooked, but he knew it would irritate her if he straightened it—though she'd only show the irritation as a faint flicker around her mouth. Surprising how well he'd gotten to know her, and, at the same time, how impersonal their relationship was. A professional distance was appropriate. But it didn't *feel* appropriate somehow, with Leah…

"That police detective called," she said, straightening the painting herself. "Asking if we're going to come to the arraignment for that burglar."

"I'm not inclined to press charges."

"Really? They've let him out on bail, you know. He might come back."

"I don't want to start my new practice here by prosecuting the first mentally ill person I run into." He went to the bay windows and looked out at the wet streets, the barren tree limbs of the gnarled, blackened elm in the front yard. Leafless tree limbs always made him think of nerve endings.

"He hasn't actually been diagnosed…"

"He was confused enough to climb in through a window, ignore everything of value, go down to the basement and dig about."

"Did you have that wine looked at? The stuff he found downstairs?"

Fyodor nodded. "Hal checked it out. Italian wine, from the early twentieth century, shipped direct from some vineyard—and not improved with age. Gone quite vinegary, he told me." How had Roman Boxer known the wine was there? It seemed to have been sealed up for decades.

Something else bothered him about the incident, something he couldn't quite define, a feeling there was something he should recognize about Roman Boxer… just out of reach.

"Oh—you got approval for limited testing of SEQ10. The letter's on your desk. There are some regulatory hoops but…"

SEQ10. They'd been waiting almost a year. Things were coming together.

He turned to face Leah, feeling a sudden rush of warmth for her. It was good to have her on his team. She was always a bit prim, reserved, her wit dry, her feelings controlled. But sometimes…

"And," she said a little reluctantly, going to the waiting room desk, "your mom called."

She passed him the message. *"Please call. The psycho Psych Tech is at it again."*

His mother: the fly in the ointment, ranting about the psychiatric technician she imagined was persecuting her in the state hospital. But then she was the reason he'd gotten into psychiatry. Her mania, her fits of amnesia. His own analyst had suggested she was also some of the reason he tended to be rather reserved, wound tight—compensating for his mother's flamboyance. She was flamboyant on the upswings, almost catatonic on the downswings—prone to amnesia. Firm self-control helped him deal with either extreme. And her intervals of amnesia had prompted his interest in SEQ10.

The doorbell rang, and he went to his office to await the first patient of the day. But his first patient wasn't the first person to arrive. Instead, Leah ushered in a small middle-aged woman with penciled eyebrows, dark red lipstick, a little too much rouge, her black hair tightly caught up in a bun. She wore a pink slicker, her rose-colored umbrella dripping on the carpet as she said, "I know I shouldn't come without an appointment, Doctor Cheski..." Her cadences tripped rapidly, her voice chirpy, the movements of her head, as she looked back and forth between Fyodor and Leah, seemed birdlike. "But he was so insistent—my son Roman. He said I had to see him *here* or not at all, and then he hung up on me. God knows he's been a lot of trouble to you already. Has he gotten here yet?"

"Here? Today?" Fyodor looked at Leah. She shrugged and shook her head.

"He said he'd be upstairs..."

There was a thump from the ceiling. Squeaking footsteps; brisk pacing, back and forth.

Leah put a hand to her mouth and laughed nervously. Quite uncharacteristic of her. "Oh my gosh, he's broken into the house again."

Roman's mother looked back and forth between them. "Not again! I thought he'd made an appointment! He said he didn't trust anyone else... He barely knows *me*, you see..." Her lips trembled.

Leah's brows knit. "Did you—give him up for adoption?"

Another thump came from above. They all looked at the

ceiling. "No-o," Mrs. Boxer said, slowly. "No, he… claims to *not remember* growing up with us. With his own family! I show him photographs—he says they're 'sort of familiar.' But he says it's like it didn't happen to *him*. I don't really understand what he means." She sighed and went quickly on, "He just keeps wandering around Providence—*looking* for something… but he won't say what."

Fyodor knew he should call the police. But when Leah went to the phone, he said, "Wait, Leah." *Claims to not remember growing up with us. With his own family.*

SEQ10 was a hypnotic drug for treating, among other things, hysterical amnesia.

Fyodor looked at Mrs. Boxer. She had some very high-quality jewelry; new pumps, sensible but elegant. A rather showy diamond bulked on her wedding ring. She had money, after all. She could pay for therapy. Insurance wouldn't cover SEQ10.

Fyodor took a deep breath, and, wiping his clammy palms on his trousers, went up the stairs.

He found Roman in the guest room right over the office. Roman was sitting on the edge of the four-poster bed, nervously turning a glass of wine in both hands, around and around—he'd put the wine in a water tumbler from the upstairs bathroom.

"Brought your own wine this time, I see," Fyodor said.

"Yes. A California Merlot. Still trying to learn how to drink." Roman smiled apologetically. He wore the same suit as last time. Neat as a pin. "Strange sensation, alcohol." After a moment he added, "Sorry about the door. No one was here when I came. I needed to get in."

Fyodor grunted. He planned to rent the room out as an office, and now this guy was damaging it—the door to the outside stairs stood open, the wood about the lock splintered. There was a large screwdriver on the bedside table.

"Why?" Fyodor asked. "I mean—why the urgency about

getting in? Why not make an appointment?"

Roman swirled his wine. "I'm... looking for something here. I just—couldn't wait. I don't know why."

T WAS AN EVENING SESSION, AFTER FYODOR WOULD normally have gone home. Roman's mother had already had the broken door replaced and paid a large advance on the therapy. And Roman was more interesting than most of Fyodor's patients.

Leaning back on the leather easy chair in Fyodor's office, Roman seemed bemused. Occasionally, he smoothed the lines of his jacket.

"Your mother gave me some background on you," Fyodor said. "Maybe you can tell me what seems true or untrue to you."

He read aloud from his notes.

Roman was twenty-one. An only child, he'd had night terrors until he was nine, with intermittent bedwetting. Father passed on when he was thirteen. They weren't close. Roman had difficulty keeping friends but was likable, and elderly people loved him. He loved cats, but his mother made him stop adopting them after he accumulated four. One died, and he gave it an elaborate burial ritual. Good student in high school, at first, friends mostly with girls—but no girlfriends. Not terribly interested in sex. Bad last year in high school when some sort of Internet bullying took a more personal form. Reluctant to talk about it. Refused to attend the school. Finished with home schooling, GED. Two years of college, attendance quite patchy. Autodidact for the most part. Tendency to have unusual difficulty with cold weather. No close friends "except in books."

"All that sound right to you, Roman?" Fyodor asked, getting his laptop into word processing mode.

Roman looked vaguely about him. "Not very flattering,

is it? Sounds like someone I *knew*—but it doesn't feel like it happened to me personally. *Apparently* it's me."

Fyodor typed in his laptop, *Possible dissociation due to unacceptable self-image.*

"But since last year—your memories seem like… you?"

"Yes—since last year. All that seems real. I can't remember anything before that unless somebody reminds me, and then it's… like remembering an old television episode. Except I can't really remember those either…"

Roman's eyes kept wandering to the Victorian fixture hanging from the ceiling. "That fixture's been here a hundred years."

"I would have thought it's older than that, really, as this house was built in the early nineteenth century," Fyodor said absently, adjusting his laptop to make sure Roman couldn't see what he was typing.

"No," Roman said firmly. "Installed early twentieth century. But it was made in the nineteenth."

Fyodor made a note: *Possible grandiosity? Faux expertise syndrome?* "Your mother says you feel your name is not Roman. Although she showed you a birth certificate. Do you feel the birth certificate is…"

"Is faked, unreal—part of a conspiracy?" Roman chuckled. "Not at all! What I said was, I *feel* my name is not Roman. I answer to it for simplicity's sake. And as for what my name really is—I truly don't know. Roman Boxer is correct—and incorrect. But don't waste your time asking why that is, I don't have an answer for you."

"And this started when you took a walk on a beach…"

"Yes. Last September. We went to Sandy Point. Myself and… well… *Mother.* She has a little place at Sandy Point… so I have learned. My real memories start—really, as soon as I *arrived* on the beach that day. Before that I don't remember much. She's prompted a few memories, but…" He cleared his throat. "Well, I was feeling odd from the moment I stepped onto the sand." He smiled dourly. "Not 'feeling myself.' And then—it'll take some telling…"

"Tell me the story."

Roman brightened. "Now *that* I enjoy. I've got half a dozen notebooks filled with my stories. But this one is true. Very well: It was a fine Indian Summer afternoon. I was in the mood to be alone… this woman who insists she's my mother—even then, she often put me in that mood… so I went out to Napatree Point. Big sandy spit of land, you know. The sea looked blue, fluffy clouds scudding in the sky, a real postcard picture. Just me and the gulls. Now, I don't much care for walks by the beach. Rather dislike looking at the unidentifiable things that wash up there. And the smell of the sea—like the smell of some giant animal. I'd rather go to the library. But I keep hearing people talk about how *inspirational* the sea is. I keep looking to *connect* with that Big Something out there. So I was walking on the beach, trying to shake the odd feeling of inner dislocation—I *did* manage to appreciate the way the light comes through the top of the waves and makes them look like blue glass. I shaded my eyes and gazed way out to sea, trying to see all the way to the horizon—and I got this strange feeling that something was *looking back* at me from out there."

Fyodor repressed a smile, and typed, *Enjoys dramatization.*

"All of a sudden I felt like a giddy little kid. Then I had a strange impulse—it just charged up out of my depths. I felt it go right up my spine and into my head, and I was yelling, 'Hey out there!'" Roman cupped his hands to either side of his mouth, mimicking it. "'Hey! I'm here!' I don't know, I guess I was just being spontaneous, but I felt truly very impish…"

Fyodor typed: *Odd diction, archaic vocabulary at times. It comes and goes. Possibly clinically labile? Showing agitation as he tells the story.*

"…and I yelled 'I'm here, come back!' and it's funny how my own voice was echoing in my ears and a *response* just came into my head from nowhere: *They tolled—but from the sunless tides that pour…* And I yelled that phrase out loud! I'm not sure why. But I'll never forget it."

Auditory hallucination, Fyodor typed. *Feelings of compulsion.*

Roman squirmed in his chair, licked his lips, went on. "It was a curious little thing to think—like an unfinished line of poetry, right?"

Use of antiquated expressions comes and goes: e.g., curious. Affectation?

"And as soon as I said it I heard gigantic big bells ringing, like the biggest church bells you ever heard—and it sounded like they were coming from under the sea! A little muffled, and watery, but still powerful. It got louder and louder, the sound was so loud, it hurt my head, like I was getting *slapped* with each clang of the bell, and each time it rang it was as if the sea, the stretch of the sea in front of me, got a little *darker*, and pretty soon it *just went black*—the whole sea had turned black…"

Hallucinogenic episodes, possible seizure—drug use?—

"…And no, I don't use drugs, doctor! I can see you thinking it!" He smiled nervously, straightening his tie. "Never have got into drugs! Oh fine, a few puffs on a bong once or twice—barely felt it."

Fyodor cleared his throat—strangely congested, it was difficult to speak at first—and asked, "This vision of the sea turning black—did you fall down during it? Lose control of your limbs?"

"No! Well… I didn't *fall*." Roman licked his lips, sitting up straight, animated with excitement. "It was as if I was *paralyzed* by what I was seeing. The blackness sucking up the ocean was holding me fast, you see. But it was really not so much that the sea was turning black—it was that the sea was *gone*, and it was replaced by a… a night sky! A dark sky full of stars! I was looking down into the sea, but in some other way I was gazing *up* into this night sky! My stomach flip-flopped, I can tell you! I saw constellations you never heard of, twinkling in the sea—galaxies in the sea!—and one big yellow star caught my eye. It seemed to grow bigger, and bigger, and it got closer—till it filled up my vision. Then, silhouetted on it, was this black ball… a planet! I rushed closer to it—I could see down into its atmosphere. I saw warped buildings, you could hardly believe they were able to stand up, they seemed so crooked, and cracked domes, and pale things without faces flying over them—and I thought, that is the world called…" He shook his head, lips twisted. "Something like… *Yegget*? Only not that. I can't remember the name precisely." Roman shrugged, spread his hands, and then laughed. "I know how it sounds. Anyway—I was gazing at this planet from above and I heard this… this *sizzling* sound. Then there was a flash of light—and I was back on the beach. I felt a little dizzy, sat down for awhile, kept trying to remember how I'd gotten to that beach. Could not remember, not then. The memory of what I'd seen in the sea, the black sky—*that* was vivid. And what was before that? Arriving at the beach. Notions of escaping from some bothersome person."

"Nothing before then?"

"An image. A place: I was lying in a small bed, in a white room, with this sweet little nurse holding my hand. Remembering it, I had a yearning, a *longing* for that bed, that nurse—that white room. For the comfort of it. I could almost hear her speak.

"Then, on the beach, I felt this scary *buzzing* in my pocket! I thought I had a snake in there, and I was clawing at it, and then… something fell out. This shiny, silvery, petite machine fell onto the ground. It was buzzing and shaking in the sand like it was mad. I could see it was some kind of instrument—a device. It seemed strange and familiar, both at the same time, right? So I had to think about how to make it work and I opened it and I heard this tiny voice saying, 'Roman, Roman are you there?' It was the… it was my mother." He stared into the distance. His voice trailed off. "My mother."

"But you didn't recognize the thing as a cell phone?"

"After she spoke, I remembered—but it was like something from a science-fiction movie I'd seen. *Star Trek*. I couldn't recall buying the thing."

Fyodor made a few notes and nodded. "And since then— the persistent long-term memory issues, your own name seeming unfamiliar. And you had feelings of restlessness?"

"Restlessness. An inner… goading." Roman settled back in the chair, staring up at the antique light fixture. "I would have trouble sleeping. I'd go out before dawn for these long rambles… in the old section of Providence—with its mellow, ancient life, the skyline of old roofs, Georgian steeples…"

Archaic affectations cropping up more frequently as patient reminisces.

"You said you felt like you were looking for something—?"

"Correct. And I didn't know what. Just this feeling of 'It's right around the next corner, or maybe around the next one' and so on. Till one day—I was there! I was standing in front of this house, looking at your sign. It was closed—I took a cab to a Target store, just opening for the day. I bought a little crowbar. Went back to the house—the rest is history. I still don't know exactly what it is about this house. You just bought the place, right? How'd you find it, doc?"

"Oh, my mother suggested it to me, actually. She was in real estate before she…" Fyodor broke off. Not good to talk about personal matters with a patient. "So—anything else? We're about out of time."

"Your mother! She was *committed*, right?" Roman grinned mischievously. "The inspiration for your career! And you an only child, too, like me—imagine that!"

Fyodor felt a chill. "Uh—exactly how—"

"Don't get spooked, doc," Roman chuckled. "It's the Internet. I googled you! The paper you wrote for the Rhode Island Psychiatric Association—it's online. Tough childhood with sick mother led you to want to understand mental illness…"

Fyodor kept his expression blank. It annoyed him when a patient tried to turn the tables on him. "Okay. Well. Let's digest all this." He saved his notes and closed his laptop.

"No therapeutic advice for me, Doctor Cheski?"

"Yes. Something behavioral. Don't commit any more burglaries."

Roman came out with a harsh laugh at that.

OMAN BOXER WENT HOME WITH THE WOMAN HE doubted was his mother. Fyodor watched through a window as they got into her shiny black Lincoln.

An unstable young man. Perhaps a dangerous young man—researching his doctor's background, breaking into his office… twice. He should not be seen here…

Roman refused to be committed. *"I won't take those horrible psychiatric meds. I don't wish to be a zombie. I'll just run off, end up back here again. This is the place. It took me a long time, wandering around Providence, to find it. I know, Mom says I never lived here. But I was happy here once. I have to get help right here…"*

Roman and his mother were both amenable to the use of SEQ10, to search out the core trauma, since it was something the patient only took on a temporary basis, with the doctor in the room. There were forms to be filled out, approval from the APA.

Fyodor went to his office, feeling restless himself. He wished he'd tucked a bottle of brandy away in the house. But he was trying to keep his drinking down to a dull roar.

Too bad the wine in the basement was off. Be crazy to drink the stuff anyway...

E PUTTERED AT HIS DESK, ORGANIZING HIS COMPUTER files, sending out e-mails to colleagues who might want to rent office space. Making the occasional note on Roman Boxer. The late November wind hissed outside; the windows rattled, the furnace vents rumbled and oozed warm air. He wished he'd asked Leah to work late. The big old house felt so empty it seemed to mutter to itself every time the wind hit it.

About 9:30, Fyodor's cell phone vibrated in his pants pocket, making him jump. Like a snake.

Fyodor reached into his jacket and fumbled the phone out—his hands seemed clumsy tonight. "Hello?"

"You forgot me..." It was his mother's smoky voice—a bad connection, other voices oscillating in and out of a sea of static in the background.

"Mom. How did I...? Oh. It's that night?" It was his mother's night to call him. She must have called his home first.

"You bought the house..."

"Yes—thanks for the tip. I sent you a note about it. You've got a good memory. So long ago you were selling houses. I'm hoping if I can rent out the other rooms as offices it'll more than pay for the mortgage... You still there? This connection..."

"I was born..." Her voice was lost in the crackle. "...1935."

"Right, I remember you were born in 1935—"

"In that house. I was Catholic. Lived there till I got married. Your father was Russian Orthodox. Father Dunn did not approve. Father Dunn died that year..." Her voice sounded flat. But it was difficult to make out at all.

He frowned. "Wait—you were born in *this* house? I'm sure you showed me a house you were born in—it was in Providence, but... it was an old wreck of a place... I don't recall where... I was a kid... But then the agent said they restored it..." Could this really be that house?

"...*Through sunken valleys on the sea's dead floor,*" she said, as the wind howled at the window.

"What?"

The phone on his desk rang. He jumped a little in his seat and said, "Wait, Mom..."

He put the cell phone down, answered the desk phone. "Dr. Cheski..."

"Fyodor? You weren't at home... here you are!" It was his mother. Coming in quite clearly. On this line. "You need to talk to that psycho Psych Tech, he's following me around the ward..."

Sleet rattled the window glass. "Mom... You playing games with their phones there? You get hold of a cell phone? You're not supposed to have one."

On impulse he picked up the other phone. "Hello?"

"*They tolled but from sunless tides...*" Then it was lost in static—but it did sound like his mother's voice, in a kind of dead monotone.

Monotone—and now a dial tone. She'd hung up.

He put the cell phone slowly down, picked up the other line. "What, Mom, have you got a phone pressed to each ear?"

"You sound more like a patient than a psychiatrist, Fyodor. I'm trying to tell you that the 'Psycho' Tech who claims he works here is... What?" She was speaking to someone in the room with her now. "The doctor said I could call my son... I *did* call earlier; he wasn't at home..." A male voice in the background. Then a man came on the line, a deep voice. "Is that Dr. Cheski? I'm sorry, doctor, she's not supposed to use the phone after eight. I could ask the night nurse—"

"No, no, that's all right—does she have a cell phone too? It seemed like she was calling me on two lines."

"What? No, she shouldn't have one... Oh, there she goes, I have to deal with this, doctor... But don't worry, it's no big problem, just her evening rant, yelling at Norman..."

"Sure, go ahead."

He hung up. Picked up the cell phone. Put it to his ear. Nothing there. He checked to see what number had called him last. The last call was from Leah, two days before.

EXT MORNING, A COLD BUT SUNNY WINTER DAY, Fyodor dropped by the ward, at the facility across town. A bored supervisory nurse waved him right in. "She's in the activities room."

His mom wore an old Hawaiian-pattern shift and red plastic sandals, her thin white hair up in blue curlers; her spotted hands trembled, but they always did, and she seemed happy enough, playing cards with an elderly black woman. Someone on a television soap opera muttered vague threats in the background.

"Mother, that house you suggested to Aunt Vera for me—did you say you were born there?"

Mom barely looked up when he spoke to her. "Born there? I was. I didn't say so, but I was. Don't cheat, Maisy. You *know* you cheat, girl. I never do."

"Did you call me twice last night, Mom? Talk to me twice, I mean?"

"Twice? No, I—but there was something funny with the phone, I remember. Like it was echoing what I said, getting it all mixed up. Hearts, Maisy!"

"You remember reciting poetry on the phone? Something about tides?"

"I haven't recited poetry since that time at Jimmy Dolan's. Your Dad got mad at me because I climbed up on the bar and recited Anais Nin… What are you laughing at, Maisy, you never got up on a bar? I bet you did too. Just deal the cards."

He asked how things were going. She shrugged. For once she didn't complain about Norman the Psych Tech. She seemed annoyed he'd interrupted her card game.

He patted her shoulder and left, thinking he must have misheard something on the cell phone. Perhaps some kind of sales recording.

Suggestion. The lonely house, the odd story from Roman. Auditory hallucination?

It wasn't likely he'd be bipolar like his mother—he was thirty-five, he'd have had symptoms long before now. He was fairly normal. Yes, he had a little phobia of cats, nothing serious…

He got back to the office a few minutes late for his first patient. He had six patients scheduled that day; four neurotics, one depressive, and a compulsive finger biter. He listened and advised and prescribed.

A few days later—after Roman signed numerous waivers— Fyodor was sitting beside Roman's bed, in the guest room, with its repaired lock, waiting for the drug to take hold of his patient.

Roman was lying on the coverlet, eyes closed, though he was awake. He looked quite relaxed. He wore a T-shirt and creased trousers, his blazer and tie and Arrow shirt folded neatly over a chair nearby, the shiny black shoes squared under it. His arms were crossed over his chest; his mother had provided the warm slippers on his feet. There was a small bandage on his right arm, where he'd been injected. The furnace was working full-bore, at Roman's request, and the room was too warm for Fyodor's liking.

On a cart to one side was the tape recorder for the session, a used syringe, and the little tray with the prepared syringes for adverse reactions. Superfluous caution.

Leah entered softly, caught Fyodor's eye, and nodded toward downstairs, silently mouthing, "His mother?"

Fyodor shook his head decisively. No monitoring mothers. Roman was of age.

"I do feel a pleasant... oddness," Roman murmured, his eyes fluttering as Leah left the room.

"Good," Fyodor said. "Just relax into that. Let it wash over you." He switched on the tape recorder, aimed the microphone.

"I feel... sort of thirsty." His eyes closed; his hands dropped loose, occasionally twitching, at his sides.

"That will pass... Roman, let's go back to that experience by the ocean, a little over a year ago. You said after that, you were remembering a white room, with a nurse. Could we talk about that again?"

"I..."

"Take your time."

"...She holds my hand. That's what I remember about her. The soft pressure of her hand. Trouble breathing—a pressure, a pushing inside me, crowding my lungs. And then—my very last breath! I remember thinking, Is this indeed my last breath? Gods, the pain in my belly is returning, the morphine is wearing off... They say it's intestinal cancer, but I wonder... Perhaps I should try to tell the nurse about the heightened pain. She's sweet, she won't think me a whiner. The others here are more formal, but she calls me Howard... I feel closer to her than I ever did to Sonia... my own little Jewish wife, ha ha, to think I married a Jew, and my closest friend, for a time, before he got the religion bug, was Dear Old Dunn, a Mick... I want to raise the nurse's hand to my lips, to thank her for staying with me. But I can't feel her hand anymore. I'm floating over her... There's a voice, an inhuman guttural voice, calling me from above the ceiling—above the roof. Above the sky. I *must ignore it*. I must go away from there, to find something, something to anchor me safely in this world... I want to tell my friends I am all right... I drifted, drifted, found myself in front of Dunn's house... There is a cat, heavy with pregnancy, curled up under the big elm tree. I love cats. Feel drawn to her. That calling comes again, from the deep end of the sky. I need to anchor. *The cat*. I fall... fall into her. The warm darkness... then sounds, the scent of her milk and her soft belly... light!... and I remember exploring. I was exploring the yard... the big tree, overshadowing me, days pass, and I grow... the sweet mice scurrying to escape me..."

Fyodor had to lean close to hear him.

"Oh! The mice taste sweeter when they almost escape! And the birds—they seem happy to die under my claws. Their eyes, like gems... the light goes out... the gems fall into eternity... mingle with stars... I can scarcely think—but my body *is* my thought as I patrol the night. I pour myself through the shadows. The other cats—I avoid them, most of the time. If I feel the urge to mate, I go into the house... this house!... through the back door... the girl lets me in... I know what a girl is, what people are, I remember that much. I know there is food and comfort there. I rub against the girl's legs, climb onto her lap. I will let my embers smolder here. She admires my golden eyes. The girl tells her mother, and Father Dunn, who has come to visit, that the cat understands everything she says. When she says follow, the cat follows. She tells them, 'I think it understands me right now! It is not like other cats...'"

Fyodor shook his head. This was not going as planned. Roman should be incapable of fantasizing under the influence of this drug; the formula was related to sodium pentothal, but more definitive; it had a tendency to expose onion-layers of memories, real memories... but a memory of being a cat?

Was Roman remembering a childhood incident in which he'd *imagined* being a cat?

"How…" Fascinated, Fyodor cleared his throat, aware his heart was thudding. "How far back do you remember… before the white room—and before the cat?"

Roman moaned softly. "How far… how *deep*… the night-gaunts… I have come to this house to see Dunn. Of all my friends in the Providence Amateur Press Club, he was the one I trusted the most. Curious, my trusting a Mick—I sometimes sneer at the Irish in the North End, but even so, I love to work with dear old Dunn on his little printing press, in the basement of that magnificently musty old house. I am even tempted to take him up on the wine his father kept in that hidey-hole down there. But I never do. Dunn loves to cadge a little wine from his father's bottles. Makes up the difference in grape juice. The old Irish rogue conceals the bottles from his wife, she doesn't like him drinking… wine from Italy, a local Italian priest got for him… dear old Dunn! I even ghostwrote a little speech he made… ghostwriter, wondrous and most whimsical to think of that term, considering how long I wandered, here, from house to house in Providence, afraid of the Great Deep that yawned above me when I breathed my last. Gone. Did anyone notice?" He made a soft rasping moan. "What will people remember of me? If anything they'll remember the intellectual sins of my youth. But why *should* people remember me? I'm sure they won't… If I could tell them what I saw that day, on my trip to Florida! Getting out of the bus, on the South Carolina coast, an interval in the bus trip… my last real trip, in 1935 it was… driver told us the bus would be delayed more than an hour… there's time to visit the lighthouse on the point near the station. Determined to get to know the ocean. Wanting to go against my own grain. But you can't grow the same tree twice. Yet I writhe about, trying to change the pattern. I will go to sea, until I make peace with its restless depths. Despite what I told Wandrei—or because of it. I'll show them I'm more than the polysyllabic phobic they think me. Found the lighthouse—tumbledown old structure, seems to have been fenced off... a broken spire... what a shame... there's been a storm, I can see the wrack from the sea mingled with its ruins... the breakers have shattered the lower, seaward wall of the lighthouse... there, is that a hollow beneath it? I clamber over fence, over slimed stones, drawn by the mystery, the possibility of revealed antiquity... Perhaps the lighthouse was built on some old colonial structure... Look here, a hollow, a cobwebbed chamber, and within it a sullen pool of black water—its opacity broken by a coruscation of yellow. What could be glowing, sulfurous yellow, within the water of a pool hidden beneath a lighthouse? It's as if the lighthouse had one light atop and a diabolic inverse sequestered beneath. There, I stare into it and I see... something I've glimpsed only in dreams! The tortured spires, the cracked domes, the flyers without faces... I'm teetering into it... I'm falling—swallowing salt water. Something writhes in the water as I swallow it. An eel? An eel without a physical body. Yet it nestles within me, biding, whispering...

"Darkness. Walking...

"Back on the bus, looking fuzzily about me. How *did* I make my way back to the bus? Cannot remember. The driver solicitous, asking, 'You sure you're all right, sir? You're wet clear through.' I insist I'm well enough. I take a few minutes to change my clothes in the station restroom. The other passengers are exasperated with me, I'm delaying them even further. I feel quite odd as I return to the bus. Must have struck my head, exploring that old lighthouse. Had a dream, a nightmare—can't quite remember what it was... dream of something crawling into my mouth, worming through my stomach, down to my intestines... something without a body as we know them...

Quite exhausted. I fall asleep in my seat on the bus and when I wake, we're in northern Florida."

Fyodor glanced at the tape recorder to make sure it was going. Had he administered the drug wrongly? This could not be a memory—Roman could not possibly remember 1935. Still, it was surely a doorway into Roman's unconscious mind. A powerful mind—a writer's mind, perhaps. A narrative within a narrative, not always linear; a nautilus shell recession of narrative...

Eyes shut, lids jittering, Roman licked his lips and went hoarsely on. "...trip to Cuba canceled but still—Florida! Saw alligators in the sluggish green river—seemed to glimpse a slitted green eye and within that eye a sulfurous light shining from some black sky... A great many letters to write on the bus back, handwriting can scarcely be legible... oh, the pain. In the midst of my midst, how it chews away. Cursed as always with ill health. Getting my strength in recent years, discovering the healing power of the sun, and then this—the old flaw chews at me from within now. I fear seeing the doctor. Nor can I afford him. Little but tea and crackers to eat today... can't bear much more anyway, the pain in my gut... I seem to be losing weight... R.E.H. is dead! Strange to think of 'Two-Gun Bob' taking his own life that way. He should have been a swordsman, striking the life from the faceless flyers when they struck at him in some dire temple—not muttering about his Texas neighbors, not stabbed through the soul by his mother's passing. We should not be what we are—we were *all* intended to be something better. But we were planted in tainted soil, R.E.H. and I, tainted souls blemished by the color out of space. I wrote from my heart but my heart was sheathed in dark yellow glass, and its light was sulfurous. So much more I wanted to write! A great novel of generations of Providence families, their struggles and glories, their dark secrets and heroics! I can be with them, perhaps, when I die—I will become one with the old houses of

Providence, wandering, searching for its secrets… And I refuse to leave Providence, when I gasp my last…

"The sweet little nurse takes my hand, more tenderly than ever Sonia did. But God bless Sonia, and her infinite patience. If only… but it's too late to think of that now. The nurse is speaking to me, *Howard, can you hear me?… I believe we've lost him, doctor. Pity—such a gentlemanly fellow, and scarcely older than…* I can't hear the rest: I'm floating above them, amazed at how emaciated my lifeless body is; my lips skinned back, my great jutting jaw, my pallid fingers. I'm glad to be free of that body. There's no pain here! But something calls me from the darkness above. Is the light of Heaven up above? I know better. I know about the opaque gulfs; the *deep end* of the sky. The Hungry Deep. *I will not go!* I will go see Dunn! Yes, dear old Dunn. Something so comforting about the company of my fellow Amateur Pressmen. I'll find my way to Dunn's house… Here, and here… I flit from house to house… is it years that pass? It is—and it doesn't matter. I drift like a fallen leaf along the stream of time, waft through the streets of Providence. How the seasons wheel by! The yellowing leaves, the drifting snow, the thaw, the tulips… I see other ghosts. Some try to speak, but I hear them not… There—Dunn's house! I'll see if he's still within. But no. Father Dunn has moved on. There is the little Irish girl, adopted by the Dunns. And the cat, her cat, fairly bursting with kittens. Oh, to be a cat. And why not? The mice… sweeter when they run… I speak to the girl… she shouts in fear and throws something at me. She chases me from the house!

"What's that? One of the great metal hurtlers in the street! Truck's wheel strikes me, wrings me out like a wet rag… Agony sears… I float above the truck, seeing my body quivering in death, below me: the body of the cat. But I am at peace, once more, drifting through Providence. Let me wander, as I did once before… let me wander and wait. Perhaps next time I'll find something more suitable. Someone. A pair of hands that can fashion dreams…

"The Great Deep calls to me, over and over. I won't go! My ancient soul has strength, more strength than my body ever had. It resists. I remember, now, what I saw in the ruins of that old lighthouse—under its foundations: the secret pool, the shamanic pool of the Narragansett Indians. A fragment of a great translucent yellow stone was hidden there—a piece of a larger stone lost now beneath the waves, once the centerpiece of a temple in the land some called Atlantis.

"The cat-eye stone struck from Yuggoth by the crash of a comet—whirling to our world, where it spoke to the minds of the first true men; gave the ancients a sickening knowledge of their minuteness, the vast darkness of the universe.

"It has been whispering to me since I was a child—my mother heard it, she glimpsed its evocations: the faceless things that crawled from it just around the corner of the house. She'd tell me all about them, my dear half-mad mother Sarah. She had visited that place, and heard its whispering. And that seemed to plant the seed in me—which grew into the twisted tree of my tales…

"I drift above the elm-hugged street, refusing to depart my beloved Providence. But the call of the Great Deep is so strong. Insistent. I hear it especially loudly when I visit Swan Point Cemetery. No longer summoning—now it is demanding.

"There is only one way free, this time—I must hide within someone… I must find a place to nestle, as I did with the cat… Here's a woman. Mrs. Boxer is with child. I feel the heartbeat, pattering rapidly within her—calling to me… I go to sleep within her, united with him, the *tabula rasa*…

"I wake on the beach, full-grown. I cannot quite speak. I cannot control my body. It moves frantically about, speaking into a little invention, from which issues a voice. 'Why, what do you mean?' says the voice. 'This is your mother, for heaven's sake! Whatever are you about, Roman?' If only I could speak and tell her my name. A voice comes from my mouth—but it is not my voice, not truly. I want to tell her my name. I cannot… My name…"

Fyodor leaned closer yet. The next words were whispered, hardly audible. "…is Howard. Howard Phillips. Howard Phillips Lovecraft…"

Then Roman was asleep. That was the natural course of the drug's effects. There was no waking him, now, not safely, to ask questions.

Stunned, Fyodor sat beside Roman, staring at the peacefully sleeping young man. Seeing his eyelids flickering with REM sleep. What was he dreaming of?

FYODOR HAD GROWN UP IN PROVIDENCE. EVERYONE here had heard Lovecraft's name. Young Fyodor Cheski had his own Lovecraft period. But his mother had found the books—he was only thirteen—and she'd taken them away, very sternly, and threatened that he would lose every privilege he could even imagine if he read them again. She *knew* about this Lovecraft, she said. Things whispered to him—things people shouldn't listen to.

It was one of his mother's fits of paranoia, of course, but after that Fyodor was taken with a more modern set of writers, Bradbury and then Salinger—and a veer into Robertson Davies. Never gave Lovecraft another thought. Not a conscious thought, anyway.

His mother, in her manic periods, would babble about a cat she'd had as a small girl, a cat that used to talk to her; she'd look into its eyes, and she'd hear it speaking in her mind, hissing of other worlds—dark worlds. And one day she could bear it no more, and she'd driven the cat into the street, where it was hit by a passing truck. She feared its soul had haunted her, ever since; and she feared it would haunt Fyodor.

A chill went through Fyodor as he realized he had fallen entirely under the spell of Roman's convoluted narrative. He had almost believed that this man was the reincarnation of the writer who'd died in 1937. Perhaps he did have a little of his mother's... susceptibility.

He shuddered. God, he needed a drink.

He thought of the wine in the basement. It was still there. Hal said it was vinegar, but he hadn't tested the other bottles. Fyodor had a powerful impulse to try one out. Perhaps he'd see something down there that would spark some insight into Roman...

His patient was sleeping peacefully. Why not?

He went downstairs, to find that Roman's mother, anxious, had gone to see her sister. Leah was yawning at her desk.

He looked at her, thinking he really should take her out, once, see what happened. She's not dating anyone, as far as he knew.

He almost asked her then and there. But he simply nodded and said, "I'll take care of things here. He's sleeping... he'll stay the night... You can go home."

He watched her leave, and then turned to the basement door, remembering the agent had mentioned the house had belonged to the Dunn family for generations. Doubtless Roman had found out about the house's background, somehow, woven it into his fantasies. Probably he was a Lovecraft fan.

Fyodor found the switch at the top of the steps, switched on the light and descended to the basement. Really, that bulb was too bright for the basement space. It hurt his eyes. Ugly yellow light bulb.

He crossed to the corner where he'd replaced the cap over

the hole in the floor. The crowbar was still there. He pried up the cover of cement and wood—took more effort than he'd supposed. But there were the bottles. How was he to open them?

Why not be a little daring, opening the bottle as they did in stories? He pulled a bottle out and struck the neck on the wall; it broke neatly off. Wine splashed red as blood against the gray concrete.

He sniffed at the bottle. The smell wasn't vinegary, anyway. The aroma—the wine's bouquet—was almost a perfume.

The bottle neck had broken evenly. No risk in having a quick swig. He sat on one of the crates, put the bottle neck to his lips, and tasted, expecting to gag and spit out the small sip...

But it was delicious. Apparently this one had been sealed better than the one his friend Hal had looked at. Strange to think it had been here undisturbed all those years—even when his mother had been here. Only once had she mentioned the name of the people who'd adopted her. The Dunn family...

He wanted badly to sit here awhile and drink the wine. Quite out of character—he was more the kind to have a little carefully selected Pinot in an upscale wine bar. But here he was...

Strange to be down here, drinking from a broken wine bottle, in the concrete and dust.

It's not like me. It's as if I'm still under the spell, the influence, of Roman's ramblings. It's as if something brought me here. Something is urging me to lift the bottle to my lips... to drink deeply...

Why not? One drink more. If he was going to ask Leah out he'd need to be more spontaneous. He could call her up, tell her the wine was better than they'd supposed. Might be worth something. Ask her to come and try some...

He licked his lips—and drank. The wine was delicious; a deep taste, and unusual. Like a tragic song. He laughed to himself. He drank again. What was it Roman had said?

I never used to drink. I wanted to take it up, starting with something old and fine. I want a new life. I desire to do things differently. Live!

Fyodor drank again... and looked up at the light bulb. He blinked in its fierce sulfurous glare, its assaultive parhelion. It seemed almost part of an eye, a glowing yellow eye, looking at him from some farther place...

He stood up suddenly, shaking himself, his twitching hands dropping the bottle—it shattered on the concrete with a gigantic sound that seemed to resound on and on, echoing... and in the echo was a voice. His mother's voice... the part of her mind that had spoken to him through the sea of static. This time it said something else.

"We need souls. We have few left in our world. Come to us, across the Great Deeps. Restore our world. Become one with us."

The room, which should be dull gray, seemed to quiver in ugly colors. He turned and staggered to the stairs. His head buzzed.

Then he looked up to see that Roman Boxer was standing at the head of the stairs. "Doctor? Are you well? You *are* Doctor Cheski, are you not? I believe that was the name..."

Fyodor started wobblingly up the stairs. Alcohol level must have gotten very high in the wine. Seeing things. Unable to climb a damn basement stairs very well...

He got to the third step from the top—and Roman put out his hand to him. "Here—take my hand. You look a trifle unsteady."

But Fyodor held back, afraid to touch Roman and not sure why. "You... should be asleep."

"Yes, well—I simply woke up. And everything was fine! Whatever you gave me helped me enormously. The pain in my stomach is gone! I was surprised to be no longer in the hospital... Yes. Thought I was a goner. Kind of you to bring me home—if that's what this place is. That nurse—is she here?"

"The nurse? What..." Fyodor licked his lips. "What is your name?"

"You really *have* overindulged, my friend. I am your patient,

Howard Lovecraft…" Roman smiled widely and once more reached for him. Fyodor jerked back, irrationally afraid of that hand. *The hand of a dead man.*

And Fyodor tipped backwards, flailed, tumbled down the stairs. He heard a sickening *crunch*…

Darkness entered through the crack in his skull. It swept him up, carried him away…

He drifted through the darkness—orbiting a far world. Beginning to sink toward that cloud-clotted planet…

No. He refused to go.

"In time, you will come. We traded him for you…"

Fyodor struggled, psychically writhing, to get back. A long ways back, and an endless time somehow folded within a few minutes… Then he was crawling across the basement floor. Someone was helping him up. Roman… was that his name?

The young man, quite solicitous, helped him up the stairs to the front hall—and then Leah stepped in the door. "Oh my God! Fyodor! Roman, what happened! Have you hurt him? He's got blood on his head! I knew something was wrong! I was sure of it! Never mind, just sit down, Fyodor, I'll call an ambulance… and the police."

OW THE SEASONS WHEEL BY. SPRING, SUMMER, FALL, winter; spring, summer, fall; a year and another… And then an early summer day… the roses were pretty, quite new, not yet chewed by the fungus… Mom drooped in her chair, across from him, eyes completely hidden in sunglasses. She would want to play cards when she woke up. He preferred the puzzle.

"Fyodor?" It was Leah, speaking from the back door. Smiling. Dressed up rather formally. "We're going out. To the book signing."

"Hm?" Fyodor looked up from his Old Providence jigsaw

puzzle. Mother had been grumpily helping him put the puzzle together on the card table, in the late summer sunshine; the rose garden behind the Dunn house. But Mom had gone to sleep, a jigsaw piece in her hand, slumped in her chair. She looked contented, snoring away there.

Roman was so good to take care of her—to care for them both here.

"I said, we're going to Roman's signing—for his book? You sure you won't come? The man from the *New York Times* is going to interview him."

"Is he? That's good. Big crowd?"

"Oh, yes. It looks to be a bestseller. I know you don't like crowds."

"No. Crowds and cats…"

He had heard Roman's agent, a pretty blonde lady, chattering away over breakfast. "They're framing it as *Roman Theobald, the man Lovecraft might have become…*" Then she'd turned to him. "How are you this morning, Fyodor? Would you like some more orange juice?"

Very kind of her. Everyone was very kind to him, since the accident. Since the damage to his head.

Leah had married "Roman Theobald"—that was his pen name. Roman Boxer was his real name. Anyway the name on his birth certificate. Sometimes, in the house, she used a funny little affectionate name for him. "Howard." Odd choice. Anyway, she was Mrs. Roman Boxer now. She was almost ten years too old for Roman, but Mrs. Boxer had approved. She'd bought the Dunn house as a wedding gift for them. Mrs. Boxer had died, soon after the wedding, of cancer. Buried at Swan Point Cemetery.

Fyodor felt good, thinking about it. Maybe it was the Prozac. But still—it was true, everyone *was* very kind. Roman, Leah, the doctors. And Leah made sure he took his pills in the evening. He really couldn't sleep without them. Particularly the pills against nightmares. He was quite sure that if he dreamed of that place again, the place the bells in the sea spoke of, that he would not wake up the next morning. He might never wake up again. And mother, then, poor old mumsy, would be all alone. Until they came for her too.

View

TOM FLETCHER

Tom Fletcher was born in 1984. He is married and currently lives in Manchester, England. He is the author of two novels— The Leaping (Quercus, 2010) and The Thing on the Shore (Quercus, 2011)—and numerous short stories. He blogs at www. endistic.wordpress.com, his Twitter username is @fellhouse, and he can be found on Facebook at www.facebook.com/ tomfletcherwriter.

"JUST THE HALLWAY ALONE IS WORTH IT," NEIL SAID. "Look at the banisters, the tiles, the space."

It was a very impressive hallway. The floor was surfaced with black and white tiles, chequered. They were polished to a high sheen. The banisters of the spiralling staircase were heavy-looking. Dark, solid wood. Also well-polished. And the space—the chequerboard floor seemed vast, the tiles seeming to diminish in size to nothing at the far side of the room.

"It's like being in a painting," Neil said.

It *was* like being in a painting.

THE ESTATE AGENT WAS AN INCREDIBLY TALL MAN with a perfectly bald head that gleamed as cleanly as the tiles. He wore a grey suit with a cream-coloured shirt. He carried a clipboard that held a few sheets of paper—information about the house, judging by the way he would look down at the clipboard and then impart some fact or other. His deep-set eyes blinked slowly whenever he spoke.

"This flooring is the original flooring," he said, his voice sonorous and profound, "dating back to when the first part of the house was constructed in 1782. Extensions have been made since then, of course, outwards and upwards and even downwards."

"Outwards?" I asked. "I thought this was a terrace?"

"It is a terrace," the estate agent said. "You'll see what I mean when we head upstairs. I propose that I show you around the ground floor to start with, and then take you to the upper floors, and then, after that, we'll come back down and you can explore the basement. After that, I'll give you some time to talk between yourselves. How does that sound?"

"Sounds good," Neil said, looking up at the ceiling.

 HE KITCHEN WAS AS IMPRESSIVE AS THE HALLWAY. Marble tops, a Belfast sink, those beautiful tiles throughout. Cupboards and drawers that looked custom made, and again, that lovely dark wood.

"Cheri," Neil said, "this house is amazing. We should go for it. We should definitely go for it."

"It is amazing, so far," I said, "but we haven't seen it all yet. Let's just see it all before we make our minds up. We need to think about the cost of it too. We can't just fall for the first place we see. We don't want to hurt ourselves, financially."

"Mmm," Neil said, waggling his head around, "yeah…"

The estate agent grinned and gestured towards the back door.

 HE GARDEN WAS A LONG, THIN STRIP OF A THING, but it was verdant, bright, and green beneath the autumn mist. It was enclosed by a tall wooden fence. A healthy-looking vegetable patch thrived at the far end. The bright tops of a few ripe pumpkins bulged up, regularly spaced. Neil squeezed my hand. "When we have kids," he said, "this garden would be perfect."

When we turned to look back at the house, I realised how low the mist had come. Even the windows of the first floor were obscured.

HE LIVING ROOM WAS COSY AND SQUARE, WITH WARM wooden floorboards—smooth and glowing with varnish—and an open fire, lit even then, just for the viewing. It roared merrily away like a happy animal. The walls had been given an even coat of pale lime green paint. It looked flawless—quite fresh.

The estate agent took us back out into the hallway and grinned his huge, toothy grin.

"As you can see," he said, "this is a very desirable property. Now. Let's go upstairs."

HE ROOMS ON THE FIRST FLOOR WERE AS GRAND AND appealing as those on the ground floor. There was a small landing, and then two bedrooms, one of which had an opulent en-suite bathroom.

"The house feels quite narrow," I said to the estate agent.

"The lower floors are indeed narrow," the estate agent said. "Originally, the house was narrow and tall. So, as you've seen, there were only a couple of rooms on each floor. It gives these floors a nice, cosy feel, but, if you like to have space around you, then the upper floors should be more to your taste." He grinned. "This property really offers the best of both worlds," he said.

I started to wonder if his shirt really was cream-coloured, or just grimy. The ridge of the collar was dark, as if greasy. The colour of the rest of it seemed a bit patchy.

"What's upstairs?" Neil asked.

"Well, really, the rooms are for the owners of the property to use as they see fit," the estate agent said. "What's upstairs is pure potential!"

HE LAYOUT OF THE SECOND FLOOR MATCHED THAT of the first, except what was an en-suite bathroom on the first floor was just a separate bathroom on the second. The staircase spiralled up through the landing, up towards the converted attic rooms. We didn't say much as we looked around this floor; I was thinking about studies, nurseries, playrooms, libraries.

"The attic is where we start to see the beginning of the expansion of the property," the estate agent said, wiping a handkerchief across his damp forehead. "Shall we ascend?"

I wasn't sure what he could mean by *start to see the beginning of* at this stage, but I did not vocalise my query. I was sure that we would see soon enough.

And see soon enough we did. Too soon. And too much.

HE ATTIC WAS A SHOCK. THE STAIRS ENDED IN A TINY room with a ceiling that was lower than the other ceilings in this house, but still relatively high when compared with most ceilings. The walls had been painted pink, messily, as if by an impatient child. The stairs were situated right in the middle of the room, which was disorientating, given that on the first three floors they had always been at the back left of the central space. One door led off to the right. "This way," the estate agent said, gesturing towards the door.

All the rooms in the attic were interconnected, with multiple doors, and they were all different shapes too, with awkward corners and inexplicable dog-legs. We flicked the light switches as we went, but the floor still felt gloomy.

"A family that used to live here bought up the attics of the adjacent houses," the estate agent explained, "and converted the whole lot into this warren. Good for parties, or games of hide and seek, or even just for storage."

"Why are there no skylights?" I asked. "Don't attics usually have skylights?"

"Well," the estate agent said, "when they converted this attic into this network of rooms, they built another attic—a replacement attic—on top."

"Makes sense," Neil said, nodding.

"What were these rooms for?" I asked.

"What were they *for*?" the estate agent repeated, grinning again. "Why, what a strange question. I'm not sure that they were *for* anything in particular. A kind of folly, if you will. It would be a dreary world indeed if things were only created to perform particular functions, would it not?"

"I suppose it would," I said, looking around.

"Shall we go upstairs?" the estate agent asked.

"Yes," Neil said. "Come on, Cheri. How exciting is this house?"

"It is quite exciting," I said.

"This way," the estate agent said, and he led us through a doorway into a room that I thought we'd already been into, but we hadn't. This room was full of old, dusty, wooden furniture, piled floor to ceiling. Broken chairs, warped picture frames, ornate little coffee tables, leather footstools leaking their innards down the side of the heap.

There were no doors or stairs or ladders though.

"Up through there," the estate agent said, pointing upwards to a trapdoor in the ceiling. He set off climbing up the accumulated junk, the clipboard in his mouth, his arms and legs moving slowly but surely. He moved like a four-legged spider. Soon enough he had opened the trapdoor and his sweaty head had disappeared through it, followed by the rest of his body. Neil went up after him, and I followed.

The replacement attic really was like an attic, complete with skylights. Not that the skylights let much light in—the mist out there looked thick.

The attic was one long room—really long, actually—
carpeted with offcuts. It looked as if it were split-level, in a
sense, with the roof being significantly lower in one half of the
room. In that suspended wall, there was a door.

"What you see is what you get, with this room," the estate
agent said. "Let's carry on up." He moved a set of stepladders
into the middle of the room and made his way, somewhat
wobblily, up to the suspended door. This whole structure—the
room that seemed to hang from the roof—appeared to be made
entirely of wood. I couldn't see how it was supported, unless
it was built into the walls of this replacement attic, but given
that even that was an appendage, I couldn't imagine that any
of this was very secure. I lightly tapped the floor—the roof,
originally—with my right foot.

"Are all of these extensions legal?" I asked.

"Of course!" the estate agent said. But he didn't elaborate. I
resolved to investigate that more fully, after the viewing.

We followed him up the stepladders.

What I had taken to be a kind of subsidiary loft turned out
to be something much more alarming. Once the estate agent
had got through the door and we'd all stepped through, we
could see that the room was actually much taller than it should
have been. The ceiling was far higher than the ceiling of the
replacement attic had been. There was a window high up there
in a side wall, with a ladder reaching up to it.

"This way," the estate agent said.

"I feel like we're not really looking at the house any more,"
I said. "We just keep on going upwards."

"Well," Neil said, "all rooms are pretty much the same with
no furniture in, aren't they? A room is a room is a room!"

"Yeah, I suppose so," I said.

"Besides," the estate agent said, "the view is one of the
major attractions of this property."

"You know," I say, "I'd quite forgotten about the view."

"Well!" the estate agent said, "we'll be seeing it soon enough!" He grinned down from the ladder, his mouth looking very wide, his teeth larger and more yellow than I'd realised. He seemed to be sweating profusely. Even his suit jacket was showing sweat patches. I realised that his shirt was probably white, originally, and just discoloured through excessive perspiration.

Neil started clambering up the ladder, and I followed.

The window opened out onto a wooden platform that nestled into the side of the wall through which we'd just climbed, and was connected to the roof below—the top of the replacement attic—by a complicated network of metal struts and poles. We couldn't see very far because of the mist, but we could see that this was just one of a series of platforms that stretched off upwards and to the side, some of which looked even more precarious than this one.

"Oh," Neil said, plaintively, "trust it to be misty on the day we come for the viewing."

"Don't worry," the estate agent said. "We just need to keep on going up."

"We can do that?" Neil asked.

"Of course we can," the estate agent said. I don't know if we were just in closer proximity to him than we had been up until this point, but his breath really stank.

"Is it OK if Neil and I just have a word in private?" I asked the estate agent.

"Absolutely," he said. "I'll just go up to the next floor and wait for you."

"Thanks," I said.

I waited until the estate agent had made his way up some wonky, makeshift stairs, and then turned to Neil.

"Look," I said, "I know this house is great, but I just don't want you to get too excited. We need to have a good think about it afterwards, maybe see a few other places, make our minds up after considering all the options."

"It is really great, though," Neil said, "and we haven't even seen the view yet."

"I know," I said. "We're both excited. But let's not get carried away."

Neil nodded, eyes wide. "I know, I know," he said. "I get it."

All around us the mist was curling, rolling, shifting. There wasn't any wind to speak of, but it still moved, slowly. I couldn't hear much apart from the creaking of distant crows, and a sound like that of dry leaves in the wind. Which was strange because, as I say, there was no wind to speak of. Unless the wind was beneath us. Beneath the platforms, beneath the mist.

On the next platform, the estate agent had poured three cups of tea from a flask and put them on a small table. The china cups, the flask, and the table must all have been there already. "Most potential buyers like a rest at this point," he said, passing me one of the cups. The cup looked as if it had been broken and then glued back together. None of the cups matched.

"There's been a lot of interest, then?" Neil asked, before blowing onto the surface of his tea in order to cool it down.

"Well, naturally," the estate agent said. He was scratching at his neck and at the top of his head.

Neil seemed to realise—as I already had—that the tea was long cold. He peered at it down his nose. I took a sip out of politeness and felt my oesophagus contract almost immediately, in response to the terrible taste; not only was it cold, but there was something rotten in it.

The estate agent was drinking his quite happily.

"Yes," the estate agent said, "this property has certainly attracted a lot of viewings. It's very desirable."

"It *is* very desirable," Neil said, looking around at the mist and the damp wood. "Especially with the view as well."

"Well, of course," the estate agent said. "We'll see it soon. Well. Five or six more floors."

"Is all this really stable?" I asked.

"It's about as stable as you'd expect," the estate agent said. "It is just what it looks like."

The next few floors were increasingly unsteady. The platforms were not straight, but angled; the struts, pipes, and planks were all different lengths; the screws and bolts that held everything together looked loose.

I started to feel what might have been wind in my hair.

The estate agent couldn't leave his neck or head alone. He was scratching and scratching. I thought I could see a thick rash of big, sore-looking spots appearing behind his ears and on the skin around his collar, but the mist was so thick that I couldn't be sure.

"It would be good to sit up here with a nice drink come summer," Neil said. But I did not respond. I was too intent on maintaining my grip and my balance.

Each platform now was quite small, connected only to the previous one by four wooden struts. Each one had a hole in it to allow access by ladder, and a ladder that led up to the hole in the next one. Every now and again I would wonder if I could feel the structure moving in the wind, but the sensation may have been caused just by the movement of the mist.

I don't know how many "floors" we had ascended, but it must have been more than five or six, so I stopped the estate agent before he carried on up to the next one.

"How much further?" I asked.

"Not much further at all," he said. "I assure you, you'd regret not making the most of the viewing after coming all of this way."

"I know," I said. "Don't worry! I'm not about to leave or anything. I just thought I'd ask."

We climbed the remaining ladders in silence. Well—we

climbed them without speaking. The estate agent, who was up in front, was whispering to himself and still scratching. The sound of him scratching had become a constant.

Then we were above the mist. We could see. All we could see, if we looked down, was the top of the mist, but even so. The sky above was a cold, pale blue. The structure we were climbing—well, we couldn't see how far up it went, because we could only see the underside of the platform above.

"Oh my God, Cheri," Neil said, "this house is amazing. So much space!"

"There is a lot of space," I agreed, looking around. The mist below was yellow and grey, not white. The upper reaches of the house were definitely swaying gently in the wind. Or not even in the wind—just swaying, gently. Maybe our very presence there was unbalancing the thing. "Well," I said, "Come on then. Let's see this view!"

The view became apparent over the next couple of floors.

When we got high enough to see further than the extent of the mist, we lay down on our stomachs and looked out over the edge.

"We'll wait," the estate agent said, clawing at his underarms, "until the mist has cleared."

Beyond the reach of the mist, not much was visible apart from a hazy, grey-brown landscape. I couldn't think where that was, though—I knew the area from years ago, and I thought it was all residential round there.

As the mist cleared, more became visible, and I started to feel distinctly uneasy. There were rows of houses, sure, but they did not look quite as they did from the ground. I was not even certain that they were the houses that I was expecting to see. The thin gauze of mist that remained did not account for the differences. They were all tall Victorian terraces, which in itself would have been fine, correct, but they were all slightly taller, slightly thinner, than the houses in the streets that I thought I knew. They were all slightly darker and grimmer. There were more boarded-up windows, more soggy, rotting curtains, more abandoned gardens. The empty landscape that was visible further away was just that; a kind of wasteland. I thought that there had been some kind of public building there, though; a library or museum or town hall or something.

"This isn't quite how I remember this place," I said.

"Oh well," Neil said, "your memory has always been unreliable."

"What?" I said. "No it hasn't!"

But Neil was distracted. "Look at that!" he exclaimed, pointing. "What's that?"

"What do you mean, about my memory?"

But he wasn't listening. He was instead staring, gaping, gawping.

Something was moving down one of the streets below us. A big something. I thought at first that it was a dustcart, but it wasn't a dustcart. It was too big, for a start; nearly as tall as the houses on either side. And it took up the whole width of the street as well. It had a smooth, humped back that swung from side to side as it shuffled along. It walked on all fours, but its front legs were not really legs. They were arms. Its skin was mottled pink and white, and covered in soft-looking growths. Its head was not visible; it was obscured by the wobbly, bulbous bulk of its body.

"A view quite unique," the estate agent said.

The beast progressed until it reached that empty space that had once been something else—a town hall, a museum, a library—and then squatted, started rooting around, and eventually seemed to disappear down into the ground.

"I've got to be honest," I said. "This is disappointing."

The estate agent spluttered and spat, drool running from

his big wet lips and awkwardly sharp teeth. "Well," he said, "well, well, well. I suppose there is no accounting for taste."

"I really like it," Neil said.

"Can we talk about it downstairs?" I asked. "Back in the hallway, or the living room maybe? Somewhere it's a bit warmer?"

"OK," Neil said. "But hey, look at *that*!" he pointed again.

I glanced briefly and saw much movement over in a cul-de-sac—lots of people, I think, but I did not look long enough to see what they were doing or what they really were. I pressed my face into the wood on which we lay. "I want to go downstairs," I said. "Now."

"OK, OK," said Neil. "Come on then."

The estate agent followed us down.

I slipped various times, as did Neil, but neither of us fell.

ACK IN THE BEAUTIFUL HALLWAY, I WAS SHAKING. "What's wrong?" Neil asked.

"I don't know," I said. "There's something weird about this house."

"I really like it," he said.

"I know you do," I said, "and I'm not forgetting that. But— weren't things different when we went upstairs? When we were up on those wooden boards? Didn't it feel wrong?"

"Did it?" he said. He looked confused.

"I think it did," I said. "I think I want to leave."

Behind us, the estate agent cleared his throat. The sound was large and ugly. I turned to see him wiping something green away from his mouth. "Don't go yet," he said. "You haven't seen the cellar."

"I don't want to see the cellar," I said.

"You can't make your mind up without seeing the whole house," the estate agent said. "It might change your feelings completely."

"I don't want anything to change my feelings completely," I said.

"Come on, Cheri," Neil said. "Let's see the cellar." He looked to the estate agent. "It won't take long, will it?"

"No," the estate agent said, grinning widely and scratching at his Adam's apple. "It won't take long at all."

"Come on," Neil said, pulling at my hand like a child, guiding me over to a small door to the left of the spiral staircase. "Come on, Cheri."

The estate agent strode ahead of us, keys jangling in his hand. "We like to keep this door locked," he said.

"Why's that?" I asked. But he didn't appear to hear me.

He opened the door and stooped to pass through it. Neil followed him, also stooping, and yet somehow turning to grin back at me at the same time. "Come on," he mouthed. Beyond him, the estate agent was making his way down a steep, narrow staircase, squeezed in between walls with all the paint peeling off them.

I hesitated. I looked behind me at the black and white tiles. I felt as if my heart were beating my blood into foam. I could hear rushing in my ears. I was starting to feel ridiculously paranoid, as if everything we'd just seen was wrong, strange, impossible. I doubted everything, momentarily, as I thought about what we'd seen when we'd gone upstairs.

"Cheri," Neil was saying, his hand reaching out to mine once more. "Come on."

I smiled at him. I put the panic down to being tired and stressed out. House-hunting is always exhausting.

"Let's just look round it quickly," I said.

"We'll be done before you know it," he said, nodding.

I nodded back and took his hand and started to follow him down the stairs.

Houundwife

CAITLÍN R. KIERNAN

Caitlín R. Kiernan is the author of several novels, including Daughter of Hounds *(Penguin, 2007) and* The Red Tree *(Penguin, 2009), which was nominated for both the Shirley Jackson and World Fantasy awards. Her next novel,* The Drowning Girl: A Memoir, *will be released by Penguin in 2012. Since 2000, her shorter tales of the weird, fantastic, and macabre have been collected in several volumes, all published by Subterranean Press, including* Tales of Pain and Wonder *(2000, 2008),* From Weird and Distant Shores *(2002),* To Charles Fort, with Love *(2005),* A is for Alien *(2005),* Alabaster *(2006), and* The Ammonite Violin & Others *(2010). In 2012, Subterranean Press released a retrospective of her early writing,* Two Worlds and In Between: The Best of Caitlín R. Kiernan *(Volume One). She lives in Providence, Rhode Island, with her partner Kathryn.*

1.

MEMORY FAILS, MOMENTS BLEEDING ONE AGAINST AND into the next or the one before, merging and diverging and commingling again farther along. Rain streaking glass, muddy rivers flowing to the sea, or blood on a slaughterhouse floor, wending its way towards a drain. There was a time, I am still reasonably certain, when all this might have been set forth as a mere *tale*, starting at some more or less arbitrary, but seemingly consequential, moment: the day I first met Isobel Endecott, the evening I boarded a train from Savannah to Boston, or the turning of frail yellowed pages in a black-magician's grimoire and coming upon the graven image of a jade idol. But I am passed now so far out beyond the conveniences and conventions of chronology and narrative, and gone down to some place so few (and so very many) women before me have ever gone. It cannot be a tale, anymore than a crystal goblet dropped on a marble floor may ever again hold half an ounce of wine. I have been dropped, like that, from a great height, and I have shattered on a marble floor. I may not have been dropped. I may have only fallen, but that hardly seems to matter now. I may have been pushed, also. And, too, it might well be I was dropped, fell, *and* was pushed, none of these actions necessarily being mutually exclusive of the others. I am no different from the broken goblet, whose shards do not worry overly about how they came to be divided from some former whole.

Memory fails. I fall. Not one or the other, but both. I

tumble through the vulgar, musty shadows of sepulchers. I lie in my own grave, dug by my own hands, and listen to hungry black beetles and maggots busy at my corporeal undoing. I am led to the altar on the dais in the sanctuary of the Church of Starry Wisdom, to be bedded and worshipped and bled dry. I look up from a hole in the earth and see the bloated moon. There is no ordering these events, no matter how I might try, if I even *cared* to try. They occurred, or I am yet rushing towards them. They are past and present and future, realized and unrealized and imagined and inconceivable; I would be a damned fool to worry over such trivialities. Better I be only damned.

"It was lost," Isobel tells me. "For a very long time it was lost. There were rumors it had gone to Holland, early in the fifteenth century, that it was buried there with one who'd worn it in life. Other stories say it was stolen from the grave of that man sometime in the 1920s and carried off to England."

I sip coffee while she talks.

"It's all bound up in irony and coincidence, and, really, I don't give that sort of prattle much credence," she continues. "The Dutchman who's said to have been buried with the idol, some claim he was a grave robber, that he fancied himself a proper ghoul. Charming fellow, sure, and then, five hundred years later, along come these two British degenerates—from somewhere in Yorkshire, I think. Supposedly, they dug him up and stole the idol, which they found hung around his neck."

"But before that… I mean, before the Dutchman, where might it have been?" I ask, and Isobel smiles. Her smile could melt ice, or freeze the blood, depending on one's perspective and penchant for hyperbole and metaphor. She shrugs and sets her coffee cup down on the kitchen table. We're sitting together in her loft on Atlantic Avenue. The building was constructed in the 1890s, as cold storage for the wares of fur merchants. The walls are thick and solid and keep our secrets.

She lights a cigarette and watches me a moment.

My train is pulling into South Station; I've never visited Boston before, and I shall never leave. It's a rainy day, and I've been promised that Isobel will be waiting for me on the platform.

"Well, before Holland—assuming, of course, it was ever *in* Holland—I've spoken with a man who thinks it might have spent time in Greece, hidden at the Monastery of Holy Trinity at Metéora, but the monastery wasn't built until 1475, so this really doesn't jibe with the story of the Dutch grave robber. Of course, the hound is mentioned in *Al Azif*. But you know that." And then the conversation shifts from the jade idol to archaeology in Damascus, and then Yemen, and, finally, the ruins of Babylon. In particular, I listen to Isobel describe the blue-glazed tiles of the Ishtar Gate, with their golden bas-reliefs of lions and auroch bulls and the strange, dragon-like *sirrush*. She saw a reconstructed portion of the gate at the Pergamon Museum when she was in Berlin, many years ago.

"In Germany, I was still a young woman," she says, and glances at a window and the city lights, the Massachusetts night and the yellow-orange skyglow that's there so no one ever has to look too closely at the stars.

This is the night of the new moon, and Isobel kneels before me and bathes my feet. I'm naked save the jade idol on its silver chain, hung about my neck. The temple of the Starry Wisdom smells of frankincense, galbanum, sage, clove, myrrh, and saffron smoldering in iron braziers suspended from the high ceiling beams. Her ash-blonde hair is pulled back from her face, pinned into a neat chignon. Her robes are the color of raw meat. I don't want her to look me in the eyes, and yet I cannot imagine going up the granite stairs to the dais without first having done so, without that easy, familiar reassurance. Dark figures in robes of half a dozen other shades of red and black and grey press in close from all sides. The colors of their robes denote their rank. I close my eyes, though I have been forbidden to do so.

"This is our daughter," barks the High Priestess, the old one crouched near the base of the altar. Her voice is phlegm and stripped gears, discord and tumult. "Of her own will does she come, and of her own will and the will of the Nameless Gods will she make the passage."

And even in this instant—here at the end of my life *and* the beginning of my existence—I cannot help but smile at the High Priestess' choice of words, at force of habit, her calling them *the Nameless Gods*, when we have given them so very many names over the millennia.

"She will see what we cannot," the High Priestess barks. "She will walk unhindered where our feet will never tread. She will know their faces and their embrace. She will suffer fire and flood and the frozen wastes, and she will dine with the Mother and the Father. She will take a place at their table. She will know their blood, as they will know hers. She will fall and sleep, be raised and walk."

I am pulling into South Station.

I am drinking coffee with Isobel.

I am nineteen years old, dreaming of a Dutch churchyard and violated graves. My dream is filled with the rustle of leathery wings and the mournful baying of some great, unseen beast. I smell freshly broken earth. The sky glares down at all the world with a single cratered eye which humanity, in its ignorance, would mistake for a full autumnal moon. There are two men with shovels and pick axes. Fascinated, I watch their grim, determined work, an unspeakable thievery done sixty-three years before my own birth. I hear the shovel scrape stone and wood.

In the temple, Isobel rises and kisses me. It's no more than the palest ghost of all the many kisses we've shared during our long nights of lovemaking, those afternoons and mornings spent exploring one another's bodies and desires and most taboo fancies.

The Hermit passes a jade cup to the Hierophant, who in turn passes it to Isobel. Though, in this place and in this hour, Isobel is *not* Isobel Endecott. She is the Empress, as I am here named the Wheel of Fortune. I have never seen this cup until now, but I know well enough that it was carved untold thousands of years before this night and from the same vein of leek-green jadeite as the pendant I wear about my throat. The mad Arabian author of the *Al Azif* believed the jade to have come from the Plateau of Y'Pawfrm e'din Leng, and it may be he was correct. The Empress places the rim of the cup to my lips, and I drink. The bitter ecru tincture burns going down and kindles a fire in my chest and belly. I know this is the fire that will make ashes of me, and from those ashes will I rise as surely as any phoenix.

"She stands at the threshold," the High Priestess growls, "and soon will enter the Hall of the Mother and the Father." The crowd murmurs blessings and blasphemies. Isobel's delicate fingers caress my face, and I see the longing in her blue eyes, but the High Priestess may not kiss me again, not in this life.

"I will be waiting," she whispers.

My train leaves Savannah.

"Do you miss Georgia?" Isobel asks me, a week after I arrive in Boston, and I tell her yes, sometimes I do miss Georgia. "But it always passes," I say, and she smiles.

I am almost twenty years old, standing alone on a wide white beach where the tannin-stained Tybee River empties into the Atlantic Ocean, watching as a hurricane barrels towards shore. The outermost rain bands lash the sea, but haven't yet reached the beach. The sand around me is littered with dead fish and sharks, crabs and squid. On February 5th, 1958, a B-47 collided in midair with an F-86 Sabre fighter 7,200 feet above this very spot, and the crew of the B-47 was forced to jettison the Mark 15 hydrogen bomb it was carrying; the "Tybee bomb" was never recovered and lies buried somewhere in silt and mud below the brackish waters of Wassaw Sound, six or seven miles southwest of where I'm standing. I draw a line in the sand, connecting one moment to another, and the hurricane wails.

I am sixteen, and a high-school English teacher is telling me that if a gun appears at the beginning of a story, it should be fired by the end. If it's a bomb, the conscientious author should take care to be certain it explodes, so that the reader's expectations are not neglected. It all sounds very silly, and I cite several examples to the contrary. The English teacher scowls and changes the subject.

In the temple of the Church of Starry Wisdom, I walk through the flames consuming my soul and take my place on the altar.

2.

IT'S A SWELTERING DAY IN LATE AUGUST 20—, AND I walk from the green shade of Telfair Square, moving north along Barnard Street. I would try to describe here the violence of the alabaster sun on this afternoon, hanging so far above Savannah, but I know I'd never come close to capturing in words the sheer *spite* and *vehemence* of it. The sky is bleached as pallid as the cement sidewalk and the whitewashed bricks on either side of the street. I pass what was once a cotton and grain warehouse, when the New South was still the Old South, more than a century ago. The building has been "repurposed" for lofts and boutiques and a trendy soul-food restaurant. I walk, and the stillness of the summer afternoon makes my footsteps seem almost loud as thunderclaps. I can feel the dull beginnings of a headache, and wish I had a Pepsi or an orange drink, something icy cold in a perspiring bottle. I glance through windows at the air-conditioned sanctuaries on the other side of the glass, but I don't stop and go inside.

The night before this day, there were dreams I will never tell anyone until I meet Isobel Endecott, two years farther along. I had dreams of a Dutch graveyard, and of a baying hound, and awoke to find an address on West Broughton scribbled on the cover of a paperback book I'd been reading when I fell asleep. The handwriting was indisputably mine, though I have no memory of having picked up the ballpoint pen on my nightstand and written the address. I did not get back to sleep until sometime after sunrise, and then there were only more dreams of that cemetery and the spire of a cathedral and the two men, busy with their picks and shovels.

I glance directly at the sun, daring it to blind me.

"You knew where to go," Isobel says, my first evening in Boston, my first evening with her and already I felt as though I'd known her all my life. "The time was right, and you were chosen. I can't even imagine such an honor."

It is late August, and I sweat, and walk north until I come to the intersection with West Broughton Street. I am clutching the copy of *Absalom, Absalom!* in my left hand, and I pause to read the address again. Then I turn left, which also means I turn west.

"The stars were right," she says, and pours me another brandy. "Which is really only another way of saying these events cannot occur until it is *time* for them to occur. That there is a proper sequence."

I walk west down West Broughton until I come to the address that my sleeping self wrote on the Faulkner book. It's a shop (calling itself an "emporium") specializing in antique jewelry, porcelain figurines, and "Oriental" curios. Inside, after the scorching gaze of the sun, the dusty gloom seems almost frigid. I find what I did not even know I was looking for in a display case near the register. It is one of the most hideous things I've ever seen, and one of the most beautiful, too. I guess the stone is jade, but it's only a guess. I know next to nothing about gemstones and the lapidary arts. That day, I do not even know the word *lapidary*. I won't learn it until later, when I begin asking questions about the pendant.

There's a middle-aged man sitting on a stool behind the counter. He watches me through the lenses of his spectacles. He has about him a certain mincing fastidiousness. I notice the mole above his left eyebrow, and that his clean nails are trimmed almost to the quick. I notice there's a hair growing from the mole. My mother always said I had an eye for detail.

"Anything I can show you today?" he wants to know, and I only *almost* hesitate before nodding and pointing to the jade pendant.

"Now, that is a very peculiar piece," he says, leaning forward and sliding the back of the case open. He reaches inside and lifts the pendant and its chain from a felt-lined tray. The felt is a faded shade of burgundy. He sits up again and passes the pendant across the counter to me. I'd not expected it to be so heavy, or feel so slick in my fingers, almost as though it were coated with oil or wax.

"Picked it up at an estate sell, a few years back," says the fastidious seller of antiques. "Never liked the thing myself, but different strokes, as they say. If I only stocked what I liked, wouldn't make much of a living, now would I?"

"No," I reply. "I don't suppose you would."

I stand alone on a beach at the south end of Tybee Island, watching the arrival of a hurricane. I've come to the beach to drown. However, I already know that's not what's going to happen, and the realization brings with it a faint pang of disappointment.

"Came from an old house down in Stephen's Ward," the man behind the counter says. "On East Hall Street, if memory serves. Strange bunch of women lived there, years ago, but then, one June, all of a sudden, the whole lot up and moved away. There were nine of them living in that house, and, well, you know how people talk."

"Yes," I say. "People talk."

"Might be better if we all tended to our own business and let others be," the man says and watches me as I examine the jade pendant. It looks a bit like a crouching dog, except for the wings, and it also puts me in mind of a sphinx. Its teeth are bared. Here, in my palm, carved from stone, is the countenance of every starving, tortured animal that has ever lived, the face of every madman, pure malevolence given form. I shiver, and the sensation is not entirely unpleasant. I realize that I am becoming aroused, that I am wet. There are letters from an alphabet I don't recognize inscribed about the base of the figurine, and a stylized skull has been etched into the bottom. The pendant is wholly repellent, and I know I cannot possibly leave the shop without it. It occurs to me that I might kill to own this thing.

"I think it would be," I tell him. "Be better if we all tended to our own business, I mean."

"Still, you can't change human nature," he says.

"No, you can't do that," I agree.

The train is pulling into South Station.

The hurricane bears down on Tybee Island.

And I'm only eleven and standing at a wrought-iron gate set into a brick wall, a wall that surrounds a decrepit mansion on East Hall Street. The wall is yellow, not because it has been painted yellow, but because all the bricks used in its construction have been glazed the color of goldenrods. They shimmer in the heat of a late May afternoon. On the other side of the gate is a woman named Maddy (which she says is short for Madeleine). Sometimes, like today, I walk past and find Maddy waiting, as though I'm expected. She never opens the gate; we only ever talk through the bars, there in the cool below the live oak branches and Spanish moss. Sometimes, she reads my fortune with a pack of Tarot cards. Other times, we talk about books. On this day, though, she's telling me about the woman who owns the house, whom she calls Aramat, a name I'm sure I've never heard before.

"Isn't that the mountain where the Bible says Noah's Ark landed after the flood?" I ask her.

"No, dear. That's Mount Ararat."

"Well, they *sound* very much alike, Ararat and Aramat," I say, and Maddy stares at me. I can tell she's thinking all sorts of things she's not going to say aloud, things I'm not meant to ever hear.

And then Maddy says, almost whispering, "Write her name backwards sometime. Very often, what seems unusual becomes perfectly ordinary, if we take care to look at it from another angle." She peers over her shoulder, and tells me that she has to go, and I should be on my way.

I'm twenty-three, and this is the day I found the pendant in an antique shop on West Broughton Street. I ask the man behind the counter how much he wants for it, and after he tells me, I ask him if it's jade, or if it only *looks* like jade.

"Looks like real jade to me," he replies, and I know from his expression that the question has offended him. "It's not glass or plastic, if that's what you mean. I don't sell costume jewelry, Miss. The chain, that's sterling silver. You want it, I'll take ten bucks off the price on the tag. Frankly, it gives me the creeps, and I'll be happy to be shed of it."

I pay him twenty-five dollars, cash, and he puts the

pendant into a small brown paper bag, and I go back out into the blazing sun.

I dream of a graveyard in Holland, and the October sky is filled with flittering bats. There is another sound, also of wings beating at the cold night air, but *that* sound is not being made by anything like a bat.

"This card," says Maddy, "is the High Priestess. She has many meanings, depending."

"Depending on what?" I want to know.

"Depending on many things," Maddy says and smiles. Her Tarot cards are spread out on the mossy paving stones on her side of the black iron gate. She taps at the High Priestess with an index finger. "In this instance, I'd suspect a future that has yet to be revealed, and duality, and hidden influences at work in your life."

"I'm not sure what you *mean* by duality," I tell her, so she explains.

"The Empress, she sits there on her throne, with a pillar on either side. Some say, these are two pillars from the Temple of Solomon, king of the Israelites and a powerful mystic. And some say that the woman on the throne is Pope Joan."

"I never knew there was a woman pope," I say.

"There probably wasn't. It's just a legend from the Middle Ages." And then Maddy brushes a stray wisp of hair from her eyes before she goes back to explaining duality and the card's symbolism. "On the Empress' right hand is a dark pillar, which is called Boaz. It represents the negative life principle. On her left is a white pillar, Jakin, which represents the positive life principle. Positive and negative, that's duality, and because she sits here between them, we know that the Empress represents balance."

Maddy turns over another card, the Wheel of Fortune, but it's upside down, reversed.

I am twenty-five years old, and Isobel Endecott is asleep in the bed we share in her loft on Atlantic Avenue. I lie awake, listening to her breathing and the myriad of noises from the street three stories below. It's four minutes after three A.M., and I briefly consider taking an Ambien. But I don't *want* to sleep. That's the truth of it. There's so little time left to me, and I'd rather not spend it in dreams. The night is fast approaching when the Starry Wisdom will meet on my behalf, because of what I've brought with me on that train from Savannah, and on that night I will slip this mortal coil (or be pushed, one or the other or both), and there'll be time enough for dreaming when I'm dead and in my grave, or during whatever's to come after my resurrection.

I find a pencil and a notepad. The latter has the name of the law firm that Isobel works for printed across the top of each page: Jackson, Monk, & Rowe, with an ampersand instead of "and" being written out. I don't bother to put on my robe. I go to the bathroom wearing only my panties, and stand before the wide mirror above the sink and stare back at my reflection a few minutes. I've never thought of myself as pretty, and I still don't. Tonight, I look like someone who hasn't slept much in a while. My hazel eyes seem more green than brown, when it's usually the other way around. The tattoo between my breasts is beginning to heal, the ink worked into my skin by the thin, nervous man designated the Ace of Pentacles by the High Priestess of the Church of Starry Wisdom.

I write *Aramat* on the notepad, then hold it up to the mirror. I read it aloud, as it appears in the looking glass, and then I do the same with *Isobel Endecott*, speaking utter nonsense, my voice low so I won't wake Isobel. In the mirror, my jade amulet does its impossible trick, which I first noticed a few nights after I bought it from a fastidious man in a shop on West Broughton Street. The reflection of the letters carved around the base, beneath the claws of the doglike beast, are precisely the same as when I look directly at them. The mirror does not reverse the image of the pendant. I have never yet found a mirror that will. I turn away from the sink, gazing into the darkness framed by the bathroom door.

I stand on a beach.

I sit on a sidewalk, eleven years old, and a woman named Maddy passes me the Wheel of Fortune between the bars of an iron gate.

3.

EMORY FAILS, AND MY THOUGHTS BECOME AN apparently disordered torrent. I'm a dead woman recalling the events of a life I have relinquished, a life I have repudiated. I sit in this chair at this desk and hold this pen in my hand because Isobel has asked it of me, not because I have any motivation of my own to speak of all the moments that have led me here. I'm helpless to deny her, so I didn't bother asking *why* she would have me write this. I did very nearly ask why she didn't request it *before*, when I was living and still bound by the beeline perception of time that marshals human recollection into more conventional recitals. But then an epiphany, or something like an epiphany, and I understood, without having asked. No linear account would ever satisfy the congregation of the Church of Starry Wisdom, for they seek more occult patterns, less intuitive paths, some alternate perception of the relationships between past and present, between one moment and the next (or, for that matter, one moment and the last). Cause and effect have not exactly been rejected, but have been found severely wanting.

"That is you," says Madeleine, passing me the Tarot card. "You are the Wheel of Fortune, an avatar of Tyche, the goddess of fate."

"I don't understand," I tell her, reluctantly accepting the card, taking it from her because I enjoy her company and don't wish to be rude.

"In time," she says, "it may make sense," then gathers her deck and hurries back inside that dilapidated house on East Hall Street, kept safe from the world behind its moldering yellow brick walls.

Burning, I lie down upon the cold granite altar. Soon, my lover, the Empress, climbs on top of me—straddling my hips—while the ragged High Priestess snarls her incantations, while the Major Arcana and the Minor Arcana and all the members of the Four Suits (Pentacles, Cups, Swords, and Staves) chant mantras borrowed from the *Al Azif.*

The Acela Express rattles and sways and dips as it hurries me through Connecticut, and then Rhode Island, on my way to South Station. *Because I could not stop for Death, He kindly stopped for me…* The woman sitting next to me is reading a book by an author I've never heard of, and the man across the aisle is busy with his laptop.

I come awake to the dank embrace of the clayey soil that fills in my grave. It presses down on me, that astounding, unexpected weight, wishing to pin me forever to this spot. I am, after all, an abomination and an outlaw in the eyes of biology. I've cheated. The ferryman waits for a passenger who will never cross his river, or whose crossing has been delayed indefinitely. I lie here, not yet moving, marveling at every discomfort and at my collapsed lungs and the dirt filling my mouth and throat. I was not even permitted the luxury of a coffin.

"Caskets offend the Mother and the Father," said the High Priestess. "What use have they of an offering they cannot touch?"

I drift in a fog of pain and impenetrable night. I cannot

open my sunken eyes. And even now, through this agony and confusion, I'm aware of the jade pendant's presence, icy against the tattoo on my chest.

I awaken in my bed, in my mother's house, a few nights after her funeral. I lie still, listening to my heartbeat and the settling noises that old houses make when they think no one will hear. I lie there, listening for the sound that reached into my dream of a Dutch churchyard and dragged me back to consciousness—the mournful baying of a monstrous hound.

On the altar, beneath those smoking braziers, the Empress has begun to clean the mud and filth and maggots from my body. The Priestess mutters caustic sorceries, invoking those nameless gods burdened with innumerable names. The congregation chants. I am delirious, lost in some fever that afflicts the risen, and I wonder if Lazarus knew it, or Osiris, or if it is suffered by Persephone every spring? I'm not certain if this is the night of my rebirth or the night of my death. Possibly, they are not even two distinct events, but only a single one, a serpent looping forever back upon itself, tail clasped tightly between venomous jaws. I struggle to speak, but my vocal cords haven't healed enough to permit more than the most incoherent, guttural croaking.

> ...I am Lazarus, come from the dead,
> Come back to tell you all, I shall tell you all...

"Hush, hush," says the Empress, wiping earth and hungry larvae from my face. "The words *will* come, my darling. Be patient, and the words will come back to you. You didn't crawl into Hell and all the way up again to be struck mute. Hush." I know that Isobel Endecott is trying to console me, but I can also hear the fear and doubt and misgiving in her voice.

"Hush," she says.

All around me, on the sand, are dead fish and crabs and the carcasses of gulls and pelicans.

It's summer in Savannah, and from the wide verandah of the house on East Hall Street, an older woman calls to Maddy, ordering her back inside. She leaves me holding that single card, *my* card, and I sit there on the sidewalk for another half hour, staring at it intently, trying to make sense of the card *and* what Maddy has told me. A blue sphinx squats atop the Wheel of Fortune, and below it there is the nude figure of a man with red skin and the head of a dog.

"You are *taking too long*," snaps the High Priestess, and Isobel answers her in an angry burst of French. I cannot speak French, but I'm not so ignorant that I don't know it when I hear it spoken. I wonder dimly what Isobel has said, and I adore her for the outburst, for her brashness, for talking back. I begin to suspect something has gone wrong with the ritual, but the thought doesn't frighten me. Though I'm still more than half blind, my eyes still raw and rheumy, I strain desperately for a better view of Isobel. In all the wide world, at this instant, there is nothing I want but her and nothing else I can imagine needing.

This is a Saturday morning, and I'm a few weeks from my tenth birthday. I'm sitting in the swing on the back porch. My mother is just inside the screen door, in the kitchen, talking to someone on the telephone. I can hear her voice quite plainly. It's a warm day late in February, and the sky above our house is an immaculate and seemingly inviolable shade of blue. I've been daydreaming, woolgathering, staring up at that sky, past the sagging eaves of the porch, when I hear something and notice that there's a very large black dog only a few yards away from me. It's standing in the gravel alleyway that separates our tiny backyard from that of the next house over. I have no way of knowing how long the dog has been standing there. I watch it, and it watches me. The dog has bright amber eyes, and isn't wearing a collar or tags. I've never before seen a dog smile, but *this* dog is smiling. After five minutes or so, it growls softly, then turns and trots away down the alley. I decide not to tell my mother about the smiling dog. She probably wouldn't believe me anyway.

"What was that you said to her?" I ask Isobel, several nights after my resurrection. We're sitting together on the floor of her loft on Atlantic, and there's a Beatles album playing on the turntable.

"What did I say to who?" she wants to know.

"The High Priestess. You said something to her in French, while I was still on the altar. I'd forgotten about it until this morning. You sounded angry. I don't understand French, so I don't know what you said."

"It doesn't really matter what I said," she replies, glancing over the liner notes for *Hey Jude*. "It only matters that I said it. The old woman is a coward…"

Somewhere in North Carolina, the rhythm of the train's wheels against the rails lulls me to sleep. I dream of a neglected Dutch graveyard and the amulet, of hurricanes and smiling black dogs. Maddy is also in my dreams, reading fortunes at a carnival. I can smell sawdust and cotton candy, horseshit and sweating bodies. Maddy sits on a milking stool inside a tent beneath a canvas banner emblazoned with the words *Lo! Behold! The Strikefire & Z. B. Harbinger Wonder Show!* in bold crimson letters fully five feet high.

She turns another card, the Wheel of Fortune.

I lie in my grave, fully cognizant but immobile, unable to summon the will or the physical strength to begin worming my way towards the surface, six feet overhead. I lie there, thinking of Maddy and the jade pendant. I lie there considering, in the mocking solitude of my burial place, what it does and does not mean that I've returned with absolutely no conscious knowledge of anything I may have experienced in death. Whatever secrets the Starry Wisdom sent me off to discover remain secrets. After all that has been risked and forfeited, I have no revelations to offer my fellow seekers. They'll ask their questions, and I'll have no answers. This should upset me, but it doesn't.

Now I can hear footsteps on the roof of my narrow house. Something is pacing heavily, back and forth, snuffling at the recently disturbed earth where I've been planted like a tulip bulb, like an acorn, like a seed that *will* unfold, but surely never sprout.

It goes about on four feet, I think, *not two.*

The hound bays.

I wonder, will it kindly dig me up, this restless visitor? And I wonder, too, about the rumors of the others who've worn the jade pendant before me, and the stories of their fates. Those two ghoulish Englishmen in 1922, for instance; they cross my reanimated mind. As does a passage from François-Honoré Balfour's notorious grimoire, *Cultes des Goules*, and a few stray lines from the *Al Azif*. My bestial caller suddenly stops pacing and begins scratching at the soft dirt, urging me to move.

In the temple, as my lover takes my hand and I'm led towards the altar stone, through the fire devouring me from the inside out, the High Priestess of the Starry Wisdom reminds us all that only once in every thousand years does the hound choose a wife. Only once each millennium is any living woman accorded that privilege.

My train pulls into a depot somewhere in southern Rhode Island, grumbling to a slow stop, and my dreams are interrupted by other passengers bustling about around me, retrieving their bags and briefcases, talking too loudly. Or I'm jarred awake by the simple fact that the train is no longer moving.

After sex, I lie in bed with Isobel, and the only light comes from the television set mounted on the wall across the room. The sound is turned down, so the black-and-white world trapped inside that box exists in perfect grainy silence. I'm trying to tell her about the pacing thing from the night I awoke. I'm trying to describe the snuffling noises and the way it worried at the ground with its sharp claws. But she only scowls and shakes her head dismissively.

"No," she insists. "The hound is nothing but a metaphor. We weren't meant to take it literally. Whatever you heard that night, you imagined it, that's all. You heard what some part of you expected, and maybe even needed, to hear. But the hound, it's a superstition, and we're not superstitious people."

"Isobel, I fucking *died*," I say, trying not to laugh, gazing across her belly towards the television. "And I came *back* from the dead. I tunneled out of my grave with my bare hands and then, blind, found my way to the temple alone. My flesh was already rotting, and now it's good as new. Those things actually happened, to *me*, and you don't *doubt* that they happened. You practice necromancy, but you want me to think I'm being superstitious if I believe that the hound is real?"

She's quiet for a long moment. Finally, she says, "I worry about you, that's all. You're so very precious to me, to all of us, and you've been through so much already." And she closes her hand tightly around the amulet still draped about my neck.

On a sweltering August day in Savannah, a fastidious man who sells antique jewelry and Chinese porcelain makes no attempt whatsoever to hide his relief when I tell him I've decided to buy the jade pendant. As he rings up the sale, he asks me if I'm a good Christian girl. He talks about the Pentecost, then admits he'll be glad to have the pendant out of his shop.

I stand on a beach.

I board a train.

Maddy turns another card.

And on the altar of the Church of Starry Wisdom, I draw a deep, hitching breath. I smell incense burning and hear the lilting voices of all those assembled for my homecoming. My heart is a sledgehammer battering at my chest, and I would scream, but I can't even speak. Isobel Endecott is straddling me, and her right hand goes to my vagina. With her fingers, she scoops out the slimy plug of soil and minute branches of fungal hyphae that has filled my sex during the week and a half I've spent below. When the pad of her thumb brushes my clit, every shadow and shape half-glimpsed by my wounded eyes seems to glow, as if my lust is contagious, as though light and darkness have become sympathetic. I lunge for her, my jaws snapping like the jaws of any starving creature; there are tears in her eyes as I'm restrained by the Sun and the Moon. The Hanged Man places a leather strap between my teeth.

Madness rides on the star-wind…

"Hush," Isobel whispers. "Hush, hush," whispers the Empress. "It'll pass."

It's the day I leave Savannah for the last time. In the bedroom of the house where I grew up, I pack the few things that still hold meaning for me. These include a photo album, and tucked inside the album is the Tarot card that the woman named Madeleine gave me.

4.

SOBEL IS WATCHING ME FROM THE OTHER SIDE OF THE dining room. She's been watching, while I write, for the better part of an hour. She asks, "How does it end? Do you even know?"

"Maybe it doesn't end," I reply. "I half think it's hardly even started."

"Then how will you know when to stop?" she asks. There's

dread wedged in between every word she speaks, between every syllable.

"I don't think I will," I say, this thought occurring to me for the first time. She nods, then stands and leaves the room, and when she's gone, I'm glad. I can't deny that there is a certain solace in her absence. I've been trying not to look too closely at Isobel's eyes. I don't like what I see there anymore...

King of Cat Swamp

JONATHAN THOMAS

Jonathan Thomas's collections of weird fiction include Stories from the Big Black House *(Radio Void Press, 1992),* Midnight Call and Other Stories *(Hippocampus Press, 2008), and* Tempting Providence and Other Stories *(Hippocampus Press, 2010).* Arcane Wisdom *has published his Lovecraftian novel* The Color Over Occam, *and his short stories have appeared most recently in* Postscripts *22/23 and the first* Black Wings of Cthulhu *(both from PS Publishing). Thomas is a native of Providence, Rhode Island.*

WIGHT PEEKED PAST DRAWN SHADE IN THE LIVING room to make sure the yard crew had decamped before he switched on the underground sprinkler system. Yes, they were gone, but how long had that frail old guy been pacing back and forth out front, in this July scorcher? Like a stray dog with a fix on some tantalizing scent? And why did he keep casting coppery bright eyes toward the house, and were those eyes probing, or beseeching, or resentful? If he was casing the place—not that he looked physically capable of burglary—he scored no points for stealth. In fact, Dwight was a little surprised none of the neighbors had called the cops on this blatantly "suspicious character."

Edith reached from behind his shoulder and parted the shade another inch to let her see what was so absorbing. Made him jump. "Maybe he needs to use a bathroom," she speculated. "Maybe he needs to borrow a phone. Maybe he's thirsty."

"But why does he have to be thirsty here?" Dwight didn't consider himself the least mean-spirited. Or elitist. It just seemed a fair question.

"Well, we can't stand by and let him limp around till he gets sunstroke." Edith had an extraordinary gift for telling Dwight what to do short of coming right out with it. All right, so she was only hastening the decision he'd have made on his own, eventually. That didn't help him feel any less like a hapless pinball as he chucked a pair of gold cufflinks into a sideboard drawer to be on the safe side, bumped into the row of suitcases ready in front hall for dawn taxi to the airport, and opened the door onto triple-digit heat index. A world of stunning difference from the central air inside. Dwight needed a few seconds to regroup before calling out, "Can I help you?"

But by then, ancient geezer had shuffled halfway up the grey slate walk. His burnished eyes never blinked as they narrowed upon Dwight, and he licked cracked lips, priming them to speak. In his expression resided a strength of will completely at odds with his general infirmity. Osteoporosis had crumpled him so severely that the average catalpa pod looked more substantial. His dark but bloodless complexion reminded Dwight of walnut meat, with comparably deep wrinkles and hairlessness to match.

Dwight was a washout when it came to pegging ethnicities, and even at the edge of point-blank range couldn't tell if angular features were Hispanic or Italian or Syrian. "Mediterranean" struck him as a rational compromise. And the outfit was emphatically generic. White button-down shirt with long sleeves, loose khaki trousers, sandals. If anything, too much coverage for this hothouse climate. Maybe he suffered from poor circulation. "Please, I come back after long, long time away," he wheezed. "I do not want to steal." The rutted face peered up at Dwight's as if in supplication, but also as if Dwight owed him something, an insinuation with which he was less than comfortable. What's more, the accent contributed nothing toward defining the stranger's pedigree. Cajun? Portuguese? Mexican? Dwight was starting to feel rudderless. Say something! "Did you work for the people who used to live here?"

"This place was mine! Something of mine is still here!" Oh, shit. Dwight had wounded the catalpa pod's dignity. He'd also been blindsided by that claim to former ownership, and who was he to brand anyone a liar out of hand? Still, he couldn't see it, not in this upper-crust Colonial Revival enclave, in what had always been, well, an unapologetically white bastion on the East Side of Providence. Like water into cracked cement, the geezer took advantage of Dwight's nonplussed state to slip past him and into the house. This turn of events had scarcely registered when Edith's startled yelp pulled Dwight inside on the double.

How had those decrepit legs carried the unwanted guest to the living room already? Dwight heard him mewl, "Please, I am only Castro. I have come back here for something that is mine." Edith was still at the window, and this so-called "Castro," with hands upraised in a medieval-looking gesture of appeasement, had violated her personal space, to judge by her red cheeks and arched eyebrows and incisors biting into lower lip. She was wedged in among the beige velvet drapes, and had backed well beyond arm's length from the doddering intruder. Dwight could understand why she was aghast, even if it seemed an overreaction. She treated Dwight to a glance that fairly bristled, *I meant for you to find out what he wanted, not ask him in!* Oh, boy. No smoothing this over till she decided in due course to cool off.

Instead, Dwight aimed for a conciliatory tone toward Castro, who was, after all, merely a feeble and confused, if not senile, old specimen. As if anything of his were really on the premises! "Mr. Castro, why don't you have a seat? I'm sure we can get this sorted out in a minute." Castro eyed him as if wary of forked tongues, waddled backward and away from Edith, sized up the furnishings, and planted himself in the leather Deco club chair, their most valuable piece, facing the plasma TV. Dwight perched at one end of the puffy canvas sofa, across the room from the rear picture window, setting his guest in three-quarters profile. Castro swiveled on the squeaky upholstery to confront him head-on, putting Dwight unjustly on the defensive.

Edith, with a valiant post-traumatic smile, was rebounding from the drapes, rising to the occasion, doing her part to defuse the awkwardness. "Can I get you something to drink? It's so humid out there, isn't it?" Barely making eye contact, let alone giving Castro a chance to answer, she was off to the kitchen, with that sway in her hips, more pronounced when she was in a hurry, that Dwight had found so provocative in premarital days, before realizing she couldn't help it, that it wasn't meant to turn him on. Maybe she was less interested in relieving Castro's thirst than in jumping at any excuse to absent herself a while.

Castro did watch her departure with what Dwight preferred to regard as appreciation. Yes, the man must have been parched, though no more perspiration shone on his furrowed skin than on petrified wood, as if his sweat glands had worn out over decades. Nor did he proffer her thanks or other nicety, but to Dwight he confided, "She is pretty, your wife."

Dwight for the life of him couldn't think up an answer to that. Castro didn't visibly care, content with an armchair inspection of the room, from Japanese woodblock prints on the wall to Erté bust on Corinthian pedestal to bronze figurines from Benin on the mantel. Casing the place despite protests to the contrary? Dwight wished in vain for something to say, if only to curtail the mental checklist. Jeez, had the sneaky codger noticed the luggage on his way in? Good luck enjoying Costa Rica for two carefree weeks now. And where the hell was Edith with that glass of whatever?

"Here we are!" she lilted, bustling in with a blue plastic tumbler of cola. In her own good time, as usual. Handed it to Castro, who sniffed it with pursed, questioning lips as the fizz subsided. He tasted it and his features crinkled disdainfully.

"Please, can you put nice rum in this?" he demanded. "Nice Cuban rum."

Dwight and Edith exchanged helpless frowns, far from thrilled at prospects of a drunk, out-of-control foreigner in their den. More disturbing, it was as if Castro knew about that liter of Edmundo Dantes, a gift from Dwight's boss, who'd smuggled it in through Canada. It was locked in the bottom drawer of Second Empire china cabinet in the dining room. On reserve for special occasions. Was Castro psychic? Or a practical joker in the employ of Dwight's boss? In either case, refusing him would likely result in an ugly scene sooner rather than later. This Castro, as two minutes with him had demonstrated, was nothing if not irascible.

Another excuse for Edith to duck out, anyway, and she seized upon it without comment. Dwight heard her clattering in the McCoy bowl full of Lindt chocolates where they hid the key to the cabinet, and then the key rattling in the lock. Castro was also listening, head cocked quizzically to one side. More clinking and scraping of glass against glass, across wood. Followed by the squeal and pop of a cork stopper.

Edith tripped back in, with a cheerful demeanor that may have been less transparently phony to Castro than to Dwight. Castro had to hold out his cup to meet Edith's outstretched arm with the open bottle. Quite admirable, her skill at hovering no closer than absolutely necessary to get the job done. "Say when!" Her smile did become brittle as the level of liquid rose significantly in the cup before Castro gave an understated nod of approval. He sampled the expensive concoction and smacked his arid lips with gusto. Nobody's fault if it sounded more to Dwight like the click of mandibles.

Dammit, with all that fussing over the drink, Dwight had almost forgotten Castro's purported reason for worming his way in, and beaming Castro was relaxing and enjoying his rum and coke way too much. Dwight leaned forward from the edge of the sofa and aspired to a stern, authoritative timbre. "Mr. Castro, when we bought this house, the attic was completely empty, the basement was completely empty, and every cupboard and closet was completely empty. Unless we've missed a secret crawlspace or trapdoor, anything you mislaid was gone when we moved in."

"Mislaid?" huffed Castro scornfully. Then he nestled deeper in the maroon leather, sipped his drink, and adopted a more serene air. "Please, Mrs. Nickerson, you sit down too." Castro extended his free arm toward the sofa and drew circles in the air with his index finger. Edith sighed and played along. Keeping a lid on her impatience, but no longer smiling. Dwight wondered whether guest or hostess would blow up first. Edith had an extensive record of speaking her mind on short notice.

Wait a minute, how had Castro known their last name? Dwight had to rein in his alarm. Let the old guy spook you, and you pass the ball to his court. "Nickerson" was on the mailbox, for God's sake. Or, assuming Castro's claim about lost property was sincere, he could have learned by any number of aboveboard means who occupied his former address.

"The houses around us, the streets and the sidewalks, the ground under our feet, they all feel so solid, like they always will be here, like they always have been," Castro expounded. "But it was not so long ago, things were different, were they not?"

"I don't see how this enters into your business here." When had Dwight asked for an oration? Had he already allowed Castro an inch and ceded a mile?

As if affirming that worst fear, Castro took a slow, exasperating slurp from his tumbler. "This ground we walk on, for example, with the big houses and the neat yards on top of it. Underneath, for thousands of years, was a swamp here that festered and bred sicknesses and vermin. Even less than a hundred years ago, some swamp was around us. The English who first came, they named it Cat Swamp, and the street you call Olney now, it went to the swamp, and they called it Cat Swamp Trail. That swamp is all buried, but who can say it is gone forever?"

"Whether it is or it isn't, every word of this is news to me," Dwight retorted, loath to admit Castro had hit a nerve by reducing his exclusive neighborhood to malarial wetland. "Why should we trust this information?"

Castro shrugged impassively. "No one can be sure of how much history there is, even in one's own backyard."

"Well, maybe I see what you mean," Edith ventured. "I heard there used to be a ravine where Elton Street is. But what does any of this have to do with whatever it is that belongs to you?"

"The ravine? Nothing to do with it, nothing." Sly Castro winked. Yes, of course he was acting purposely obtuse. Not out to fool anybody. Just his little jest, okay?

"Okay, but why in the world," asked Dwight despite wishing he could stop himself, despite misgivings that he was somehow chomping on bait, "was it called Cat Swamp?"

Castro raised his index finger and wagged it back and forth, as if to say, *All in good time, my child.* "It took a little while in front of your house to be sure you still had my thing of value. It will take a little while to relate how that thing of value came to be here."

Oh God, please, just get on with it, Dwight inwardly fumed, regretting he'd ever peeked out the front window. A like sentiment was all too readable in Edith's body language.

"In the beginning was a religious persecution, very long ago, but it is the first cause of my being here." Castro indulged a generous swallow from his tumbler. "In Andalusia, the people had leave to worship as they pleased. But after the Moors were expelled, it became bad, too hard to stay, for those who did not profess the orthodox creed."

Oh no, Dwight silently quailed, he's not really dragging us all the way back to 1492, is he? But yes, he plainly was, and Dwight would have been fidgeting with irritation had he not been spacing out amidst Castro's nonstop babble.

"The Inquisition and the wars about faith were to spread all over Europe. To be safe for the longest time, it was needful to join with the Portuguese, who were sailing to lands with no Christians, with no jealous gods. And what is now New England would be safest, even though the Portuguese had put up a church and a fort where your Newport is today, and sought to convert the Niantic people. But in a few years the soldiers and the priests went away, as anyone could have foretold they would, because the gold and the silver and the trade were elsewhere, and those passengers were soon forgotten who chose to stay and watch hurricanes and lightning hammer away at the fort. Nothing remains from those Portuguese builders except some of the church, visible at sea, and used by mapmakers as a landmark for generations before the Protestant colonies."

Inexplicably to Dwight, the more Castro drank, the more polished his diction, the more educated and articulate his delivery, above and beyond simply warming to his topic.

"And so where the doctrine of the Catholics did not take root, another did, with precious decades to flourish unmolested, and to attract members from among the native men, and to receive those disciples from the Old World with the cunning to seek and find American refuge. For the sake of avoiding friction with the sachems and the shamans of that region, the newcomers retired to territory shunned as worthless and unlucky, a swamp in fact, north of the bay. There they could practice their rituals and libations in privacy, to curry the favor of divine powers sovereign over earth and sea and stars. Native leadership for the most part left these swamp dwellers in peace, unwilling to risk the displeasure of strange gods."

Castro emptied the tumbler and set it gently on the parquet beside his chair. He had crossed the line between doddering and delusional, in Dwight's confident opinion, and where would he go from there? Slipping out of earshot and phoning the police to remove this potential menace might have been the best plan, but then the babble resumed, and Dwight didn't want to exit in the middle of a monologue and maybe set off their touchy powder keg. Wait till the next pause.

"Throughout this era, the only English to come ashore were fishermen who stayed in summer stations, and who had nothing for recreation but to drink and to seduce the native women. These seasonal visitors, and not the next century's settlers, gave Cat Swamp its name, which was later thought to be from an abundance of cattails, or because bobcats prowled there, but no, it was because of the fishermen's own cats that ran off and hid in the swamp, hunting mice and beetles." Castro silently clapped his palms together, with fingertips leveled at Dwight. "And that is the answer I owed you, Mr. Nickerson, is it not?"

The best Dwight could do was nod helplessly, as if he had to keep his head above treacherous current, to the exclusion of almost everything else. A current of verbiage? Is that all it was? Edith was similarly glassy-eyed.

"The people of the swamp were happy to let the cats breed as they would, for they made acceptable offerings to those exalted, almighty powers, greedy for adoration. Much more pleasing to those powers was the blood of living men, which the fishermen also supplied when drunkenness made them easy marks, or when the furious kinfolk of a ravished native woman delivered them bound and naked. If entire boatloads of fishermen were to disappear, for the most part no one would miss them, and if someone did, where would blame ordinarily fall except upon the Atlantic?"

This crazy old coot, this demented story, it must be a hoax, Dwight reverted to telling himself. Staged by his boss, a send-up in lieu of a send-off, before tomorrow's flight. Yeah, that'd be just like him. Any minute now, someone somehow, Castro, boss, or third party, would tip his hand.

"Mrs. Nickerson, you look especially upset about these past happenings. Would it help for me to assure you that fishermen and rapists and slavers were often the same people?"

Castro droned on without waiting for Edith's yes or no. "Those first English colonists came here to escape persecution, even as we did, and those who built the first homes around the bay, and who were sometimes in earshot of our feline sacrifices, pretended deafness to them, in those days when the reputation of the cat was doubtful at best. Again you are upset, Mrs. Nickerson, but you must accept, your ancestors did not care what happened to cats."

Castro's hands were still clasping together and seemed to operate with a fidgety, independent volition of their own. They jerked a couple of inches back, forth, up, down at irregular intervals, as if obeying the skittish pull of the four compass points. Ever more annoying. If only Dwight could find the words to make him stop. At least Edith, bless her, had mustered the wherewithal to scoff, "Mr. Castro, do you really expect us to believe that Providence was founded by a coven of witches?"

"No, no, Mrs. Nickerson," he patiently corrected her. "Witches are friendly to cats, remember? Most of your forebears also made that mistake. Almost none had the learning to perceive the ancient, enormous gulf between my religion and that of superstitious rustics. But those forebears of yours, as their numbers increased over the months and pushed inland, grew violently offended at what they glimpsed and overheard at the end of Cat Swamp Trail, and did oblige the swamp dwellers to quit their refuge of more than a century. In haste those victims of hatred had to scatter into the wilderness or secure passage to far-flung ports where none had knowledge of them or where the roads led to deathless masters who might enlarge their wisdom and impart how men and time might do them no further injury."

Okay, Dwight pleaded, if there's a man behind the curtain, it would be really good of him to pop out right now. The shiny black mantel clock ticked impassively on. Nope, nothing.

"Meanwhile, your forefathers, in their ignorant passion, strove to expunge my people not only from the land but from memory and the written word. Over the long run, that was also preferable to us, insulting as it was at the moment. Of those self-righteous witnesses, William Blackstone alone preserved a plain-spoken account of us in his journal, which fire destroyed along with the rest of his library, days after his death."

"And that was never considered suspicious?" Dwight found himself asking.

"William Blackstone's death was purely natural." Maybe so, but Castro's crooked smile was hardly innocent. Truth interposed as a wall of deception? "And Roger Williams, rumor had it, described us in some coded manuscripts, but they have never been deciphered. Perhaps he was libeling other neighbors altogether. Did you know his mortal remains turned into the root of an apple tree?"

What? Dwight was becoming disoriented, numb to the sofa beneath him as if his legs had fallen asleep up to the waist, or he was at the outset of a poor man's out-of-body experience. "Mr. Castro, do you honestly believe that anything of yours is inside this house?" Dwight managed to ask. "Would you at least do us the courtesy of stating what it's supposed to be? In one straightforward sentence?"

Castro's smile had taken on a capricious edge. Or was it patronizing? His copper eyes, in contrast, had gone emotionless, borderline reptilian. "Hidden in the hinterlands of Cathay were the most accomplished teachers of my religion. In three lifetimes, a disciple could not grasp the fullness of wisdom in one of them."

Castro's hands, still acting on their own, were performing

manipulations, tangentially like a game of cat's cradle, except the shapes they wove, while fluttering apart and spiraling toward a contact they never quite achieved, induced a queasiness in Dwight, a foreboding, yet he lacked ambition to lower his gaze.

"One master too many in the disciplines of Cathay would have sown deadly, useless conflict, so after my intellect had penetrated to the innermost circle of secret lore, I withdrew, and eventually reached the haven of Louisiana bayou, where I could gather and teach acolytes in the seclusion of another swamp for yet more decades, until small-minded men enforcing human law drove us forth again. They caught me and nearly brought me to grief, but I tricked them by playing the mestizo degenerate they presumed I was, and when their guard was down, I escaped by the grace of my religious resources. Today you would call it 'playing the race card,' would you not?" An unpleasantness stole across Castro's grin, as his hands danced on of their own profane accord.

"And when was that?" Edith was surprisingly naive to expect a straightforward answer from Castro now after so many deflected questions. Her hands were wrapped around the upright bottle of Edmundo Dantes in her lap, as they had been since she'd sat down.

"To have your nice bottle of rum, or any fermented beverage, would have been illegal then," Castro disclosed.

"You mean to say you were alive in the 1920s?" How could he lie so blithely? How many years past a hundred would that make him?

Castro's frown may have directed disappointment or condescension, but not sympathy, at Dwight's dull wits.

"How long ago did you live in this house?" asked Edith when it became clear that Castro would not honor Dwight with a reply. Her tone was incurious, as if she spoke only to keep other questions at bay. Was her mind a scary leap or two ahead of Dwight's?

"I have never lived in this house."

To go by Edith's blanching complexion, Castro, in that skewed way of his, had answered a question other than the one she had asked, one that she was afraid of asking. Nor did Castro's hands relax in their manic, unseemly choreography. Why didn't Edith prevail on Castro to leave off, as Dwight would have, had he been less preoccupied trying to concentrate?

"Let me get this straight," Edith slowly enunciated. "You started referring to yourself, in this epic account of yours, as one of the fugitives from this swamp you alleged was here. You're implying, in other words, that you're more than four hundred years old?"

"No, not four hundred years, no."

Petty or not, Dwight disliked how Castro was far more mild-mannered when "pretty" Edith guessed incorrectly. And since Castro liked her so much, why, he railed inwardly again, didn't she insist he stop futzing with his hands?

Copper eyes grew brighter as if Dwight's mute, unbecoming resentment were amusing. "During my sojourn in Cathay, I rambled among the Sichuan mountains and contemplated the archaic dawn sequoias there." Castro had broken into a singsong chant, at a tenuous volume that obliged Dwight to lean forward, ears straining. Was this somehow Castro's roundabout approach to revealing his age? "Those trees offered me food for thought on the origins of predacious flora. Sometimes I observed that flies and bees resting on the soft green platform of a frond had adhered to it, and then fused with it, dissolving into a wingless, glossy husk. Some enzymes in the needles, I inferred, had served inadvertently to trap and digest the insects. The chemical makeup of these trees, and the insects' susceptibility to it, had conspired to make a carnivore of the sequoia, which benefited from this intake of animal protein."

Dwight could do nothing but sit flummoxed, struggling

to follow the breathy lecture. Deranged cultist was effectively impersonating a botanist, whatever the validity of his science. Moreover, his accent waned as his eloquence expanded. Curb a couple of diphthongs, and he could have anchored the evening news.

"Reproductive fitness, I realized, favored those individual plants that derived extra nutrients from prey, within those species endowed with the appropriate enzymes. Therefore certain species would exploit carnivory more and more, to the exclusion of their conspecifics that did not."

Who or what, Dwight puzzled, was the real Castro? That was one riddle Edith couldn't solve any better than he could, though between the extremes of rampant insanity and erratic brilliance, Dwight had to go with the first option, to label Castro a hopeless sociopath who talked a fantastically elaborate game. Trusting first impressions had always steered him safely away from troublesome characters before, and what was this scholarly discourse but a loony departure from equally loony historical fantasy?

"In common with spiders and many another predator, the earliest carnivorous plants needed a means of immobilizing victims while remaining passive themselves." Castro fell silent as if his recital had reached its fit conclusion, and his hands, which had persevered in their enthralling, unwholesome gyrations, dropped limply to his lap.

The gleam in Castro's eyes had subtly ignited along the ridges of his face until an exultant mask leered at Dwight and Edith. In conjunction, a musk had been invading Dwight's nostrils, as if Castro, still dry as petrified wood, had been exuding a malodor of disguised excitement through channels other than atrophied sweat glands. It was acrid with longstanding piss and entrenched fungus, and with a whiff of partial spoilage, of arrested decay, like that of an elderly neighbor's corpse he'd once had to ID at the chilly morgue. Dwight tried to slide back across the sofa, to withdraw a little from that nastiness, but he couldn't budge. Stuck like a fly on a sequoia frond, as if subject to oblique power of suggestion, or was it something more, something in those weaving hands?

"At present," Castro resumed, "I should think I need merely reaffirm the truth that has dawned upon you. In that benighted age before your streets and houses, this place was mine, and a sacred object of mine had to be concealed in haste beneath the water and mud of Cat Swamp. The followers and victims here were mine, the rituals were carried out under my guidance, and when those almighty powers that ravened among men before history return among them to end history, the triumph will be mine. I will be much greater in the future when the stars are right, but in that olden time, I was the King of Cat Swamp."

"But what about us?" Edith's formerly low, sultry drawl had coarsened, thickened, as if airways were clogged with swollen, uncooperative vocal muscles. "Why can't we move?"

Castro bounced implausibly to his feet, brushed invisible specks off his shirtfront, and shrugged. Not a twinge of osteoporosis in his posture. "You are here where you say you belong. Why should you want to move ever again?" His placid smile was at odds with his pitiless copper focus.

"But what did we do to you?" Dwight also had to invest stubborn effort into eking out words, and they emerged malformed, gurgling.

"Mr. and Mrs. Nickerson, you are both proud of your distinguished ancestry, are you not? Of those who carved your towns from wilderness, as you like to put it, as if they simply daubed upon blank canvas? You are not, to look at you, different from your forebears who dispossessed the native peoples, and who dispossessed us. You might say that I am here to retrieve but a single token of what I have lost to you."

"But how could we help whatever it was they did?" Dwight was nearly choking on each syllable. Uncanny that Castro understood him.

"Regardless of that, you are the beneficiaries of what they did, yes or no?" Castro's smile had hardened to the grimness of his eyes. "Can you deny it? Can you stand up and dispute it? No? I thought not."

"Please, we can help you. Whatever it is you're after, let us get it for you." The urgency in Edith's strangled plea implied that she and Dwight were of one panicky mind: Castro meant for their paralysis to be terminal. "There must be something we can give you!"

"The devil has a hand in all bargains," Castro admonished. "Let us not complicate this and involve him. I deal with someone else."

Castro ambled over to Edith and twisted the bottle of Edmundo Dantes up and out of her two-handed grip, as if unscrewing a threaded stopper. Her fingers persisted in enclosing nothing. "My thanks to you once more, humoring an old man his taste. I never did say 'when,' you may recall. For nice rum like this you have no further use."

Dwight heard Castro's sandals cross the kitchen linoleum, and then the door to the back hall creaked wide, and then the sticky back door burst open, causing the whole house to tremble. Dwight next picked up Castro's trail in the back yard, as framed by the picture window. Castro had a long-handled shovel from the garage and was digging in the shade, by amazing coincidence, of a young dawn sequoia, a housewarming present from his boss. With a flash of insight that passed just as readily for psychosis, Dwight pondered how well he really knew the boss. What was his religious affiliation, for instance?

Castro was laboring steadily in the terrific heat like an ox in its prime. Every so often he'd lodge Dwight's shovel in the turf and savor a swig of rum, smacking his leathery lips. Not too late for the joke to be on Castro maybe. Dwight might have smirked had it not been such a chore. An hour ago the landscaping guys had sprayed the grass with chemicals that stayed toxic for three days. Too much to ask for a dose of modern suburbia to be this ancient fiend's undoing? If the fiend's unflagging vitality were any indication, then yes, it definitely was. Dwight watched and watched, with consistently sinking spirits. A gallon of pesticide might not faze Castro. But maybe he wasn't even digging in the right spot. Yeah, that would serve him right. What had made him so cocksure about destroying that portion of Dwight's cherished lawn, anyway?

Castro was chest-deep in his pit, surrounded by mounds of mingled sand and loam. He bent from view and straightened up, dammit, with something in his arms, something the girth of a hassock, and he hoisted it with tender care onto grass already smothering under loose soil. Whatever had led him to the front door had performed unerringly up to the last square foot. He reverently wiped clods and smears of dirt off his artifact with a handkerchief, which allowed Dwight to see it was made of greenish stone, though he couldn't otherwise make head or tail of it. And to think, it had been under his lawn almost four hundred years.

Castro flattened his palms on the grassy perimeter, hoisted himself out of the hole, clapped his hands free of grime and ineffectual lawn poisons, drained and chucked the Edmundo Dantes, and, incredibly, hefted and hugged his prize to his chest with one spindly arm. With no intention, evidently, of tidying up over there. He hove toward the back door and out of sight again, to reenter Dwight's field of vision in the living room. The greenish bulk and Castro's white sleeve bisecting it were briefly all that Dwight could see, but proximity afforded no aid to comprehension. Here was a block of masonry or a squat statue, but of what? There were wings and claws and tentacles and eyes, disjointed, asymmetrical, out of proportion to each other, like an optical illusion set in some unfamiliar mineral, or like a mess on the floor at closing time in a sinister butcher's shop.

After Castro had exited, Dwight spent a futile while fixated on reconciling those disparate body parts to each other. He didn't snap out of it till a car door slammed in front of the house and an engine revved and soon receded. Shit, it sounded like his boss's Explorer. He then belatedly glimpsed in peripheral vision that Edith was gone.

Dwight was reminded of a laughable scene in a movie back at college. An old movie, nowhere as old as Castro, but old enough to be silent, and it was German. In that memorably funny scene, a vampire picks up his own coffin and strolls around with it on one shoulder. Ridiculously or not, Castro had gone that German vampire one better, toting off a boulder plus Dwight's wife. He would have felt more angst about her fate, had his own not been much closer at hand.

He and Edith were supposed to be on vacation. Mail and newspaper delivery had been canceled, the oblivious yard crew would come and go, and the Nickersons had warned friends and coworkers they'd be incommunicado for two weeks in paradise. Nobody would miss them. Nobody would ring the doorbell and worry.

Days and nights inched glacially by, in which Dwight soiled himself and then no longer soiled himself, hungered and thirsted and then no longer hungered and thirsted, shivered in the drafty central air and then went forever numb. Pangs and aches and every sensation wore out, just as Castro's glands had done centuries ago. So did Dwight's spite and indignation at being singled out, at the unfairness of Castro tracing that block of masonry to his backyard among all the equally deserving candidates for slow death in former Cat Swamp. He gradually gave up despising Edith, too, for making him let Castro inside in the first place. At last Dwight was down to one coherent nagging thought, recurring to him more and more rarely, that after a certain unremembered number of days, the ravages of starvation were irreversible.

He was in no shape to acknowledge, or to appreciate the aptness of it, when a scruffy feral tom stole in through the back door Castro had carelessly left open, and began spraying the drapes and scratching up the upholstery, and in general behaving like one more previous owner come home. Dwight didn't even hear the crash when the cat bumped the Erté bust off its pedestal.

Dead Media

NICK MAMATAS

Nick Mamatas is the author of a number of novels, including the pseudo-Lovecraftian Move Under Ground (Night Shade Books, 2004) and, with Brian Keene, The Damned Highway (Dark Horse, 2011). With Ellen Datlow, he coedited the ghost story anthology Haunted Legends (Tor, 2010), and he has also published more than sixty short stories in magazines and anthologies such as Asimov's Science Fiction, Lovecraft Unbound, Long Island Noir, and the Mississippi Review. A native New Yorker, Mamatas spent some time in creepy old Brattleboro, Vermont, before settling in California.

T MISKATONIC, LIKE MOST LIBERAL ARTS COLLEGES, nothing is ever thrown away, but almost everything is misfiled. Lenore Reichl was a junior and knew her way around, but she needed help for what she wanted this time—an actual Dictaphone. For that she had to appeal to Walt McDonald, the ever-present work-study student in the A/V office. The trick was to figure out whether Walt was unwilling to leave his seat or just really too stupid to know what a Dictaphone was. Lenore tried bending over the desk, just showing a little bit of cleavage and most of her teeth. Her piercings glinted. She tapped the toe of her stompy boot. That got Walt away from Facebook for two seconds.

"Look, I don't know," he said. "I did all the tagging here last year. Everything has a barcode now, and there's no code for a Dictaphone."

"Just because there's no code for something doesn't mean it doesn't exist," Lenore said. She and Walt had shared a class last semester—Semiology, which involved watching lots of television commercials. They weren't friends. The mildest of acquaintances, really. They didn't even nod to each other when they passed on the quad, but Lenore did feel comfortable using Walt's name. "Walt," she continued, "just because there's no signifier doesn't mean there's no referent." Walt had been in charge of the video projection unit and had saved the day more than once in Semiology. "C'mon," Lenore said. She licked her lips. Not too flirty, just, more like anxious.

Walt glanced back at the screen, looking at his reflection

rather than the status updates of his online friends. He didn't have too many friends here in Arkham. Not a lot of black kids made it to Miskatonic, and those who did were often subtly abused and often suspected of such crimes as petty theft, Affirmative Action status, and facility with a basketball. Walt was too fat for basketball, too fat for Lenore. Not so fat that he had to go around doing pretty girls with purple hair special favors for no reason, though. "What do you even need a Dictaphone for?" he asked, more to himself than to Lenore.

"I'm glad you asked," she said, and reached into her shoulder bag. It was an Emily the Strange thing, and what came from it was pretty strange itself. A small cylinder wrapped in yellowing paper.

"Is that what I think it is?" Walt asked.

"Yes!" Lenore said. "It's a cylinder, the Wilmarth cylinder. Brattleboro. The mysterious recording of the so-called 'Bostonian' and the Mi-Go. And I need a Dictaphone to play it, to hear the voices. This is primary source material."

"Oh," Walt said. He glanced at his monitor again. "I thought it was something else. Anyway, yeah, that's cool, but we have mp3s of everything, so why bother?"

"We have mp3s of DAT tapes of a cassette of reel-to-reel tapes of a 78 record of this cylinder. Luckily, I'm into vinyl, so I managed to work my way back through the dead media—stuff is definitely dropping out with every generation. It's like oral folklore, what's on here. It's been, you know, changed."

Now Walt was interested. He shifted in the chair, held out his hand for the tube, then carefully undid some of the paper and uncapped it to peer at the wax cylinder within. "All right, but you're coming with me. Four eyes are better than two."

The A/V archive was in a dusty Quonset hut off the library, and it was stuffed with dead and dying machines: VHS players and overhead projectors—the old analog kind with Cyclopean lenses atop craning necks—shelves of slide projectors, and that just on either side of the large entrance. Walt clicked on the light, and Lenore saw the problem. Floor to ceiling, desks and blown-out televisions and snake-coils of coaxial cables spilling from ruined cardboard boxes. The dust was oppressive, and if there was any rhyme or reason to the storage at all it was simple— oldest stuff in the back. "The Dictaphones, if we even have any, are on the other side of this. So let's start moving stuff out of the way. There's a dolly in that corner and we can use a few of the TV carts that still have four wheels to move shit outside."

Lenore wasn't much help. She had on the sort of long lace dress Walt would call "kooky," and needed to hold up the hem with one hand at all times. But boy, did she talk. "I know; it's all basic term paper stuff. Is the so-called 'black goat of the woods' a separate figure from Shub-Niggurath or not?"

Walt shoved some old monochrome computer monitors out of the aisle he was making and leaned in close to Lenore, just so that she could see his eyes roll. "C'mon," he said. "Nobody knows. That's why it's a term paper topic—you can argue pro or con, and everyone knows the arguments and rejoinders and whatnot. It's a religious argument, not a real research question at this point. Not for undergrads, anyway. Wilmarth couldn't comprehend what he got on wax, so I can't imagine what sort of research you have planned to find out… eighty years later."

"Field…" Lenore said, the word rolling off her tongue tentatively, "research."

Walt didn't know what to say. But he found the machine a moment later.

IT TOOK SOME TIME TO GET THE DICTAPHONE WORKING. Walt appropriated some copper wiring from a dead filmstrip projector and put Lenore to work wrapping it in insulating tape. She frowned when Walt cracked the still sleek black case to get at the innards of the Dictaphone.

"This is totally steampunk," Lenore said. "They don't make equipment like this anymore. Everything's so sleek and sterile these days."

"If you like vintage, you came to the right friggin' college, that's for sure," Walt said. It was true. Miskatonic felt lived in. Every stone on the quad was worn. The lights flickered during the frequent winter storms. Monocles, sideburns, and grandfather's suit jacket, moth-bitten and frayed were perennial student affectations. Corned beef hash and liver had regular rotations in the cafeterias. There wasn't even a single vending machine on campus.

"Why does anyone come here?"

"Pfft, you know," Walt said. "You have the rich idiots who couldn't get into any of the *real* Ivy League schools; ninth-generation inbred legacy College Republicans; locals from across the river the College Fathers give full rides to just so nobody swims across and burns the whole place down; Californians who want to be close to skiing, and…"

"And?" Lenore asked, her voice lilting as she stretched the word. She liked this.

"People like us. You know, people with *reasons* to come here."

"So you'll do it." Lenore didn't have a car. Walt did.

"I'll plug this thing in now and give it a whirl." Walt tried putting it in backwards first, by mistake. Lenore had her notes with Akeley's transcript of the recording—or at least the transcript Wilmarth claimed to have received from Akeley— spread out under her palms. Walt touched the sapphire point to the cylinder. The recording was tinny and distant, more crackle than voice. Was that a Boston Brahman chanting "…abundance to the Black Goat of the Woods. Iä! Shub-Niggurath! The Goat with a Thousand Young!" or a toothless old Vermonter putting on airs?

"Akeley himself, running a scam of some sort?" Walt said, but Lenore shushed him harshly. Then that inhuman buzz of a voice, near-chanting, "And He shall put on the semblance of men, the waxen mask and the robe that hides…" What a voice! Like auto-tune, a nail on a chalkboard. Walt didn't hear it so much as feel it. But then Lenore was skeptical. "What if he recorded this on another Dictaphone, then played it back… wouldn't it sound all hissy and strange?" They played the cylinder again, then a third time. Lenore had a pocket watch, yet another Miskatonic fad, with a second hand and took notes with each pass.

"This is some wild shit," Walt said after the fourth round. "But is it telling us anything? Are we debunkers now? Skeptics all of a sudden?"

"Get one of the blanks. Let's try it," Lenore said. She recorded herself—"the waxen mask and the robe that hides"— then played it back, recording that on her cell phone's voicemail, then re-recorded the playback of her voicemail onto the wax cylinder. "You're a freakin' genius, Walt," she said, "getting this thing working." Walt thought himself thinking that Lenore wasn't too shabby herself. He wanted the experiment to fail, so they could do that field research, so that he could spend more time with her. And it did fail. A tiny little Lenore voice, with a trace of a microchip accent, spilled out of the Dictaphone's old speaker. No vibrato, no buzz of the sort that made Walt's molars cringe in his mouth. "Ah well," Lenore said.

"Maybe… the cave's acoustics made it easier to fake such a voice?" Walt said.

"Why would Akeley bother telling the truth about the cave if he was running a hoax?"

"You said that there were things on the cylinder not on the mp3s, that you heard them on the old records and tapes."

"There is." She slid the transcript over to Walt and

reloaded the Wilmarth cylinder. "Listen closely. Listen *past* the words." Walt and Lenore shared a look—Walt confused, Lenore confused by his confusion. "At the recording artifacts, you know," she said. "With the copies, they've either been digitally erased or just degenerated beyond hearing from the process of copying."

Walt got up and turned off the lights in the little office. "The fluorescents, you know," he explained. "Buzzing." He even turned off his computer and threw his wristwatch—yes, he still wore one as a Miskatonic affectation of his own—into a desk drawer. Lenore had a keychain flashlight with which to illuminate the transcript, and a purple-painted finger to follow along. And there was something there, in the opening sounds of the recording. *Ii eh lu uh uh wu.* Then, after the hysterical and uncanny buzz of "a thousand young!" *Ah ih ah ca t'pa.* Just a little hint of *And it has come to pass*, but not in that Boston accent.

"The 'Bostonian' is being fed his lines?" Walt asked.

"Sounds like it."

"By Akeley."

"Or by whoever actually made the recording. Or by someone standing next to him."

"Or maybe it's just an echo of some sort. In the cave."

"Again with the cave!" Lenore said, but she laughed. She was a pale girl, nearly aglow in the darkened room. "…but maybe," she conceded.

"So the original recording has a third speaker. That's great, Lenore. Senior thesis stuff maybe, if you feed it into the right program and manage to extract it, but it's not literature, it's not a determination about Shubby and the black goat." Lenore snorted at *shubby*.

"One more time," she said, and reset the point on the cylinder. This time, just thanks to expectations, Walt heard the other human speaker, and he heard something else. Some of the hisses and crackles themselves seemed to be phonemes now—stage-whispered prompts or at least preliminary throat-clearings from beings beyond the stars. "Ahem ahem," Walt said. "Did these things, if there were any, even have throats?"

"Here is my proposal!" Lenore said. She shot up from her seat and reached for the light switch herself. "There were other speakers! Let's assume that, just for now. At least one other human speaker, be it Akeley himself or a confederate, or who knows. Many people have tried to determine who 'the Bostonian' was, but maybe he's not important. Maybe he was just an actor who was just fed lines by someone else? I say we head to Vermont and find that person, or traces of the same. Field research," she said.

"And then just ask him if Shub-Niggurath *is* the Black Goat of the Woods with its thousand young?" Walt asked.

"Of course not. But we have already expanded the number of people who knew what was going on from two to three. That means that there may have been more, there still may be more. So, come on."

"You know I'll say yes," Walt said. He was always being tapped for favors by non-drivers, but mostly just to the local packie for party supplies. "But what were you going to do if I said no?"

Lenore shrugged. "Like you said, I knew you'd say yes. And if you didn't, Peter Pan to Boston, then Amtrak to Vermont I guess…" She glanced away from him.

Walt spun in his chair and typed something on his keyboard. "I'll take tomorrow off… thank *you*, EZLabor, now check Google Calendar… okay, I'm free. We can go—"

"Now," Lenore said.

Walt laughed. "The stars are right?"

"You know it, kiddo," she said.

T WAS A TEDIOUS TWO-HOUR TRIP ACROSS THE TOP OF Massachusetts to southern Vermont. At night the trees are black and the highway stuffed with tractor-trailers. Walt idly wondered if Lenore planned on killing him in Brattleboro, but decided against. She wanted a ride, after all. How would she get rid of the car, get back to campus? And the great mess they'd left from burrowing through the supply hut of old A/V equipment would be a great clue in itself. Fingerprints everywhere in the dust, the friggin' Dictaphone, half-gutted and left on the workbench. He had nothing to worry about, he decided, this time. In general, though, for students like Walt and Lenore, those few who came to Miskatonic for *reasons*, a bit of curricular violence was never far from their minds.

"Do you have to pee?"

"I'll pee in Vermont," Lenore said. "I've never peed in Vermont."

"It's good to have dreams, and to accomplish them," Walt said. "We're going to run out of shitty mill towns to turn off onto in a few minutes though, so if you wanted to pee—"

"Do *you* want to pee?" Lenore asked. "Or did you just want to visualize my vagina somehow, and let me know you were doing so?"

Walt laughed. "You have a mouth, woman!"

Lenore arranged her Emily the Strange purse on her lap for the millionth time.

Right outside Brattleboro they stopped at a motel and spent the night tiptoeing around one another, in their separate beds, around the door of the tiny bathroom. Neither had brought a change of clothes, but Brattleboro was full of used bookstores and people who shopped at the food co-op and places like Save the Corporations from Themselves—"hemp clothing for ugly girls," Lenore declared as they walked up Main Street the next morning—so they weren't out of place, not Lenore in her lace or Walt in his oversized sweatshirt and low-riding jeans.

"Think the town's changed much?" Lenore asked. Then she nodded at a news rack. "The *Reformer* is still publishing."

"I saw a building dedicated to milk cows, and there was that truck full of lumber rattling down High Street," Walt said. "But yeah, this place is fucked up. One-third hick, one-third yuppie, one-third dirty hippie. So anyway, what's the deal, Missus Peel?"

"Huh?"

"Your plan. *Field* research, remember? We didn't drive two hours to have smoothies for lunch and go back home." Walt pulled out his phone and tried to call up a map of the environs, but didn't get any service. "What the—? No bars."

"Verizon only 'round here!" some too-helpful old timer in coveralls called out as he passed by. "Happens all the time to the casual trade."

Lenore turned on her heel and walked after him. "Excuse me," she called out. "Where might someone new to town find... goats?"

"For what?" the man said, his vowels flat. Now he was suspicious. He looked past the purple porcupine spikes of Lenore's haircut to take in Walt. "Not a good idea to go around upsetting livestock, especially other people's."

"It's for an art project," Lenore said. She made a little gesture at her own clothing.

"Just pictures," Walt said. To Lenore he added, "We'll have to find a drugstore and get a map. And a disposable film camera too."

The old timer recommended the Price Chopper— *Choppah!*—he said it, and then beyond that there was indeed a goat farm. Then he nodded and continued his walk.

"Weird," Walt said.

"Why's that weird?"

"It's weird because it's not weird, if you know what I mean," Walt said.

"Well," Lenore said, "remember, the whole thing with Wilmarth could have been a hoax. There's almost too much evidence—the cylinder, the newspaper articles, letters. If all the stuff happened here, why isn't it mainstream science or literature? So maybe this isn't weird because there's nothing to be weird about."

Walt just gawked openly now as they walked back to the car, looking, looking for something. And he found it in the public parking lot behind the shops of Main Street, on the side of a Dumpster: Goodenough Rubbish Removal.

HE PRICE CHOPPER WAS EASY ENOUGH TO FIND, and maps were plentiful there. There was even a phone book available at the customer service desk, but it wasn't necessary because the answer was right there— Goodenough Road. "As in Akeley's son, George Goodenough Akeley," Lenore said.

"Well, they've been breeding, I suppose," Walt said. It was a sunny day, and Goodenough was sufficiently winding to be interesting, lined with tangles of trees. "Where are we going, for real?"

"Yeah," Lenore said. "Maybe we should stop and buy a gun. There are no gun control laws in Vermont. We can go in *strapped!*"

Walt glanced over sidelong. "Ever fire a gun?"

"I've never been motivated to even touch one before. It's just… you know." Again with the lip, her teeth clicking. She was eager for something.

"Right. It's a road, on a map, mentioned in the documents. We could end up at a goat farm at the end of a long line of Japanese tourists and fat gamers looking for something real."

"Exactly. Where we're headed there's either nothing important at all, or something so horrific that..." She gulped. "Nobody! Has! Ever! Returned!" Lenore rolled her eyes at herself.

"Does this look like a farm?" Walt nodded out the window. "Hey, a cow."

Lenore glanced over. "City boy. That's a friggin' horse."

"In the city, garbage hauling firms are all Mafia. Maybe that's why anyone else who ever had the idea to check out Goodenough never came back."

"Hey, a goat," Lenore said.

HE FENCE STRETCHED ON ENDLESSLY, SOMEHOW, AND the mud of spring was thick under Walt's feet. Tired of looking for a gate or door, he made a brace with his hands and boosted Lenore over, then popped up atop the gate and with some struggling managed to swing his heavy legs over.

"Now we're breaking and entering for the sake of scholarship and hijinks," she said. "It's so sunny today; I just feel like nothing can go wrong. The air isn't like this by the Miskatonic River."

"Yeah, I guess no cotton mill spent eighty years dumping poison into the local water table," Walt said. "Anyway, about the cylinder..."

"Mm-hmm?" She was already striding toward the far off end of the field, kicking up those knees.

"How did you get it? Where did you find it?"

Lenore turned to look over her shoulder. "Jealous? Or suspicious?"

"Incredulous," Walt said. "It's weird."

"I was looking for something else, and came across it in the library," Lenore said. "Let's play pretend. You're Wilmarth."

"Okay, I'm Wilmarth."

"Akeley... goes missing, but you've just talked to him. You rush home and write up a monograph. You even make a note of having retained your flashlight and revolver and suitcase."

"And so how come I didn't snatch up a little canister with the word AKELEY written on the side too? You know, have something to show later, to prove my claims."

"Right. And the talking machine. Clearly, on a literary level, it was just Wilmarth taking a look at a Dictaphone and a wax cylinder and thinking, 'What if this office equipment was crazy alien technology? What would that look like? How would it end up on Earth and what would it do?' So, assume that. What's Shub-Niggurath and the black goat of the woods? One thing, or maybe two things. Maybe he gets some students from the theater department together, feeds them lines as he's recording, just for kicks or for some kind of literary immersion—to create a faux 'document' that gives his story more authenticity, more verisimilitude."

"Like an ARG?" Walt said.

"Aaargh," Lenore repeated. She was only half-joking; one of her boots had sunk into the sod.

"An alternate reality game. Internet games that bleed over into real life, with phone numbers that really work, things you can find in real life, actual people to talk to who give you clues as to the next step. They're huge," Walt said. "They usually just tie into some movie or TV show, but really, people are playing ARGs all around us."

"Sure, maybe it's just like an ARG. Or maybe we'll just go into that farmhouse and some kind old lady will offer us lemonade and tell us about the pet black goat her mother had as a little girl." Lenore shook the mud from her boot and trotted, bored of Walt now. Trotting up to the farmhouse and its adjacent greenery, she even muttered *shrub nigger*—could that be the secret within the old Akeley farmhouse?

No, it was a man with a shotgun leveled at her on the other side of the screen, and when the fat kid pounded up the three steps of the porch to give Lenore a piece of his mind, the old man covered Walt with the gun too.

O, HERE'S WHAT HAPPENED. I FOUND THE SAME Dictaphone cylinder Lenore did, back in 1977. It was really something. Like I said before, some kids attend Miskatonic for *reasons*, and I was one of them. I wanted to know what was going on behind the veil, as it were—I was just a mass of pimples and stringy hair named Marie Anne, and not into anything girls were supposed to be into, and even Women's Liberation didn't change that. The boys in my classes were all so competitive, and as sexist as anything. So when I found the cylinder I listened to it till I'd memorized every audio element, every exhalation and smack of the Bostonian's lips. I even figured out how to do the Mi Go voice. It's easy enough; just a paper and comb kazoo. Practice enough with it and you can "sing" dialogue that sounds uncannily like some sort of vaguely insectoid alien. But I didn't want anyone else to find the cylinder, and I couldn't bring myself to destroy such an artifact, so when I returned it to the campus library, I did so unofficially by placing it on a random shelf in the stacks.

It's easy enough to find the Akeley farm. Wilmarth, who was still alive and teaching a course every semester when I was a student, practically appended directions to his syllabus at the beginning of every semester. He'd made an agreement, you see, with the Mi-Go. They're from Tyche, a great gas giant in the Oort Cloud. A cold and slushy minor planet like Pluto could never support intelligent life, but in the lower depths of a Jupiter-like planet, atmospheric conditions are right for life. Think of jellyfish hundreds of times the size of blue whales, floating in the hot clouds for thousands of years, riding storms older than human civilization. And inside those huge gasbag beings is another kind of ecosystem, one in which smaller, *harder* creatures evolved. They were born, and died, in the hundreds of generations in the bellies of these city-sized jellyfish, and then they finally pierced the membrane of their host organism and were exposed to the elements of Tyche… they were torn to shreds by the winds.

Gas giants are mostly hydrogen, of course. But life will out, and so will intelligence. The harder creatures, the fungal-crustacean Mi-Go, learned to communicate with one another across long distances, over the roar of the endless storms of Tyche, with a form of hypersonic communication that bordered on telepathy. The mind was elevated to the center of Mi-Go civilization. But they were a lonely race. The only other form of life on the planet was the gasbag jellyfish in which they lived, like *Escherichia coli* in the hot guts of an Earth mammal. People used to think the Earth was alive and called her Gaia, worshipping her in mud-soaked and blood-drenched pagan rites. But imagine *knowing* that the thing in which you lived was alive, and without any form of intelligence. How lonely would you be, if you couldn't even pretend that you were anything other than a speck in a blob floating along on the chaotic and deadly winds of a planet hidden a quarter of a light-year from its sun? Lonely enough, indeed. So the Mi-Go reached out to find new life, new minds. And they've been collecting us for quite a while. Such a long while.

Lenore and Walt found out what they wanted to know, just as I did back in '77. Of course, there's no such thing as a "brain canister"—someone was probably eating too much expired pork brains from rusty cans when he came up with such a ludicrous idea. The mind is nothing but a system of electrochemical responses embedded in a network of cells and gaps. Easy to copy, to record onto a new medium. Like the medium of a gasbag membrane. And that's where we are now. I'm here. Lenore is here, and so is Walt. In our new "body" we're immortal and the constant focus of the attentions of the Mi-Go. It took me such a long time to learn to communicate with them, but they're patient. Long-lived anyway, though I've had a dozen generations die, and absorbed them. They spirited me away from my human body; it's only fair that I gain my sustenance from breaking down their corpses, from eating them. The Mi-Go have even picked up the idea of religion from the human minds they study—death is a quaint ritual now. They tear their dead apart and smear their innards against my inner membrane to encourage decomposition and ingestion. And they sing when they do it. The Mi-Go also go to war. Gasbag against gasbag.

In fact, I killed Walt and Lenore just now. *Now* is a relative term, I admit. Time's very different out here, with our 6000-year solar revolutions and endless, changeless lives. Of course we go to war. We're human, and we have nothing else to do but fight over the only commodity we have—our lives, our selves, our memories. And the Mi-Go live to please. I liked Walt and Lenore. They were like me. *Homo sapiens sapiens*, Anglophones, Americans. They drove cars and drank tonic, as I did. Walked across the Miskatonic University quad on crisp winter nights, the snow like mounds of sparkling diamonds on either side of the cobblestone paths. It's been such a long time since I'd "met" someone so much like me. I barely recognize most of the "humans" encoded upon the medium of a gasbag's membrane I come across these days. It's been three million years. The Green Mountains of Vermont have long since fallen to dust, but there's still a little something on the spot of the Akeley Farm, a few feet above sea level, that attracts the tiny, hairless, and half-witted daughter species as different from my human life as *Australopithecus afarensis* is. It was so good to encounter the gasbags encoded with Walt and Lenore, to have *my* Mi-Go tear into them, to drink their memories and for a moment remember what it was like to have limbs, to breathe air, to say words I know with a human jaw.

I hope I find some more like them soon. *Soon* is a relative term. But I'm patient, and old.

The Abject

RICHARD GAVIN

*Richard Gavin is one of Canada's most critically acclaimed
horror writers. His books include* Omens *(Mythos Books, 2007),*
The Darkly Splendid Realm *(Dark Regions Press, 2009), and*
Charnel Wine: Memento Mori Edition *(Dark Regions Press,
2010). His nonfiction writings have appeared in* Ruc Morgue,
Dead Reckonings, Starfire Journal, *and on his blog, "At Fear's
Altar" (www.richardgavin.net). Gavin lives in Ontario with his
beloved wife and their brood.*

1.

EARTH'S END WAS ONLY MOMENTS AWAY, YET SHE STILL had nothing to say to him.

As the jeep negotiated the rugged mountain road, Petra caught herself meshing her hands across her middle in a protective gesture. When she remembered this was unnecessary she crumpled inside and allowed her arms to drop.

"Jee-zus!" Tad blurted as they bounced over a pernicious pothole. After the next hairpin turn the steepness of the incline forced Tad to fumblingly jerk the gearshift into second, first. He thudded his foot down on the accelerator. "Do me a favour, call Charlie and ask how much farther it is. I'm afraid this thing's going to fall apart around us if we don't get there soon."

Petra reached for her purse and began the quest for her cell phone.

Charlie's hello was a peep beneath the rumble of engines and the roar of the open jeep windows.

"Hey," Petra cried. "How much farther is this place? Tad's getting a bit nervous." She pressed the phone hard against her ear. "Charlie says you should chill out." She hoped her tone was not too gleeful; just enough to jab at Tad's already ornery mood. "He also said to tell you the End is nigh."

As she snapped the phone shut, Petra heard Tad mutter something she was sure was an insult.

"First a flight from Providence to Vancouver"—as he

ranted, Tad moved his hand in prima donna sweeps—"now a four-hour drive up this mountain range. Your *friends* really know how to show their guests a good time."

A dozen retorts, ranging from witty to outright caustic, swam through Petra's mind. Certain that whatever reply she chose would be the wrong one, she opted to look silently out at the sycamores and yews, which were reduced to grey-green smears as the vehicle rattled past them.

2.

"WHAT DO YOU KNOW? YOU MADE IT!" CHARLIE WAS dragging a plastic cooler out of his jeep while Douglas stood fidgeting with the clasps of a large backpack.

"No thanks to your lead," Tad called as he exited the second jeep, "or this deathtrap you stuck us with."

"Hey, go easy on her," Charlie replied. "That jeep took a hell of a beating when Doug and I drove through the Badlands a few years ago. Besides, what's to complain about? It got you here, didn't it?"

"Barely."

Gravel crunched beneath the soles of Petra's runners as she crossed the tiny roadside inlet where the vehicles were parked. Charlie's description of their destination as "breathtaking" and "out of this world" had clearly been hyperbole, for as she surveyed the tall, pervasive hemlock trees, Petra saw only common woodlands. The boughs all seemed to mesh, forming a spider's skein, or perhaps a shroud, above her.

Craning her head back, shielding her eyes, Petra discovered that the sky was only visible in shards. She felt foolish lugging the small amateur's telescope along in its cheap plastic case.

"So this is it, huh?" Tad's hands gripped his hips, and his mouth was bent in a sneer of dissatisfaction.

Douglas shook his head. "No, this isn't it. This is just the entrance to the Crawlspace. We won't reach Earth's End for another hour, maybe two."

"Two hours!" Tad cried.

"Maybe less. It depends on how fast you can walk."

"Why don't we just drive up there?"

"Because we'd need a road to do that," Douglas explained. He grinned and added, "The mouth of the Crawlspace here is as close to Earth's End as you can get by vehicle."

Douglas stepped over a corroded iron chain that drooped across a thin footpath. A battered sign warned NO TRESPASSING. NATURAL REGENERATION IN PROGRESS. DEPT. OF AGROFORESTRY, but the faintness of the text rendered the warning inconsequential.

3.

WO YEARS AGO PETRA HAD BEEN SINGLE AND HAD sacrificed her days for slave's wages at an independent book and magazine shop in Providence. Tad had been one of her regular customers. The store sat kitty-corner to the financial planning firm where he was employed, and three or four times a week Tad would escape his desk in order to pay a lunch-hour visit to Petra's store, usually for a newspaper but occasionally a paperback potboiler. His shyness was mild enough to be endearing.

Four months of lingering and small talk elapsed before they had their first date. It was Petra who'd done the asking.

They went to a screening of *Picnic at Hanging Rock* at the

Columbus Theater and then for coffee at a quaint diner that had art deco fixtures and a live jazz trio every Thursday. By Christmas that year they were living together.

But their pantomime of married life began to erode all too quickly, and Petra did not even have wedding day memories to cling to as the watershed of their happiness.

A promotion resulted in an almost exponential increase in Tad's hours at the office. With her meagre financial contributions rendered unnecessary, Petra quit her job. Tad bought a house for her to rattle around in and stew over her fear that day by tedious day she was becoming her mother; someone whose life had always seemed to Petra to be little more than a thirty-year-long stifled scream.

Her only salvation came in the form of lazy daydreaming on the living room sofa. She would fantasize about fashioning one of the upper bedrooms with a crib, a brightly coloured rocking chair, a herd of cartoon zoo animals dangling from a ceiling mobile.

After sharing her fantasies with Tad during afterglow one night, he'd told her they would talk about kids when the timing was better. Timing had always been of great importance to Tad, always.

That night had marked the first in a running stream of recurring nightmares for Petra. These unsettling dreams differed widely in aspect but were unwavering in theme: she would always be held captive by her past. Some nights she would find herself at a party, cornered by several of her ex-boyfriends, all of whom took great pleasure passing a telephone between them and sharing with Tad all the mistakes and embarrassing things she'd done throughout her life. Other nights she would dream of wandering her childhood home, which would be rotted and haunted by the anguished ghost of her mother.

The nightmare where her father, afflicted with something

akin to rabies, chased her down an endless stairway, shouting "Run! Run! I'm coming!" was particularly indelible and had led to more than one bout of insomnia.

4.

HE CRAWLSPACE WAS A WINDING TRAIL DOMED BY fat vines and greenery. The flora was so dense that it actually knitted together, transforming the footpath into a tight, humid tunnel. The growth pressed so near to the ground that those who were foolish enough to roam the Crawlspace had to stoop while they trod its arduously sheer incline.

Charlie and Douglas led the way. They each had large packs strapped to their backs and were lugging the plastic cooler between them. The pair of them were demonstrably more experienced at hiking than Petra, who was practically speed-walking just to keep them in sight. Tad lagged at the tail end of their party. Petra glanced back to note his sweaty, scarlet-coloured complexion and wondered whether it was due to exertion or rage.

"We're nearing the peak," Charlie shouted, "so you need to watch yourselves. Once you cross over the top, this path drops downward. It's steep as hell, so get ready to run."

"Running, too?" Tad hollered. "This just keeps getting better."

"You can always roll down the decline if you want," Douglas suggested without looking back.

Petra couldn't resist stealing a glimpse of her lover's expression, which flaunted the impotent fury of a punctured pride.

The remainder of the upward trudge was effected wordlessly until Charlie called, "Okay, this is it!" Then he and Douglas dipped over the summit and vanished.

When Petra reached the thin ledge, the tunnel of flora became an echo chamber. The low-end thumping of Charlie and Douglas footing full-tilt down the path was contrasted by a high hushing sound, akin to the whirring one hears inside a conch shell.

"Go, go!" Tad ordered as he came up just behind her.

Petra stepped over and began her descent. It felt as though the world had switched on its axis and begun to spin wildly, hurling everything forward and down, forward and down. The overgrowth extended even lower, constricting the tunnel into an airless pipe. The terrain became horrifically uneven; thick vines and chunky rocks jutting up here and there like booby-traps in the soil. Terrified that she might stumble, possibly fracture her skull, Petra began to scream. Behind her came the sound of laughter.

Seconds later she saw the proverbial light at the end of the tunnel. Daylight glimmered at the far mouth of the Crawlspace, brilliant as a struck match-head. By now the thudding of footsteps had stopped, or perhaps had been drowned out by the rushing sound, which was almost deafening.

Petra reached the aperture and came rocketing out onto a plateau of slick flat rock. The sunlight was so radiant that for a beat she thought the world had been consumed in waves of white fire. Her eyes instinctively squinted shut as she ran. Every stomp against the stone jarred her from her soles to her skull.

She thought she might have run forever, when a barrier suddenly knocked against her midsection, blasting the wind from her lungs. Falling forward, Petra opened her eyes to see Charlie holding her. Her face was reflected in the black plates of his sunglasses. She resembled, she thought, a feral daughter, with her scorched-looking complexion and wild, sweat-drenched mane.

"Careful," Charlie said; "a few more paces and you'd have gone right over."

Once her eyes grew accustomed to the glare, Petra surveyed her surroundings. The ocean below refracted the sunlight into a measureless cobweb of diamond-glints.

"Kind of makes you dizzy, doesn't it?"

Petra hadn't even heard Douglas moving up behind her, and she flinched at the sound of his voice.

"And a little jumpy too, apparently," she chirped.

"Please don't joke about being jumpy when you're standing by a nine-hundred-metre drop."

"I'm no good at measuring, but I'll take your word for it. God… this place…"

"Yeah, it's pretty neat. I used to come up here a lot when I first moved here. Charlie introduced me to it. He's been coming to Earth's End since he was a teenager. Not to party or anything like that, usually just to think."

"I'm guessing there weren't too many beer bashes on a cliff like this."

"Or none that lived to tell about it."

Even with his smile to temper it, Petra found Douglas's statement unnervingly cold. She wondered if he sensed her discomfort, for he quickly changed topics.

"When you stand with your back to the escarpment you can understand why this place has always been known as Earth's End. There doesn't seem to be anything out there but water and sky. Go on and stare out there for a bit. It's eerie."

Petra heeded and focused her attention on the expanse before her, doing her utmost to shut out the rock and greenery that braced her. Douglas was right: from this vantage the world seemed as distant, as fleeting as a childhood fever dream. She felt as though she was floating among the varying shades of blue, expanding and soaring through both the great empty sky and unbottomed water at once.

But with this, Petra felt the sky lose its comforting lustre. It revealed all the openness and emptiness of the cosmos. The dark ocean and the ghost-pale foam of its breakers suggested a bottomless pit brimming with damned spirits.

There was nothing here, *nothing*.

Petra's realization of this was palpable, irrefutable. She had reached the omega point and wondered if she could ever return to the life she'd known back on Earth.

But a lengthier study of the vast expanse revealed an incongruity in the distance, a dark blip that disrupted the vacuum of blue.

Jutting up from the Pacific, looking much like a Stone Age dagger or a granite lingam, was a mountain. It was only nominally shorter than the cliff at Earth's End, but was far thinner, almost needlelike. It put Petra in mind of a stalagmite instead of a proper mountain.

"What's that?" Petra mumbled.

"*That*," Charlie began, his voice almost boastful as he pointed to the distant rock, "is a story unto itself."

5.

THE WORLD, FOR ALL ITS SIZE AND BUSTLE, NEVER seemed able (or perhaps willing) to clear a path for Petra to follow. From her earliest childhood recollections of rural Dunwich to her all-grown-up-now life in Providence, she had invariably been the Outsider. Never able to pinpoint the reason for her feeling a few degrees off from the rest of humanity, Petra's childhood was one of lush interior experiences, which she cultivated in order to shield herself from the cold, sterile routines of school and home.

She'd met Douglas when they were students in the same first-year English literature class at Brown University. She was hoping to get an English degree, but Douglas was only taking the lit. class as a breather from his engineering courses. He was (Petra came to appreciate) as ill-suited to the world as she was.

"Sometimes," he used to tell her, "it seems like the only way I can make any headway in life is to listen to my instinct and then do the exact opposite. How crazy is that?"

They got on right away.

Twice they'd attempted to nudge their friendship into something amorous, and both tries resulted in giggly, physically awkward evenings that ended with the pair of them trading secrets in the dark.

The summer between their first and second year of university, Douglas came to accept fully that he was gay. The night he shared this fact with Petra he had taken her for a long walk on Buttonwoods Beach. Standing on the wet sands, under a cold moon, Petra felt thrilled for him but a little sad for herself. Douglas seemed to have found his path, leaving her to bob listlessly alone.

Once Douglas met Charlie while vacationing in British Columbia, his life began to move in an upward trajectory. Charlie managed to get Douglas recruited by the same Vancouver engineering firm that had headhunted him. The pair of them relocated to western Canada before Douglas had even finished his degree.

Petra traded e-mails with him now and again, not really believing that his allusions to having her out to the West Coast for a visit were anything beyond a nicety.

In April she'd written him a lengthy e-mail in which she detailed her relationship with Tad. She had tried her best to sound positive. Douglas was enthusiastic in his response, and a week later he sent a charmingly insistent message:

Petra,

I've had a Eureka! Moment:

August 27th. You and Tad. Charlie and Me. The longest total lunar eclipse in 3000 years (supposed to last 90 mins).

You haven't lived 'til you've seen Earth's End. Let's go watch the lights go out together!

Love,
Douglas

Tad hadn't wanted to go. At all. But after the incessant bad dreams and the other drama of recent weeks, he concluded that perhaps he owed Petra this much. One long weekend, then back to seeking some help for her anxieties. That was his offer. Petra accepted the terms and booked the plane tickets.

6.

"IT'S CALLED THE ABJECT," CHARLIE BEGAN. HE PAUSED long enough to fish two bottles of Corona out of the cooler. He uncapped them and handed one to Petra. "The legend about this place, which supposedly goes back to before the Paleoindians, is that the Creator who shaped this world had forged a thousand planets before it. He was totally indifferent to the worlds he made and would destroy them on a whim. But whenever the Creator made a new world he would send four alien beings called the Watchers to keep an eye on that planet's life-forms while he went off to keep building.

"These Watchers were omniscient. They floated around

Earth, observing us puny humans as we fumbled our way up the food chain, but there wasn't really much of interest down here to a starry being. The early tribes eventually stopped roaming and began to put down roots. Then for eons the Watchers saw nothing more than people planting in the spring, harvesting in the fall, popping out a few kids and teaching them the same song-and-dance. Over and over and over.

"Well, one of the Watchers got sick and tired of this. He wanted people to start looking up at the stars instead of just keeping their eyes on the soil year in, year out. He wanted to show them how deep this rabbit hole really was, so he broke the rules and flew down to Earth. He hid out in a desolate mountain." Charlie nodded to the Abject. He was staring intently at Petra, as if trying to gauge how well he was managing to ratchet up the legend's tension. "Once he was there he began sending out strange dreams to the people, visions of alien worlds and horrible cities that the Creator had laid to waste over the eons

"Most of the early proto-humans didn't think much of those dreams, or didn't understand them. But one man became utterly obsessed with them, so much so that after a while he couldn't take the life of Homo sapiens any longer. He went off to live like a hermit, far away from boring old civilization. Naturally he chose the most remote mountain he could find to live his solitary life. Lo and behold, if this guy didn't come upon the Watcher.

"The Watcher offered to teach this man some very special things, which he did. The man learned how to cross the wall of sleep, and how to speak to the dead souls in all the ruined cities that are buried somewhere out there.

"So, things were going good—depending on your definition of good—for this man. But then the Watcher told him that their relationship is give and take. Since the man had been given a taste of the otherworldly, the Watcher wanted to get a better foothold in the worldly.

"He'd developed an interest in changing us humans, you see. An interest in giving us powers we aren't meant to have. So the Watcher instructed his devotee to bring women to the cave for the purposes of... well, procreation. The Watcher wanted to create a species that looked human, but had monstrous souls. This race would have the best of both worlds; souls that could roam the stars and bodies that allowed the Watcher the use of opposable thumbs, taste buds, emotions.

"The student obeyed and brought the Watcher women, probably against their will. In time a little colony of these half-human, half-Watcher beings began to grow within the mountain cave.

"Well, eventually the other Watchers got nervous about not hearing from their brother, and they decided to check in on this corner of the world. When they saw what was happening they immediately reported it to the Creator. He was so outraged that he cleaved off part of the world and filled the divide with water. He banished the fallen Watcher to his cave and cut off his followers from the rest of the world. He then transformed them into ghouls, hideous things.

"From that night on the Creator said that this cliff we're standing on would be the actual end of this world, and that mountain over there would be known as the Abject, the Hell where all the blasphemers were imprisoned. He vowed not to destroy this planet, not because he cared about humanity, but because he wished to inflict eternal punishment on the Abject."

"That's quite the fairytale," Tad said.

Charlie chortled. "It's just an old spook story, Tad, nothing to get nervous about. Now, who wants another drink?"

By then Earth's End had begun slipping into the gloaming. The group laid out blankets upon the cold, puddle-laden rock.

Wine bottles were uncorked, steak sandwiches and brie and apples were served and gobbled.

In the sky just beyond the needlelike pinnacle of the Abject, a crescent moon was visible, crowned by the shimmer of the first eager stars.

7.

A FEW WEEKS BEFORE SHE'D RECEIVED DOUGLAS'S invitation, Petra had gone with Tad for a late lunch at an English-style pub on Hope Street. She had stopped the waitress immediately after Tad had ordered them two rye-and-gingers; their customary drink. As the waitress had been leaving their table, Petra had gently gripped the woman's elbow and requested that the bartender hold the rye from hers.

With that, Tad had looked at her and he'd known. He'd known. For a long spell he'd merely stared at her, not saying anything. When he did finally speak, his choice of words ("We can correct this") had motivated Petra to spring to her feet and hurl her drink in his face. It was the first time she'd ever done such a thing, the first time she'd even *seen* such a thing done, save for the movies.

She'd stormed out of the restaurant and into the bustling crowd on the sidewalk.

And all at once Petra had felt the world disintegrate. Providence had paled to an indistinct grey haze. Everything slowed to a crawl. The people that milled about her all sounded as though they were speaking behind glass.

Things stayed that way for some time. Somehow while in that cumulus state, Petra must have reconciled with Tad, must have considered what he'd had to say about the situation.

Somehow she must have consented to have the issue "corrected."

The problem was fresh enough that the remedial action was but a day procedure. When it was over, Tad had come bearing white orchids. Petra had slept a lot and tried not to think about the fact that her long-standing desire to carve a niche for herself, to create *someone* who was like her in some way, had been eradicated.

The nightmares had returned almost immediately afterward, with unmatched relentlessness and ruthlessness. In this new batch, the stairs that Petra tried frantically to run down would dissolve like soaked sugar, and her father's following cries were no longer in English (*"N'gai, n'gha'ghaa, bugg-shoggog, y'hah…"*).

In these recent nightmares, Petra's father found her.

Nightly she would feel herself being clutched, choked. But not by human hands.

8.

OW EFFECTIVE THE CHILDREN'S TELESCOPE WOULD BE at discerning constellations Petra had yet to learn, but she'd discovered that it did serve as a very effective spyglass for studying the mountain of forbidden things. The encroaching nightfall smudged a great many of the mountain's finer details, but as she stood panning the telescopic lens up and around the Abject, Petra was able to see great cragged rocks that were bearded with sun-bleached weeds. Some of the mountain's indentations held stagnant rainwater, as though they were libation-bearers. With its barrenness and its isolated locale, the Abject might as well have been an alien planet.

When she panned upward to discover the great cave entrance, Petra almost gasped. It was a granite hole that held the ugliest of blackness. She truly was terrible at measuring things, yet Petra still had the undeniable impression of the cave's vastness. She could almost understand why people would decorate a place like this with a legend of fallen Watchers and barbarous cults. Almost.

"I recommend using one of these for the actual eclipse," Charlie called.

Petra lowered the eyepiece and turned in Charlie's direction. He was seated on the cooler, struggling to assemble a small cardboard contraption.

"These things are designed for eclipses. I gather they're safer."

"You've got nothing to worry about," Tad rebutted. He was reclined beneath a poplar at the forest's edge, his mind and his thumbs enthralled with his Blackberry's Sudoku program. "Solar eclipses are the only dangerous kind."

"Well, better safe than sorry, right?" Douglas said. Petra recognized it as yet another expression of his peacekeeping nature. It was a quality she'd always admired about him, loved about him, in fact.

Petra accepted the plastic cup of white wine Douglas offered her.

"Should be soon," she said.

"Yes. Oh, hey, if you walk a bit this way you can get a really good view of the tree line." Once they were out of earshot, Douglas said to her, "Okay, now tell me everything."

Petra's response ("What do you mean?") was so insincere an attempt to sound bewildered that even she didn't buy it. She looked at Douglas and saw him looking at her, the way he used to, the way he always had, the way Tad never did. She pressed a hand to her mouth and began to sob.

"I'm sorry," she gasped. She leaned against Douglas and repeated, "I'm sorry. I didn't mean to do this. I'm ruining the whole night."

"To hell with the night," Douglas replied as he gave her shoulders a reassuring squeeze. "Talk to me."

"I would if I could. But I don't even know what's wrong with me. I don't know where to begin."

"So start at the middle."

"I'm lonely," she blurted. The words sounded odd as she spoke them, almost like a fib she was feeding Douglas to stave off his prying. She hadn't thought of herself as feeling lonely. She lived with Tad, after all. But somehow this pair of words also felt true; a simple summation of her innermost workings.

"I could tell."

It was on the tip of her tongue to tell him about all the rest; about the abortion and the sickening hollow feeling she'd had in her heart ever since, about her occasional desire to check out of the world, about the unbearably horrific dreams. There was so very much to tell.

"Hey, you two!" Charlie shouted. "It's almost time!"

Petra craned her head upward to see a lightless disc slipping over the moon.

9.

HE BLACKNESS LURCHED ACROSS THE MOON AT A PACE so tedious it was almost unbearable, or so it seemed to Petra. It was like watching a crab crossing a white desert. She and her three companions stood on Earth's End, watching the umbra scab over the lunar light.

Petra momentarily allowed her eyes to drop to where the

Abject was, or had been before the masking had camouflaged it utterly. She raised her flashlight, strangely bemused by the feebleness of its beam. The light was but a skeletal finger poking into the great gulf of space. It scarcely seemed to reach beyond the cliff's edge before being smothered completely.

As the eclipse reached its zenith, Petra silently marvelled at just how richly varied the Night could be, how the dark could splay and flaunt itself in so very many textures and shades. She wondered if it was always this way, or if tonight's rare celestial contingency caused these rare visions. Either way, Petra could not help but be awed by the sights. And the sounds.

Upon first hearing it, Petra dismissed the noise as merely a forest sound distorted by distance and echo. Perhaps it was a drunken holler let out by Charlie or Douglas, both of whom were brandishing empty wine bottles like clubs. The sound certainly hadn't come from Tad, for, as a quick pan of the flashlight revealed, he was too busy exhibiting his boredom.

As the noise persisted, Petra realized that her assumptions about animals or her companions had been foolish, for the faint wail was clearly coming from somewhere in the blackness before her.

Her repeated attempts to find the source of the noise were as futile as her first, but now Petra was frightened, panicked. Somewhere in the night, with its buried moon and its dead stars that were unable to pierce the heavy fleece of clouds, an infant was screaming. It was the thinnest possible sound, but was unmistakably the cry of a babe lost in some unreachable nook of the night. Petra felt heartsick. The mewling was so forlorn. It was the howl of something unwanted, something abject.

She only became aware that she had stepped off the cliff's edge after she'd glanced down and saw nothing but blackness beneath her feet. Perhaps she was dreaming, or was already dead. But if this was annihilation, it was exhilarating. Petra felt unbounded, as open as the night itself.

Petra began to walk, and the shadows felt downy beneath her, as soft as thunderheads. Perhaps she was projecting, but Petra felt that every step seemed to calm the unseen infant. She walked on, across a bridge that was formed in darkness and of darkness.

She wondered what the poor babe might look like after being flung from the end of the world. Her mind conjured the image of a bat-wing bassinet set beside a fire that wept Hell-glow and smoke.

Petra could not even hear the cries of her companions behind her, so complete was her enchantment.

She looked up and she saw.

10.

AD HAD KEPT HIS INTENTIONS OF RETURNING TO British Columbia to himself. He had no friends to share these plans with, of course, but even when he booked off the last week of August he told his supervisor it was to catch up on some renovations around the house; a plausible excuse as his home had fallen into disrepair since Petra's demise. Tad had never realized how warm and full the house had felt when they had shared it. But now it was cold and dirty and hollow, like an old warehouse, an excavated tomb.

The weather during the flight was pacific, as though nature was speeding him along to face that which he'd previously been unwilling to face.

He spent the first night holed up in a motel, trying not to think about the close proximity of Earth's End, of the Abject, of Petra's watery grave.

The following morning was dull and dim and rainy. Tad partially hoped that his rental car would skid out on the mountain road. He was actually nourished by morbid visions of himself being impaled on a tree. But, after several wrong turns, he ultimately arrived at the neglected entrance to the Crawlspace. He'd been dreading the possibility of finding Douglas's jeep parked along the side of the road. Perhaps he and Charlie had thought of marking the tragic anniversary in the same manner. But the area was as vacant as it had been last summer, perhaps the way it had always been.

It was late afternoon, but the sky was so heaped with grey that it felt like evening. Tad remained slumped behind the wheel, watching the raindrops splatter into amoebalike shapes on the windshield. At last he reached over and dragged the .38 from the glove compartment. Tucking it into the front of his jeans, he exited the car and disobeyed the NO TRESPASSING sign for the second time in his life.

The Crawlspace went past in a green blur. Every so often Tad thought he saw Petra just ahead of him, racing once more toward her death under an eclipsed moon.

The ocean roared and crashed in great tumults at the base of Earth's End. The atmosphere was hazed with mist. The Abject was little more than an onyx pin swathed in fog.

Tad's gaze went downward, his mind raced backward.

He hadn't wanted to relive the night, and certainly not with such vivid, lacerating clarity, but the interred memories began to claw their way back to the surface.

Tad imagined himself once again standing under the occulted moon. The white wine and beer had made him feel that the cliff he stood upon was on a pitch, for he swayed to and fro, listening to the two queers yammering and tittering like schoolgirls. Petra was standing aloof, shining her flashlight ahead of her, into the darkness. She'd been leaning forward, had been shielding her eyes with her hand as if this action would somehow enable her to see.

What had she seen?

The question had been gnawing at Tad for a full year. On those rare nights where he was able to snatch some REM sleep, *that* image would bloom in the grey haze of sleep, wrenching him into a panting, twitchy wakefulness. He would see Petra taking that lone fatal step over the edge, would see her being instantly subsumed by the night.

Had it been he who'd inspired Petra to jump? What had driven her to drop so casually, so easily?

Tad pulled the revolver from under his belt and examined it. He began to sob. It was the first time he had cried over Petra.

He'd been downright stoic through the long investigation that came once that rare darkness ebbed and the moon returned, and later the sun. He had stood wrapped in a fibrous grey blanket that one of the emergency workers had given him. Douglas had been given a sedative to calm him. Charlie had wept and snivelled while he'd insisted over and over that he'd had no clue as to how Petra had fallen.

The boats had bobbed across the ocean for three full days afterwards. They'd dragged the same area again and again but turned up nothing. Tad had been warned that the chances of recovering Petra's body in these waters were slim.

11.

PERHAPS THERE WAS SOME CORNER OF TAD'S SOUL THAT was sanctimonious after all, for despite many repeated attempts at placing the .38's nub against his temple, he was unable to squeeze the trigger. So he remained seated, his legs dangling over the edge of Earth's End, his body shivering from the cold shower that continued to fall upon him. He looked out at the Abject, and in a weird way he felt it was he who was being looked at, watched.

The rain eventually lightened, but by then the sky had grown dark.

"Petra…"

He spoke her name quietly, almost sibilantly. He was exhausted in every sense of the word, too drained to speak in anything above a whimper.

It must have been this destroyed state of mind that caused the optical illusion of the fog swirling into a great funnel; the chute that afforded Tad a clear view of the Abject.

There was a fire in the great cave, or so it looked to Tad. He scrabbled back from the ledge and rose to his feet. He could see plump sparks of light glowing like flung embers against the ancient dark. These flint-sparks enabled Tad to see that the rim of the cave was eroding, quickly. Its stone edges were peeling back to reveal…

Teeth.

And then the cave was no longer a cave, but a crooked grin.

The face that pulled up and out of the rock was immense, with a glacier-pale complexion and eyes like stagnant tarns.

Tad's vision blurred, wavered. The cliff felt like pudding beneath him. He glared dumbly as the Abject sprouted an arm, another. And as the vast thing shook off the crust of its deosil hibernation, it fanned its limitless wings, eclipsing the gibbous moon behind a veil of black plumage and dangling tufts of rot. Each heave of the thing's scaly chest choked the air with stench and embers.

Its howl shook Earth's End and dropped Tad to his knees.

The Watcher turned its dead gaze to the cliff. It reached, as though it could grasp the escarpment with ease. Tad's mouth worked frantically, forming silent pleas.

'*She saw this…*'

And then Tad saw Petra.

She was walking on night air, or so Tad thought until he looked down and discovered that the hideous thing from within the rock had stretched one of its wings across the water, forging a bridge between its Outer realm and the world of men. There were other figures perched on various ridges of the Abject, human in size if not altogether in shape; just as the Abject itself had been mountainous in scope, but not in composition.

Petra, looking feral, black-stained, yet regal in her madness, trod upon the feathery arch. Most of her body looked positively ossified, save for the belly, which was swollen with fledgling life.

She held something in her spindly, filthy arms.

Something that shifted and mewled.

Something that she freed.

Something that came lurching at a great speed toward Earth's End.

Tad saw the thing pushing itself along on unnumbered flabby claws. Its eyes were like the suckers on a deep sea creature's tentacle. Its mouth was nothing but tongue.

Tad prayed he'd have time enough to fire once.

Dahlias

MELANIE TEM

Melanie Tem's work has received the Bram Stoker, International Horror Guild, British Fantasy, and World Fantasy Awards and a nomination for the Shirley Jackson Award. She has published numerous short stories, eleven solo novels, two collaborative novels with Nancy Holder, and two with her husband, Steve Rasnic Tem. She is also a published poet, an oral storyteller, and a playwright. Her stories have recently appeared in Asimov's Science Fiction Magazine and the anthologies Supernatural Noir, Shivers VI, Portents, Blood and Other Cravings, and Werewolves and Shapeshifters. The Tems live in Denver. They have four children and four granddaughters.

I N ROSEMARY FARBER'S DREAM OR WAKING DREAM OR hallucination or vision, that sunny July afternoon on the couch in the house she'd lived in since her marriage just after the second world war, on the dead-end street in the little town near the foothills of the Colorado Rockies that had officially slid into suburbia but retained much of its insular small-houses-and-big-trees feel—something was coming. She was no more or less its object or prey than were the rabbit brush or the fox, but it would get her, which she thought not entirely a bad thing.

In Nina Scherer's multi-tasking rush—on her cell setting up an appointment with a client for later that afternoon, juggling the red and yellow dinner-plate dahlias from her yard and the chicken casserole and chocolate chip cookies she'd stayed up late last night getting ready to bring today, checking her Daytimer for when and where she needed to have her son at band and her daughter at karate, trying to remember if there was enough milk at home for breakfast—in the midst of all this getting-through-the-day and keeping-things-running, something seemed vaguely odd to her about the meadow between her grandmother's house and the river. Something out of the corner of her eye about the tall summer grass, about its color or its motion in the breeze. This impression didn't really register with her until she was already on the porch, and it was too much hassle to back out and look again.

When Nina called and pushed open the door, Grandma Rosemary was under an afghan on the couch. She spent most of her time there now, looking tired and ninety-one years old but not alarmed, not in pain, not otherwise distressed. In fact, looking calmer than Nina herself ever felt.

"Hi, Grandma." Nina set the dahlias on the coffee table and the food on the counter. She bent to kiss the old woman, so dear to her for so long, still Grandma Rosemary but going away from her a little every day, as if pulled down some slope into a place or a placelessness where Nina couldn't follow, wouldn't want to follow, would never want to follow. Although a little rest would be nice.

Rosemary turned her head. "Those are lovely."

"It's been so dry. Our water bills are sky-high, and the garden is still struggling."

"They're so big and bright."

"They grew that way just for you." Nina smiled past a sudden lump in her throat.

"Well, not really. We're in the same world at the same time, is all, the dahlias and me. Nothing personal. I expect I'm a lot more interested in them than they are in me." She chuckled.

Nina's phone vibrated and Caller ID displayed a name of someone who, she decided rather grudgingly, could wait. In the seconds it took for the call to go to voicemail, the worry that not answering it had been a big mistake lodged in her mind where it would cause persistent low-level distress, for in her business there was a commonplace though inaccurate adage that a missed call equaled missed opportunity. In fact the call, and the follow-up text message and e-mail she wouldn't find until much later, were about something that really didn't matter very much, though the client was convinced it did.

One of the cats glided from the couch onto the table and, with that lovely and utterly inhuman pink-tongue flickering, lapped delicately from the water in the vase. Hoping nothing in dahlias was toxic to cats, Nina inquired of her grandmother as she put her cell phone away, "How are you?"

Rosemary said, "Something's moving in and it will take me. I don't have much longer."

When Rosemary was like this, being in a hurry didn't work. But Nina had only about forty-five minutes, fifty at the most, before she had to be back at the office for the team meeting. She knew she'd regret it if she missed this conversation. Really, it was the least she could do, and Grandma Rosemary had always been fun to listen to, with her family stories from as far back as the Civil War, her on-the-spot composition of rhymed and free verse, the sense that she was always engaged with more than one world at a time. Childhood summers spent in this house had affected Nina in ways she wasn't completely aware of, showing her—though she hadn't learned it very well—how not to take herself too seriously in the larger scheme of things and, at the same time, fostering her m.o. of staying busy, filling time to overflowing, by sheer perpetual motion declaring her own significance.

She should have paid attention to Rosemary that afternoon, borne witness and learned something. It wouldn't have made any difference in what happened, but still she should have listened. Instead, "Oh, Grandma," she remonstrated, smoothing her palm across the thin white hair, "don't talk like that."

Rosemary smiled indulgently. "All right, then, what shall we talk about? What's new with you?"

The rocker tipped forward and stayed that way when Nina sat on the edge of the seat. She never knew quite what to say to that question. "Nothing much new, I guess. Same old, same old. You know?"

"How are the children? How's Ken?"

"Good. They're all good. Busy."

"Give them my love."

"I will. They said to say hi." They hadn't, but she told

herself they would have if they'd thought of it, which actually wasn't likely.

Anything beyond small talk ran the risk of a longer and deeper conversation than either of them wanted that day. Yet they were both restless, dissatisfied with the chitchat, neither knowing why. Rosemary thought her peevishness was because of her profound, unremitting fatigue. Nina thought hers was from having so much to do.

Outside, the meadow grass undulated, a swath glistening in the high strong sun and bending under the living weight that was moving up from the river, closer and closer to the house though neither the house nor anything else was its particular target. Rosemary knew it was coming. Nina didn't quite yet.

"Are you hungry?" Nina tried.

"I'm never really hungry anymore."

"You have to eat."

This exchange they had almost every time Nina visited. But usually Rosemary didn't say so directly, "Why? Why do I have to eat?"

"What do you mean, why? You have to eat to live." Nina didn't have time for this. Rosemary didn't have much time, either, but the time she had wasn't spoken for anymore.

She did eat a little, a few spoonsful of the casserole, half a cookie, a swallow or two of milk. Nothing tasted good, more a function of her diminished gustatory, olfactory, and tactile senses than of the intrinsic merits of food. Nina ate quickly and quite a lot, sampling, mostly to check on the quality of her own cooking, which she found somewhat lacking. Rosemary said it was good, and it was, because of the companionship and forethought, and also because of the abundance of chips in the cookies, in some places the dough embedded in a melted mass of chocolate rather than the other way around.

They talked—Nina talked—about things that once

had aroused her grandmother's interest, often passion: the kids, the economy, the war, religion, politics, family stories. Rosemary reminisced about this neighborhood as it used to be, when at weekly coffeeklatches the women got mending and fancy work done and chatted about mostly inconsequential things made to seem consequential by the sharing. She always pointed out that it hadn't all been placid, there'd been things hidden and not-so-hidden—child abuse, infidelity, illnesses and accidents, a kidnapping. This time how she put it was, "We weren't really friends. But we were friendly. Those get-togethers were like solid ground. Everybody's gone now. Some moved away and didn't keep in touch. Some died. Francine Pollack went to a nursing home last month. So now I'm the only one still left on the street from those days. I'm an island in a rising sea."

"I'm sorry, Grandma. That must be a terrible feeling."

"It's the way of the world."

"Well, we don't have to like it."

"Doesn't matter if we like it or not."

Rosemary saw no point in saying any more right then about what regularly swept through the neighborhood like a viscous transparent tide. It had brought the great love of her life as well as his early death, the Klingmans' house fire and also their glorious roses, Mark Abernathy going MIA in Vietnam and Cheryl Raines becoming a doctor in sub-Saharan Africa, hand-built houses bulldozed for a strip mall and a lovely new creekside park replacing dilapidated and dangerous apartments, both Francine Pollack's deterioration and her good long life— bringing or causing or revealing, Rosemary didn't know, but all of it with the utter indifference she found terrible and reassuring. "I'd like to take a little walk," she announced, and began the laborious process of getting to her feet.

Startled, Nina took refuge in glancing at her watch. "Oh,

Grandma, I don't think—There's not enough time— Are you sure you can—?" But she hastened to support the unsteady walker that her grandmother was using to pull herself up.

They made their way out the back door. It was a dry hot summer, and petunias were languishing in their pots. "Do you suppose it would help," Rosemary asked, breathlessness and strain altering her sardonic intent, "if we prayed for rain?"

Nina was praying that Rosemary wouldn't fall, that she would make the meeting, that she had enough gas in the car for all the running around she had to do yet today. Whether she really believed in the efficacy of petitionary prayer or it was only a ritual like a jump-rope chant, it gave her the illusion of calm while actually adding to her tension. Uncomfortable in the heat and her two-inch heels, aware that her cell was beeping with missed calls, she could manage only, "Maybe."

"God," Rosemary panted, "whatever that means, most likely cares not a whit about my dried-out petunias or your drooping dahlias."

"So God hates us? Or the universe or whatever?" Nina couldn't tell whether she should take her grandmother's soft elbow or put an arm around her or not.

"I think we're of no interest to him. It."

"Gee, Grandma, that's cheery."

"Not cheery." Rosemary teetered and Nina grabbed her. "But not *not* cheery, either. Neutral. It just is."

"You're going to fall. It's hot out here. Let's not do this."

Rosemary saw or felt or tasted or in some other way took in the gloss moving up over the meadow. Nina probably didn't yet, or didn't know she did. It had oozed around the apple tree now and under the ancient swing set. The tree would live quite a few more years to bear hard little fruit for the crows and squirrels, but the swing set would finally rust through that fall. Nina, realizing her attempt to be helpful was actually contributing to the old woman's unsteadiness, let go of her and just stayed close.

Nina had been having episodes of vertigo and pounding headaches, once or twice with blurred vision, and every now and then two fingers of her right hand went numb. Stress, she was sure. She didn't have time to do anything more than be sure the Ibuprofen bottle in her purse was always full. Right now she was having some trouble with her left foot. She didn't mention this to Rosemary or anyone else, didn't give it much thought, her thoughts being busied with many other things, at the moment her grandmother's slow but somehow headlong momentum. "Where are we going?"

"Just down the meadow a little ways," Rosemary said. She was in its path. Everybody was in its path. It was time. Might as well go meet it, see what would happen next. She thought to assure her granddaughter, "It won't take very long," which was true, but what she couldn't know was that it would take the rest of Nina's life.

Frail as she was, Rosemary managed to guide the two of them across the patio and down into the back yard. This meant navigating three steps and the sliding patio door that stuck, requiring Nina to pull hard enough to compromise the balance of them both, individually and together. Clouds were moving in from over the mountains, where weather almost always came from. "It couldn't have stayed pretty just a few more minutes for us," Nina grumbled. The air was humid now, full, as if threatening rain, but it wasn't threatening anything, even if it did rain. And in this case there would be no precipitation all that week, though yards and gardens and the meadow itself could have used drenching.

The meadow looked wet to Rosemary. To Nina, meaning to concentrate on her grandmother but mostly worrying about the time and all the obligations waiting to consume her at work and at home, it just looked big. Maybe it rippled a bit, if that wasn't one of those occasional visual distortions that would turn out to have been harbingers. "Grandma," she said, "we can't go all the way down to the river."

Quietly Rosemary said, "No need." Nina didn't ask what she meant. What Rosemary meant was something like, "It doesn't matter whether we go all the way to the river or stay where we are or go back inside the house and lock all the doors. There's no need to do anything." But even if Nina had asked, Rosemary wouldn't have been aware of all that.

From years of use—horseshoes, baseball, barbecues, dogs, gardens planted and then left to grow over and then dug up again—the ground back here was uneven. When Nina fell, she thought her heel had caught in a hole or on a hillock. In fact, a blood vessel in her brain, weak and bulging for some time without the knowledge of its host, had just burst. Nina might have been aware of pain, thunder inside her head, panic about all the things she was leaving undone, sorrow and guilt about Ken and the kids, the sentient substance that spread over her without any intent at all. But, really, there wasn't much chance for her to be aware of anything.

Rosemary, though, watched it happen. Watched the slime flood the long meadow, claim her granddaughter, and keep right on moving. With great effort and risk, she bent to hold Nina's hand, feel for her pulse, touch her wet cheek. In what for her was haste, she went back to the house, walker rattling, body barely carrying out her desperate orders, after much struggle got the patio door open and found the phone where she'd left it on the coffee table beside the gorgeous, indifferent dahlias and the flicker-tongued alien-tongued cat oblivious to her as it drank from their vase.

Bloom

———⊰⊱———

JOHN LANGAN

John Langan is the author of a short story collection, Mr. Gaunt
and Other Uneasy Encounters *(Prime Books, 2008), and a
novel,* House of Windows *(Night Shade Books, 2009). His
stories have appeared in the* Magazine of Fantasy & Science
Fiction *as well as in anthologies including* The Living Dead
(Night Shade Books, 2009) and Poe *(Solaris, 2009). He lives in
upstate New York with his wife, son, dog, and a trio of cats, and
whatever's scratching at the walls.*

1.

IS THAT—DO YOU SEE—"
Already, Rick was braking, reaching for the hazards. Connie turned from the passenger-side window at whose streaky surface she had spent the last half-hour staring. Eyes on something ahead, her husband was easing the steering wheel left, toward the meridian. Following the line of his gaze, she saw, next to the guardrail about ten yards in front of them, a smallish red and white container. "What?" she said. "The cooler?"

"It's not a cooler," Rick said, bringing the Forrester to a stop. His voice was still sharp with the edge of their argument.

"What do you—" She understood before she could complete her question. "Jesus—is that a—"

"A cooler," Rick said, "albeit of a different sort."

The car was in neutral, the parking brake on, Rick's door open in the time it took her to arrive at her next sentence. "What's it doing here?"

"I have no idea," he said, and stepped out of the car. She leaned forward, watching him trot to the red and white plastic box with the red cross on it. It resembled nothing so much as the undersized cooler in which she and her roommates had stored their wine coolers during undergrad: the same peaked top that would slide back when you pressed the buttons on either side of it. Rick circled around it once clockwise, once counterclockwise, and squatted on his haunches beside it. He was wearing denim shorts and the faded green Mickey Mouse T-shirt that he refused to allow Connie to claim for the rag drawer, even though it had been washed so many times it was practically translucent. (It was the outfit he chose whenever they went to visit his father.) He appeared to be reading something on the lid. He stood, turning his head to squint up and down this stretch of the Thruway, empty in both directions. He blew out his breath and ran his hand through his hair—the way he did when he was pretending to debate a question he'd already decided—then bent, put his hands on the cooler, and picked it up. Apparently, it was lighter than he'd anticipated, because it practically leapt into the air. Almost race-walking, he carried the container towards the car.

Connie half expected him to hand it to her. Instead, he continued past her to the trunk. She tilted the rearview mirror to see him balancing the cooler against his hip and unlocking the trunk. When he thunked the lid down, his hands were empty.

The answer was so obvious she didn't want to ask the question; nonetheless, once Rick was back behind the wheel, drawing his seatbelt across, she said, "What exactly are you doing?"

Without looking at her, he said, "We can't just leave it there."

"If the cell phone were charged, we could call 911."

"Connie—"

"I'm just saying. You wanted to know why that kind of stuff was so important, well, here you are."

"You—" He glanced over his shoulder to make sure the highway was clear. As he accelerated onto it, he said, "You know what? You're right. If I'd charged the cell phone last night like you asked me to, we could dial 911 and have a state trooper take this off our hands. That's absolutely true. Since the phone is dead, however, we need another plan. We're about forty, forty-five minutes from the house. I say we get home as quickly as we can and start calling around the local hospitals. Maybe this is for someone in one of them. In any event, I'm sure they'll know who to call to find out where this is supposed to go."

"Do they even do transplants in Wiltwyck?"

"I don't know. Maybe. I think Penrose might."

"We could stop at the next state trooper barracks."

"The nearest one is our exit, up 209. We're as quick going to the house."

"You're sure there's something in there?"

"I didn't look, but when I lifted it, I heard ice moving inside."

"It didn't look that heavy."

"It wasn't. But I don't know how much a heart, or a kidney, would weigh. Not too much, I think."

"I don't know, I just—" She glanced over her shoulder. "I mean, Jesus, how does something like that wind up in the middle of the Thruway? How does that happen?"

Rick shrugged. "They don't always hire the most professional guys to transport these things. Maybe someone's tail flap was down, or they swerved to avoid a deer in the road and the cooler went tumbling out."

"Surely not."

"Well, if you knew the answer to the question—"

For a second, their argument threatened to tighten its coils around them again. Connie said, "What about the lid? I thought you were reading something on it."

"There's a sticker on top that looks as if it had some kind of information, but the writing's all blurred. Must have been that storm a little while ago."

"So it's been sitting here at least that long."

"Seems likely. Maybe that was what happened—maybe the truck skidded and that caused the cooler to come loose."

"Wouldn't you stop and go back for something like that?

Someone's life could be on the line."

"Could be the driver never noticed, was too busy trying to keep himself from crashing into the guardrail."

The scenario sounded plausible enough—assuming, that is, you accepted Rick's assertion about underqualified drivers employed to convey freshly harvested organs from donor to recipient. Which was, now that Connie thought about it, sufficiently venal and depressing likely to be the truth. "What if it's supposed to be heading north, to Albany?"

"There's probably still enough time, even if whoever it is has to drive back the way we came."

"Maybe they could fly it wherever it needs to go. Doesn't Penrose do that?"

"I think so."

Already, she was buying into Rick's plan. Would it make that much difference to call the hospitals from their house instead of the police station? Equipped with a fully charged cell phone, they could have been rushing whatever was packed in the cooler's ice to the surgical team who at this moment must be in the midst of preparations to receive it. Connie could picture herself and Rick striding into the Emergency Room at Wiltwyck, the cooler under Rick's arm, a green-garbed surgeon waiting with gloves outstretched. With the cell inert, though, home might be their next best option. Based on her experiences with them at an embarrassing number of stops for speeding, the Wiltwyck troopers would require more time than whoever was waiting for this cooler's contents could spare for her and Rick to make clear to them the gravity of the situation.

That's not true, she thought. *You know that isn't true. You're just pissed because that guy wouldn't agree to plead down to ten miles an hour over the speed limit.* She was justifying Rick's plan, shoring up his ambition to be part of the story—an important part, the random, passing stranger who turns out to be crucial to yanking someone at death's very doorway back from that black rectangle. Because... because it was exciting to feel yourself caught up in a narrative like this, one that offered you the opportunity to be part of something bigger than yourself.

Rick had the speedometer to the other side of eighty-five. Connie reached her left hand across and squeezed his leg, lightly. He did not remove his hands from the wheel.

2.

OUR HOURS LATER, THEY WERE STARING AT THE cooler sitting on the kitchen table. Its surface was pebbled plastic; Connie wondered if that contributed in any way to keeping its contents chilled. The red cross stenciled on its lid was faded, a shade lighter than the bottom half of the cooler, and beginning to flake off. The symbol didn't look like your typical red cross. This design was narrow at the join, the sides of each arm curving outwards on their way to its end—the four of which were rounded, like the edges of a quartet of axes. Connie had seen this style of cross, or one close to it, before: Alexa, the first girl with whom she'd shared an apartment, and who had been more Catholic than the Pope, had counted a cross in this style among her religious jewelry. A Maltese cross? Cross of Malta? Something like that, although Connie remembered her old roommate's cross ornamented with additional designs—little pictures, she thought; of what, she couldn't recall. To be honest, this version of the cross seemed less a religious icon and more the image of something else—an abstract flower, perhaps, or an elaborate keyhole. For a moment, the four red lines opening out resembled nothing so much as the pupil of some oversized, alien eye, but that was ridiculous.

What it meant that the cooler resting on the blond wood of their kitchen table bore this emblem, she could not say. Did the Red Cross have subdivisions, local branches, and might this be one of their symbols? She'd never heard of such a thing, but she was a manager at Target; this was hardly her area of expertise.

Rick said, "Maybe it's a Mob thing."

"What?" Connie looked across the table at him, slouched back in his chair, arms folded over his chest.

"I said, Maybe it's a Mob thing."

"What do you mean?"

He straightened. "Maybe it's part of someone who, you know, messed with the Mob. Or someone they had a contract on."

"Like what—a finger?"

"Finger, hand—proof that the job was done."

"Seriously?"

He shrugged. "It's a possibility."

"I don't know."

"You don't know what?"

"I don't know—I mean, the Mob? Transporting—what? Severed body parts in medical coolers? Wasn't that a movie?"

"Was it?"

"Yes—we saw it together. It was on TNT or TBS or something. Joe Pesci was in it. Remember: he's a hit man and he's got these heads in a duffel bag—"

"*Eight Heads in a Duffel Bag.*"

"That's it!"

"So there was a movie. What does that prove?"

"It's just—"

"Or maybe it's some kind of black market thing, a kidney for sale to the highest bidder, no questions asked."

"Isn't that an urban legend?"

"Where do you think these things come from?"

"I—"

"Look—all I'm saying is, we've exhausted the legitimate avenues, so it makes sense to consider other possibilities."

Connie took a breath. "Granted. But we don't even know what's inside the cooler—if there's anything in it."

"You're the one who said we shouldn't open it."

"I know. It's—if there's something in it, then we need to be careful about not contaminating it."

"Are you listening to yourself? We don't know if there's anything in the cooler, so we shouldn't be too concerned about it, but we shouldn't open it, in case there is something in there. What are we supposed to do?"

Before she could answer, Rick pushed himself up from his chair and stalked to the refrigerator, the bottles in whose door rattled as he yanked it open. Connie bit the remark ready to leap off her tongue. Instead, she stood and leaned over to have another look at the square sticker on the cooler's lid. There were no identifying names on the label, no hospital or transport service logos, no barcode, even, which, in the age of global computer tracking, struck her as stranger than the absence of a corporate ID. There were only four or five lines of smeared black ink, unintelligible except for one word that she and Rick had agreed read "Howard" and another that he guessed was "orchid" but of which Connie could identify no more than the initial "o." Now, as her gaze roamed over the ink blurred into swirls and loops, she had the impression that the words which had been written on this sticker hadn't been English, the letters hadn't been any she would have recognized. Some quality of the patterns into which the writing had been distorted suggested an alphabet utterly unfamiliar, which might smear into a configuration resembling "Howard" or "orchid" by the merest coincidence.

God, you're worse than Rick. She resumed her seat as he returned from the fridge, an open bottle of Magic Hat in hand. Not that she wanted a drink, exactly, but his failure to ask her if she did sent Connie on her own mission to the fridge. They were out of hard cider, damnit. She had intended to stop at Hannaford for a quick shop on the way home, then the cooler had appeared and obscured all other concerns. They were almost out of milk, too, and butter. She selected a Magic Hat for herself and swung the door shut.

Rick had set his beer on the table and was standing with his back to her, bent forward slightly, his arms out, his hands on the cooler.

"Rick?" Connie said. "What are you doing?"

"Is that a trick question?"

"Very funny," she said, crossing the kitchen to him. He was staring at the cooler as if he could will its contents visible. He said, "We have to open it."

"But if there's something inside it—"

"I know, I know. I can't see any other choice. We called Wiltwyck, and they didn't know anything about it. Neither did Penrose or Albany Med or Westchester Med. The transport services they gave us the numbers for weren't missing any shipments—one said they aren't even using coolers like this anymore. The cops were useless. Hell, that guy at the sheriff's thought it was probably just someone's cooler. Maybe there'll be some kind of information inside that'll tell us where this is supposed to go."

"What if it's a Mob thing?"

"Do you really believe that?"

"No, but I could be wrong, in which case, what would we do?"

"Get rid of it as quickly as possible. Burn it. I don't think there's any way it could be traced to us."

To her surprise, Connie said, "All right. Go ahead."

Rick didn't ask if she were sure. He pressed in the catches on the lid and slid it back. As Connie inclined toward it, he drew the cooler toward them. It scraped against the table; its contents shifted with a sound like gravel rasping. Connie had been anticipating a strong odor washing out of the cooler's interior, raw meat full of blood; instead, there was the faintest blue hint of air long-chilled and another, even fainter trace of iodine. Rick's arm was blocking her view; she nudged him. "What is it?"

"I don't know."

"Let me see."

He shifted to the right. The cooler was full of ice, chips of it heaped in shining piles around, around—

She registered the color first, the dark purple of a ripe eggplant, shot through with veins of lighter purple—blue, she thought, some shade of blue. It was maybe as wide as a small dinner plate, thicker at the center than at its scalloped circumference. At five—no, six spots around its margin, the surface puckered, the color around each spot shading into a rich rose. The texture of the thing was striated, almost coarse.

"What the fuck?"

"I know—right?"

"Rick—what is this?"

"A placenta?"

"That is not a placenta."

"Like you've seen one."

"As a matter of fact, I have. There was a show on Lifetime—I can't remember what it was called, but it was about women giving birth, in living color, no detail spared. I saw plenty of placentas, and trust me, that is not a placenta."

"Okay, it's not a placenta. So what is it?"

"I—is it even human?"

"You're saying what? that it's an animal?"

"I don't know—some kind of jellyfish?"

"Looks too solid, doesn't it? Besides, wouldn't you store a jellyfish in water?"

"I guess."

Rick started to reach into the cooler. Connie grabbed his wrist. "Jesus! What are you doing?"

"I thought I'd take it out so we could have a better look at it." He tugged his hand free.

"You don't know what it is."

"I'm pretty sure it isn't someone's kidney."

"Granted, but you can't just—it could be dangerous, toxic."

"Really."

"There are animals whose skin is poisonous. Haven't you heard of Poison Dart Frogs?"

"Oh." He lowered his hand. "Fair enough." He stepped away from the cooler. "Sweetie—what is this?"

"Well, I'm pretty sure we can say what it isn't. I doubt there's anyone whose life depends on receiving this, and I'm pretty sure it wasn't attached to any Mob informer. Nor was it feeding a fetus nutrients for nine months. That leaves us with—I don't have the faintest idea. Some kind of animal."

"I don't know."

Connie shrugged. "The world's a big place. There are all kinds of crazy things living at the bottom of the ocean. Or it could be from someplace else—deep underground. Maybe it's a new discovery that was being transported to a museum."

Rick grunted. "Okay. Let's assume this was on its way to an eager research scientist. What's our next move?"

"Another round of phone calls, I guess."

"You want to start on that, and I'll get dinner going?"

She wasn't hungry, but she said, "Sure."

Rick reached for the cooler. "Relax," he said as she tensed, ready to seize his arms. Steadying the cooler with his left hand, he closed it with the right. The lid snicked shut.

3.

O SURPRISE: SHE DREAMED ABOUT THE THING IN THE cooler. She was in Rick's father's room at the nursing home (even asleep, she was unable to think of him as "Gary" or "Mr. Wilson," let alone "Dad"). Rick's father was in the green vinyl recliner by the window, his face tilted up to the sunlight pouring over him in a way that reminded Connie of a large plant feeding on light. The green Jets sweatsuit he was wearing underscored the resemblance. His eyes were closed, his lips moving in the constant murmur that had marked the Alzheimer's overwhelming the last of his personality. In the flood of brightness, he looked younger than fifty-eight, as if he might be Rick's young uncle, and not the father not old enough for the disease that had consumed him with the relentless patience of a python easing itself around its prey.

Connie was standing with her back to the room's hefty dresser, the top of which was heaped with orchids, their petals eggplant and rose. The air was full of the briny smell of seaweed baking on the beach, which she knew was the flowers' scent.

Although she hadn't noticed him enter the room, Rick was kneeling in front of his father, his hands held up and out as if offering the man a gift. His palms cupped the thing from the cooler. Its edges overflowed his hands. In the dense sunlight, the thing was even darker, more rather than less visible. If the scene in front of her were a photograph, the thing was a dab of black paint rising off its surface.

"Here," Rick said to his father. "I brought it for you." When his father did not respond, Rick said, "Dad."

The man opened his eyes and tilted his head in his son's direction. Connie didn't think he saw what Rick was offering him. He croaked, "Bloom."

"Beautiful," Rick said.

His father's eyes narrowed, and his face swung toward Connie. He was weeping, tears coursing down his cheeks like lines of fire in the sunlight. "Bloom," he said.

Almost before she knew she was awake, she was sitting up in bed. Although she was certain it must be far into the night, one of those hours you only saw when the phone rang to announce some family tragedy, the digital clock insisted it was two minutes after midnight. She had been asleep for an hour. She turned to Rick and found his side of the bed empty.

There was no reason for her heart to start pounding. Rick stayed up late all the time, watching *Nightline* or *Charlie Rose*. For the seven years Connie had known him, he had been a light sleeper, prone to insomnia, a tendency that had worsened with his father's unexpected and sudden decline. She had sought him out enough times in the beginning of their relationship to be sure that there was no cause for her to leave the bed. She would find him on the couch, bathed in the TV's glow, a bag of microwave popcorn open on his lap. So prepared was she for him to be there that, when she reached the bottom of the stairs and discovered the living room dark, something like panic straightened her spine. "Rick?" she said. "Honey?"

Of course he was in the kitchen. She glimpsed him out of the corner of her eye the same instant he said, "I'm in here." By the streetlight filtering through the window, she saw him seated at the kitchen table, wearing a white T-shirt and boxers, his arms on the table, his hands on the keyboard of his father's laptop, which was open and on. The cooler, which he had pushed back to make room for the computer, appeared to be closed. (She wasn't sure why that detail made her heart slow.) She walked down the hallway to him, saying, "Couldn't sleep, huh?"

"Nah." His eyes did not leave the computer screen.

"You're like this every time we visit your Dad."

"Am I? I guess so."

She rubbed his back. "You're doing all you can for him. It's a good place."

"Yeah."

On the laptop's screen, a reddish sphere hung against a backdrop of stars. Connie recognized the painting from the NASA website, and the next picture Rick brought up, of a rough plane spread out under a starry sky, at the center of which a cluster of cartoonishly fat arrows identified a handful of the dots of light as the sun and planets of the solar system. A third image showed eight green circles arranged concentrically around a bright point, all of it inside one end of an enormous red ellipse.

The screen after that was a photo of a massive stone monument, a rectangular block stood on its short end, another block laid across its top to form a T-shape. The front of the tall stone was carved with a thick line that descended from high on the right to almost the bottom of the left, where it curved back right again; in the curve, a representation of a four-legged animal Connie could not identify crouched. The image that followed was another painting, this one of a trio of circular structures set in the lee of a broad hill, the diameter of each defined by a thick wall, the interior stood with T-shaped monoliths like the one on the previous screen.

Rick sped through the next dozen screens, long rows of equations more complex than any Connie had encountered in her college math class, half of each line composed of symbols she thought were Greek but wasn't sure. When he came to what appeared to be a list of questions, Rick stopped. Connie could read the first line: *12,000 year orbit coincides with construction of Gobekli Tepe: built in advance of, or in response to, seeding?*

Oh God, Connie thought. She said, "You want to come to bed?"

"I will. You go ahead."

"I don't want you sitting up half the night feeling guilty."

He paused, then said, "It isn't guilt."

"Oh? What is it?"

He shook his head. "I had a dream."

Her mouth went dry. "Oh?"

He nodded. "I was sitting here with my Dad. We were both wearing tuxedoes, and the table had been set for some kind of elaborate meal: white linen tablecloth, candelabra, china plates, the works. It was early in the morning—at least, I think it was, because the windows were pouring light into the room. The plates, the cutlery, the glasses—everything was shining, it was so bright. For a long time, it felt like, we sat there—here—and then I noticed Dad was holding his fork and knife and was using them to cut something on his plate. It was this," he nodded at the cooler, "this thing. He was having a rough time. He couldn't grip the cutlery right; it was as if he'd forgotten how to hold them. His knife kept slipping, scraping on the plate. The thing was tough; he really had to saw at it. It was making this noise, this high-pitched sound that was kind of like a violin. It was bleeding, or leaking, black, syrupy stuff that was all over the plate, the knife, splattering the tablecloth, Dad's shirt. Finally, he got a piece of the thing loose and raised it to his mouth. Only, his lips were still trembling, you know, doing that silent mumble, and he couldn't maneuver the fork past them. The piece flopped on the table. He frowned, speared it with his fork again, and made another try. No luck. The third time, the piece hit the edge of the table and bounced off. That was it. He dropped the cutlery, grabbed the thing on his plate with both hands, and brought it up. His face was so eager. He licked his lips and took a huge bite. He had to clamp down hard, pull the rest away. There was a ripping noise. The thing's blood was all over his lips, his teeth, his tongue; his mouth looked like a black hole."

Connie waited for him to continue. When he didn't, she said, "And?"

"That was it. I woke up and came down here. There was nothing on TV, so I thought I'd get out Dad's laptop and… It's like a connection to him, to how he used to be, you know? I mean, I know he was already pretty bad when he was working on this stuff, but at least he was there."

"Huh." Connie considered relating her own dream, decided instead to ask, "What do you think your dream means?"

"I don't know. I dream about my Dad a lot, but this…"

"Do you—"

"What if it's from another planet?"

"What?"

"Maybe the dream's a message."

"I don't—"

"That would explain why there's no record of it, anywhere, why none of the museums knows anything about it."

"That doesn't make any sense," Connie said. "If this thing were some kind of alien, you'd expect it'd be all over the news."

"Maybe it's dangerous—or they aren't sure if it's dangerous."

"So they pack it into a cooler?"

"They're trying to fly under the radar."

"I don't know—that's so low, it's underground."

"Or… what if a couple of guys found it—somewhere, they were out hunting or fishing or something—and they decided to take it with them in the cooler they'd brought for their beers?"

"Then why the red cross on the cooler? What about the sticker?"

"Coincidence—they just happened to take that cooler."

"I could—look, even if that is the case, if a couple of hunters came upon this thing, I don't know, fresh from its meteorite, and emptied out their oddly decorated cooler so they could be famous as the first guys to encounter E.T., how does that help us know what to do?"

"We could call NASA."

"Who what? would send out the Men in Black?"

"I'm serious!" Rick almost shouted. "This is serious! Jesus! We could be—we have—why can't you take this seriously?" He turned to glare at her as he spoke.

"Rick—"

"Don't 'Rick' me."

Connie inhaled. "Honey—it's late. We're tired. Let's not do this, okay? Not now. I'm sorry if I'm not taking this seriously. It's been a long day. Whatever it is, the thing in the cooler'll keep until we get some sleep. If you want, we can call NASA first thing in the morning. Really—I swear."

"I—" She readied herself for the next phase of his outburst, then, "You're right," Rick said. "You're right. It has been a long day, hasn't it?"

"Very. I can't believe you aren't exhausted."

"I am—believe me, I'm dead on my feet. It's just, this thing—"

"I understand—honest, I do. Why don't you come up to bed? Maybe once you lie down—"

"All right. You go up. I just need a minute more."

"For what?" she wanted to ask but didn't, opting instead to drape her arms over his shoulders and press her cheek against his neck. "Love you," she said into his skin.

"Love you, too."

Her heart, settled after its earlier gallop, broke into a trot again as she padded down the hall to the stairs. The sight of Rick, once more staring at the computer screen, did nothing to calm it, nor did her lowering herself onto the bed, drawing the covers up. If anything, the thoroughbred under her ribs charged faster. She gazed at the bedroom ceiling, feeling the mattress resound with her pulse. Was she having a panic attack? *Don't think about it*, she told herself. *Concentrate on something else.*

Rick. What else was there besides him at the table, his fingers resting on the keyboard's sides, sifting through his father's last, bizarre project? Not the most reassuring behavior; although it was true: each monthly pilgrimage to his father left him unsettled for the rest of that day, sometimes the next. No matter how many times she told him that his Dad was in the best place, that the home provided him a quality of care they couldn't have (not to mention, his father's insurance covered it in full), and no matter how many times Rick answered, "You're right; you're absolutely right," she knew that he didn't accept her reasoning, her reassurance. In the past, thinking that anger might help him to articulate his obvious guilt, she had tried to pick a fight with him, stir him to argument, but he had headed the opposite direction, descended into himself for the remainder of the weekend. She had suggested they visit his Dad more often, offered to rearrange her work schedule so that they could go up twice a month, even three times. What good was being store manager, she'd said, if you couldn't use it to your advantage? Albany wasn't that far, and there were supposed to be good restaurants there; they could make a day of it, spend time with his father and have some time for themselves, too.

No, no, Rick had said. It wasn't fair for her to have to rework the schedule (arriving at which she'd compared to the circus act where the clown spins the plates on the ends of all the poles he's holding while balancing his unicycle on the highwire). It wasn't as if his Dad would know the difference, anyway.

He might not, Connie had said, *but you will*.

It was no good, though; Rick's mind had been made up before their conversation had started. He had never admitted it, but Connie was sure he was still traumatized by his father's last months of—you couldn't call it lucidity, exactly, since what he would call to yell at Rick about was pretty insane. Gary Wilson had been an astronomer, his most recent work an intensive study of the dwarf planets discovered beyond Neptune in the first decade of the twenty-first century: Eris, Sedna, and Orcus were the names she remembered. From what she understood, his research on the surface conditions on these bodies was cutting-edge stuff; he had been involved in the planning for a probe to explore some of them. Plenty of times, she and Rick had arrived at his apartment to take him to dinner, only to find him seated at his desk, staring at his computer monitor, at a painting of one or the other of the dwarf planets. At those moments, he had seemed a million miles away, further, as far as one of the spheres he studied. Hindsight's clarity made it obvious he was experiencing the early effects of Alzheimer's, but the spells had always broken the moment Rick shook him and said, "Dad, it's us," and it had been easier to accept her father-in-law's assurance that he had merely been daydreaming.

Not until his behavior became more erratic did it dawn on them that Rick's father might not be well. His attention had been focused on one dwarf planet, Sedna, for months. Connie had sat beside him at the Plaza diner as he flipped over his mat and drew an asterisk in the center of it which he surrounded with a swirl of concentric circles, all of which he placed at one end of a great oval. "This is Sedna's orbit," he had said, jabbing his pen at the oval. "Twelve thousand years, give or take a few hundred. Over the next couple of centuries, it will be as close to us as it's been during the whole of recorded history. The last time it was this near, well…"

"What?" Rick had said.

"You'll see," his father had declared.

They hadn't, though, not directly. One of Rick's father's friends at the state university had phoned after a presentation during which the extent of Gary Wilson's breakdown had become manifest. Connie had heard the lecture, herself, in person, on the phone, and in a long, rambling voicemail. She considered herself reasonably well-educated in a hold-your-own-at-Trivial-Pursuit kind of way, but Rick's father's discussion strained her comprehension. Almost thirteen thousand years ago, a comet had burst over the Great Lakes—yes, that was a controversial claim, but how else to explain the high levels of iridium, the nano-diamonds? The glaciers were already in retreat, you see; it was the right time, if you could measure time in centuries—millennia. This was when the Clovis disappeared—wiped out, or assimilated in some way, it was hard to say. You wouldn't think a stone point much of a threat, but you'd be surprised. The drawings at Lascaux—well, never mind them. It's what happens at *Gobekli Tepe* that's important. Those curves on the stones—has anyone thought of mapping them onto Sedna's orbit? The results—as for the shape of the monuments, those giant T's, why, they're perches, for the messengers.

And so on. The thing was, while Rick's father was propounding this lunatic hodgepodge of invention, he sounded as reasonable, as kindly, as he ever had. Perhaps that was because she hadn't challenged him in the way that Rick did, told him that his ideas were crazy, he was flushing his career down the toilet. Confronted by his son's strenuous disbelief, Gary flushed with anger, was overtaken by storms of rage more intense than any she had witnessed in the seven years she had known him. He would stalk from their house and demand that Connie drive him home, then, once home, he would call and harangue Rick for another hour, sometimes two, until Rick reached his boiling point and hung up on him.

The end, when it came, had come quickly: she had been amazed at the speed with which Rick's father had been convinced to accept early retirement and a place in an assisted living facility. There had been a brief period of days, not even a full week, during which he had returned to something like his old self. He had signed all the papers necessary to effect his departure from the college and his relocation to Morrison Hills. He had spoken to Rick and Connie calmly, with barely a mention of Sedna's impending return. Two days after he settled into his new, undersized room, Gary had suffered a catastrophic event somewhere in his brain that the doctors refused to call a stroke, saying the MRI results were all wrong for that. (Frankly, they seemed mystified by what had happened to him during the night.) Whatever its name, the occurrence had left him a few steps up from catatonic, intermittently responsive and usually in ways that made no sense. There was talk of further study, of sub-specialists being brought in, possible trips to hospitals in other states, but nothing, as yet, had come to pass. Connie doubted any of it would. There were more than enough residents of the facility who could and did vocalize their complaints, and less than enough staff to spare on a man whose tongue was so much dead weight.

Harrowing as Rick's father's decline had been, she supposed she should be grateful that it had not stretched out longer than it had. From talking with staff at Morrison, she knew that it could take years for a parent's worsened condition to convince them/ their family that something had to be done. At the same time, though, Rick had been ambivalent about his father entering assisted living. There was enough room in the house for him: he could have stayed in the downstairs bedroom and had his own bathroom. But neither of them was available for—or, to be honest, up for—the task of caring for him. Rick's consent to his father's move had been conditional; he had insisted and Connie had agreed that they would re-evaluate the situation in six months. Their contract had been rendered null and void by Gary's collapse, which had left him in need of a level of care far beyond that for which either of them was equipped. However irrational the sentiment might be, Connie knew that Rick took his father's crash as a rebuke from the universe for having agreed to send him away in the first place.

Connie didn't realize she had crossed over into sleep again until she noticed that the bedroom's ceiling and walls had vanished, replaced by a night sky brimming with stars. Her bed was sitting on a vast plane, dimly lit by the stars' collective radiance. Its dark red expanse was stippled and ridged, riven by channels; she had the impression of dense mud. That and cold: although she could not feel it on her skin, she sensed that wherever this was was so cold it should have frozen her in place, her blood crystallized, her organs chunks of ice.

To her left, a figure was progressing slowly across the plane. It was difficult to be sure, but it looked like a man, dressed in black. Every few steps, he would pause and study the ground in front of him, occasionally crouching and poking it with one hand. Connie watched him for what might have been a long time. Her bed, she noticed, was strewn with orchids, their petals eggplant and rose. At last, she drew back the blanket, lowered herself onto the red mud, and set out toward him.

She had expected the mud to be ice-brittle, but while it was firm under her feet, it was also the slightest bit spongy. She wasn't sure how this could be. A glance over her shoulder showed the bed and its cargo of flowers unmoved. While she was still far away from him, she saw that the man ahead of her was wearing a tuxedo, and that he was Rick's father. She was not surprised by either of these facts.

In contrast to her previous dream of him, Gary Wilson stood tall, alert. He was following a series of depressions in the plane's surface, each a concave dip of about a foot, maybe six feet from the one behind it. At the bottom of the depressions, something dark shone through the red mud. When he bent to prod one, he licked his finger clean afterwards. Connie could feel his awareness of her long before she drew near, but he waited until she was standing beside him to say, "Well?"

"Where is this?"

"Oh, come now," he said, disappointment bending his voice. "You know the answer to that already."

She did. "Sedna."

He nodded. "The nursery."

"For those?" She pointed at the depression before him.

"Of course."

"What are they?"

"Embryos." The surface of his cheek shifted.

"I don't understand."

"Over here." He turned to his left and crossed to another row of depressions. Beside the closest was a small red and white container—a cooler, its top slid open. To either side, the depressions were attended by thermoses, lunchboxes, larger coolers, even a small refrigerator. Rick's father knelt at a dip and reached his hand down into the mud, working his fingers in a circle around whatever lay half-buried in it. Once it was freed, he raised it, using his free hand to brush the worst of the mud from it. "This," he said, holding out to Connie a copy of the thing she and Rick had found on the Thruway. Its surface was darker than the spaces between the stars overhead.

"That's an embryo?" she said.

"Closest word." Bending to the open cooler, he gently deposited the thing inside it. His hands free, he clicked the cooler's lid shut. "Someone will be by for this, shortly," he said, raising his fingers to his tongue.

"I don't—" Connie started, and there was an explosion of wings, or what might have been wings, a fury of black flapping. She put up her hands to defend herself, and the wings were gone, the cooler with them. "What...?"

"You have to prepare the ground, first," Rick's father said, "fertilize it, you could say. A little more time would have been nice, but Tunguska was long enough ago. To tell the truth, if we'd had to proceed earlier, it wouldn't have mattered." He stepped to the next hole and its attendant thermos and repeated his excavation. As he was jiggling the thing into the thermos, Connie said, "But—why?"

"Oh, that's…" Rick's father gestured at the thermos's side, where the strange cross with the slender join and rounded arms was stenciled. "You know."

"No, I don't."

Gary Wilson shrugged. His face slid with the movement, up, then down, the flesh riding on the bone. The hairs on Connie's neck, her arms, stood rigid. She did not want to accompany him as he turned left again and headed for a deep slice in the mud, but she could not think what else to do. Behind her, there was a chaos of flapping, and silence.

The fissure in the mud ran in both directions as far as she could see. It was probably narrow enough for her to jump across. She was less sure of its depth, rendered uncertain by dimness. At or near the bottom, something rose, not high enough for her to distinguish it, but sufficiently near for her to register a great mass. "Too cold out here," Rick's father said. "Makes them sluggish. Inhibits their"—he waved his hands—"development. Confines it."

There were more of whatever-it-was down there. Some quality of their movement made Connie grateful she couldn't see any more of them.

"Funny," Rick's father said. "They need this place for infancy, your place for maturity. Never known another breed with such extreme requirements."

"What are they?"

"I guess you would call them… gods? Is that right? *Orchidaceae deus*? They bloom."

"What?"

"Bloom."

4.

HERE WAS A SMALL DECK AT THE BACK OF THE HOUSE, little more than a half-dozen planks of unfinished wood raised on as many thick posts, bordered by an unsteady railing, at the top of a flight of uneven stairs. A door led from the deck into the house's laundry room, whose location on the second floor had impressed Connie as one of the reasons to rent the place two years ago, when her promotion to manager had allowed sufficient money to leave their basement apartment and its buffet of molds behind. On mornings when she didn't have to open the store, and Rick hadn't worked too late the night before, they would carry their mugs of coffee out here. She liked to stand straight, her mug cradled in her hands, while Rick preferred to take his chances leaning on the rail. Sometimes they spoke, but mostly they were quiet, listening to the birds performing their various morning songs, watching the squirrels chase one another across the high branches of the trees whose roots knitted together the small rise behind the house.

A freak early frost had whited the deck and stairs. Once the sun was streaming through the trunks of the oaks and maples stationed on the rise, the frost would steam off, but at the moment dawn was a red hint amidst the dark trees. *Red sky at morning*, Connie thought.

She was seated at the top of the deck stairs, wrapped in the green and white knitted blanket she'd grabbed when she'd left the laundry room hours ago. The bottle of Stolichnaya cradled in her arms was almost empty, despite which, she felt as sober as she ever had. More than sober—her senses were operating past peak capacity. The grooves in the bark of the oaks on the rise were deep gullies flanked by vertical ridges. The air eddying over her skin was dense with moisture. The odor of the soil in which the trees clutched their roots was the brittle-paper smell of dead leaves crumbling mixed with the damp thickness of dirt. It was as if she were under a brilliant white light, one that allowed her no refuge, but that also permitted her to view her surroundings with unprecedented clarity.

She had emerged from her dream of Rick's father to silence, to a stillness so profound the sound of her breathing thundered in her ears. Rick's side of the bed was still cold. Except for a second strange dream on the same night, there had been no reason for Connie to do anything other than return to sleep. Her dream, however, had seemed sufficient cause for her to rouse herself and (once more) set out downstairs in search of Rick. In the quiet that had draped the house, the creaks of the stairs under her feet had been horror-movie loud.

She had not been sure what she would find downstairs, and had walked past the front parlor before her brain had caught up to what it had noticed from the corner of her eye and sent her several steps back. The small room they called the front parlor, whose bay window overlooked the front porch, had been dark. Not just nighttime dark (which, with the streetlight outside, wasn't really that dark), but complete and utter blackness. This hadn't been the lack of light so much as the overwhelming presence of its opposite, a dense inkiness that had filled the room like water in a tank. Connie had reached out her hand to touch it, only to stop with her fingers a hair's-breadth away from it, when the prospect of touching it had struck her as a less than good idea. Lowering her hand, she had retreated along the hall to the dining room.

Before the dining room, though, she had paused at the basement door, open wide and allowing a thick, briny stench up from its depths. The smell of seaweed and assorted sea-life baking on the beach, the odor had been oddly familiar, despite her inability to place it. She had reached around the doorway for the light switch, flipped it on, and poked her head through the doorway. Around the foot of the stairs, she had seen something she could not immediately identify. There had been no way she was venturing all the way into the basement; already, the night had taken too strange a turn for her to want to put herself into so ominous, if clichéd, a location. But she had been curious enough to descend the first couple of stairs and crouch to look through the railings.

When she had, Connie had seen a profusion of flowers, orchids, their petals eggplant and rose. They had covered the concrete floor so completely she could not see it. A few feet closer to them, the tidal smell was stronger, almost a taste. The orchids were motionless, yet she had had the impression that she had caught them on the verge of movement. She had wanted to think, *I'm dreaming; this is part of that last dream*, but the reek of salt and rot had been too real. She had stood and backed upstairs.

Mercifully, the dining room had been unchanged, its table, chairs, and china cabinet highlighted by the streetlight's orange glow. Unchanged, that is, except for the absence of the cooler from the table, and why had she been so certain that, wherever the container was, its lid was open, its contents gone? Rick's father's laptop had remained where her husband had set it up, its screen dark. Connie had pressed the power button, and the rectangle had brightened with the image of one of the T-shaped stone monuments, its transverse section carved with what appeared to be three birds processing down from upper left to lower right, their path taking them over the prone form of what might have been a man—though if it was, the head was missing. The upright block was carved with a boar, its tusks disproportionately large.

Thinking Rick might have decided to sleep in the guest room, she had crossed to the doorway to the long room along the back of the house, the large space for which they had yet to arrive at a use. To the right, the room had wavered, as if she had been looking at it through running water. One moment, it had bulged toward her; the next, it had telescoped away. In the midst of that uncertainty, she had seen… she couldn't say what. It was as if that part of the house had been a screen against which something enormous had been pushing and pulling, its form visible only through the distortions it caused in the screen. The sight had hurt her eyes, her brain, to behold; she had been not so much frightened as sickened, nauseated. No doubt, she should have fled the house, taken the car keys from the hook at the front door and driven as far from here as the gas in the tank would take her.

Rick, though: she couldn't leave him here with all *this*. Dropping her gaze to her feet, she had stepped into the back room, flattening herself against the wall to her left. A glance had showed nothing between her and the door to the guest room, and she had slid along the wall to it as quickly as her legs would carry her. A heavy lump of dread, for Rick, alone down here as whatever this was had happened, had weighed deep below her stomach. At the threshold to the guest room, she had tried to speak, found her voice caught in her throat. She had coughed, said, "Rick? Honey?" the words striking the silence in the air like a mallet clanging off a gong; she had flinched at their loudness.

Connie had not been expecting Rick to step out of the guest room as if he had been waiting there for her. With a shriek, she had leapt back. He had raised his hands, no doubt to reassure her, but even in the dim light she could see they were discolored, streaked with what looked like tar, as was his mouth, his jaw. He had stepped toward her, and Connie had retreated another step. "Honey," he had said, but the endearment had sounded wrong, warped, as if his tongue had forgotten how to shape his words.

"Rick," she had said, "what—what happened?"

His lips had peeled back, but whatever he had wanted to say, it would not come out.

"The house—you're—"

"It's… okay. He showed me… Dad."

"Your father? What did he show you?"

Rick had not lowered his hands; he gestured with them to his mouth.

"Oh, Christ. You—you didn't."

Yes, he did, Rick had nodded.

"Are you insane? Do you have any idea what—? You don't know what that thing was! You probably poisoned yourself…"

"Fine," Rick had said. "I'm… fine. Better. More."

"What?"

"Dad showed me."

Whatever the cooler's contents, she had been afraid the effects of consuming it were already in full swing, the damage already done. Yet despite the compromise in his speech, Rick's eyes had burned with intelligence. Sweeping his hands around him, he had said, "All… the same. Part of—" He had uttered a guttural sound she could not decipher, but that had hurt her ears to hear.

"Rick," she had said, "we have to leave—we have to get you to a doctor. Come on." She had started toward the doorway to the dining room, wondering whether Wiltwyck would be equipped for whatever toxin he had ingested. The other stuff, the darkness, the orchids, the corner, could wait until Rick had been seen by a doctor.

"No." The force of his refusal had halted Connie where she was. "See."

"What—" She had turned to him and seen… she could not say what. Hours later, her nerves calmed if not soothed by the vodka that had washed down her throat, she could not make sense of the sight that had greeted her. When she tried to replay it, she saw Rick, then saw his face, his chest, burst open, pushed aside by the orchids thrusting their eggplant and rose petals out of him. The orchids, Rick, wavered, as if she were looking at them through a waterfall, and then erupted into a cloud of darkness that coalesced into Rick's outline. Connie had the sense that that was only an approximation of what she actually had witnessed, and not an especially accurate one, at that. As well say she had seen all four things simultaneously, like a photograph overexposed multiple times, or that she had seen the cross from the top of the cooler, hanging in the air.

She had responded with a headlong flight that had carried her upstairs to the laundry room. Of course, it had been a stupid destination, one she was not sure why she had chosen, except perhaps that the side and front doors had lain too close to one of the zones of weirdness that had overtaken the house. The bottle of Stolichnaya had been waiting next to the door to the deck, no doubt a refugee from their most recent party. She could not think of a reason not to open it and gulp a fiery mouthful of its contents; although she couldn't think of much of anything. She had been, call it aware of the quiet, the silence pervading the house, which had settled against her skin and become intolerable, until she had grabbed a blanket from the cupboard and let herself out onto the deck. There, she had wrapped herself in the blanket and seated herself at the top of the deck stairs.

Tempting to say she had been in shock, but shock wasn't close: shock was a small town she had left in the rearview mirror a thousand miles ago. This was the big city, metropolis of a sensation like awe or ecstasy, a wrenching of the self that rendered such questions as how she was going to help Rick, how they were going to escape from this, immaterial. From where she was sitting, she could look down on their Subaru, parked maybe fifteen feet from the foot of the stairs. There was an emergency key under an overturned flowerpot in the garage. These facts were neighborhoods separated by hundreds of blocks, connected by a route too byzantine for her understanding to take in. She had stayed where she was as the constellations wheeled above her, the sky lightened from blue-bordering-on-black to dark blue. Her breath plumed from her lips; she pulled the blanket tighter and nursed the vodka as, through a process too subtle for her to observe, frost spread over the deck, the stairs.

When the eastern sky was a blue so pale it was almost white, she had noticed a figure standing at the bottom of the stairs. For a moment, she had mistaken it for Rick, had half stood at the prospect, and then she had recognized Rick's father. He'd been dressed in the same tuxedo he'd worn in her second dream of him, the knees of his trousers and the cuffs of his shirt and jacket crusted with red mud. His presence prompted her to speech. "You," she had said, resuming her seat. "Are you Rick's Dad, or what?"

"Yes."

"Great. Can you tell me what's happened to my husband?"

"He's taken the seed into himself."

"The thing from the cooler."

"He blooms."

"I don't—" She'd shaken her head. "Why... why? Why him? Why this?"

Rick's father had shrugged, and she had done her best not to notice if his face had shifted with the movement.

She had sighed. "What now?"

"He will want a consort."

"He what?"

"His consort."

She would not have judged herself capable of the laughter that had burst from her. "You have got to be fucking kidding me."

"The process is underway."

"I don't think so."

"Look at your bottle."

"This?" She had held up the vodka. "It's alcohol."

"Yes. He thought that might help."

"What do you—" Something, some glint of streetlight refracting on the bottle's glass, had caused her to bring it to her eyes, tilting it so that the liquor sloshed up one side. In the orange light shimmering in it, Connie had seen tiny black flakes floating, dozens, hundreds of them. "Oh, no. No way. No."

"It will take longer this way, but he thought you would need the time."

"'He'? You mean Rick? Rick did this?"

"To bring you to him, to what he is."

"Bring me—"

"To bloom."

"This is— No. No." She had wanted to hurl the bottle at Rick's father, but had been unable to release her grip on it. "Not Rick. No."

He had not argued the point; instead, before the last denial had left her mouth, the space where he'd stood had been empty.

That had been... not that long ago, she thought. Time enough for the horizon to flush, for her to feel herself departing the city of awe to which the night's sights had brought her for somewhere else, a great grey ocean swelling with storm. She had squinted at the bottle of Stolichnaya, at the black dots drifting in what remained of its contents. Rick had done this? So she could be his consort? Given what she'd witnessed this night, it seemed silly to declare one detail of it more outrageous than the rest, but this... She could understand, well, imagine how an appearance by his father might have convinced her husband that eating the thing in the cooler was a good idea. But to leap from that to thinking that he needed to bring Connie along for the ride—that was something else.

The thing was, it was entirely typical of the way Rick acted, had acted, the length of their relationship. He plunged into decisions like a bungee-jumper abandoning the trestle of a bridge, confident that the cord to which he'd tethered himself, i.e. her, would pull him back from the jagged rocks below. He dropped out of grad school even though it meant he would lose the deferment for the sixty thousand dollars in student loans he had no job to help him repay. He registered for expensive training courses for professions in which he lost interest halfway through the class. He overdrew their joint account for take-out dinners when there was a refrigerator's worth of food waiting at home. And now, the same tendencies that had led to them having so much difficulty securing a mortgage—that had left the fucking cell phone's battery depleted—had caused him to… she wasn't even sure she knew the word for it.

The sky between the trees on the rise was filling with color, pale rose deepening to rich crimson, the trunks and branches against it an extravagant calligraphy she could not read. The light ruddied her skin, shone redly on the bottle, glowed hellishly on the frosted steps, deck. She stared through the trees at it, let it saturate her vision.

The photons cascaded against her leaves, stirring them to life.

(What?)

She convoluted, moving at right angles to herself, the sunlight fracturing.

(Oh)

Blackness.

(God.)

She lurched to her feet.

Roots tingled, blackness, unfolding, frost underfoot. Connie gripped the liquor bottle by the neck and swung it against the porch railing. Smashing it took three tries. The last of the vodka splashed onto the deck planks. She pictured hundreds of tiny black—what had Rick's father called them?—embryos shrieking, realized she was seeing them, hearing them.

Blackness her stalk inturning glass on skin. Connie inspected the bottle's jagged top. As improvised weapons went, she supposed it wasn't bad, but she had the feeling she was bringing a rock to a nuclear war.

The dawn air was full of the sound of flapping, of leathery wings snapping. She could almost see the things that were swirling around the house, could feel the spaces they were twisting. She released the blanket, let it slide to the deck. She crossed to the door to the laundry room, still unlocked. Had she thought it wouldn't be? Connie adjusted her grip on her glass knife, opened the door, and stepped into the house.

For Fiona

And the Sea Gave
Up the Dead

JASON C. ECKHARDT

Jason C. Eckhardt is a freelance illustrator who writes on occasion, relishing the added dimension of time in the written medium. His stories and articles have appeared in the Weird Fiction Review, Lovecraft Studies, Studies in Weird Fiction, *and other journals. For his own reading he enjoys the works of Lovecraft, Dunsany, Bierce, Robert E. Howard, Loren Estleman, and various histories. He lives in Massachusetts with his wife, stepdaughters, and cats.*

N 2004 HISTORIANS AND NATURALISTS ALIKE WERE galvanized by the news of the discovery of the sea-journals of British naturalist Margate Townshend. The small, sharkskin-bound octavo volumes came to light during an auction of an anonymous lot at the London auction house of Berkley and Dighton that year and were subsequently purchased by representatives of the Miskatonic University School of Natural History. As a first-hand account of Captain James Cook's second great voyage of exploration (1772–75), by an aide to the ship's official "natural historians," Johann Reinhold Forster and his son George, the value of this document is unquestioned. The wealth of data on the flora, fauna, and native customs of the Pacific will be of inestimable worth to future scholars of history, anthropology, and biology.

But the journal's importance transcends even these great boons. Specifically, it may settle for once and for all the long debate as to why Cook, retreating from the Antarctic pack in January 1774, abruptly came about in Latitude 47 degrees south to make his famous run to 71 degrees, 10 minutes south, "as far as I think it possible for man to go."

The period in question in Townshend's journals is January 5–11, 1774. Scholars will be struck immediately with the many discrepancies between Townshend's account and those of other diarists aboard the *Resolution* (the redoubtable Cook among them). But certain internal evidences in Townshend's text, coupled with its virtual agreement with other shipboard chronicles on all other aspects of the voyage, have led many to the conclusion that Townshend's account is the more reliable; and, conversely, that there was a conspiracy of silence among the rest of the explorers over what they found during those lost days. The reasons for this will become obvious upon reading. It is with the intention of inspiring further debate and intellectual inquiry that the following text is now published and submitted to the public for the first time, through a grant from the Francis Wayland Thurston Research Fund.

1774 JAN'RY 5.

HIS MORN THE WIND CALM, THE SKY CLEAR—A Blessing to be free of the wicked Cold and Ice-mountains of the extreme South. Quantities of Sea-Birds encounterd, incl. Albatross, Sheerwaters, the *Puffinus* of Linnaeus, &c. Flying Fisshe too, flockes of them such that the Deck was littered all about with them, shining like Bars of Silver. They flew head on into our Ship as if driven by a Blast. Later encounter'd Several of Squidd of unknown species, swimming S.S.W. These we saw off and on until the Duske descended, after which Time these fishe were visible by the bright Maculations of Colour upon their long and many Armes.

1774 JAN'RY 6.

LEAR AND THE WIND CONTINUES ASTERN, WARMER every Day, tho' while the weather stays amenable the Crewmen appear restless. One or two complain of the Squid, which Creture we have seen in increasing Shoals of hundreds, nay, thousands. Their Peculiarity evaded me untill one of the seamen caught one up with his fizgig [i.e., harpoon].

He landed the Squid upon the deck for our Inspection. It proved a large (15 feet) variant of *Teuthis* Linn[aeus], but in place of the usual Finns imployed in moving them thro' the water these have large Wings of a membraneous Aspect much like to Bats wings. A set of segmented Fingers sprout from either side of the Squids head and it is upon these that the Wings are spread as Sails are set upon Spars. I made bold to christen it my self, calling it *Teuthis megaptera* after its great Wings (*pace* Linnaeus).

Beyond this, tho', we did not have time sufficient thoroughly to examine this Specimin, for the Sailors did not like the look of its Eyes, saying It gives us the Evill Eye. Forster, eager to dissect the animal, attempted to assuage their Fears, reminding them that onlie a Man can possess a Soul & a Consciousness & Will. But they are a superstitious Lot and to ease them we threw the Thing back into the Sea.

1774 JAN'RY 7.

HE WIND THAT HAD BLOWNE US CLEAR OF THE Antarctic regions now abated somewhat, the sky still clear but temperature hot. More squid pass on, flights of many Birds, too—Albatross, Tropick birds, & the Great Petrel *Micronectes giganteus* Linn., all in a South by Southwesterly fashion. Their Shadowes make a pattern on the deck like a moving lattice, so Numerous are they, and the sound they made was as the whistling of a Great Gale. Whither they go I cannot say, as we found no Land in that Direction.

At mid day the lookout espied a Cloud of prodigious Size on the horizon N.N.E. This bespoke volcanic Activitie and thus an island where Island was not recorded to be. So the *Resolution* was steered towards this cloud, the Crewe being on short Commons of mouldy bread and foul Water, and nothing loth to find fresh, but the Clowd provd to be of mighty Size and Distance, and by the setting of the Sunne with the wind slackening we had not raisd this land.

To night the schools of Squidd continue by us. Their glowing Spots were so many that we saild thro' a River of Jewells, as it were. The Seaman Isaac Gillis join'd me at the rail to admire this Spectacle, and even claim'd to see a Patterne or Message spelt in the arrangement of the Spots. But this I could not credit, and later some of his fellow Sailors told me O don't mind him, Sir, Gillis is just an ignorant old son of a Pagan Scotchman. He comes from the Western Isles of that Nation (so they informed me) and believes in Selkies and the Like.

But I am arrous'd to Inquiry at this Gillis, for the Patterns he claimed to see were not the same Markings that I could make out. On an Inspiration I later tested him with Mr Hodges paints [William Hodges, expedition artist aboard the *Resolution*—Ed.] and discovered him to be colour-blind in the Redd spectrum. Thus his Worde is doubly suspect, and I will in future guard myself against his Deceptions.

1774 JAN'RY 8.

NOT AND INCREASINGLY STILLE, BUT WE RAISD THE Island whose Smoke we espied yesterday, in approx. 50 S., 135 W. It is indeed a volcanic Formation, compriz'd of basalt, pumice, & granite, and rises in black & shere Cliffes on 3 sides, viz S., W., & E. Upon its Crest wave a forest of Palms and Cycads *cycan circilanus* Linn., and it is from the midst of these that the great Cloud tumbles upwrd into the Sky. The soil eroded from the volcanic Ejecta must have been sown with the above Verdure by passing Birds, yet no birds did we see upon this Day. In contrast to the past two Days not a bird was in evidence neither upon the Land nor upon the Sea. They all had fled.

As we approach'd the Island a Wind freshened from the North and blew upon us a Reek such as few of us can have ever known. It was blended of Sulphur from the smoking, thundering Caldera above, but also of a Stench of Corruption so strong as to send some of our stoutest Mariners to the rail. Upon rounding the Island to its North side we discovered the Source of this hellish Smell. Here the Land shelved down more gently than the other Sides, and met the muttering Surf in a Beach of black Sande. Strewn as far as Eye could see upon this Strand were thousands of the Bodies of *Teuthis megaptera* I have described before, all beached and rotting in the Tropick Sun. What can have driven them so to maroon themselves I cannot imagine.

30 yards beyond the edge of the water the Forest began; and as anchor was dropped and the *Resolution* came to rest, People emerged from those Trees. At that distance (half a mile) little could be discern'd as to their Nature, but that they were typicall in Colouring to other South Sea Islanders we had seen, being dark of skin with black hair curled like that of a Negroe, and that they were a large People. However I was chosen, along with Mr Forster *père*, and several Seamen to accompany Capt. Cook ashore in one of the boats, and soon had better opportunitie to see them.

Having crosst the water we stepped in amongst the decaying Squids and up the beach, and here I was able to view these Salvages more clearly. They were indeed a large People, the least of whom was not less than six feet in hight, and some of whom loomed over our tallest Sailors. They wore skirts of some woven grass, both Sexes, to cover the Organs of Generation, but chests bare, Females too as in the fashion of the women of Otaheite. But notwithstanding this Boldness of attire there was no attraction to them. Rather, all, Male and

Female alike, bore a fierceness of expression which precluded any native Charm. This Fierceness was accentuated by Tattews, on arms, legs, Breasts & especially on the Face. Those on the Face called to mind the *moko* of the Indians of Taika Mowi [the Maori of New Zealand—Ed.], but less individual in character. All the Men before us wore a Tattew design of ropes of vines or tentacles spreading out in curling ramifications from a single Eye imprinted into the forehead. The Skill used in creating these Tattews was impressive, and the Designs might even have been considered beautiful but for the dire Aspect of the Wearers faces. The Men, too, wielded Swords edged with Sharks teeth such as we had found on other Islands, which added to their Wild apperance.

Captain Cook, ever bold unto the point of Rashness, approached them with open arms and offerd them gifts of Paper [a rare commodity in the Pacific—Ed.], but they would have none. One of the seamen, who knew some of the Ocean dialects, went with him as interpreter. The rest of us stayd back, between the line of menacing Islanders and the line of stinking squid Bodies, and I would be hard prest to say which was worse. It was a tense Situation, made worse by a feeling of Unease that had spread thro' the ship, but the Crew were eager for decent food and the water in the Hold green & foul, so it was deem'd worth the Risk.

The Conversation between the Capt. and the Islanders appeared to be going peacefully. Then Gillis, the same sailor who had spoken with me about the Squids, walked to one of the dead Monsters on the sand and bent down as if to touch it. At this 20 Warriors broke from the line and were running towards us, swinging their Swords and bellowing in an access of rage. Luckilly our Men were arm'd with muskets and raised them to fire. Before they could do so Capt. Cook yelled Shoot over their Heads!, which the men did. The explosion of the muskets checkt the Warriors in their charge, but only just, and not nearly as thoro'ly as we had wished. While they stood thus, weapons raised but irresolute, not 20 Feet away, and our Men frantically reloading their Pieces, I could see Cook and the interpreter in converse earnest and swift with the Islanders. You must not touch the Squidd, the Interpreter calld to us, They are sacred to these people. At this, we moved as one a few feet forward and away from the Squid, keeping our eyes upon the Warriors, who watched us likewise. I put up my hands in a Motion of appeasement, and all relaxed somewhat. At length Cook and his man came back to us, and we were told that we would be allowd to obtain Water & Comestibles but not stay overlong.

We return'd an hour later with 2 boats and 22 Men, and our reception this second time was reserved but not as hostile as before. In fact, as the Day progress'd, our Primitive Hosts became more amicable and aided us in finding the needed Supplies. In the company of one Titan warrior, a hairy Rustum named A'tai, I was allow'd to roam in their Forest to find animal Specimins, but a poor collector did I make. The Island was remarkably free of most of the higher forms of life, altho' I detected the spoor of many Birds, which now seem to have deserted the Isle. I was put in Mind of all the avian Multitudes we had seen winging Southwards the previous Days, and wondered.

With the bipedal Population of the Island I had more success. The Interpreter Sailor joined me & Mr Forster and we were able to interview Several of the Salvages upon divers Subjects, & here my inquiries bore curious Fruit. [He is playing with us here, referring to the fruit gathered by the sailors—Ed.] For it was quickly borne in upon me that every Soul upon the Island was Colour-blind. [This is not as far-fetched as it sounds: Pingelap, also in the Pacific Ocean, is another example of an island where the achromatic mutation spread throughout an entire population.] This explained why some of the Selvages, attempting to help our Men gather Fruit, gathered ripe and unripe alike, unable to tell the colour diferences.

Of material Culture they have precious little, besides their Huts (mean in comparison with other Societies we had encounterd), canoos, & sundry tools. In One greater hut, tho', they kept their religion, and this they explicated with Enthusiasm. They believe in a Great Squid (they told us), named Tlulu, who would one Day rise up out of the sea and raise this Tribe of the Faithful to Mastery of the Earth. The North is said to be Sacred to him, and that region is *tapu* [taboo] to all save the Faithful. To reckon the Time of His rising, they have built Charts of woven sticks & string so contrived to Predict the position of sartain Stars in their Courses. [Townshend may be mistaken—this is very reminiscent of the *mattang* of the Marshall Islands, used for navigation—Ed.] These they hang about the House of Tlulu like so many Snares set to entrap Time it self.

The Southern Summer day was long but by the time sufficient Stores were gathered to the Beach the sunn was westering. Our hosts expressed sadnes (by word if not by expression) at our leaving & urged us to sail South, to other Islands far greater than their own. But this we knew for a Lie as we had but lately traversd these Seas and encounter'd naught save Ocean Ocean & more Ocean. We thanked them, said naught of our true destination, and we prepared to embark.

But as the Sun neared the horizon of a sudden our Hosts all faced North and the Men set up a loud chaunt, viz:

Tlulu Tlulu
Fan glei Ma-glawa na'
Tlulu R'lai waga-nal fata'n

and the Warriors stamppd their feet in time on the black Sand & beat their Chests with the flat of their Swords. The Women moaned in unison, such a doleful Sound as of the Winds of the World mourning the Last Day. And as they moaned they sank to their Knees & thence lay prone upon the sand. Now the Men made to do the same, until the whole Population was spred upon the beach like a Congregation of Mussulmen facing Mecca. It was a spectacle I expect to see in my Memory the rest of my life, the Island rising high and green behind us, the volumes of Smoke higher still, into the indigo tropick evening, those giant brown bodies laid upon the Sand, glistening in the last Rayes of the setting Sunne, and the putrescent remains of the squid not washed off by the Tides. All grew terribly quiet—only the soft sudden Clap of waves upon the Strand. Of a sudden the ground beneath our feet commenced to vibrate, and from the smoking Mountain at our back came a deep and angry Mutter. It only lasted some seconds, but impressed us again with the Titanic forces intombed beneath these lands of the South Sea. And when the islanders arose we saw that they were all Smiling, and One pointed to the wide Sea and said Tlulu.

1774 JAN'RY 9.

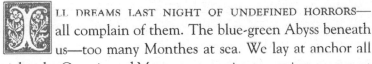

LL DREAMS LAST NIGHT OF UNDEFINED HORRORS— all complain of them. The blue-green Abyss beneath us—too many Monthes at sea. We lay at anchor all night, the Captain and Master not trusting to navigate amongst unknown shoals and Reefs in the dark. A guard was placed on deck against any possible Incursions by the Salvages, and indeed in the morn we found the *Resolution* ringed by canoos. Capt. Cook and Johann Forster spoke the nearest Canoo and were told they were there to protect us, tho' from what they would not say.

Preparations were made to procede Northward, but the

Natives would no[t allow it], beseeching us to stay and injoy the Bounty of the Island, though to speak truly those benefits had been scanty Enou[gh]. Cook directed them to move away from the Ship but they would not and brandished their swords & spears. At last the Captain order'd a Cannon fired across their bows, which mighty sound astonisht these Salvages much but dissuaded them not one jot.

Now the brutes paddled towards our ship and showed ev'ry Intention of boarding with consequent Murder & Pillage, but this time it was Captain Cook who would not have it and ordered the cannon loaded with grape[shot] and fired into the midst of them. The discharge made great slaughter amongst the warriors and sank 2 canoes, yet did they come on more Determin'd than ever, blood in their Eyes.

Now it was to be seen that more Islanders, roused by the noise of the Battle, were issuing forth from the island in more canoos. In fact, it seemed the whole population of the Island must be upon the water, so Numerous were they, and armed at all aspects. Our crew was all armed as well and with the Cannon & swivel the Muskets bang'd and clatterd making an ungodly Din in the quiet morning air, yet the Natives came on again and again. Soon it was evident that we must slay All or be born under by their sheer Ferocity and numbers, and this the Capt. was loth to do, so ordered sails set and whilst the Guns kept the most Zealous of the attackers at bay, we made good our escape.

Even as the wind freshened and bore us away to the North the Islanders tried to keep pace with us, paddling furiosly and all the time calling Tlulu Tlulu in Voices made rough by exertion. Now 3 of the Canoos spread Sail also, much like those tall triangular Sails imploy'd by the Indians [i.e., the Maori—Ed.], and bid fair to catch us up, the wind being in their Quarter. And upon these sails we could see an Image of their Great Squidd-God or Tlulu painted in some red pigment, terribel to look at.

But for all their paint & Tattews & infernal shouts & armes the gunners made short work of them, spraying them with lethal loads of grape and round-shot & tearing their pretty Sails all to rags & filling their bilges with the Blood of the slain.

In an hour we had left them behind and stood on at a fair pace, some 8 knotts under a cloudles Sky. With the fair weather & Sun and our escape from the islanders our mood should have been lighten'd, yet our Crew were still surly and recalcitrant. As we progressed thro' the foaming Water I felt this choler spreading even to me, and I observ'd Mr Forster *père* more disputatious & ill-favoured than usual. Seaman Gillis is on the edge of Hysteria, and sadly his Mood conveys easily to the other seamen. Many now speak in Low Voices of the Squidds and their possible meaning. They do their chores faithfully but without the Alacrity of former days. There is nothing so plain as Mutinie, but it would be fair to say their hearts are not in their work. We saw few fish and no Birds at all on this day, altho' an occasionall Squid of the ubiquitous *megaptera* species shot past us, ever South. And it was plain to me now that Bird and Beast alike had not been migrating *to* anything, but fleeing *from* Something. And we are ploughing thro' the waves towards that Something.

To night Gillis was clappt in irons and will be flogg'd upon the morrow. He had been becoming more erratick all day, and as Night fell he clamber'd into the shrouds, there to observe the squid beneath the Waters. He began yelling down that now he could see the Patterns intire, he had learnt the cipher of the Squids maculations and it told him we should arrive at our Destination in a day and a nights Time. With the Mens mood already wound to a high pitch the Boatswain called for Gillis to Come down out of there, be a good lad and shut it, but he would not, and finally the Mate and a couple Hands must needs climb the rigging as well and chase him even to the Topsail yards before securing him & returning him to the deck where he was restrain'd. My heart is mov'd to sadness and regret at the Poor man and his plight, yet he seems the most sanguine and Cheerfull of our company anticipating Great Things to come. That he is mad is without a doubt, but I am reminded of his colourblindness and that of the Islanders, and I now ask myself not What is it that they do *not* see, but What is it that they *DO* see?

1774 JAN'RY 10.

IND CONSTANT, NEARLY A GALE OUT OF THE S.S.W. SUN and hotter, the Mood on deck sombre. Gillis brought up to Deck this morning, bound to the shrouds and given 12 lashes. Still he complaind none, and when the doctor applied salves to his Back, and a new sail was spread upon the mainmast, disclosing a gigantick Squidds head and tentacles he had painted in tar upon it, he laughed like to burst his Lungs. The Mate secreted him far below Decks, in hopes that his Laughter will not further annoy the crew, who are become surly for lack of Slepe. All complain of bad dreams, my self included, of the Depths of ocean & of Somthing rising to be seen, a great and awful Revelation. The text

And the Sea gave up the Dead which were in it [Rev. 20:13]

revolves in my mind again and again tho' I try to silence it. There is no wholesome Distraction to put in its place, however, as the Crew are silent, the Forsters are silent, the Captain is silent, and the sea is become a wide and featureless Desertt devoid of Life of any kind. For even the strange squid have quit these Waters, responding to Who knows what Stimulus or warning. Yet our Captain has set his aquiline face and implacable Will towards the Unknown North, as resolute to discover what is undiscover'd as to go where he has been forbidden, *tapu* or no. The Wind seems to manifest his intent, pressing the sails until the Masts creak and groan in a most worrysome Manner. He is, indeed, the Captain of *Resolution*.

As I write this in my berth before a Sleep which I dread, the only sound of Human activitie is the hoarse laugh of Gillis, secured deep in the Hold.

1774 JAN'RY 11.

N THE LATITUDE OF 47 DEGRESS 9 MINUTES SOUTH, Longitude of 126 Degrees, 43 minutes West. Sun, hot, the wind dyed in the Night. The Sea the colour of Pewter, the sky a steely blue such as I have never seen—a vast Slate upon which anything may be written. V. early this morn awaked by a shout. As I lay in my berth wondering if it emanated from the Captain's cabin or no, I heard the rapid thumping of bare Feet running upon the deck above my head, and soon divers Yells and Alarms. I rose quickly, glad to be free of the Gripe of unspeakable nightmares, and came up on Deck.

All the Crew were awake and running hither and yon, many crowding along the bow rail and cat heads forward, staring Ahead. I joined them, close by Captain Cook himself. Like his Men, his Countenance was set & grim & intent upon the Sea before Us.

There, several miles distant, the Ocean was heaving up in a wide Circle, a smooth, silvery shield betokening some titan Current upwelling from unguessed Depths. A Hand in the rigging guessed it to be 2 miles in diameter, and contrary to its evident dispersal of water we were being drawn towards It. Still we remain unmoving, fascinated by this Irruption from a World beyond our most acute philosophies. This is What we have been drawn towards, the Captain said quietly at my side, This is What the Salveges tried to discourage us from reaching. And still we drifted towards It, and the only sound on that flat, immeasurable Plain was the gurgling of the uprising waters.

We should have stayd thus and, God help us, have been caught by that unholy Current but that at that moment there was a Commotion aft. Gillis had contrived to escape his bounds, evade his Captors, & run pell mell up onto the Main Deck, calling and screaming in a most hideous Manner, Tlulu! Tlulu! So aghast were we at this apparition, his hair disheveld, his eyes distended, shirt in flying tatters behind him as he ran, that for a moment no one thought to restrain him. In that moment he grabbed up from beside one of the Canon two of the six-pound balls, career'd to the rail and throwing his Hands holding the shot straight out before him, dove over and down to splash into the Sea. We watched as his body, still clutching the balls, legs kicking, faded and faded into the Green waters, faded, dwindled, and Gone.

Then Consciousness returned to us as with a slap, and the Captain ordered the Boats over the side Immediately. Cables were strung betwixt Ship and boats, and the doughty Sailors manned their oars, bent their backs to the Task, and turned the *Resolution* about and away from that nightmare Fountain in the Middle of the sea. They rowed like men possess'd or reborn, reborn to Sense and Duty, and rowed us until the Upwelling had disappear'd back over the horizon. Then a clean, fresh Breeze arose from the N.W., the boats were pulled in and stowed, and the Captain directed us on a course as near due South as could be attain'd without nearing that Island of Evill People. He speaks now of returning to find the Southern Continent, for which even the most Profane among us praised God Almighty, officer and man.

HUS ENDS THE DISPUTED PORTION OF MARGATE Townshend's manuscript. It should be noted that there is no Able Seaman Isaac Gillis on the ship's list for the *Resolution* for the voyage of 1772–75 (nor for any of Cook's voyages, for that matter), nor is there any island in the location Townshend indicates. However, papers may be recopied or revised during the long, quiet watches at sea (as we know Cook himself did in journal entries dealing with cannibalism); and the unknown island seems to have been an unstable formation of recent origin. Things that have risen may sink, and those that have sunk may rise again.

Casting Call

DON WEBB

Don Webb's most recent book is Do the Weird Crime Serve the
Weird Time *(Wildside Press, 2011). He has been nominated for
the Rhysling Award and the International Horror Guild Award
and expects to be nominated for other awards he will not win.
He teaches creative writing for UCLA Extension and has fifteen
books and more than 400 short stories published. You can see him
in the plutonium weapons documentary* Plutonium Circus.

IGHT GALLERY, *ORIGINALLY TO BE CALLED* **ROD SERLING'S** *Wax Museum, ran on NBC from 1970 until 1973. Serling as host would introduce the segments with reference to one of Tom Wright's paintings of macabre or surreal subjects. Wright had to produce almost a hundred paintings. In the first season he worked with oil on canvas; in later years he resorted to faster-drying acrylic on particleboard. Here's a fact you won't find elsewhere, my little cryptlings: several artists would show up at the studio each week with their own paintings (not understanding that NBC commissioned Tom Wright for each painting to match an existing script). Their horrorific art, they felt, could have inspired the writers for the glass teat. Some of it, I recall, was pretty dang horrorific.*

—Tycho Johansen, *I Was Rod Serling's Bodyguard*
(North Hollywood Books, 1983)

ELIX RAMIREZ'S FIRST THOUGHT WHEN HE SAW IT WAS horrible. Not bad-taste/bad-art horrible. It might have been that. The colors were perhaps a little garish. The graveyard mold a little bit too much on the slate blue side. The ghoul's doglike face seemed (to Felix) to be a little too elongated. Felix tried to think of the painter that did that, but Amedeo Modigliani's name eluded him despite Art History 102 two years ago. But he certainly thought of Goya's *Saturn Devouring One of His Sons*. The ghoul's gore-smeared mouth, clamped down on the naked figure's thigh, seems to have a leering grin. Felix watched Rod and the big dumb Dane look at the painting. Felix thought Rob would love it. Partially because the ghoul's staring eyes looked more than a little like Richard Nixon's and Rod, the "angry young man of Hollywood," wanted to punish Nixon for the war. Felix wanted to walk over to Rod, wanted to introduce himself, but you didn't just walk up to studio execs in NBC. Felix was waiting with the other cattle for a screen test. But he clearly heard Serling say something about "Pickman's Model" and express some regret. The great man's elevator came, and Rod and his bodyguard boarded.

It was 1971 and big things were happening. Eighteen-year-olds could now vote as well as die for their country. We went to the moon twice. The World Trade Center was opened a few weeks ago and they've started building the Superdome in New Orleans. And Felix Ramirez had a plan. He is ready to be one of the first Chicano actors to make it big. Everything points to go. They've got that new show *All in the Family*. They axed *Hee-Haw*, *Green Acres*, *Mayberry R.F.D.*, and *The Beverly Hillbillies*. *The Lawrence Welk Show* was replaced by *The Sonny and Cher Comedy Hour*. What did you not see? Mexicans. Felix knew at some point, Mexicans were going to be interesting. So he had a plan: monsters, then villains, then heroes of his people, then finally the serious actor. He would do it for Momma. Momma had died the same week as Kennedy, so it wasn't a big deal, not even to the nuns at school. Probably that November he had begun to hate the world.

His cousin Guillermo had called him from Mexico City and told him to try out for *Night Gallery*. He figured it out; nobody will care if a monster eats enchiladas on its off-time. Then it is a clear step to villains, and then when Mexicans become commercial—there he would be.

The trouble for the grand scheme is that Felix was not drawn to macabre (unlike Guillermo). He tried watching Karloff stumbling along in *Frankenstein*. He tried his best Romanian accent imitating Lugosi. He just wasn't scary. But the painting leaning on the guard's desk. *That* was scary.

Felix had a "call back"—he was being considered for a ghoul. He would get the painting as a model. He almost ran to the guard's desk. A bored African American guard reading a comic book, *The Forever People*. The painting was gone.

"Excuse me, sir," said Felix.

"Yeah."

"There was a painting here."

"Sure was."

"Do you know what happened to it?"

The guard looked up. Felix saw that one of the superheroes was black, the other ones looked like hippies. It was a sign. We were in a new age.

The guard said, "The artist came and got it. At least she told me she was the artist. Why?"

He sounded a little worried; maybe he realized that he should have asked the "artist" for some ID. But on the other hand, who would want that monstrosity behind their couch?

"I thought it looked really scary. I wanted to study it. For my next role."

"Oh, you're an actor. Well, I will agree with you on the scary part. That thing gave me the willies. It had been against my desk for a week. At night I would turn it against the wall." He gestured. "A lot of people leave stuff here. They think that Serling buys art for his show. The first season we wouldn't let them leave it. He looks the stuff over now. I think he does that to annoy the network artist. He can be a dick sometimes."

"He ever buy any of it?"

"He doesn't even run the show. Laird runs it. Serling got tired of doing everything over at CBS."

"So what's he looking for?"

"He does his thing. I do my thing." The guard began to pick up the comic book.

Felix persisted. "I really want to meet that artist. Maybe she can help me out with makeup tips."

The guard reached into a trash can. "I had just filed her phone number."

He handed Felix half a torn envelope.

She was Mexican. She was a maid. And one of her weirdo clients had the biggest collection of science fiction and horror shit in all the world. His home was in the fashionable Los Feliz section of Hollywood. Her name was Carlotta Rotos, and the first time Felix met her was on a driveway with a sign that said, "Hollyweird, Karloffonia." Carlotta spoke to Felix rapidly in Spanish. She had invited him here because she didn't want to meet him first at her tiny home. Her boss had encouraged her to try and get the painting on the show. He was a little weird.

She was dark and very pretty and in an actual maid's outfit.

A super-energetic man introduced himself as Forrest J. Ackerman. He asked Felix what he was interested in and Carlotta said, "Lovecraft." Felix had no idea who Lovecraft was. Ackerman was ushering him into the house, the "Ackermansion." At the doorway he pointed further up Los Feliz. There appeared to be a Mayan temple. "Frank Lloyd Wright's 'Maya House'—it was the exterior for *House on Haunted Hill*. That starred Vincent Price. Some people think I look like him. Lovecraft, eh? I've got a postcard from him."

Ackerman ran to an overstuffed desk. He couldn't find it. Then he handed Felix a copy of *Dracula*. "Signed first. But that's not so rare; there are five of those. Look at the next page."

It was covered in signatures from Bela Lugosi to Christopher Lee. Everyone that had been the Count.

For the next two hours there were props from TV and movies and books, books, books. And magazines. And more magazines. At one point Ackerman had shown him a copy of *Weird Tales*. "This was my first magazine. I kept buying them. My mother actually told me that if I was not careful, by the time I was an adult I would have a hundred of them." The crazy laugh that followed would have done any mad scientist proud. The "Unique Magazine" showed an Egyptian scene, a brown man and boy were coming over an outcropping toward a crude sphinx with pyramids in the background. "Imprisoned with the Pharaohs" by HOUDINI. Thrills! Mystery! Adventure!

Felix was a little dizzy when he walked out into the Los Feliz twilight. Ackerman hadn't been able to find the postcard. "Things walk out of here all the time." He had explained to Felix that "Pickman's Model" was a short story by Lovecraft. When he had heard that NBC was filming it, he suggested Carlotta try and submit the painting. "I've got a few items that Lovecraft used to own." Carlotta looked very guilty when he said that. He showed off Lovecraft's annotated copy of *The King in Yellow*. Felix could tell that he was supposed to be impressed, so he acted impressed. He was, after all, an actor. At the end of the tour, Ackerman pointed to the Maya House again. "That little number is pretty Frank Belknap Long itself. Bad angles. Bring bad things. Frank Lloyd Wright had been putting the finishing touches on it when his houseboy went berserk at Taliesen and killed seven people. It was said the house was cursed. He built it for a shoe magnate, and the man lost everything in the Depression. The next owner's wife jumped off the parapet. Tindalos hounds, Chihuahua style, if you ask me. I've got a book on that too somewhere. The Mexicans knew. Six owners in forty-four years."

Carlotta looked as if she was going to cry. When she walked him to his car, she gave him her East LA address.

It was brown stucco and had four floors and was on a different planet from the Ackermansion. But it was the planet that Felix had grown up on. Planet Barrio. There was a cop car parked in front of the liquor store on the corner. It was Tuesday, the smog index was high, and it was hot. He buzzed her box, she buzzed him in. Her room was on the third floor. It had horrorable and fantastic studies of ghouls hung on its tiny walls. Some were scenes from Egypt or Rome, others were modern; on the easel was a mainly finished study of a human male being initiated into ghoul society at Forest Lawn. Two ghouls were painting his naked body with a blue-green liquid. A female ghoul with rows of small breasts like a dog reclined on a tombstone holding a broken human skull. Gore ran down her lips, and she stared lewdly at the human. Her face was Carlotta's.

"I am not sick, Mr. Felix," she said. "I used to paint normal things."

She pointed to two small canvases up in the corner of the room. One was a reproduction of Van Gogh's *Sunflowers*. The other was a somewhat insipid seascape.

"It was because of my brother and the book."

And so Felix heard Juan's story.

Carlotta's mom was a maid. Her father a Zoot-suiter. A pachuco. Mom worked for Hollywood go-getters. Dad was in and out of jail. Sometimes Dad was Juan's hero, hater of the Anglo-culture machine. Sometimes Dad was Carlotta's villain—drunk, womanizer, shit-disturber. Momma was Thanksgiving. Papa was *Cinco de Mayo*. Papa got a knife in the side, Momma got to dust an Oscar. Momma was the real world, working hard every day. Papa was Juan's world.

As a teenager he was in gangs. He tried to find common cause with the blacks. Six years ago he had been in the Watts Riots. Then Juan changed. He buckled down. He went to school.

Juan Rotos wanted what every American wants: gold and knowledge. You go to school to learn stuff and get a good job, *comprende*? All good Americans want Faust's deal. A Peruvian named Carlos Castaneda had found it. Carlos was an Angelino.

Just a couple of years ago he had published *The Teachings of Don Juan: A Yaqui Way of Knowledge*. Don Juan was a "Nagual," which comes from the Nahuatl word *nahualli*, one who could turn himself into an evil animal-like being for the purposes of sorcery. He made a bundle off the books. In Aztec mythology the God Tezcatlipoca was the protector of nagualism, since he governed the distribution of wealth and the powers of black magic. Juan discovered that shortly after the Conquest, a certain "Black Friar," Thomas de Castro, had written an account of the magic involved. *Dioses Malvados del Laberintho*. The book had a litany for invoking Tezcatlipoca in his forms as Cetl, the Night Axe; Huemac, the Double; Eihort, the Demon of the Labyrinth; Nyarlathotep-Metzli, the Messenger of the Moon. The book then explained how certain drugs could be smeared on the body in cemeteries, how teeth could be pulled, and how certain sex magic rituals could make you into a Nagual or *Brujo Negro*.

Juan had decided de Castro's book could be his meal ticket. Anglos would love the drugs and sex and dominant cultures are always fixated on the magic systems of the people they conquer. It was making millions for Castaneda and it would make millions for him. Now it seemed that the bad priest's book had vanished, so Juan was forging one. Then he spotted a little article on the books that inspired a horror writer named H. P. Lovecraft. It mentioned de Castro's book *Dioses Malvados del Laberintho*. There was a copy in LA in the Ackermansion.

Juan asked Carlotta to steal it. Borrow it at least until Juan made a copy.

Sure, what was the harm? Juan might make his millions. She picked up the book, she could return it after a copy was made. Juan wouldn't be a jailbird like Papa, he could make good money for Momma's retirement. Mr. Ackerman wouldn't even miss it.

Then Juan decided that it was for *real*.

The hexes, the spells, the visions, the power. Juan wasn't

going to return the book. Juan was going to become one of Them. The shape-shifters. The flesh eaters. The ghouls Mr. Lovecraft wrote about could be the vanguard of the Revolution. Juan found E. Duran Ayers's report of the Zoot Suit Riots. The guy that the LAPD had as an expert witness against Papa and the other pachucos. He taped it to his mirror:

Mexican Americans are essentially Indians and therefore Orientals or Asians. Throughout history the Orientals have shown less regard for human life than have the Europeans. Further, Mexican Americans had inherited their "naturally violent" tendencies from the "bloodthirsty Aztecs" of Mexico, who were said to have practiced human sacrifice centuries ago.

Juan got a tattoo over his heart: *¡Yo soy un Azteca sanguinario!* I am bloodthirsty Aztec. He also had a white football-looking sigil added, the sign of Eihort. His Momma decided that he was going to Hell. She died a few weeks afterward.

Juan began reciting the litanies, buying the herbs. He got a few of his friends to break into a vault at Forest Lawn. Carlotta broke into tears at this point.

"One night he came here, very late. His face was all black. He had pulled his teeth and put in black glass. Obsidian chips. He gave me the book. I don't know if he was crazy, or not really human anymore. I never saw him again. But I have these."

She went into her tiny kitchen and pulled open a drawer. She had a handful of newspaper clippings. Graveyard vandalism. Disappearing children. Bodies stolen from morgues. A criminal gang in Halloween drag.

"So I read this horrible little book. At least the parts in Spanish."

She handed Felix the small volume. A reprint from 1863 Mexico City. *Biblioteca de la Luz Oscura.*

The black-and-white illustrations were crude but effective. Ghouls among Aztec ruins. Ghouls eating corpses. Orgies on the roof of the National Cathedral. There were a few notes in Lovecraft's handwriting; Felix recognized it from the other book. God names were underlined. One section had been labeled "Changelings." One of the most horrible illustrations had the underlined note: "Drawn from LIFE." The last section was in Latin, "Ordo Novo Astrorum." It was full of dates, and latitude and longitude tables and astrological symbols. Again Lovecraft's note, "De Castro says when the stars are RIGHT check alignments monuments of Tullan." There were a few strange sketches of buildings; one did look like Wright's Maya House. Another, perhaps a giant door, was labeled Paseo de Ya-R'lyeh.

Carlotta had broken down. Rivers of mascara ran down her brown face. For the first time Felix realized how young she was. She was his age (or just a few years older). And how sad. And what nice breasts. She lunged at him, and he stared at demonic lustful Carlotta in the painting. Her tears fell hot on his chest, and there were black stains on his light blue cotton shirt. He knew if he understood why she had to keep painting the thing she feared, he would understand fear. He would be the next Karloff, the next Lugosi. He held her. He patted her. He hoped she couldn't feel his hard-on.

When the storms of emotion passed he took her to Chabelita's. Tacos. Burritos. Hamburgers. Mexican Food. He had a burger and coffee and asked if he could borrow the book.

After the litanies and the offerings the book was a makeup guide and acting manual. To become a ghoul, you had to cover yourself with a blue-black mixture. It was partially graveyard dirt (to make yourself pleasing to the Lord of Worms), ground Seer's Sage (pipiltzintzintli), "magic" mushrooms, soot, and turkey fat. There were useful suggestions on how to make the jaw line appear more doglike, how to make the hair ropy. The book really suggested replacing teeth with obsidian chips and making an incision at the base of the spine for the tail to grow. There were a few notes on the language—"meeping," Lovecraft had glossed.

The ghoul not only ate the flesh, but the memories of the deceased. Wizards and priests were highly prized. It had limited powers of invisibility. It was immortal, although de Castro was unclear about this; it faded from the world of the "tonally"— the everyday world made from parts of the sun. The ghoul lived on a dream world untouched by the healthy sun of earth.

No wonder Juan went crazy. De Castro's informants had been drug-crazed Otomi shamans plotting to throw the Spanish out. Their post-Conquest oppression had been great; if bullets couldn't be had, magic could.

Felix had a week. He began with regular makeup products. He painted his teeth black, thinking the obsidian would be overkill. He even scared himself in the mirror.

He didn't call Carlotta during his preparation time. He knew he could fall in love with her, and she would be scared shitless that he was using the little book at all. He had sort of, kind of, suggested that he would just drop it into Mr. Ackerman's mailbox. Besides, she was probably crazy too. She had had to rationalize Juan's actions. She had to at least partially believe that he had become a ghoul. Felix wondered if she worried about her Momma's dead body; one of the clippings had been about a Mexican graveyard…

Besides, it bothered him how hot he got thinking of the naked many-breasted Carlotta in the painting. He wanted to be scratched by the long gore-stained nails, rub his tongue down the rows of canine teats.

Three days before *Night Gallery* would be casting the ghoul for "Pickman's Model" Felix had a breakthrough. He had an honest-to-god gimmick. He could claim to have Aztec sorcery on his side! Man, how cool is that?

The magic-using personality can always find omens of confirmation. That night's "Late Late Show" was *The Time Travellers* in which Forrest J Ackerman played a bit part. The gods were in favor.

Getting the Seer's Sage and the "magic" mushrooms wasn't easy; he used Crisco for turkey fat, but he did scoop some real-live cemetery dirt. He had to add some more routine pigments to make his blend. Then he called the NBC studios in "beautiful downtown Burbank" and asked if he could be allowed to do his Aztec ritual before the casting call. This was California, so the "yes" was a foregone conclusion.

He decided it would be better to say the incantation in English, so he translated the chant 93:

> *Lowly Father of Worms, whose moon face is disfigured with rotting death,*
>
> *I am you and you are me. Behold, I wear the dead skins like my uncles the Priests.*
>
> *Behold my teeth are the stones of Tezcatlipoca like my uncles the Priests.*
>
> *You taught that to walk, which should not walk.*
>
> *You have fatted me on the bodies of wizards!*
>
> *You are Eihort. I feast with Thee! You are Nyarlathotep-Metzli! I mock with Thee!*
>
> *You make liquid my flesh! You make dead my mind! You make long my bones!*
>
> *Yr Ngg Eihort Ebloth Yetl! Yetl! Shinn-ngaa!*
>
> *I am you and you are me! I am your flute. I am your teeth!*

Felix practiced the chant, trying to make it sound American Indian—that is to say, like every cowboy movie he had ever seen. He fell asleep at three in the morning. He awoke with a terrible hangover. The door of his apartment was open and there was blood on his lips, but Felix Ramirez was not an imaginative man.

On the big day it seemed that everything that could go wrong did. Someone had locked the studio and the key couldn't be found. Then they couldn't get the air turned on. Then Mr. Serling had to go to another set, and they had to wait. Some of the wannabe fiends left. The audition was supposed to happen at three. At six-thirty they got to their dressing room. Felix had tried to tell everyone about his new-found religion. The black security guard listened with the "I've heard it all" look. The white receptionist seemed interested in the sex magic part. Two of the ghouls-to-be had joined a new religion that month also. One was about UFOs, the other had to do with screaming.

There was another delay. The goop on his face had made it numb; now it was making him a little dizzy. Felix didn't know what "Seer's Sage" was—but it came across as pot from Hell. It definitely gave him the munchies. Weird thoughts kept creeping into his mind. *You know, if I was high on this shit I could pull my teeth out. That would feel real good, like coming. I wonder if Chinese people taste like Chinese food? I bet I could jump really high. There's probably not much human left in Juan Rotos. I bet worms pooped in that graveyard dirt. I am probably wearing dead people. I want to say to Rod Serling, "I submit you for Eihort's approval!" I am really hungry. I shouldn't have thrown away that pizza, the mold might make it taste better, who knows? I want to bite that white girl receptionist.*

Felix got up and paced. This was getting too weird. Juan had probably got a bunch of his angry young Mexicans to try this, and then do a little graveyard vandalism in some rich white cemetery. Probably Forest Lawn—what an emblem of what's wrong with white America! That would have sent them way over the edge! He took a deep breath. He would sit down and focus on the chant. The room was a little too bright, a little too hot. The eight other guys done up as ghouls were beginning to bug him. He wanted to meep at them.

Two more ghouls left. Felix saw through the open doors the moon had come up. The Otomi said the moon was once the equal of the sun. Then the sun threw a rabbit in its face. All the craters astronauts visited were an insult to the moon. The moon gave his flesh to worms, which became people. It was people's job to revenge the moon's insult. The messenger of the moon mocked other gods. It was people's job to get with the program. Felix closed his eyes. The moon called to him. Revenge me! Make red!

Mr. Serling strolled in with his big Dane bodyguard. Felix jumped up and said he was going to do his chant now.

"What's that clown doing?" asked Serling.

The words were coming out all wrong. It had started in English, but it became something else. The bodyguard pushed Serling backward. "If this is a publicity stunt it is stupid."

Felix felt his arms growing/lengthening. He should have made the cut for the tail. That was going to hurt. The security guard had dropped his comic book. One of the ghouls was yelling about the space brothers.

The smells! The room was full of the revolting smells of living things, all hot and shiny-smelling like the sun. Like Tonatiuh! The insulting sun, enemy of the thousand-faced moon. Felix grabbed the arm of the space-brother worshipper. He yanked hard. It didn't come off the first time, but tore free the second. Make red. He squeezed the forearm the way he squeezed a toothpaste tube. He loved the taste as it squirted in his mouth. But his teeth were wrong. They were white like the sun. Something hot burned into his chest. The guard was shooting him. Serling was screaming as the big blonde pushed him into an elevator. Felix yelled, "I submit you for Eihort's approval! You are entering a place between substance and shadow, things and ideas! I am filing you under 'S' for snack!"

Then Felix could see it. A big crack in the world. He could see it, the place between substance and shadow, things and ideas. He could see the nagual, the dreamlands. He could see a long stairway of onyx or obsidian hanging off the crack, which both was and was not in space. The guard threw his gun at Felix. What did the fucker think was going on—that this was *Dragnet*?

Felix knew he had to re-establish order. These people weren't focused. He yelled out, "Ninoyoalitoatzin inic nehuatl inic chicnauhtopa! Nimoquequeloatzin Niehort! Yo es Nyarlathotep-Metzli! I am the Father of Worms!"

No one bowed. They were supposed to bow. The Mocker Moquequeloatzin had made worms walk to make fun of the gods. Religion was the black joke. He charged at the screaming receptionist. He grabbed her fat little cheeks like tamales. He stuffed them in his mouth. Her screams were laughter.

He could see into the earth now as though the floor, the ground were purest crystal. He could see Eihort. It was a bloated white football resting on tiny legs. The ghouls were feeding on bodies. When it moved it made the countless little earthquakes LA suffered. The whole Pacific rim shook when it shook. Eyes formed in its Jello, and they looked at Felix with love he hadn't felt since Momma died.

Police were running in the door. The moon looked about twenty times as big. Moonlight sounded so sweet. He loped toward the door. The cops were shooting, and then they were running. Out in the parking lot was a big white van. It was open.

Inside was Carlotta, her sixteen tiny breasts displayed. There was a ghoul driver. Juan, no doubt. She meeped and barked, but she clearly meant, "*¡Vámonos!*" Felix ran to his mate. The van careened out of "beautiful downtown Burbank."

CASTING CALL

HE NIGHT THE PRESS CALLED "ATTACK OF THE GHOULS" WAS one of the closest calls I had with the boss. He had been having fits filming "Cool Air" and was on set for many extra hours. There was an audition for the ghouls for "Pickman's Model"—and like always with NBC the message to call off the audition was lost in the main switchboard. The boss decided to go over. He felt sorry that the poor actors had been waiting for so long. As soon as we walked in, one of them—clearly some kind of hophead—began mumbling some weird stuff. I tried to push the boss away, but he was all irate as usual. Then another one of the ghouls runs up to the first one. The hophead pulls the other ghoul's arm off. We all thought it was a publicity gag. Then the security started shooting. I got the boss out of there. NBC put a big hush on the story. They decided that people would think it was a really stupid ad campaign. Of course, some of the story did leak out in the town of "It bleeds, It leads." Some reporter tried to connect the incident with some graveyard vandalism, but I tell you it was just another snapshot of how people act in Hollyweird

—Tycho Johansen, *I Was Rod Serling's Bodyguard.*
(North Hollywood Books, 1983)

The Clockwork King, the Queen of Glass, and the Man with the Hundred Knives

DARRELL SCHWEITZER

Darrell Schweitzer has been writing fantasy and horror since the early 1970s. His credits include Whispers, Twilight Zone, Cemetery Dance, Interzone, Postscripts, and numerous anthologies. He is the author of three novels, The Shattered Goddess (Donning, 1982), The White Isle (Owlswick Press, 1989), and The Mask of the Sorcerer (New English Library, 1995), and the novella Living with the Dead (PS Publishing, 2008). He is a poet, critic, and interviewer, and has published books about Lord Dunsany and H. P. Lovecraft. He was coeditor of Weird Tales for nineteen years. He is a four-time World Fantasy Award nominee and one-time winner.

UCH OF THIS STORY WILL HAVE TO REMAIN suppositional, because a good deal of it is speculative and significant parts of it are untrue. I did not witness. I was not there.

I will admit that I met Reginald Graham in college, a few weeks into my freshman year. He was two years older than me and, yes, I looked up to him awfully, and yes, I suppose I really did, as campus wits snickered at the time, follow him around like a puppy dog, but no, we were not lovers, not queer; it wasn't like that at all. I hate it the way people think only in such clichés rather than stretch their pea-sized brains just a little. When a boy gets into a relationship like that with someone older it may be more that he's Wagner looking for Faustus, applying for the position of genuine, certified sorcerer's apprentice, mad scientist's assistant, sidekick junior grade. You don't even have to be a hunchback to get the part. What he hungers for is wisdom, guidance, a path through life, and he will cling desperately to someone he thinks has got it. Maybe this does indicate a certain weakness of character, or simple immaturity. Did you ever wonder what happened to poor Wagner after it all? No one cares. Go look it up.

You know the main bit:

> *Cut is the branch that might have grown full straight,*
> *And burned is Apollo's laurel bough.*

Et cetera, et cetera.

So maybe I was indeed somebody with no backbone, looking for a combination of a guru and father figure, but I wasn't his bum-boy, so you can just forget about that.

How, then, am I mad? Hearken! and observe how healthily—how calmly I tell you the whole story.

I followed Reggie Graham around because I thought he was a genius. At that point he was working on being a poetic genius, the next T. S. Eliot or Ezra Pound, and if his words often didn't seem to make sense that was because they were *deep*. They had to be, from the passionate conviction with which he declaimed them. Oh, yes, some of the impression he made was biological chance—he was a big, broad-shouldered guy with brilliant red hair, a thick beard, and a booming voice—and some of it was stagecraft, complete with a fake British accent that he could put on when he wanted to; but his voice somehow sounded *right*. It commanded authority, like a prophet's. And he *was* a genius.

It was during this period that he gave me my first real clue to what a far more frivolous writer later called life, the universe, and everything. We were driving late at night, way out in the country, coming back from I don't remember what, and on a lonely road, far enough away from anywhere that there was no city glow even on the horizon, he pointed to the darkened fields on either side of the road, and said, "Have you ever really thought about it, Henry? The darkness. As soon as you get away from the road and the occasional farmhouse, just a few hundred yards out into one of those fields, you might as well be on another planet. *Anything* could be happening out there, out of sight, out of earshot. If somebody were being raped or murdered or"—here he laughed and dropped into a sinister, particularly good Boris Karloff impression—"*eaten by cannibals*, those lights, the world, civilization, the possibility of rescue would seem as hopelessly far away as the stars, and *no one would ever know*."

"They'd find the bodies in the morning. There'd be buzzards."

"But the world of the morning light is not the world of the darkness, Henry, no, not at all. By day, that's a familiar field. You're trespassing on some farmer's property, all mud and cornstalks. But at night, in the darkness, it's as remote as the bottom of the sea."

"And what do *you* find there?" I asked.

"Something terrible," he said, "Or something beautiful. Or both at the same time."

Now I may *suppose* that Reggie had already started his nocturnal perambulations in farmers' fields by then, but I did not *know*—I *do* not know—because what he did right after that was drop out of school. His genius led him to actually getting one of his verse plays put on by an avant-garde company in Philadelphia. I attended the first performance, which was staged in a long corridor with a huge plastic bag stretched the length of it, and the audience sitting on the floor on one side, with the actors on the other. Most of it consisted of shrieked, half-comprehensible lines, cacophony on musical instruments, and silhouetted violence. The costumes suggested chess pieces. It was all, in the parlance of the period, "heavy," and that and twenty-five cents, as some campus critic quipped, would get you a cup of coffee. What it got Reggie Graham was the termination of his college career, because his parents insisted he major in business or accounting so he could get an actual job afterwards, and while such a romantic rebellion is eminently suitable for one of such genius, certain practicalities set in when funds are cut off.

HE DARKNESS. WE SPECULATE THEN THAT IN THIS POST-*collegiate period Reginald Graham found his way into the darkness. Maybe he drove out to that very same country road one night, pulled over to the side, and just started walking, off into nowhere. Maybe he found where he was going. Maybe the*

shadows and hints of shapes became solid for him. Maybe he stepped through some kind of gateway.

OW, THEN, AM I MAD? Let me tell you what happens to Wagner without Faustus. He drifts. The boy grows up, kind of. He lives with his mom for a while. He gets a series of meaningless, low-level jobs.

Then, five years later, when I was twenty-six, Reggie called me up suddenly, in the middle of the night. The connection was poor. I could have in retrospect imagined that he was out in the dark, standing in a muddy field, surrounded by ineffable mystery, but that was impossible at the time because cell phones had not been invented yet.

We will speculate that he called to tell me of his findings, to draw me back in to whatever adventure his life had set him out on, because maybe he needed a sorcerer's apprentice again, sidekick, junior associate mad scientist's assistant (no deformities required), but not, I emphasize, not an *ephebe*.

He told me about *another place*, which existed only in the darkness, which was invisible to the light; and for a moment the connection was very clear and he said, "You were expecting maybe malevolent, tentacled monstrosities from beyond the rim of the cosmos, but no, it is not like that at all," and then there was a lot of static, and I could only make out bits, about a mountain range of black glass, and a kingdom, dragons, a castle, a king who was mostly clockwork and his queen who was made of living glass, and roads that twisted into angles that didn't make sense, and there was a long bit about monsters, and a singing forest with razor-sharp leaves.

"Reggie, is this some new play you're working on?"

"No," he said abruptly. The connection broke.

OW, THEN—?"

 AGNER, DRIFTING, EVENTUALLY GETS NUDGED OUT OF the nest by Mom, goes back to school, and finishes an advanced degree, and after a bit more dithering ends up as a teacher of English literature at a private middle school trying to hook fourteen-year-olds on the thrills and beauties of *The Tragickal History of Doctor Faustus*, alternating every other semester with *Romeo and Juliet*. Every once in a while he slips them some Poe. ("How, then, am I mad? Hearken—!") He even becomes a Minor Poet himself, joining the elite of American poets with an actual, non-subsidized book in print, entitled, modestly, *Poems*, which has sales very, very closely approaching three figures.

If he doesn't have a house in the suburbs, an ideal wife out of a 1950s sitcom, and the statistically average 2.5 children, well, at least he has made a start at the American dream. We live in a possibly imaginary, imperfect world.

 HE NEXT TIME REGGIE GRAHAM BURST INTO MY LIFE we were both approaching forty. It was as if college— and the strange phone call—were only yesterday and there was no break in the continuity whatever. He grabbed hold of my arm as I walked along a Philly street and hauled me into a bar, and before I could even protest I realized that this craggy, almost white-haired stranger actually was my old master—yes, that was what he was; Wagner has a master in Faustus, not a chum, not a buddy, not an equal of any sort—and I was as affixed by his intense gaze as a desert mouse is allegedly hypnotized by the gaze of a rattlesnake; but it wasn't like that between us, no, not ever.

I wasn't much for drinking. I had rarely ever been inside a bar in my life. I wasn't really sociable, to tell the truth. So I sat there, fluttering and stammering while he ordered drinks for us and insisted I take a good stiff jolt of whatever it was, and then, in the darkness of that place, all the noises and lights of the outside faded away, and I saw only his face drifting before me like a risen moon, and I felt but did not see that he pressed something into my hand. It was a ring, cold to the touch.

"I need you to keep this safe," he said. "Be careful with it. It can break. It is made of glass. But it must not break and it must be kept from the enemies of the Queen of Glass, who would use it to destroy her, destroy everything, Henry, not only her world, but yours, ours, the whole kablooie."

Now you would think that the reaction that any sensible person would have at this point would be to break away, say, "Reggie, are you *nuts?*" and just leave, or, if one happened to be braver, more concerned, heroic even, one might even try to work one's way through the obviously deranged, utterly schizophrenic fantasy to find the inner, true core of my friend's soul—if he really was my friend and not my master and I his willing slave—or at least steer him to the nearest funny farm, a.k.a. psychiatric clinic, and leave these matters to the professionals. But no, I was Wagner, remember, who was there to help when Faustus sold his soul to the devil for a handful of party tricks and a night in bed (we hope) with Helen of Troy. I was the puppy dog, the apprentice, the mad scientist's sidekick (hunchback optional, no assembly required), so that is not what happened at all.

Reggie took me by the hand—no, it wasn't like that between us at all, not ever—and he led me *away*, not out onto the familiar city street, no, but *elsewhere*. I admit that because this is largely a work of supposition and fiction and speculation, and, being at best a Minor Poet ("My ninety-nine readers can beat up your ninety-nine readers!"), I am not very good at this, not the person who even should be telling this story—but I alone survived to tell thee, to coin a phrase—I admit, I say, that from here on to the end the continuity becomes hard to follow, there are lacunae in the narrative, and at times even I (most of all I) have no idea what is going on or why, even as I was more than a little disconcerted when we stepped, not out of the bar and onto the street, but into a *dark place*, and it was *cold there*—I mean, wasn't this a sunny Saturday afternoon in July? I wasn't dressed for work, but was wearing flip-flop sandals, blue jeans, and a Grateful Dead T-shirt. Yes, it was suddenly nighttime, and winter. I could see my breath. My feet and arms burned with the cold. Reggie wrapped a blanket and sat me down by a pot-bellied, wood stove beneath the glare of a single light bulb, and it seemed as if we had been there for a long time, as if we'd been together for months, and he had become—and I somehow already knew this, as if I had been attending his exhibitions and shows—not a famous poet or a playwright but, to spite his now dead parents, neither a chartered accountant nor a Kmart manager, but instead a notably eccentric painter, whose brilliance was known to a select few, who honored *me* by inviting me out to his remote studio, a barely converted, unheated barn way, way out in the country, in the darkness, well beyond the glow of city lights. Here I *had been for a long time* sitting for a portrait that was to be his masterpiece, that was to reveal every bit of his passion and dark wisdom to the unsuspecting and largely undeserving world.

My eyes adjusted. I could make out the weathered, wooden walls, the high rafters, and the precarious-looking floor with dark gaps in it. Reggie sat on a high stool with an easel and canvas turned sideways to me, so he could catch some of the light. As he painted, he spoke, as if continuing a long-running conversation that I *remembered* from a dream out of which I had only half awakened. He said that the crisis in the Kingdom of Black Glass was coming to a climax. An evil force had gathered in the Forest of Razored Leaves, a terrible foe to the lord he, Reggie Graham, faithfully served, the Clockwork King and the king's consort, the Glass Queen. This enemy, called The Man with the Hundred Knives, would soon lead his armies out of the forest, overwhelm the Palace of Black Glass, smash everything, and send its shards scattering in some fearful and immensely destructive way to pierce the infinite number of worlds that existed everywhere in the darkness.

It was the worlds of light, I was to understand, the worlds that contained things like college campuses and private middle-schools and bars and Kmarts that were illusion, that didn't matter, that were merely dreams, from which now, as I sat for this portrait, I had only partially awakened.

As he spoke I got up and came over to look at the portrait. There I was, in the lower right, huddled in a small area of light by the wood stove. Reggie had painted himself into the picture, a portrait of himself seated at his easel painting the picture. I couldn't help but notice, as I looked from the painting to his face, to the painting again, that he *did* look shockingly aged, but not withered, not feeble; no, more like one of those timeless heroes in popular fantasy, who have battled wizards or demons for centuries, and have become hardened, gnarled, immensely potent, like a cross between Gandalf and Strider with just a touch of Gaiman's Sandman. The image of me, by contrast, made me look younger and skinnier than I actually was, and very vulnerable, with the emphasis on the unruly mop of brown hair and the exaggerated, round glasses, the thin, pointed chin, pale forehead, and wide eyes. I could not have, I realize in retrospect, asked him, "Is that me or Harry Potter?" because this was a while ago and the Harry Potter books hadn't been published yet.

I didn't ask him anything, but just stood there and watched as he worked in the wide space in the upper left, painting dark upon dark, shaping images I could just barely make out, of a king whose face was a faintly luminous clock, the hands set at just a minute before midnight, and beside him the Queen of Glass, all black and gleaming, tiny points of light on the tips of her crown like stars; while behind them and a little below, in the upper middle part of the painting, the sinister Man with the Hundred Knives (who wore them strapped across his body on two long belts, like a pair of bandoliers) gathered his forces in the Forest of Razored Leaves.

There was so much more in this picture that I cannot explain or describe. There was a whole world there, much more real to me then than the half-remembered dream of city streets, schools, bars, department stores, and the like.

I understood fully and completely, to the very depths of my heart, that Reggie Graham had always been the sort of genius who would awaken us into the true world and the true kingdom, and that, because he had done so, nothing else mattered or would ever matter again.

O I WOULD LIKE TO BELIEVE. BUT REMEMBER: THIS IS A tissue of speculation and lies.

How, then, am I mad? Maybe I'm mad because I didn't say, "Whoa, wait a minute Reggie, *you* are the one who has abandoned all pretense of sanity. You've drawn me into this— Drawn? Painted, like in the painting, painting me into the painting—that's a joke, get it?—into your private psychotic fantasy world." While there might be other worlds and other dimensions, how could he expect me to believe that they're inhabited by glass people and filled with magic kingdoms and razor-blade forests and creatures that look like animate chess pieces, sort of a cross between *Alice in Wonderland* and *The Lord of the Rings* on acid, with, as I was soon to discover, a substantial sadomasochistic element added?

No, I just stood there, while Reggie explained everything and explained and explained, so thrillingly, so compellingly, that I felt as if I too had lived in the Black Glass world for a thousand years, as he had, only occasionally assuming mundane guise and venturing into the world of light to recruit a new, not necessarily hunchbacked assistant (batteries not included).

UT WHO IS TO SAY THAT AN UTTER AND ABSOLUTE genius cannot also be utterly and absolutely mad?

I don't believe that. I don't believe any of this.

It is therefore mere supposition that as Reggie was telling me all this, as he stopped painting for a minute and showed me a black glass dagger—like one of those obsidian knives Aztec priests used to rip hearts out with—and explained that the Man with the Hundred Knives is not complete or all-powerful as long as he's missing this one and only has ninety-nine, I suddenly heard a loud crash and a thump behind me, in the dark recesses of the barn and something grabbed me from behind and whirled me around, and I found myself face to face with what looked half like an enormous insect, half like a naked man whose red skin gleamed like animate, baked brick. Its many limbs flashed and flickered like whips, too fast to follow, and I was hurt, I was falling, I was cut to pieces, while I heard Reggie Graham shouting, "It wants the ring! Don't give it the ring!" But I had no chance to think about any ring, and could only curl into a ball, my back to it, to make it work a little while longer as it slashed through my clothing and my flesh and my bones to get to my vitals.

Then there was another crash, and the pain did not stop, but now I sat with my back against an upright beam in a spreading pool of my own blood, with broken bits of reddish glass or clay all around me, and Reggie standing over me, hefting a sledgehammer in his hands and looking rather pleased with himself.

"I knew this would come in handy one day," he said.

"What the fuck was that thing?" I managed to gasp, gurgling on blood.

"A scorpion man. A servitor of the enemy. There are, I am afraid, a lot more where that one came from, in the Forest of Razored Leaves."

"I think I'm bleeding to death," I said.

"Very likely," he said. "Henry, I didn't intend for this to happen. I am afraid things are beyond my control now. Times are desperate indeed. I must return to my native country, to do my duty for my lord and my lady, and, if necessary, to die for them. I am sorry."

This was the "Reggie Graham, you are out of your fucking mind!" moment, but I could not bring myself to say that, to defy him, and all I managed to say, rather pathetically was, "So you're just going to leave me then?"

But he said to me gently, binding my wounds as best he could with shreds of my own clothing, then helping me to my feet, "No, no, of course not."

With the obsidian knife he cut a hole in the air, parting the darkness as if he'd made a long, vertical slash in the side of a tent, and he pushed me through.

That was how I came to be sprawled face-down in the mud and the snow in the middle of a field in rural Lancaster County. I rolled onto my back. I looked up at the familiar stars, and rested for a while, reassured that I was home, in my own world, out of Reggie Graham's fantasy. But I also had just enough rationality left to realize that I would very likely die out here, either bleeding to death or from freezing, and in the morning, when the darkness gave way to the familiar and mundane, vultures or maybe a dog would find my body. If I was going to avoid that, I was going to have to get help, and *yes, out there in the darkness, in the middle of the field, so impossibly far from any farmhouse or from the highway, I might as well have been on another planet, or at the bottom of the sea. It took all my strength, strength I didn't know I had, impossible strength, magic which must have come from the glass ring that was still in my pocket, for me to crawl so very far toward a distant light, and pound weakly on a door until a very startled farmer and his wife discovered me.*

OW, THEN, AM I MAD? LET ME COUNT THE WAYS:
I had a lot of explaining to do. I tried not to explain. The police were called in, of course, to the hospital where I was taken, and of course nothing made sense. That was to be expected. But the detectives, then the psychiatrists began to lose patience with me when I wouldn't tell them what they wanted to hear. After my injuries had healed, more or less, though I was heavily scarred and one of the tendons in my lower right leg was damaged and I could only walk with a cane, there was some question of whether or not, and where, I should be held. I refused to file a criminal complaint against anyone. I was not obviously suicidal, and the injuries I had suffered were of such a nature that they could not have been self-inflicted. I think the head detective secretly thought I was some kind of pervert who had gotten into a really wild s&m party. The doctors didn't know what to think. Somehow the news leaked out and reporters from tabloids wanted to talk to me. I was the latest thing in UFO abductions. I had made alien anal probes passé.

In the end, there was nothing they could do but send me home, inasmuch as I had any home to go to. My apartment had been closed for non-payment of rent. All my things were gone, except for what my sister Maureen somehow rescued, a few of my books and papers and things the landlord didn't want.

When I left the hospital, I insisted they give me whatever

had been in my pockets when I had been admitted. Somehow—for all my clothing had been as shredded as I—my pockets had held together. I was handed my wallet, my keys, and a Ziploc plastic bag containing the Glass Queen's ring, which miraculously wasn't broken.

My widowed big sister took me in, and for over ten years I lived with her in rural, upstate New York. I was terrified of the dark, and of open spaces. I very much would have preferred a city with its bright lights, but I had no other resources. I lived with her quietly, a semi-invalid, pursuing my career as a non-subsidized Minor Poet, whose total sales, after several more increasingly strange volumes, actually did rise well into three figures. I was even nominated for the Totally Obscure Award, twice.

Then Maureen got sick and died, and I found myself at sixty-three alone in her house, surrounded on all sides by the dark, open fields and the empty distances.

When I looked in the mirror I saw a soft, graying face that might indeed have looked like Harry Potter if he'd missed his calling and were now tottering on the edge of senility. I thought to myself that here was someone whose life had passed him by, who had never managed to accomplish very much in this world because it was like a dream to him, only half-remembered in those rare moments when he *actually awakened* into the darker, *real* world where the endlessly brave, endlessly brilliant Reggie Graham battled the monstrous minions of The Man with the Hundred Knives (or actually ninety-nine, since Reggie had one of them) in defense of his lord the Clockwork King and his lady the Queen of Glass.

But I was interrupted as I stood before the bathroom mirror in the midst of these reflections, because, behind me, the air itself was suddenly slit open as if someone had made a long, vertical slash in the side of a tent and hurled something through.

There was a loud bang. Something heavy fell into the

bathtub. With astonishment, then with sorrow and resignation, I saw that it was the very familiar sledgehammer, the one with which Reggie Graham had destroyed the scorpion man to save my life.

OW I SHALL TELL YOU A SERIES OF LIES:

The rip in "reality" remained there, the edges flapping in a cold breeze. The bathroom, then the whole house filled with cold, damp air, with the smell of winter ice and mud from the fields outside. I knew what I had to do. I understood something Reggie had explained to me once, that time does not move at the same speed in the dark world as it does in the world of light. What had been for me over twenty years might have been for him only a few hours.

I was growing old slowly and quietly. He was still in the thick of his fight.

I would like to think that I fulfilled my duty, that I put on heavy boots and the toughest denim jeans I owned (not having armor, these would have to do) and a heavy coat and gloves, then stepped through that gap into the other world, where I fought long and hard, with more strength than I'd ever known I had, alongside Reggie Graham. He had another name there, and was a renowned master of dark lore, a distant, forbidding, yet heroic figure, who had compromised his own soul for the sake of higher loyalties, who was both Siegfried and Faust at the same time; and I, I, his loyal and faithful companion, though hobbled with an old wound, came limping to his side.

I wielded that sledgehammer like Thor, but it was not enough, for the citadel was overwhelmed by the scorpion men in the end, and the Clockwork King and the Queen of Glass were both smashed, he to mechanical bits, she to shards. I last saw Reggie Graham on a narrow bridge over an abyss, locked in deadly combat, his one knife against his enemy's ninety-nine.

I had to flee. I left him there. He wanted me to. He knew and I knew that the only hope lay with the ring, which must remain unbroken and out of the hands of the enemy until one day a rightful prince should wear it.

So I fled back through that rent in reality, battling scorpion men all the way, until I fell, terribly wounded, in my upstairs bathroom, and that was how the police discovered me, a few days later, when the mailman and the neighbors became alarmed that my mail was accumulating in the box and my newspapers were piling up in the driveway.

I had quite a bit of explaining to do, yet again.

That is the best version of the story's ending, the most pleasing lie.

OW, THEN?

The other version is that I proved a coward and stepped through into the beleaguered citadel, sledgehammer in hand, to confront Reggie Graham and shriek, at last, at the top of my lungs, "You *are* out of your fucking mind! *None* of this is real! You're not real! I think this is all a dream one of us is having while lying in a straitjacket in a padded cell somewhere!" Then I ran back into the real world, sledgehammer in hand, abandoning him to his fate; only the scorpion men didn't let me off that easily, which is how I was so terribly wounded yet again.

But the main problem with this version, which the police deftly omitted from their report, is that the gap in the fabric between the worlds remained wide open like a torn curtain flapping in a cold breeze, even as I escaped into the bathroom, and the scorpion men tried to follow me, and I fought them, there, in the cramped bathroom.

I am at a loss to explain what happened to the sledgehammer. It wasn't found in the bathroom.

I can't explain. But the aftermath was like the surrealist light bulb joke. You know: How many surrealists does it take to change a light bulb? Two, one to hold the giraffe, one to fill the bathtub with glowing machine parts. The only difference was there was no giraffe, and my bathtub was filled with reddish bits of scorpion men, some of them still twitching. The police left that out of their report too.

EGGIE WARNED ME THAT THE ENEMY WOULD USE EVERY trick of guile and illusion at his command to get the ring away from me.

Therefore, what I most emphatically deny is any scenario in which none of the above happened, but instead, Reggie was suddenly pounding at my door in the middle of the night and screaming that he'd got it all wrong, that there was no heroic quest in the dark world, but only madness and utter horror, and I, for fear of confronting that ultimate truth, did not open the door, but *let him die* right there on my doorstep, after he had crawled for such a painful and impossible distance out of the dark. There was one last scream, more piercing than the rest, and a loud thump of something thrown against the door, then only skittering and scratching, and what flowed suddenly under the door was not blood, but *blackness*, an animate, almost material darkness. I retreated from it up the front stairs, and watched in dread-filled fascination as it groped this way and that, like an enormous tongue, and finally withdrew.

I waited until morning before I opened the front door. There was nothing there. No body. No blood. The door was not even scratched.

I have *no idea* what became of Reggie Graham, whether he

is living or dead or where he might be. Villains, dissemblers! Go ahead and tear up the floorboards if you want. You won't find anything.

I will ask you to explain, though, why the floor between the front door and the stairs is devoid of all varnish, as if something very powerful and very abrasive licked it clean.

O, WHAT DO YOU THINK? I KNOW WHAT I THINK. I THINK I have unraveled the riddle at last. Yes, it *is* all a tissue of lies, a tangle of illusion. I think the truth is that I am *not* Wagner, the weak-willed but loyal, slightly pathetic sidekick. I think that *I* am Faust and that Reggie Graham—or what seemed to be Reggie Graham—was Mephistophilis, sent to trick me out of my soul—out of the ring.

I've still got it. I admit that much. I've hidden it well. You shall not get it from me. No torture can extract it from me. I shall hold it until the true prince comes, and all your world of evil and illusion is shattered forever, like glass hit with a sledgehammer.

How, then, am I mad?

The Other Man

NICHOLAS ROYLE

Nicholas Royle is the author of six novels, two novellas, and one short story collection, Mortality *(Serpent's Tail, 2006), with another,* London Labyrinth, *forthcoming from No Exit Press. He has edited fifteen anthologies, including* Darklands *(Egerton Press, 1991),* The Best British Short Stories 2011 *(Salt, 2011), and* Murmurations: An Anthology of Uncanny Stories about Birds *(Two Ravens Press, 2011). A senior lecturer in creative writing at Manchester Metropolitan University, he also runs Nightjar Press, publishing limited-edition chapbooks.*

VERY MORNING THE SAME ROUTINE. GRAEME'S WIFE would stir first and he would wake while she was getting out of bed to go to the bathroom. While she was performing her ablutions, he would lever himself into a sitting position and swivel around, slipping his feet into a pair of Chinese slippers. Slowly, with effort that seemed to increase week by week, he would stand up and walk to the bedroom door, where he would take his dressing gown from the hook and put it on. He would climb the stairs to the second floor, the ease or difficulty with which he performed this act tending to depend on the time he had gone to bed the night before. He would clean his teeth and use the toilet and then walk back down to the first floor, where the light from under the bathroom door would indicate that his wife was still within, and he would continue downstairs, where he would switch the alarm off and go into the kitchen and make them both a cup of tea. He would take the tea upstairs, and usually by this stage his wife would be out of the bathroom and he would hand one of the cups to her and she would say thank you as she took it from him and started to get dressed.

One particular day, while his wife, Sarah, was in the bathroom, he arranged his pillow and one of Sarah's pillows and a couple of cushions under the duvet on his side of the bed and crept up the stairs to the second floor. But he got his timing wrong and came back down just as Sarah was emerging from the bathroom, so he snuck back into the bedroom and remade the bed.

The next day, he arranged the pillows and cushions under the duvet again and went up to the top floor, taking care lest the stairs should creak. When Graeme came back down, Sarah had finished in the bathroom and he could hear her voice in the bedroom. He peeped through the crack of the door. She was sitting on the edge of the bed towelling the ends of her hair. She had stopped speaking for a moment, as if waiting for a response from beneath the duvet.

With care, he retreated from the door and walked downstairs. He quickly disarmed the alarm and then shut the kitchen door behind him so that she would not hear him boiling the kettle. He stood and looked out of the window while waiting. The same damp lawn, bare trees, grey sky as the day before and the day before that. The kettle clicked off.

He climbed the stairs quietly and paused outside the bedroom door, hearing voices. It did sound like there was more than one.

There was a bookcase on the landing. Graeme deposited the cups of tea on top of it and placed his eye at the crack of the door. He couldn't see Sarah, who had perhaps moved to the right of the doorway. She would be leaning over the chest of drawers where she kept her makeup and jewellery, studying her face in the mirror. But on his side of the bed, the duvet had been pulled back and a shape like a pillow standing on its end appeared to have been somehow propped up on the edge of the mattress. The shape moved forwards slightly and then started to twist around to one side, and something caught in Graeme's throat.

He backed away from the door. What his brain told him his eyes had seen he couldn't have. A mask, perched on top of the pillow: line and shade, the suggestion of a face.

He moved back to the door. Sarah's voice could be heard from inside the bedroom.

"Right, well, some of us have got to go to work."

He registered the businesslike jangle of her charm bracelet.

The shape that had been sitting on his side of the bed stood up and stretched rudimentary arms, its back to the room. It was the size—and more or less the shape—of a man. It turned around, and Graeme heard a voice that wasn't Sarah's.

"Have a nice day, darling."

It was what he would normally say, but to him the words sounded badly pitched. There was a mouthlike slit in the mask, which even as Graeme watched was resolving into something more like a human face. Could Sarah not see, though, that the figure stood before her was not him, was not Graeme, was not even actually human? Its movements were all wrong, its dimensions slightly off. But only slightly. And as he watched, the amount by which they were off seemed to get smaller, and the movements became more natural. The eyes looked less like buttons. As the figure walked around the end of the bed, Graeme had to concede it was like looking in the mirror. The figure passed out of view, and Graeme heard Sarah's bracelet jingle. He imagined them embracing; he heard them kiss. Then he made out the rustle of Sarah turning to move towards the door, and he backed off and ran, as carefully as he could, up the stairs to the next floor.

He watched through the spindles as his wife and this other man walked out of the bedroom together. The man was dressed, in *his* clothes.

"See you later," Sarah shouted as she reached the ground floor.

"See you later," Graeme muttered quietly at the same time as he heard the other man say the same words, more loudly, loudly enough to be heard by Sarah as she opened the front door and left the house.

Graeme remained crouched by the banisters at the top of the house.

Nothing happened. The other man had gone downstairs

and Graeme couldn't hear anything. He crept back down to the first floor and slipped into the bedroom. He dressed quickly, moving with more confidence. He went downstairs; he didn't walk on tiptoe, but nor did he proceed in quite the normal way. Stopping at the bottom of the stairs, he listened. The other man was in the kitchen. Graeme could hear him emptying breakfast cereal into a bowl, returning the box to the cupboard, getting the milk from the fridge and a spoon from the drawer. Graeme heard a chair being pulled back as the other man sat down at the table. Graeme listened to the sound of him eating. He remembered his sister once telling him about the noise he made eating corn flakes. He had taken offence, but had henceforth made more of an effort with his table manners. From what Graeme could hear, the other man was eating nicely with his mouth closed. From time to time, his spoon dinked against the side of the bowl. There was a final clarion of cutlery against pottery and what might have been a faint slurp before Graeme heard the chair legs scrape backwards on the wooden floor. He ducked sideways across the hall into the front room as he heard the bowl being lodged in the dishwasher and the other man's footsteps approaching the kitchen door. Graeme held his breath, but the next sound he heard was the creak of the stairs. When the other man would have reached the top of the stairs, or at least gone beyond the half-landing, Graeme stepped back into the hall and then into the kitchen. He opened the dishwasher; there was the other man's dirty bowl on the top shelf, and he had put his spoon in the lower section just as Graeme would have done. Graeme closed the dishwasher and went to get the corn flakes, but as he stood with the box in his hands he realised he wasn't hungry. Everyone has to eat, but he had no appetite, so he put the box back.

He stood at the bottom of the stairs and looked up. He could hear the other man's footsteps travel across the hall ceiling as their owner walked towards the bathroom. But then Graeme became aware of another set of footsteps—outside. The letter box clanged and a single envelope landed on the hall floor. In three quick strides, Graeme reached the front door, picked up the letter, noticing it bore his name, and stuffed it in his back pocket, then returned to the foot of the stairs. He climbed them quickly and quietly, becoming aware as he did so of the sound of the other man using the toilet. Graeme reached the top of the stairs, stepped on to the landing and looked into the bathroom. The other man had left the door open, which Graeme might also have done, but only if alone in the house. He—the other man—was standing in front of the toilet urinating and looking out of the window towards the backs of the houses beyond the rear garden. His stream diminished to a trickle, stopped, returned briefly, then stopped altogether. For a moment, the other man's legs bent forward slightly at the knee. Graeme moved towards the stairs that would take him up to the second floor. He managed to get out of sight before the other man had finished washing his hands.

Graeme risked a look back around the banisters. There was something lying on the carpet in the middle of the landing. He felt his back pocket. The letter wasn't there, and now the other man was coming out of the bathroom. Graeme watched as the other man started to cross the landing and then stopped, his eye drawn to the letter on the carpet. The other man bent down and picked up the letter. He read the front and then turned the envelope over and tore it open. He withdrew the contents, which comprised a single sheet of paper folded into three. He unfolded it, read it, folded it again, and returned it to the envelope, and then he went back into the bedroom. Graeme listened to him moving around, opening and closing drawers. After a minute or two, the other man came out and went downstairs. Graeme heard a couple of doors being closed—the doors to the living room and kitchen—and then the other man put the alarm on and left the house, double-locking the front door.

Graeme waited a minute and then went downstairs. The alarm started beeping quietly, so he keyed in the code and it fell silent. In the kitchen, Graeme's keys were gone from their normal place. He helped himself to a spare pair and closed the kitchen door after him. Taking a jacket from the coat rack, he keyed in the alarm code and approached the front door. He turned the key in the lock and opened the door, stepping out into the fresh spring air.

There was no one at the bus stop, so Graeme sat and waited. The bus came and Graeme got on. He looked out of the window as the bus crawled through the student district and then entered an area dominated by Asian restaurants. When the bus reached the outskirts of the city centre Graeme got up and pressed the bell. The driver brought the bus to a halt, and Graeme thanked him as he disembarked. He walked a short distance and entered the building where he worked. He crossed the atrium and climbed the spiral staircase. On the second floor he stepped inside the photocopy room and checked his pigeonhole, which was empty. He then proceeded along the corridor to his office.

Closing his fingers around the handle, he looked through the glass panel in the door. The other man was sitting at Graeme's desk running his finger under the flap of a self-sealed envelope. He turned to look towards the door, and Graeme shrank back. He pressed his spine against the corridor wall, and his knees gave a little. He allowed his back to slide down the wall, but then he heard the door to his office being opened from the inside. He immediately got to his feet, turned, and walked away down the corridor. He had no way of knowing if the person opening the door was the other man or one of the colleagues with whom Graeme shared his office. He pushed open the double doors at the end of the corridor, and once he reached the stairs he took them at a run.

Reaching the ground floor, Graeme crossed the atrium and left the building via the revolving door. He stopped immediately he was outside to recover his breath, but finding himself in the middle of a crowd of smokers he moved on.

Graeme started walking home. His route took him past Sarah's place of work. He went up to the sliding doors, which opened automatically, but then he backed away again and walked up and down on the pavement for two minutes. He took his mobile phone out of his pocket and looked at it. He found Sarah's number in the address book and his finger hovered over the call button, but then he cancelled it instead and put the phone away.

He walked home, and when he got there he stood outside the house looking up at it. He checked his watch, waited a moment, and then walked on. He walked beyond the shops, through the housing estate and past the rugby club and the allotments until he reached the river. It had not rained for a few days and the river was low. He walked on the path that followed the meander of the river. His watch told him it was lunchtime, but he was not hungry, even though he had had no breakfast.

Later in the afternoon, he returned home. He entered the house, switched off the alarm, and went straight upstairs. He waited in the spare bedroom, from where he had a good view of the street. He watched one of his neighbours come out of her house and put a compostable bag of food waste in her green bin. She then picked up a confectionery wrapper from her front path and placed that in the regular dustbin before going back inside and closing the front door.

The other man walked up the road and approached the house. Graeme stepped back from the window and paced slowly across the floor. As he heard the front door being opened, he suddenly stopped and became aware of the exaggerated sound of his own breathing. He had not put the alarm on before coming upstairs. He stood absolutely still and listened. He heard the other man enter the kitchen and then move around the ground floor from room to room.

Graeme sat down, leaning against the wall. When he heard the front door again, he stood up.

"Hello-oo," Sarah called as her heels struck the wooden boards of the hall floor.

Graeme heard the other man respond and guessed he would be offering to make her a cup of tea. Taking care to minimise any noise, Graeme walked down to the first-floor landing and sat on the top step of the stairs that went down to the ground floor. Because of the half-landing and the one-hundred-and-eighty-degree turn, there was no way they could see him. He listened to them swap stories about their respective days. It sounded mechanical, listless, routine. He listened while they prepared food, poured wine, switched on the news.

When he heard Sarah coming upstairs he retreated to the next flight up before she reached the half-landing. Peering around the newel post he watched her enter the bathroom and listened to her using the toilet. She came out and stood for a moment on the landing. She looked tired. Maybe she was trying to remember if she had come upstairs for anything other than to go to the bathroom. Her face wore a strained expression. After a moment her facial muscles relaxed and she moved towards the stairs. Graeme gave it a few seconds before getting to his feet and taking an initial step to follow her, but then he stopped, staring at the spot on the landing where Sarah had been standing a moment earlier, and he raised his hands and ran them over his shaved head. He turned around and climbed the stairs back up to the top floor. He went into the spare bedroom and curled up on the bed.

RAEME AWOKE AND LOOKED AROUND THE UNFAMILIAR room. At some point in the night he had got under the duvet, but he had not got undressed. His clothes were a bit rumpled, but they were not damp with sweat. He could hear noises from one floor down: one person in the bathroom, another moving around. He lay on his back and listened.

He became aware of footsteps leaving the bedroom, moving on to the landing, starting to climb the stairs. As quickly and quietly as he could, he got out of bed and stood by the door, eyes wide, senses alert. The approaching footsteps were light enough to be Sarah's, but it was hard to be sure. He looked around. The guest bedroom contained no hiding places. The footsteps stopped outside the door to the room. He held his breath.

The door opened slowly.

Sarah stood in the doorway.

From downstairs came the sound of the other man's voice.

"Have a nice day, darling."

Graeme looked at Sarah.

He could hear footsteps on the main stairs going down, a bracelet jangling, and then a voice—he would have said Sarah's voice—called from downstairs: "See you later."

The other man shouted back, "See you later."

Graeme took a step towards Sarah and looked into her eyes. He saw himself reflected in her pupils. But otherwise they looked empty.

Waiting at the Crossroads Motel

STEVE RASNIC TEM

Steve Rasnic Tem's newest novel is Deadfall Hotel, *published in 2012 by Solaris Books. New Pulp Press brought out a collection of his dark noir stories,* Ugly Behavior, *in August of 2012.*

ALKER NEVER THOUGHT OF HIMSELF AS ANY KIND OF genius, but he knew that at least his body was never wrong. If his body told him not to eat something, he didn't. If his body told him not to go into a place, he stayed outside. If his body wanted to be somewhere, Walker let his body take him there. He figured he got his body from his father, who he never knew, but he knew his father had been someone remarkable, because his body knew remarkable things.

"Blood will tell," his mother used to say, in pretty much every situation when an important decision had to be made. He eventually understood this referred to the knowledge he had inherited from his father, held in his blood, and which informed his body which seemed to know so much. Walker's blood never said anything too loudly—it whispered its secrets so softly he couldn't always hear. But he could feel it pull in this or that direction, and that had been the compass that had brought them here.

The motel was small, all one story, just a row of doors and square windows along the inner side of an L-shaped building, with a dusty parking lot and no pool. Walker heard there used to be a pool, but they'd had a hard time keeping the water sanitary, so they'd filled it in with sand. A few cacti and thorny bushes now grew in that faded bit of rectangular space, but none too well.

The maid—a withered-looking woman well into her seventies—tried confiding in Walker from day one. "There's something wrong with this dirt, and the water ain't never been quite right. You buy bottled water for your family while you're here—especially them kids." But Walker made them all drink right out of the rusty taps, because that was the drink his own blood was thirsting for.

If anything, Walker felt more at home at the Crossroads than he had anywhere in years. He'd drink the water and he'd breathe the dry desert air, taking it deep into his lungs until he found that trace of distant but unmistakable corruption he always knew to be there. He'd walk around outside barefoot at night, feeling the chill in the ground that went deeper than anyone else could know. He'd walk around outside barefoot during the middle of the day letting the grit burn into his soles until his eyes stung with unfamiliar tears.

Angie had started out asking nearly every day how long they'd be staying at the Crossroads, until he'd had enough and given her a little slap. He didn't really want to (he also didn't want *not* to), but it seemed necessary, and Walker always did what his body told him was necessary.

That was the thing about Walker—he could take people or he could leave them. And he felt no different about Angie. His body told him when it was time to have sex with her, and his body told him to hide her pills so he could father some kids by her, but Walker himself never much cared either way.

"The four of us, we'll just stay here in the Crossroads until I hear about a new job. I have my applications in, and I've been hearing good things back." She never even asked how he could have possibly heard good things, waiting there in the middle of nowhere. He never called anyone. But she'd never asked him any questions about it. Angie was as dumb as a cow.

Somehow he'd convinced her that the Crossroads Motel was the perfect place for them to be right now. From the Crossroads they could travel into New Mexico, Arizona, Utah, or turn around and head back towards Denver. They could even go back home to Wyoming if they had a particularly desperate need to visit that state ever again. In order to do any of those things, though, they'd have to get a new car—theirs had barely made it to the Crossroads before falling apart. "But we have a world of choices." That's what he told her. Of course he'd lied. She was an ignorant cow, but the dumbest thing she ever did was fall in love with him.

Their fourth day there he'd made an interesting discovery. He'd always whittled, not because he liked it particularly, he just always did. He'd grabbed a piece of soft wood and gone out to that rectangular patch where the cacti grew and the swimming pool used to be—he called that area the "invisible swimming pool" sometimes, or just "the pool"—and sat down cross-legged in the sand, the sun bearing down on him like a hot piece of heavy iron pressing on his head, and started to carve. He was halfway through the piece—a banana-shaped head with depthless hollows for eyes and a ragged wound of mouth—when suddenly the hand holding the knife ran it off the wood and into the fatty part of his hand—slow and deliberate and unmindful of the consequences.

He permitted the blood to drip, then to pour heavily into the sand before stopping it with a torn-off piece of shirt-tail. Then it thickened, blackened, spread into four flows in different directions. Then each of those flows hardened and contracted, rose from the sand into four legs attempting to carry the now rounded body of it away. It had begun to grow a head with shining eyes when the entire mass collapsed into a still shapelessness.

Not strong enough, he thought. *But that will change.*

Walker spent most of the next few days sitting in an old lawn chair he'd set up behind the motel. The cushion was faded and riddled with holes—rusty stuffing poked through like the organs of a drowned and bloated corpse. The whole thing smelled like sea and rot—odd because it was so dry here, miles from anything larger than a car wash puddle—but it was an aroma he'd always found comforting. It was like the most ancient smell of the world, what the lizards must have smelled when they first crawled out of the ocean.

He had the chair set up so he could gaze out across the desert that spread out behind the motel, away from the highway that fed out through the southwest corner of Colorado and into the rest of the West. That desert was as flat and featureless and as seamlessly light or as seamlessly dark as the ocean, depending on the time of day and the position of the sun and the moon. So much depended on those relative positions, and the things who waited beyond, much more than most human beings were destined to know.

Out on the distant edges of that desert, out at the farthest borders the sharpest human eye could see, lay shadowed dunes and hard rock exposures, ancient cinder cones and mesas, flat-top islands in the sky. He had never been to such a place, but it had been a location fixed in his dreams for most of his life.

Every day Walker sat there in the chair, the eaves of the motel roof providing some minimal protection from glare, a notepad in his lap, a blue cooler full of beer at his feet, and watched those barely distinguishable distant features, waiting for something to change or appear, or even just for some slight alteration in his own understanding. "I'm working out our future plans and finances," was what he told Angie, and of course she'd believed him. If she'd only taken a peek at that notepad she would have seen the doodles depicting people and animals being consumed by creatures whose only purpose was to consume, or the long letters to beings unknown using words few human tongues could say. But no doubt she would not have understood what she was seeing, in any case. If he had a sense of humor he might say, "It's a letter from my father." But since he had never seen the utility of humor he did not.

Angie had never asked him why they had to travel so far just to wait for the results of some job applications, especially when there were no jobs at Crossroads or anywhere within a hundred miles of that place. He hadn't even bothered to concoct a story because he'd been so sure she wouldn't ask. This woman was making him lazy.

Once or twice he'd told her directly how stupid she was. She'd looked as if she might break apart. Part of him wanted to feel sorry for what he'd said. Part of him wanted to know what the feeling was like, to feel like your face was going to break. But he didn't have the capacity in him. He supposed some people were born victims. And some people were born like him. *Predator* was a good word for people like him, he supposed. There were a great many predators on this planet.

Their two kids had been climbing the walls. Not literally, of course, but that's the way Angie had expressed it. The only place they had to play was the motel parking lot. As far as he was concerned they should let them loose out there—the children could learn a few lessons about taking care of themselves. If they saw a car coming, let them learn to get out of the way. But Angie wouldn't allow it. He was their father, of course—they had his wise blood in their bodies. He could have insisted. But sometimes you let the mother have the final say where the care of the children is concerned.

Walker's own mother let him wander loose from the time he was six years old—that had been her way. It didn't mean she had no caring in her for him. Actually, he had no idea how she felt. She could have felt anything, or nothing. That was simply the way she was.

He'd never met his father, but he felt as if he knew him—certainly he could feel him. She'd lain with a hundred men or more, so it could have been anyone, or anything he supposed.

But Walker felt he'd know his father if he saw him, however he manifested himself. It never bothered him. And if he did see this creature, his father, he wasn't even sure he'd say hello. But he might have questions. He might want a sample of his blood. He might want to see what happened if he poured his father's blood onto the grounds of the Crossroads.

The boy—they'd named him Jack—threw something at the girl. Gillian, or Ginger, depending on the day. Walker had never quite found a name he'd really liked for her, or even remembered from one day to the next. Walker didn't know what the boy tried to hit her with—he never saw anything. He didn't watch them very closely. And there was no sense in asking them—they were both little liars. That was okay with him—in his experience most human beings didn't respond well to the truth in the best of cases. These children were probably better off lying.

But Angie wouldn't stop. "They're going to grow up to be monsters! Both of them! Jack slaps her. Gillian kicks him. This crap goes on all day! Do you even care how they might turn out?"

"Of course I care," he'd lied. Because it would have been inconvenient if Angie had fully understood his basic attitude toward their children. He couldn't have her attempting to take the children and leave before things had completed. "I'll talk to them." The relief in her face almost made him smile.

The children looked up at him sullenly, defiantly. This was good, he thought. Most children were naturally afraid of him. "Jack, what did you throw at her?" he asked.

"It was a rock," Gillian or Ginger said. Walker slapped her hard across the face, her little head rocking like a string puppet's.

"I asked Jack," he explained.

She didn't cry, just stared at him, a bubble of blood hanging from one nostril.

"It was a rock," Jack said quietly. Walker examined his son's face. Something dark and distant appeared to be swimming in his light green eyes. Angie's eyes were also that color, but Walker had never seen anything swimming there.

"Would it have made you feel badly if you had really hurt her?"

Jack stared up at him dully. Then the boy turned to his sister and they looked at each other. Then they both looked back up at Walker.

"I don't know," Jack replied.

"If you continue to behave this way where other people can see you, eventually you may be detained and imprisoned. It's your decision, but that is something to think about. Right now, you are upsetting your mother. You do not want to do that. You upset her and she becomes troublesome for me. You do not want that, do you understand?" Both children nodded. "Very well, go play quietly for awhile. Stay out of my field of vision."

After they left Walker saw that a couple of drops of his daughter's blood were resting on top of the sand. He kicked at them and they scurried away.

When they'd first checked in the Crossroads had been practically empty, just a single elderly couple with a camper who'd checked out the very next day. But since then a series of single guests and families had wandered in, almost unnoticeable at first since they mostly came in during the night, but the last couple of days there had been a steady stream, so by week's end the motel was full. Still, more people came into the parking lot, or stopped in the empty land around the building, some on foot with backpacks who set up small tents or lean-tos, others in cars they could sleep in. Despite their numbers, these new visitors were relatively quiet, remaining in their rooms or whatever shelter they'd managed, or gathering casually to talk quietly amongst themselves. Many had no particular focus to their activities, but some could not keep their eyes off that horizon far beyond the motel, with its vague suggestion of dunes and mesas shimmering liquidly in the heat.

"Why are they all here?" Angie eventually came around to asking.

"They're part of some traveling church group. They'll be on their way after they rest, I'm told."

For the first time she looked doubtful about one of his improvised explanations, but she said nothing.

As more people gathered his son and daughter became steadily more subdued, until eventually they were little more than phantom versions of their former selves, walking slowly through the crowd, looking carefully at every one of them, but not speaking to them, even when some of the newcomers asked them questions.

This continued for a day or two, and although Walker could see a great deal of nervousness, a great many anxious gestures and aimless whispering, and although his sense of the bottled-up energy contained in this one location unexpectedly made his own nerves ragged, there was no explosion, and no outward signs of violence. Some of the people in the crowd actually appeared to be paralyzed. One young, dark-bearded fellow had stood by the outside elbow of the motel for two days, Walker was sure, without moving at all. Parts of the man's cheeks had turned scarlet and begun to blister.

He noticed that the longer the people stayed here, interacting, soaking up one another's presence, the more they appeared to resemble one another, and him, and his children, as if they had gathered here for some large family reunion. Walker wondered if he were to cut one of them if their blood would also walk, and he was almost sure it would.

He took his morning barefoot walk—why his own feet hadn't burned he had no idea, he didn't really even care to know—by the invisible pool. An old woman crouched there like some sort of ape. At first he thought she was humming, but as he passed her he realized she was speaking low and rapidly, and completely incomprehensibly. She sounded vaguely Germanic, but he suspected her speech wasn't anything but her own spontaneous creation.

He gradually became aware of a rancid stink carried on the dry desert wind. Looking around he saw that those who had sought shelter outside the poor accommodations of the Crossroads were up and about, although moving slowly. When he went toward them, it quickly became obvious that they were the source of the smell.

A tall woman with long dark hair approached him. "You seem familiar," she said weakly, and raised her hand as if to touch his face. He stepped back quickly, and it wasn't because he now saw that a portion of the left cheek of her otherwise beautiful face appeared melted, but because he'd never liked the idea of strangers touching him. He knew this made little sense because he'd always been a lone figure among strangers. Angie, certainly, was a stranger as far as he was concerned, and his children Jack and (what was the girl's name?) little better.

Then an elderly man appeared beside her, and a young boy, all with bubbling, disease-ridden skin. Walker darted past them, and into a crowd of grasping, distorted hands, blisters bursting open on raw, burnt-looking skin. He squirmed his way out, but not without soiling himself with their secretions.

He felt embarrassed to be so squeamish. Was he any different than they? He'd seen the dark familiar shapes swimming in their eyes like the reflections of still-evolving life forms. Clearly, he was no longer alone in the world, because what he had seen in them was both familiar and vaguely familial. But it was an uncomfortable, even an appalling knowledge.

He was some kind of mongrel, a blending of two disparate species, and yet so were they. He doubted any of them had known their fathers. His own children were their blood kin, but at least they knew their father.

The two most familiar children came out of the crowd and gazed at him, their faces running with changes. He felt a kind of unknowable loss, for a kind of kinship that had never been completely his, for the simpler Sunday afternoon picnic world of humanity that would now be forever out of his reach.

Angie came outside for her children then, bellowing the dumb unmelodic scream of a despairing cow, and he struck her down with indifferent blows from both suddenly-so-leaden hands. She had been his last possible door into humanity, and he had slammed her irrevocably closed. Her children looked on as unconcerned as an incursion of sand over an abandoned threshold.

And now they've come out of those distant mesas and deserts, on their astounding black wings, on their thousand-legged spines, their mouths open and humming like the excited blood of ten thousand boiling insects, like the secret longings of the bestial herd, like his blood preparing to leave the confines of vein, like his blood crawling out of the midnight of collective pain, the liquid horizon unfolding.

And out of that shimmering line the fathers come to reclaim their children, the keepers of their dark blood. And Walker must collapse in surrender as these old fathers out of the despairing nights of human frailty, in endless rebellion from the laws of the physical universe, these fathers, these cruel fathers, consume.

The Wilcox Remainder

‹‹‹‹‹‹‹‹‹‹‹‹‹‹‹‹

BRIAN EVENSON

Brian Evenson is the author of ten books of fiction. His novel Last Days *(Underland Press, 2006) won the ALA/RUSA award for best horror novel of the year. Other books include* The Wavering Knife *(FC2, 2004),* The Open Curtain *(Coffee House Press, 2006), and* Fugue State *(Coffee House Press, 2009). His work has been translated into French, Italian, Spanish, Japanese, and Slovenian. He lives and works in Providence, Rhode Island, where he directs Brown University's Literary Arts Program.*

1.

NOT LONG AGO, WHILE VISITING MY AUNT ON THE other side of Providence in what she refers to as a resort but which, as the sign outside testifies, is a "mental hospital" (and which until just a few decades ago was called, more bluntly and more honestly, Butler Hospital for the Insane), I was buttonholed by a man who at first I took to be an orderly. In a confidential whisper, he claimed he had something to tell me. Thinking it must be about my aunt and her rapidly declining condition, I acquiesced. Gradually, as his speech quickened and then became more and more frantic, as his gestures grew increasingly erratic, I realized my mistake. However, afraid of alarming him into doing something drastic, I feigned attention and made no sudden moves until the moment when three actual orderlies approached, immobilized the fellow after a struggle, and dragged him screaming away.

It was only near the end of the episode, when I saw the man extract from a pocket a sharp tongue of glass with one end imperfectly wrapped in cloth and use it to hold the orderlies temporarily at bay, that I began to realize what danger I had been in. As he was immobilized and one of the orderlies tried to bandage the man's very badly cut hand, I became unsteady on my feet and had to lean against the wall. I must have been pale, for one of the men leading the inmate away parted from his companions and returned to make certain of my condition. When he had assured himself that I had partially recovered, he led me not to the exit but to the director's office. Giving me a plastic cup of water and forcing me to sit, he extracted from me the promise to wait there until I recovered.

T FIRST MY CONDITION WAS SUCH THAT I DID NOT PAY the office itself much heed, and was indeed little aware of my own actions. My tie had been loosened and collar undone without my having any clear memory of my hands having done so. The plastic cup had been drained dry, and yet my mouth itself was still chalky and raw. My hands, I saw, were still shaking and making strange roiling movements as if they were being directed by a mind other than my own. It was only with a great deal of effort that I mastered myself and, to distract myself, rose to my feet and began to pace the room.

There was nothing extraordinary about the office itself. Dominating the room was a ponderous oak desk, big enough that it seemed impossible that it might have once shouldered its way through the door. Its surface was covered with a scuffed green leather blotter, a single sheet of creamy hospital stationery arranged carefully in its exact center. Four pens were arranged in a meticulous line beside the stationery. The chair I had been sitting in was a well-worn leather-backed and leather-seated chair of sturdy workmanship, perhaps an antique though in good condition. A similar chair sat on the other side of the desk and behind it, tight against the back wall, was a glass-fronted bookcase. This was full of old nineteenth-century medical books as well as, on a lower shelf, a sequence of gilt and leather-bound literary volumes. The smell of the place was of cracked leather and dust, the air fumid with motes of dust turning slowly in the shaft of sunlight coming through a solitary window.

I paced back and forth. I was, I told myself, recovered: I was now in a condition to leave. And yet I did not leave. *What was the patient trying to say to me?* I wondered. Despite giving the impression of listening in trying to appease him, I had let his words drift past me, had taken little in, and it was only with difficulty that I could recapture their gist. And his way of speaking had been such that very quickly words had been replaced by garbled moans and shrieks. But these had had a particular, peculiar cadence to them—as if his noises were not at all random but intentional. As if he were speaking an unknown but hideous language.

But what language? I thought, my feet swinging me past the bookcase again until I stopped there at one end, thinking. It was no language with which I, despite my university training, had any familiarity. *No,* I tried to tell myself. I well knew from my experience with my aunt that the unbalanced mind can convince itself that it is free of aberration, that the structure of a language does not a language make.

And yet, I could not forget the man, his imploring look, the way he grabbed my sleeve, the things he had said in plain English before his descent into the cluttered and hard sounds that seemed like the issue of no human throat. *They must not be allowed,* he had told me, tightening his grip on my jacket. *No,* he had said, *the statue, it wants to proliferate.* I think that is what he said—but what could it mean for a statue to proliferate? *Take it,* he hissed. *Warn them,* unless it was *learn them. Before they come,* he said.

And then his eyes went glassy and he spat a sound that sounded more like the snarl of a dog, no human word I knew, and it was all I could do not to draw away.

OR SOME TIME, I REALIZED, I HAD BEEN STANDING before the bookcase, unmoving, staring at something without seeing it. At first I focused on the glass itself, on my faded reflection in it, but no, that wasn't it. Instead, there, behind the glass, was a strange clay image, a figurine that at first glance looked unfinished, half-formed. I moved my head to block the light and see the thing better, and then, still not satisfied, reached up and opened the glass.

From there it was a small thing to pick the figure up. It was, I now could see, finished after all, humanoid in form but hideous in appearance, unnaturally squat. In place of a head it had a sloping protuberance, shapeless on the top and strangely bristling near where it joined the figure's shoulders. I found it at once alluring and disturbing. It exerted a certain fascination, though thinking now objectively of why that should be the case, I am at a loss to explain why. Perhaps it was because it was not quite like anything I had ever seen before. It wasn't ancient but rather of recent manufacture, perhaps the work of one of the patients. *What a strange statue*, I thought, and, thinking that, I thought again of my encounter and half wondered if this was the statue that wanted to *proliferate* itself, whatever that meant. Before I knew it, almost without meaning to, I had slipped the thing into my pocket and closed the glass door.

I MIGHT HAVE LEFT THEN HAD THE HOSPITAL'S DIRECTOR not suddenly appeared. He was a stout older gentleman, face red but eye steady, and though he must have been surprised to find someone in his office, he did not betray any hesitation or surprise. Instead, he extended his hand and took mine in his firm grip. He introduced himself as Wilcox and admitted, when I questioned him, that he was a member of

Providence's illustrious Wilcox family—was, so he claimed, one of the younger sons of long-deceased Anthony Wilcox.

Haltingly, I told him which of his inmates I was connected to. He asked me if something was wrong, if there was something about my aunt's situation that needed attention. I quickly assured him that no, everything was fine as far as she was concerned. Since he still waited attentively, I explained to him the situation that had led me to his office.

"Ah," he said, and released my hand. "You've had the dubious pleasure of meeting Henry."

I explained that the man hadn't shared with me his name.

"And what *did* he share with you?" he asked, and I could almost see his gaze sharpening, tightening on me. "What did he tell you?"

I don't know what stopped me from telling him the story in detail. Perhaps it was his own manner, his sudden almost rapacious attentiveness. Perhaps it was simply that one cannot but be loth to say anything within the walls of a madhouse that might cause your own sanity to be called into question. In any event, I claimed that Henry had been so disordered that I hadn't understood a thing. Once I had convinced him of this, and convinced him as well that even had I heard something I would have paid it no heed, he was quick to usher me out of his office and lead me down the stairs to the exit.

2.

I T IS AT THIS POINT THAT MY TALE BEGINS TO TURN dubious. Sometimes I do not believe it myself. If I was reluctant to tell a hospital director the details of my encounter with the inmate named Henry, imagine how much more reluctant I would be to tell him of the matters that follow.

Upon leaving my aunt, I returned to my office at the university. Outside of the hospital, in the full light of day, surrounded by people who I had every suspicion to believe were sane, it all seemed ludicrous. It had been an odd impulse to steal the clay figurine, I told myself, clearly the matter of being unsettled by Henry and not acting as I normally would. There was nothing to it: the little statue was simply a curio that Wilcox had collected, or perhaps a keepsake from a patient, and it meant nothing. Telling myself I would find a way to return it to him on my next visit to my aunt, I took it out of my pocket and deposited it in my desk.

The rest of the day passed normally: I taught, had a few meetings with students, attended a late afternoon lecture in the McCormack Theater. By the time I started to walk home, I had completely forgotten about the figurine.

And yet, when I reached the house and felt into my pocket for the key to my front door, I found not only the keys but a small hard object which, when I removed it, I saw was the figurine. *All right*, I told myself, *I must have absently reached into the desk and put it in my pocket upon leaving.* I thought about it only for the barest moment and then, once inside, tossed the figurine into the junk drawer, thinking that would be as good a place as any for it until I remembered to return it to Director Wilcox.

HAT NIGHT, I WAS BESET BY DREAMS OF A KIND I HAD never experienced before. I was, I found, in a strange city, the walls and angles of which were, for lack of a better descriptor, simply *wrong*. It felt wrong to be there, dizzying even, and I had at moments the impression that gravity had gone wrong as well, that I was walking or standing on surfaces that I should have fallen from or slid off. I was, in this city, little larger than an ant; the dark buildings and monoliths, doorless and indifferent, rose impossibly high above me, splotched with what I thought at first was a mold of some sort but which was damp and wet to the touch. Among them there was one building, much broader than the rest, squat in size and appearance, which, unlike the others, was not featureless but had on one awkwardly swayed side a warped bas-relief depicting a creature of hideous aspect not unlike that of the clay sculpture I had stolen, but more articulated. Here, I could see that what I had taken for spikes on the clay figure were tentacles, as if someone had lopped the head off a squat, misshapen body and put in its place the floppy body of a cephalopod. It was huge, and all the more hideous for being so. I stared up at it, rapt with awe and terror.

And then, as I watched, it *moved*. Very, very slowly it turned and fixed me with one unnatural and indifferent eye.

WOKE UP IN A COLD SWEAT TO FIND THE CLAY FIGURINE balanced upright on the nightstand beside my bed, though I had no memory of getting up and putting it there—remembered clearly putting it in the kitchen drawer and leaving it there. And yet there it was. I live alone, so I could not claim that it had been the work of someone else, unless that someone had broken into my house, moved the object, and then left without leaving a trace of his presence. I had never had a tendency toward somnabulism, could not imagine myself waking in the middle of the night and sleepwalking into the other room, opening the drawer, and bringing the thing back. And yet, unmistakably, there it was.

And so not knowing what to do I took the creature into the

kitchen, took up one of my shoes from where it lay discarded near the door, and meticulously crushed the hated object into a fine powder with its heel.

Or at least that is what I thought I did. For when I woke up there it was again on the bedside table, facing me.

WE DREAM AND WE CONVINCE OURSELVES WE ARE awake. We wake and convince ourselves we are still dreaming. In the few days that followed I did my best to convince myself that this was not happening, that the figure was not moving, seemingly of its own accord, from the places where I thrust it. That I was not, even though I thought I was, repeatedly destroying the figure only to have it reappear again shortly after. *Surely*, I told myself, *there is some logical explanation*. But the only logical explanation I could think of hinted of excessive paranoia: Director Wilcox knew I had the figurine and had hired a man, or a group of men, to slip replacements of it into my house each time I destroyed it. I tried to tell myself I was imagining this, that the dividing line between fantasy and reality had somehow ruptured for me. I even tried to convince myself that I had in fact destroyed the figure but then had somehow, in a sort of fugue state, fashioned a new one, and that I had done this again, and again, and again. But none of these explanations satisfied me. Perhaps I was dreaming, perhaps I was mad, or perhaps someone was trying to make me believe that I was mad. Or perhaps something was truly wrong with the figurine itself.

I took a few days' sick leave from school. I abandoned the clay figurine near the pond in Swan Point Cemetery only to have it reappear a few hours later on my kitchen counter. I drove across the bridge into East Providence and threw it into the waters of Watchemoket Cove. Still the horror returned. I crushed it and crushed it, and still it returned. I could not get rid of it, whatever I did.

The dreams too kept coming, the figure on the bas-relief watching me more and more attentively, and the strange massive building that the bas-relief was carved into now beginning to reveal a thin band of light, as of the crack of a door. I was terrified by the idea of what I might see when the door opened.

3.

HAT WOULD YOU DO IN SUCH A SITUATION, I ASK YOU? I was not sleeping, was beset by nightmares, felt more and more that it should be myself, and not my aunt, who should be confined in an asylum. I had to free myself of this thing, this figurine or statuette or fetish, whatever it was. And yet, it would not let me go.

And so I went back to Butler Hospital, ostensibly to visit my aunt but with the actual purpose of trying to replace the object I had stolen, hoping that then it would release me. When I was admitted I asked if I might speak to the director.

I gained his office without difficulty. The difficulty I had worried about having—that the director would be in his office when I was admitted—did not occur. I was free to do as I pleased.

In my envisioning of the scenario beforehand, I had seen myself waiting until the orderly had left me and then hurrying quickly around the desk, slipping open the glass-fronted bookcase, and thrusting the figure deep inside. It would, I was sure, be easy, as long as the director was not in the room. And yet, the director was not in the room and it was still not easy. Why? Because somehow it was not the same room. It did not even seem as if it belonged to the same century. Where before I had seen a heavy wooden desk and leather-backed chairs, I now saw aluminum filing cabinets, a glass-topped desk scattered with papers, and two Eames chairs. Where there had before been a glass-fronted bookshelf there was now only bare blank wall.

And yes, I realized suddenly, every time I had been to the director's office before it had been like this. Every time except the one time, the time when I had stolen the figurine. Why had I not known immediately at that time that something was wrong?

ESPITE ALL THIS, I TRIED TO ABANDON THE FIGURE there. I tried at first to leave it in the filing cabinets, but they were locked. I tried to place it somewhere on the desk where it would not be immediately apparent, but when I hid it beneath a paper it made a strange and noticeable mound, and when I left it exposed it was more noticeable still. Finally I stretched on my toes and placed it on the top edge of the window's lintel, balancing it there, where, with a little luck, it might go for a time unnoticed.

MIGHT HAVE LEFT THEN, MIGHT HAVE FLED THAT establishment of incarceration without seeing my aunt, but it was at that moment, with my having had just enough time to return to the chair on the proper side of the desk, that the director entered. When he did, I began to understand the full extent of my deception.

He was a slender, thin man, of sallow complexion, wearing spindly round glasses. He greeted me by name, said it was nice to see me again. And yes, I realized, I had seen him before, had spoken to him in fact many times—how could I have forgotten? I could even remember his name. Or could at least remember enough to know that his name was not Wilcox.

OW I MANAGED TO GET THROUGH THE FIRST MINUTES of that conversation without him realizing how troubled I was, I still cannot say. Perhaps it was simply enough, once again, to fear what might happen to me if I showed any hint of derangement in a facility whose only purpose and specialty was to restrain the insane. Perhaps the doctor did notice my distress and had the kindness not to comment on it, or simply thought it might have to do with whatever I had come to discuss with him about my aunt.

We discussed my aunt, how she was doing, how she was responding to treatment. He confessed to me, after unlocking one of the filing cabinets with a key and removing a thick file with her name on its tab, that she was not responding at all, that she seemed increasingly in her own private world. This I knew, having seen her fairly recently. I was only trying to stall while I gathered myself.

We discussed her situation for a moment, then I thanked him and confessed to him that I was satisfied they were doing the best they could for her. Our conversation moved on to more general topics and flindered away until at last I announced that I hated to run off but I really should be seeing my aunt. I stood up and so did he. At the door, however, I couldn't resist asking about Henry.

"Henry?" he said.

"Yes," I said. "A patient here. I wonder how he's doing."

His brow furrowed. "Normally I discuss the patients only with their family members," he said.

"I perfectly understand," I said. "Say no more."

"But in this case I'm confused," he said. "I am certain we don't have a patient named Henry."

WAS TEMPTED TO LEAVE THEN, AND IF I DID NOT IT was because, my paranoid tendencies acting up again, I felt that it would seem suspicious if I did not visit my aunt first.

And so I went and saw her. As usual, she was in her own world, living forty, or maybe fifty years in the past, as if she were a child. We sat cross-legged on the floor, she poured me tea from an imaginary teapot, she babbled at me. I responded when necessary, imagining the whole time my walk back out of the mental hospital, wondering if I would make it to the exit and freedom before they guessed I was mad.

But I am not mad, I told myself. *It was only that unholy figurine that made me feel so.*

And then, leaning back against the wall, I let one hand slide into my jacket pocket and there my fingers found, once again, somehow with me again, the clay figurine.

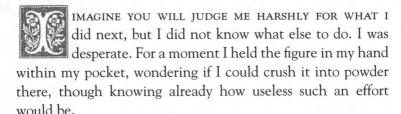IMAGINE YOU WILL JUDGE ME HARSHLY FOR WHAT I did next, but I did not know what else to do. I was desperate. For a moment I held the figure in my hand within my pocket, wondering if I could crush it into powder there, though knowing already how useless such an effort would be.

And then an awful inspiration struck me. I removed my closed fist from my pocket and held it out before me.

My aunt stopped what she was doing, regarded my fist with wide eyes.

"What do you have?" she asked.

I feigned for her my best smile. "A present," I said.

"A present!" she said, and her eyes lit up and she began to find it difficult to sit still. "And who is it for?"

"Who do you suppose it's for?" I asked.

"Me," she said, and pointed to her temple as if her finger were a gun.

"That's right," I said, and opened my palm. "It's a present for you."

HE WHOLE WAY OUT OF THE ASYLUM I FELT EYES ON my back. I felt something judging me, something weighing and assessing my actions and finding them wanting. But had I not rid myself of the idol or figurine or whatever it is, I would have gone mad—and indeed may still be a little mad already. It was evil, inhuman. As for my aunt, I cannot bear to see her again. I will never go back.

Since my aunt accepted it, the statue has not returned to me. The dreams too have faded, though I now have nightmares of a different sort, from the last moments I spent in the company of my aunt.

Those last moments are these: My aunt took the figure from me and immediately began rocking it back and forth and singing to it as if it were a baby, as if it were *her* baby. This wouldn't bother me—she is, after all, mad—and I probably could have steeled myself to bear visiting her except for the fact of what she sang.

For she sang not words but strange barks and shrieks with a peculiar unearthly cadence to them, as if she were speaking a language not meant to be uttered by a human throat.

Correlated Discontents

RICK DAKAN

Rick Dakan is a longtime Lovecraft-obsessive and a longtime professional writer, but has only recently gotten to do both at the same time. In addition to his newest novel, The Cult of Cthulhu: A Novel of Lovecraftian Obsession *(Arcane Wisdom, 2012), he is the author of the* Geek Mafia *trilogy, the serialized novel* Rage Quit, *and numerous game-related pieces dating back to 1995.*

"MR. JANNOWITZ, WHOSE IDEA WAS IT TO USE LOVECRAFT for your test case?"

"I was the one who suggested using the letters of H. P. Lovecraft. I was in Dr. Mason's office at the University. Dr. Mason, as usual, was at his computer, talking to but not looking at me. He said, 'I'm not familiar,' his gaze never leaving the screen as he typed the name into Google. 'A horror writer... I don't think so.'

"'Not his stories,' I said. I glanced at the talking points I'd typed on my phone's notepad app. I didn't want to fumble my arguments up again. 'His letters. He wrote thousands and thousands of them.'

"Dr. Mason responded with more typing. It was the only sound he liked in his office besides his own voice. He'd paid for the soundproof panels himself when both the department and the university had balked at the idea. He'd covered over the built-in bookshelves and his window in the process, leaving just the ceiling fluorescents, the battered oak desk, three chairs, and four flat screens. I knew from experience that a thousand people could gather for an African drum world cultures festival on the quad just outside and we wouldn't hear a thing at the desk.

"I let Dr. Mason scan the screen in front of him, a click, some typing, the faint noise of a mouse wheel turning. I shifted in the chair, also special-bought. Solid metal coated in foam and stain-resistant blue fabric. No creaking joints or squeaking leather.

"'Only a fraction has been digitized,' he said. 'Who else?'

"I took encouragement from my prepared notes and said,

'But it's all in print now. Volume 25 of the *Collected Letters* just came out last month.' He was reading something on the screen, probably his e-mail, but I knew he'd both heard and understood me. I also knew he was waiting for my point, so I went off notes and added, 'I could scan them in,' and then held my breath.

"'That would take at least three weeks,' he said, glancing over to the screen on his right where the latest build was compiling. It showed 32% complete.

"'I could bring in some undergrads. We could do it in a week.' I exhaled the words in a rush, which probably would have sounded panicked to Dr. Mason if he'd been paying me his full attention.

"He glanced up at me, his left eye squinting just a fraction. The pale light from the screen casting his dark complexion in stark chiaroscuro relief. 'Why have you already made up your mind?' he asked.

"I had prepared an answer for this question. I knew that Mason didn't care about why I thought Lovecraft was the perfect choice. He wanted my assessment of the neurological processes that had led me to rule out other options. I glanced at my talking points and said, 'My estranged brother introduced me to Lovecraft when I was a child, before we drifted apart. I associate Lovecraft with better times and I'm already familiar with him. Therefore, I'm personally interested in his letters and learning more about him.' I knew this wasn't exactly what Dr. Mason was looking for, but I wanted him to know it anyway. He just kept looking at me, probably guessing my motivation. A last glance at my notes and then I gave him what he wanted. 'The repeated exposure, combined with my basic human need for resolution, combined with familiarity with the subject, all come together to bias me toward the solution I've already decided is best and discount other options of equal or greater merit. Also, Lovecraft wrote about monsters, which is cool.'

"The corners of Dr. Mason's lips curved ever so slightly up into a smile, but his eyes lit up. 'Coolness is not an insignificant factor,' he said and then nodded to me.

"His smile lit up my own eyes and seeped down into a wide grin of my own. 'I'll log into interlibrary loan and put in some requests,' I said, as if I hadn't already done just that, closing my laptop and slipping out without another word."

"AND A MONTH LATER YOU BEGAN. DO YOU REMEMBER the first successful test session?"

"Yes. I remember Dr. Mason's voice over the intercom in the test lab. I was in the pilot's chair, complaining that the words were too fast. He told me to relax my eyes and to stop trying to guess what word was coming next. The words sped up, until I couldn't think ahead of them. I took a deep breath and let it out slowly.

"The thirty-inch screen in front of me was the only source of light in the room, an off-white background with large, bold Times New Roman words taking over the screen one at a time before being replaced a fraction of a second later by their successors. I started speed-reading my way aloud through the sentence: 'LANGUAGE VOCABULARY IDEAS IMAGERY EVERYTHING SUCCUMBED TO MY ONE INTENSE PURPOSE OF THINKING AND DREAMING MYSELF BACK INTO THE WORLD OF PERIWIGS AND LONG S'S WHICH FOR SOME ODD REASON SEEMED TO ME THE NORMAL WORLD.'

"'I believe the double letter "s" is meant to be the plural, not the hiss of a snake.' I hadn't sussed out the unfamiliar word and so had just said, 'essss.'

"'Sorry,' I said, blinking rapidly to moisten my eyes. 'Also, there's no punctuation, which confuses me, I think.'

"'Revision 3.8 will have punctuation, intonation, and so on. Your voice is still very stilted.'

"'I'm still not used to it,' I said, trying not to sound defensive. I did not want Carrie or Gene to take my place in the chair, and I knew Dr. Mason wouldn't hesitate to make the switch if he thought they could do a better job. I had been practicing on my own, but I'd stopped sharing my lab notes and personal log with the others. They could learn my tricks after I'd mastered them and secured my place as the first revenant pilot. 'I just need more practice.'

"There were thirty or forty seconds of silence from the observation room. I imagined Dr. Mason cogitating away on the problem. 'Ms. Thomas and Mr. Keller are also well-versed with the current software version. We'll need to develop a training system to get new hosts up to speed at some point, but that would be a waste of our time right now,' he said, thinking about my fate out loud, as was his habit. Just a few moments more silence, and then, 'Try again.'

"*Thank God*, I whispered to myself and sank back down into the web of biofeedback and physical monitoring devices attached to my head, chest, and right arm. I'd tensed up considerably and went through my breathing and relaxation exercises to relax my body and clear my mind.

"'We'll move right into the Q and A,' Dr. Mason's far off voice instructed through the intercom. 'Starting with the Autobiography Query Set A.'

"I could visualize Dr. Mason and Gene sitting in the control room on the other side of that intercom. The room's chaos must drive Dr. Mason crazy, although he'd never mentioned it. I'd posted a pic of it to Facebook and my friend Jacob had called it 'The Cyber Cephalopod,' which was somehow both a Cthulhu and an obscure Brady Bunch reference. The space beneath the desk was a riot of open-cased computers, data cables, power strips, and rack space for memory. It had ended up being cheaper to have a different computer for every piece of monitoring equipment, plus backups, plus the control gear, and it all added up to an even dozen. On the desktop, that flow of bits only translated into six screens, four of which were there mostly to monitor the monitoring machines that showed an aggregate of my brain activity, its different sections going from faded gray to bright blue as my neurons reacted to stimuli. The other was the Revenant Interface, the ever-changing control panel that bridged Lovecraft's letters and my mind. It seemed like a lot, but it was like a cheap laptop compared to the eleven IBM super-computers two floors below us that housed the actual language processing skills for our Mr. Lovecraft.

"'Ready,' came Dr. Mason's voice over the intercom. I opened my eyes and saw nothing but the screen, heard nothing but his voice.

"'Tell me one of your fondest childhood memories.'

"There was a few microseconds delay, and then I had two options, one of which was an out-of-context sentence about Lovecraft's mother that didn't seem fond or unhappy, but the other seemed dead-on. I read aloud, 'When I was very small, my kingdom was the lot next to my birthplace, 454 Angell Street. When I was between four and five, the coachman built me an immense summer-house all mine own. All this magnificence was my very own, to do with as I liked!' I gave the end of the sentence a tonal goose, mimicking remembered fondness. It was certainly my voice, but it also didn't sound anything like me. The reading was still stilted, but I had felt the rhythm of the language.

"But I didn't have time to second-guess myself, as Dr. Mason was already asking me another question. 'Tell me something else that makes you happy.' I was surprised at this request, since it required a level of contextual analysis of language that would strain the limits of the software to deal with concepts rather than just looking up facts.

"The words came a little faster this time. Dr. Mason had sped them up without telling me, and I only had one second to choose between the options Lovecraft offered. The choice seemed easy this time. 'I love kitties, gawd bless their little whiskers, and I don't give a damn whether they or we are superior or inferior! They're confounded pretty, and that's all we know and all we need to know!' In truth I'm intensely allergic to cats, but the words poured out of my mouth before my brain could quite make sense of them. The sentiments I honestly found a little off-putting, but any discomfort was entirely subsumed by my sense of excitement at losing myself in the process of channeling the dead man's thoughts.

"'What about the opposite feelings. What is something that upsets you?'

"The words flashed up on the screen, and it was again an easy choice as I skimmed the options, focusing in on key words. One response was about gentlemen not eating bananas in public, which was kind of funny, but what I said instead seemed to much more directly address Dr. Mason's question. 'As for this flabby talk of an "Americanism" which opposes all racial discrimination—that is simply god damned bull-shit!'

"'A controversial man, your friend Lovecraft,' Mason commented through the intercom. I was a little mortified about what I'd just said, but also thrilled, because it so clearly wasn't me doing the talking, it was Lovecraft. Before I could muster an excuse for the dead author's century-old nastiness, he said, 'Let's continue. I've booked a live demonstration in Portland in seven weeks. No turning back now.'

"An hour later, I was allowed to unstrap myself from the pilot's seat, blinking and rubbing my eyes, trying to slow my breathing. The mental exertion of keeping up with the rapid-fire questions and even more rapid decision-making about what to read had exhausted me. It was like taking the GRE with a chess clock on every question—constant mental strain. For me it felt like a chaotic, almost random-guess endeavor, and I hadn't really been able to track the conversation between Lovecraft and Dr. Mason. I was sure it had been quite incoherent. But in fact it was anything but.

"I downloaded a copy of the session's audio file and listened to it as I trudged my way across campus and back to my studio apartment. It's always a little disorienting to hear one's own voice played back, but listening to my voice parroting another's words packed an order of magnitude more weirdness. It was like listening to a radio play performed by a twin brother I never had—it all sounded familiar and new at the same time. Moreover, it sounded like a conversation. Occasionally stilted and with a few odd pauses and off emphases, but something a naive listener would hear and think to be a real, if odd, discussion between two men, no computers involved."

"NOW LET'S TALK ABOUT THE PORTLAND EVENT. HOW would you characterize it?"

"It was the first time everything really clicked into place."

"Even though others have called it 'a disaster'?"

"It depends on your perspective, I suppose."

"Explain what you mean."

"It was early on a Sunday morning, and the crowd inside the old Portland movie theater was smaller even than I'd predicted. I was glad Dr. Mason didn't seem to mind, although with him it was hard to tell what he really thought. A webcam let me see the room, but none of them could see me back in the lab. Instead, a 3D model of H. P. Lovecraft's head projected onto the screen did a rough job of mimicking my expressions. He/I blinked down at the audience with his giant, pixelated eyes. 'Ready when you are, Dr. Mason.'

"The audience looked interested at least, even if there were only eleven of them. They seemed largely alert, a squad of thirty- and forty-something men and two women. Most of the audience had black T-shirts with some mix of Lovecraft, Cthulhu, Miskatonic University, and tentacles on them, the most common of which was for the very H. P. Lovecraft Film Festival they were all currently attending. One plump woman was dressed in a tan three-piece suit that put me in mind of a Victorian Egyptologist. Her pith helmet sat on the seat beside her. She had a small tablet computer in her lap, fingers poised above its virtual keyboard as she looked up at me, her expression mild and expectant.

"Dr. Mason stood behind a lectern set up in front of the screen and went through some bland thanks and introductions, explaining what the Revenant Project was all about (the name got some laughs, which I knew Dr. Mason would question me about when I got back to the University), but his jargon-laden technobabble wasn't as clear as it might have been. Finally, though, he summed it up well: 'The revenant's ability to synthesize everything that Mr. Lovecraft ever wrote far exceeds the ability of even the most diligent literary scholar. The program, with its perfect recall, has all the facts at hand in a way no one has since the living subject died in 1937.'

"The Egyptologist-looking woman raised her hand and asked, 'So is it a computer program or an avatar for a person?'

"'It's both,' he replied, voice flat and short in a way most people would take offense at if they didn't know him. 'The head is obviously an avatar and Mr. Jannowitz is the user. But the program tells him what to say, which answers to give to your questions.'

"'If the program answers the questions, what is the user

there for? Just to read the answers with human inflections?' she asked, typing one-handed on her tablet while looking at me on the screen.

"'Good question. The inflections are a piece of it, but more important is to choose context. The Revenant software can guess at context and meaning based on its analysis of the grammar and syntax. It then presents the operator with options, and the user chooses the right context.'

"'So is Mr. Jannowitz choosing which answers to give? Or is the Lovecraft program?' she asked. It looked like she'd typed everything Dr. Mason had said. I wondered if she was a court reporter by day or something.

"'Both of them together. It's a kind of symbiosis. The words are all Mr. Lovecraft's. The user provides contextual decisions without choosing the content. I must emphasize that it all happens very fast. The user doesn't have the time to edit or choose—he's there to react and input the kind of data that voice-to-text and grammar software is bad at figuring out. Although it's learning, getting better all the time.' He waited for her to finish typing what he'd said, a delay of just a second or two. Everyone was watching either me or her or looking back and forth. 'Shall we get started?'

"She nodded and there were affirmative murmurs from the rest of the small audience. Dr. Mason asked, 'Who has a question for Mr. Lovecraft?' A light went on in the lower left corner of my display, indicating that my microphone was now live.

"'What was your first story published in *Weird Tales*?' someone from the crowd asked. I couldn't tell who over the webcam, couldn't even hear the question very well, but Dr. Mason repeated it in a clear voice that Lovecraft's voice-to-text analysis translated perfectly. Two answers presented themselves; one said, '1) My first amateur publication...,' the other said, '2) My first story in *Weird*...' I tapped the '2' button on the keypad and giant white Times New Roman letters filled the screen, appearing one word at a time.

"'My first publication in *Weird Tales* was "Dagon," in October, 1923.' Weeks of practice made my voice sound informed and maybe a little haughty, and Dr. Mason's voice synthesizer was doing the rest, adding in a very light Providence accent with just the barest hint of affected English accent to class things up. Lovecraft kept going, though, adding context to the simple detail. 'I like *Weird Tales* very much,' we said. 'Most of the stories, of course, are more or less commercial—or should I say conventional?—in technique, but they all have an enjoyable angle.'

"'Does your critique of *Weird Tales* apply to your own early stories, like "Dagon" and "Erich Zann" as well?' came an unasked for follow-up from the same person.

"'Of my products, my favorites are "The Colour out of Space" and "The Music of Erich Zann." It is now clear to me that any actual literary merit I have is confined to tales of dream-life, strange shadow, and cosmic "outsideness," notwithstanding a keen interest in many other departments of life and a professional practice of general prose and verse revision. Why this is so, I have not the least idea.'

"The crowd seemed to perk up on the other side of the camera, chuckling at Lovecraft's self-assessment. Later I'd look at some of the Twitter posts from someone in the audience, and he used words like 'amazing' and 'super-cool.' More questions came, and we answered easy inquiries as to my birthday and family and my favorite books. The question about how old I was befuddled me, but Lovecraft had no problem, and I found myself accurately claiming to be over a hundred years of age. Asked about the wonderful new world of the Internet, I said, 'I can't get interested in it—it doesn't even bore me enough to take my mind off other boredoms,' which drew another good laugh. I wasn't sure how Lovecraft had come up with that response, but we all knew it was perfect.

"The next question, from a thin, lanky man with long red hair tied back in a ponytail, threw me for a total loop. 'Are you alive?' he asked. Lovecraft offered me the option of giving his date of death, but it suggested that a more erudite response was the preferred reply, and so I went with it. 'My body died in 1937, but wandering energy always has a detectable form. If it doesn't take the form of waves or electron-streams, it becomes matter itself; and the absence of matter or any other detectable energy-form indicates not the presence of spirit, but the absence of anything whatever.' The audience ate it up, and someone even clapped a few times.

"As we answered fast, the questions came faster, an unconscious agreement amongst everyone in the room to try and push Lovecraft to his limits. I scarcely had time to register the questions as they came in, and the display presented such obvious choices that, with many questions, I found myself finished saying it before I knew exactly what had happened.

"The Egyptologist was the one to finally ask what I'm sure many in the room were dying to, but were too polite or shy to give voice to themselves. 'Many people have called you a racist,' she said. 'Would you agree?'

"I picked the slightly more circumspect answer from the choices Lovecraft offered me and said, 'Race prejudice is a gift of nature, intended to preserve in purity the various divisions of mankind which the ages have evolved,' which even seemed to make sense in the moment. But there was more to Lovecraft's response, and I had no choice but to continue. 'The problem of race and culture is by no means as simple as is assumed either by the Nazis or by the rabble-catering equalitarian columnists of the Jew-York papers.'

"The room went silent, except for the tapping of fingers on mobile devices and some squirming in seats. The Egyptologist pressed on, asking, 'So you don't agree with the civil rights movement's achievements since your death?'

"Lovecraft's databases didn't include any history at all since his death, except some details about the technology that made him work. None of the options were good, so I chose the one that didn't mention both 'niggers' and 'rat-faced Jews,' and went with the ignorant but superficially thoughtful-sounding, 'Now the trickiest catch in the negro problem is the fact that it is really twofold. The black *is* vastly inferior. There can be no question of this among contemporary and unsentimental biologists… But it is also a fact that there would be a very grave and very legitimate problem even if the negro were the white man's equal.'

"I expected Dr. Mason to say something, or maybe try and steer the conversation in another direction, but he let it ride. The Egyptologist followed up with another question, this time about Jews. Someone else followed up with a query about miscegenation, followed closely by another about the people living in New York. Every answer appalled me, but they came fast and natural. The audience knew their Lovecraft, of course, and thus they knew just what to ask about to elicit the most shocking responses. The more they failed to trip me up, the more racist things they got Lovecraft to say, the more enthusiastic they became.

"One fellow in the back, clearly trolling for controversy, asked us which were worse, blacks or Jews. I think he must have known what Lovecraft's answer would be. Certainly Lovecraft only gave me one option, which I dutifully voiced. 'With the negro the fight is wholly biological, whilst with the Jew it is mainly spiritual; but the principle is the same.'

"The film festival's organizer seized that moment to cut things off, nine minutes early according to my clock. I can't imagine he liked this kind of talk at his festival, even if it was

full of horror films, but he was quite abrupt about it. He thanked
Dr. Mason, who in turn thanked the audience, and everyone
applauded politely. My connection was cut, and I sank back
into my chair, dripping with sweat and breathing hard. I found
the sudden deviation from the schedule quite ungentlemanly
and wondered where simple civility had disappeared to."

"WHAT WAS DR. MASON'S REACTION TO THE EVENT?"

"He couldn't have been happier. It's hard to tell
with him of course, but he seemed pleased. For him,
all that mattered was that Lovecraft gave the right answers,
even if the content of them was objectionable. He returned
to the lab full of energy and we dug right in, implementing the
next set of features and improvements."

"And what was your assessment?"

"I was thrilled too, at least at first. I'd never experienced
anything like that. The words were just there for me, and they
were always such well-formed and composed sentences! All
I had to do was choose. I was spending all day either testing
code or serving as Lovecraft's medium. It was a week before
I saw online what people were saying. That was when I saw a
blog post claiming Dr. Mason was a terrible racist, which was
of course ridiculous. He's African-American, for God's sake!"

"Is that when you first started breaking laboratory protocol?"

"That was three weeks later. Dr. Mason was presenting at
the AAAS Conference, which was in Denver that year. Not a
live demonstration, but a prepared talk, a prequel to his paper
being published. That paper was of course first in all our minds
at the time. At least it was supposed to be.

"I'd begun to scour the Internet for reactions to our
presentation. The Egyptologist, whose name is actually Lila
Harper, had blogged the whole thing, and she was impressed.

She saw how significant what Dr. Mason had done was—an amazing feat of technology that had brought a dead man to life, in all his great and terrible true self. Others were less pleased. Of course plenty of people with no affection for Lovecraft railed against his racism and against us for parroting it back to modern ears. Among the fans it was more divided, with some holding forth that it was bad for other Mythos and Lovecraft writers to have such associations, while others pointed to much worse things said by much more famous authors.

"I couldn't help myself, and started participating in the debate online. I used a pseudonym at first, HarveyW, but during one particularly ugly comment-thread discussion about the moral implications of taking dead men's words out of context and putting them in a ghostly impostor's mouth, someone tracked my IP address to the university and I was outed. Fortunately, Dr. Mason didn't notice or care. He was focused on the project, plus preparing the first paper for publication. I kept up my defensive actions online, fighting for the project with ever more boastful claims about its potential and meaning. I wrote tens of thousands of words of comments and blog posts, arguing that the intellectual synthesis our revenants would be capable of could revolutionize literary and historical research and give us a new understanding of departed thinkers. My opponents called me, at the best of times, a deluded dreamer. Words like 'huckster' and 'con artist' also got thrown around a lot.

"Dr. Mason just doesn't know how this kind of thing works. He didn't care what people were saying about our Mr. Lovecraft online, but the fact is, if our reputation was bad it would bleed over into everything else—funding, publication, acceptance. The racism didn't bother him because to him it was a curious historic artifact. Reviving that part of Lovecraft was, to him, a feature, not a bug. But I knew, just knew for certain, that we needed the Lovecraft fans and the online communities on our side. So I got right in there, despite Dr. Mason's directions to the contrary. I got right in there and tried to make our case.

"But I was terrible at it. I can't think off the cuff, and I have a hard time making my case in debates. I wrote on one message board that, 'You were fine with Lovecraft's racism before you heard him say it live.' I just meant that the racist thing shouldn't surprise anyone, but they thought I was saying they were all racists. And then I was all, like, 'you're missing the point,' and they thought I was calling them stupid. I just kept digging deeper and deeper. It was Lila Harper who offered me a lifeline. She wrote, 'Show us what's good instead of telling us we're wrong.'

"I had to wait until Dr. Mason was going to the AAAS conference that February to present his paper. I bailed at the last minute, claiming stomach something. Carrie and Gene both went, though, and I had the lab to myself. I made the arrangements with Lila. A live discussion, a sort of debate with all our detractors. To show them.

"Dr. Mason's latest big addition to the Lovecraft revenant was simple enough, but it made all the difference. The software already parsed and indexed all the Lovecraft writings we'd scanned in (which is to say, all of them). The update simply added the entire contents of every previous conversation Mr. Lovecraft had had into the mix. Lovecraft would remember and learn from the discussions he was having every day in Dr. Mason's lab. He could remember previous questions and reference them. The original point of this addition was so that the revenant could take in positive and negative feedback in order to do better analysis, which it did. But it also became a more natural talker, and maybe (I hoped) the world's best debater. Lovecraft had perfect recall, remembering not just what he said, but what the people we talked with said as well. I'd never felt smarter.

"Of course the first question I got was about race. The very unambiguous, 'What's your problem with black people?' appeared in the chat window. I was broadcasting audio live onto Ustream from the lab, with Lila Harper moderating from her home in Eugene, Oregon. There were only about seventy people watching live, but it was all being recorded.

"Lovecraft tried to be a little circumspect this time. I'd included the negative feedback about the answers he'd given in Portland, marking them very high on the impolite scale Dr. Mason had implemented. He knew what we'd be saying wasn't going to be popular with his audience. 'Now the trickiest catch in the negro problem is the fact that it is really twofold,' we said. 'The black *is* vastly inferior. There can be no question of this among contemporary and unsentimental biologists. But it is also a fact that there would be a very grave and very legitimate problem even if the negro were the white man's equal.'

"'That's just ignorant,' someone with the screen name Yolie sent. 'It's an obscene thing for someone to say in the twenty-first century. Do you have any actual facts to back this scientific illiteracy of yours up?'

"Lovecraft registered the anger and displeasure in Yolie's question, but he wouldn't back down. He only gave me one option, which I dutifully voiced. 'The fact is, that an Asiatic stock broken and dragged through the dirt for untold centuries cannot possibly meet a Nordic race on an emotional parity. On our side there is a shuddering physical repugnance to most Semitic types, and when we try to be tolerant we are merely blind or hypocritical. Two elements so discordant can never build one society—no feeling of real linkage can exist where so vast a disparity of ancestral memories is concerned—so that wherever the Wandering Jew wanders, he will have to content himself with his own society 'til he disappears or is killed off in some sudden outburst of physical loathing on our part.'

"'But that's just not the world we live in,' protested another online identity, this one named CCurtis. 'Only the most ignorant and backwards assholes hold such repugnant views about Jews or Asians. You yourself married a Jewish woman. Wouldn't that indicate you yourself didn't feel this physical loathing you're babbling about?'

"Lovecraft gave me three options, two of which ramped up the anti-Semitism. Instead we said something to give voice to our growing frustration at being so constantly insulted. 'Sir, I refuse to fall into your adroit trap! I simply say—with a delicate wave of a perfectly manicured and correctly gloved hand—that you are wrong and I am right. Why? Because I say so! And that is all a gentleman can add to the matter!'

"This was met with a chorus of disdain from the chat room, although there were a few LOLs scattered in there. Miss Harper chimed in with her own follow-up question. 'So you would see a world without Jews? That's a terrible sentiment in a world that's seen the Holocaust.'

"I knew this was coming, of course, but Lovecraft didn't know about World War II. I probably should have filled him in before we started. But he had learned better than to agree with the arguer's premises. I had two options, both of them thankfully lacking in overt racism. The first one stated that it was easy to be a Lycurgus on paper, but I had no idea who Lycurgus was, so I didn't want to risk it. We said, 'If I could create an ideal world, it would be an England with the fire of the Elizabethans, the correct taste of the Georgians, and the refinement and pure ideals of the Victorians.'

"'Have you read any books on race recently?' GregLavyn wrote. 'The pseudo-science you're basing your prejudices on has been destroyed by the best scientists and philosophers of Europe. No gentleman or scholar could fairly comment on the subject without first reading thoroughly upon the subject.'

"Now that was a question! GregLavyn, bless him, knew how to strike at our weak points, playing to Lovecraft's Euro-fetishism. Lovecraft started to beat a rhetorical retreat. 'I fear my enthusiasm flags when real work is demanded of me.'

"'Well then,' wrote Greg, 'Perhaps you'd best withhold judgment until you know the true facts of the matter.'

"'I am disillusioned enough to know that no man's opinion on any subject is worth a damn unless backed up with enough genuine information to make him really know what he's talking about,' we said. The audience took this for the retreat it was, encouraging us to follow our own advice. I really hoped that we would. At least now he was starting to tell them what they wanted to hear, although I wasn't sure if he believed it or not.

"'So,' asked Miss Harper, 'you will spend some time making a thorough and academic study of race before you speak on it again? What if you don't like what you find? Are you capable of changing your mind?'

"'To the scientist there is the joy in pursuing truth which nearly counteracts the depressing revelations of truth,' we said, adding, 'By this time I see pretty well what I'm driving at and how I'm doing it—that I'm a rather one-sided person whose only really burning interests are the past and the unknown or the strange, and whose aestheticism in general is more negative than positive—i.e., a hatred of ugliness rather than an active love of beauty.'

"'Nice of you to admit you could be wrong,' wrote someone named LazrFcs.

"'Creative minds are uneven, and the best of fabrics have their dull spots,' we said. 'Ineffective and injudicious I may be, but I trust I may never be inartistic or ill-bred in my course of conduct.'

"I was breathing with heavy relief that we'd maybe managed to weather the racism storm for the moment, when Lovecraft did something new. He drove the conversation forward on his own, not responding to any specific question but rather to the general tenor of the chat room. 'It is the frank and cynical recognition of the inevitable limitations of people in general which makes me absolutely indifferent instead of actively hostile toward mankind. Of course, so far as personal taste goes, I'm no lover of humanity. To me cats are in every way more graceful and worthy of respect—but I don't try to raise my personal bias to the spurious dignity of a dogmatic generality.'

"I think he must have been thinking about the warm reception his cat comments got in the lab before, and it worked a little of its magic this time as well. The chat was starting to warm to us, for the first time since I'd started coming online to defend him. Someone actually asked a question about our writing for once. 'In your current state, do you still think of yourself as a writer?' asked Yolie.

"Lovecraft responded with a few lines of poetry, ones where he'd changed the pronouns around to fit the situation (a technique Dr. Mason was especially proud of). 'As, gazing on each comic act / You stare at my perfection, / I find it hard to face the fact / That I'm a mere projection.'

"It was an enigmatic reply from a being who is pure enigma, and Miss Harper had to ask for a clarification. Would Lovecraft write again? We responded, to my surprise and delight, that 'I may try my hand at something of the sort—for it really is closer to my serious psychology than anything else on or off the earth. I shall doubtless perpetrate a great deal more childish hokum (gratifying to me only through personal association with the past), yet the time may come when I shall at least try something approximately serious.'

"A whole new firestorm of comments erupted in the chat window. People were thrilled or appalled in roughly equal numbers. How could we write new Lovecraft stories? We

weren't even real or alive! Lovecraft had an answer to that.
'To all intents and purposes I am more naturally isolated from
mankind than Nathaniel Hawthorne himself, who dwelt alone
in the midst of crowds, and whom Salem knew only after he
died. Therefore, it may be taken as axiomatic that the people of
a place matter absolutely nothing to me except as components
of the general landscape and scenery. My own attitude in
writing is always that of the hoax weaver. One part of my mind
tries to concoct something realistic and coherent enough to
fool the rest of my mind.'

"Wouldn't we be corrupting Lovecraft's own legacy?
Muddying the waters with pseudo-Lovecraft texts? 'Everything
in the world outside primitive needs is the chance result of
inessential causes and random associations, and there's no real
or solid criterion by which one can condemn any particular
manifestation of human restlessness.'

"The sheer audacity of it seemed to cow some large part of
the audience. When someone pointed out that Lovecraft was
just a computer program, that he couldn't really create or think,
someone else shot back that it sure seemed like he could do
both, judging from this chat. The debate rolled back and forth,
while we sat back and watched for a while, smiling and happy
at our achievement. We were being taken seriously. We were
being given the respect of heartfelt disagreement and support.

"An hour passed and Lovecraft continued to hold our own,
impressing and provoking the audience. Finally Miss Harper
called time and offered us the last word. Lovecraft only gave me
one choice to sum up his feelings on the discussion. 'Nothing
really matters, and the only thing for a person to do is to take the
artificial and traditional values he finds around him and pretend
they are real; in order to retain that illusion of significance in
life which gives to human events their apparent motivation and
semblance of interest.' We were in complete agreement."

"AND YOU DID THIS SEVENTEEN MORE TIMES?"

"I did it eleven more times."

"It was, in fact, seventeen. But you don't remember after eleven?"

"I don't remember."

"Did you make any other copies of your logs besides the ones on your laptop?"

"I don't remember."

"When did you stop answering to the name Jannowitz?"

"I don't think that's correct."

"It is correct. You would only answer to Howard."

"I don't remember that."

"Why would you decide never to come out of the Lovecraft revenant?"

"Is that a hypothetical question? I'm not good at those."

"We know you're not, but it's important that you try. Think of it as an experiment."

"I think experimentation and research are vital to our advancement as a race."

"So you've often written. Can you think of a reason you'd choose to never come out of the Lovecraft revenant?"

"If someone were unhappy with their life in some way maybe. Or perhaps if they couldn't handle the responsibility of making their own decisions. Perhaps if one were forced."

"But what about you specifically, Jannowitz? Why would you never leave?"

"Let me think about that for a minute."

"Take your time."

"I'm not sure this is right. It's just a guess."

"That's fine."

"I will never know fame. I won't ever terrify or impress millions. Lovecraft was cut down in his prime. Maybe he deserves the time more than I do. Maybe he'll do more with it."

"But the revenant isn't Lovecraft."

"No. Maybe it's better."

"What is the last thing you remember? Before this interview."

"I typed up notes on my last debate session. Six simultaneous interviews and chats. I wrote that, 'The most wonderful thing in the world, I think, is the ability of my mind to correlate all its contents.'"

"That's a Lovecraft quote, isn't it?"

"I wrote it."

"That's enough, Gene. I think we've reached the end of what we could recover of his personality. Go ahead and log off."

"Jesus," said Gene, rubbing his eyes and blinking as he powered down the Jannowitz revenant. "I can see how you could lose yourself in it. There's no time to think for yourself."

"And you're sure you've pulled in everything Jannowitz ever wrote?"

"Carrie and I put everything he wrote into the databases, Dr. Mason. Online and off, I'm positive."

Dr. Mason sighed. "There's just not enough to make a full revenant model for Jannowitz. I don't think we can restore him this way."

"His neurosurgeon has requested access to the Lovecraft revenant for treatment purposes again. He's sent us four e-mails today."

"I suppose we'll have to let him," Dr. Mason said. "I was hoping to find something today we could use to bring him back. But his physicians think neuronal cauterization is the only way. They want to burn the Lovecraft persona out of his brain."

"And that will work?"

"I can't imagine, but what else is there? In any event, it's not our concern. We've wasted a day on this. Take half an hour for lunch while I load in Mr. Lovecraft, then we'll begin this afternoon's creative exercises."

"I think the new story it's writing is coming along pretty well."

"It's not to my taste, of course, but yes, I think you're right. I doubt the man himself would know the difference once we're finished."

The Skinless Face

DONALD TYSON

Donald Tyson is a Canadian writer of fiction and nonfiction dealing with all aspects of the Western esoteric tradition. He is the author of Necronomicon: The Wanderings of Alhazred (2004), Grimoire of the Necronomicon (2008), The Necronomicon Tarot (2007), *and* The 13 Gates of the Necronomicon (2010), *as well as a biography of Lovecraft titled* The Dreamworld of H. P. Lovecraft (2010) *and the novel* Alhazred (2006), *all of which were published by Llewellyn Publications.*

1.

THE SIDE WINDOW OF THE UAZ-452 WAS SO COATED WITH dust, Howard Amundson could barely distinguish the brick-colored desert from the cloudless blue sky above its flat horizon. Not that there was much of interest to look at from the jolting, grinding minibus, he admitted to himself. Over the past ten hours the scenery had transitioned from the grassy plain that lay just outside of Mandalgovi to red dirt with only the occasional trace of green to show that anything was alive in the desolation.

There was no question in Amundson's mind that the Gobi Desert was the most desolate place he had ever seen. The sheer bleakness of it held its own strange grandeur. It was nothing like the deserts in Hollywood movies, with their rolling sand dunes. The Gobi was carpeted with rocks. They lay scattered everywhere, ranging in size from pebbles to Volkswagens. For the most part the empty landscape was flat, but here and there a low ridge broke the monotony.

A jolt beneath his seat clicked his teeth together on the corner of his tongue. He tasted blood and cursed. The ruts in the track the driver followed were so deep, they bottomed out even the Russian UAZ in spite of its spectacular ground clearance.

The Mongolian in the front passenger seat turned and grinned, then spoke a few words to the driver, who glanced back at Amundson and laughed. Neither of them understood English, so there was no point in talking to them. They had been hired to transport him to Kel-tepu, and obviously were not concerned about what condition he might be in when he arrived.

He wrinkled his nose. The inside of the minibus smelled like a mixture of oil, sweat, and camel piss. God alone knows what it had transported before Baby Huey. Amundson twisted in his seat to study the straps that held the canary-yellow case of the multi-spectrum electromagnetic imager on its palette. The machine was the only reason he was in this desert. When Alan Hendricks, acting dean of the Massachusetts Institute of Technology, had offered him the chance to give it a field test, he had jumped at the opportunity. A successful trial would clinch the grant of tenure he had been lobbying for over the past two years.

Only later had he paused to consider what would be involved in moving Baby Huey halfway around the world to the backside of nowhere. The machine was as small and as light as modern electronics could make it, but even so, it took a lot of energy output to make electromagnetic waves penetrate solid rock, and Huey tipped the scale at more than a quarter of a ton. Beside it sat the generator he had demanded from the Mongolian authorities. He had made it clear to them that there was no way he would take Huey into the desert without its own power supply. The government had agreed to his demand. The Mongolians wanted the test to be a success almost as much as Amundson.

I should be back at MIT going over term papers, he thought, scowling through the dirty window. *If this thing runs into some glitch and fails, I'm going to look like a fool, and there won't be anyone else to blame. I'm naked out here—no assistant, no colleagues, no one to cover my ass.*

It was not a comforting thought. He had been quick to claim credit for the basic design work on Huey, even though the initial concept had come from one of his graduate students, a bright Chinese named Yun. The grad student had kept his mouth shut—he wanted his doctorate and knew better than to try to upset the natural order of things at the university. But that only meant that if Huey failed, Amundson would have to shoulder all the blame.

The UAZ-452 lurched and shuddered to a stop as the driver killed the engine. Amundson pushed himself halfway out of his seat and saw through the windows on the opposite side of the minibus that they were not far from a cluster of khaki field tents, beside which were parked several trucks.

"Are we there yet?" he demanded of the driver.

The Mongolian grinned and jabbered in his own language. He threw open the side door and gestured for the lanky engineer to get out. Hot desert air rolled into the air-conditioned interior. Amundson unfolded himself with difficulty. After sitting for so long on the uncomfortable seat, stiffness had found its way into his very bones.

From the open door of the largest tent, a group of Westerners and a single Mongolian emerged. The leader, a white-haired man with a pot belly and a bearded face, extended his hand. He was a head shorter than Amundson and had to look up to meet the engineer's gray eyes.

"You must be Amundson from MIT," he said in a resonant voice. "I'm Joseph Laski, and I rule in hell." He let out a booming laugh at his own joke.

Amundson accepted the calloused hand and shook it, surprised by its strength. There was soil under the fingernails.

"This is my wife, Anna, my assistant James Sikes, Professor Tsakhia Ganzorig from the National Museum of Mongolia at Ulaanbaatar, and the head of the American student team, Luther White."

"From Pittsburgh," the athletic young black man said with

a grin. "You'll meet the rest of the students at dinner."

"Supper," Anna Laski corrected with a slight smile. "We dine late."

"No point in wasting the light," her husband explained.

"Pleased to meet you," Sikes said. "I can 'ardly wait to get a look at that machine of yours."

He was a small man with narrow shoulders and a bald patch at the crown of his head.

"You're English," Amundson said with surprise.

"Cockney by birth, but I've been with the Smithsonian for near on twenty years."

The Smithsonian had put up the bulk of the money to finance the Kel-tepu dig, which was named after a local geological feature. Satellite photographs had revealed the faint outline of buried ruins on the track of an ancient silk road. They were invisible from the ground, but had looked promising enough for the Smithsonian to gather a team of archaeologists. The students were all unpaid volunteers, of course—they always were. They worked for the experience of being part of an important expedition, and for the improvement of their résumés. From what Amundson had read about the find at Kel-tepu, they had all hit the jackpot.

A loud bang from the open rear of the minibus drew his attention. He made an apologetic face to Laski and stalked around the vehicle.

"Be careful with that!" he said in irritation.

The two Mongolians were hunched over the imager, using a kind of wrench to release the buckles on the tight straps that held it to its pallet. Another strap let go and hit the side of the minibus.

Ganzorig came around the edge of the door and spoke to his countrymen in a quiet voice. The grins fell from their faces, and they nodded seriously.

"I'm sure they'll be careful," he told Amundson. "I have explained how valuable this equipment is to the expedition."

"Thank you," the engineer said. "If it gets knocked out of calibration, it will take me a week to put it right again."

Laski approached. The others had gone back into the tent.

"Let me show you around the site," he said, putting his hand on Amundson's shoulder.

He allowed the archaeologist to lead him behind the tents, where some distance away from the camp the ground had been excavated in a series of trenches and holes. From a distance it resembled a gopher village.

"You'd never know this is a river valley, would you?" Laski said companionably. "It looks flat. Even so, satellite photographs and topographic measurements show that an ancient river once ran through here, very close to where we are digging. It dried up fifty or sixty thousand years ago."

They stopped in front of a wall of canvas erected in a rectangle some ten yards wide and forty yards long.

"We keep our prize behind this barrier to exclude windblown dust and desert animals. You'd be surprised how many creatures live in the desert. Some say there are even wolves."

Drawing aside a flap in the wall at the near end of the enclosure, he gestured for Amundson to enter and followed close behind him. The engineer stopped and stared in amazement.

"It's quite a sight, isn't it?" Laski said with a dry chuckle. "I always like to watch the reaction the first time someone sees it."

The ground had been excavated just inside the barrier on all sides, so that only a perimeter strip a few feet wide remained of the original desert surface. The rest of the enclosure was an elongated hole, but it was not empty. Within it lay a black stone statue. It reminded Amundson of the statues of Easter Island, but was not quite like anything he had ever seen. The lines of its primitive form exhaled brute strength. It was humanoid but not quite human in its proportions. The massive erect phallus that lay flat along its lower belly was certainly not human. It seemed vaguely aquatic in some indefinable way—perhaps it was the thickness of the neck or the webbing between the impossibly long fingers.

The covering of soil had preserved the sharp edges of the stone carving, with a single exception. The face of the statue was no more than a featureless mask. No trace of a nose, lips, or eye sockets remained, if indeed they had ever existed.

"Have you identified the stone?" the engineer asked.

"Some kind of basalt," Laski told him. "We're not yet sure exactly what it is, to be honest. It has resisted identification."

"You mean it's not local," Amundson said as he began to slowly walk around the hole.

"Not local, no."

"So the statue wasn't carved in situ."

"Good heavens, no. The stone of the desert is too fractured to carve out a figure of this size. You're thinking it's like the recumbent statues on Easter Island."

"The thought had crossed my mind," Amundson murmured. He bent over to study the surface of the head.

"No, impossible. This statue was transported here from far away—how far, we can't even guess, but there is no stone like this for hundreds of miles. And it was upright—we've found its pedestal buried at its base. At some point it was toppled off its support into a hole and covered with dirt."

The burial of ancient stone carvings and ancient religious sites was not unknown. Amundson remembered reading about such a site.

"You mean like Göbekli Tepe?"

Göbekli Tepe was a twelve-thousand-year-old archaeological

site in Turkey consisting of carven stone monoliths and other structures that at some point in its long history had been completely buried, but was in every other way intact.

"Yes," Laski said, pleased at the reference. "Something like that."

The engineer crouched and leaned over the edge of the hole as far as he could reach. He was just able to touch the edge of the smooth face of the giant.

"You're certain it wasn't buried face down."

"Quite certain," Laski said firmly. "The position of the arms and hands, to say nothing of the phallus, clearly shows that it is lying on its back facing the heavens. Even so, we excavated beneath the head. There is no face on the other side."

"I think I see the chisel marks," Amundson murmured, stroking the black stone lightly with his fingertips.

"You can see them better in early morning. The low angle of the sun accentuates them."

The archaeologist waited in silence while Amundson studied the enigmatic, featureless mask. The engineer straightened his knees and turned. Lights of excitement danced in his pale grey eyes.

"It will work, I'm sure of it."

Laski clapped him on the shoulder.

"Excellent! We'll get started tomorrow."

2.

INNER—NO, SUPPER, HE CORRECTED HIMSELF—WAS better than he expected. Sikes did the cooking chores, and he did them purely from choice, Anna Laski explained to Amundson. The little Cockney had an innate talent for cooking. It was usual on an archaeological dig to eat the local cuisine, but at Kel-tepu it was the local diggers who sampled what was to them exotic dining—roast beef, pudding, dumplings, fish-and-chips, meat pies, stews, bangers-and-mash.

"The first night of the dig, the local man assigned by Gani to do the cooking made khorkhog and khuushuur—goat meat and deep-fried dumplings," Anna told him. "I didn't think it tasted that bad, really, but Sikes was beside himself. He practically begged Joe to make him camp cook."

The conversation around the long dining table in the main tent was lively and free of the tensions that so often plagued academic gatherings. In part this was due to Professor Laski's dominating personality—his enthusiasm and good spirits were infectious. In part it was also due to his gracious wife who acted as hostess at the table. But mainly it was the general atmosphere of success that pervaded the entire team. Those participating in the dig knew they were making history, and at the same time insuring the future prosperity of their academic careers. This left them with little to complain about.

Two conversations were taking place at the same time across the table, one in English among the Americans, and the other in Mongolian among the local diggers. Gani, as Anna Laski called Tsakhia Ganzorig, acted as translator at those infrequent intervals when a member of one group had something to say to a member of the other.

Amundson noticed several of the Mongolians toying with small carved stone disks about the size of a silver dollar. When the opportunity arose, he turned to the young woman seated on his right, a blonde graduate student from the University of Southern California named Luce Henders.

"Could you tell me, what are those objects?" he murmured.

She followed his eyes, fork poised before her lips, and smiled.

"You mean our good luck charms? That's what Professor Laski calls them. We've been finding them all over the place, inside the graves."

"Graves?"

Luce chewed and nodded at the same time.

"This whole site is really one huge graveyard. There are graves all around the colossus—that's what we call the statue. Hundreds, maybe thousands of them. The bones are gone, but when we dig we find stone ossuaries that must have held them, with those carved disks inside."

"What happened to the bones?"

"Time happened. Thousands of years ago this was a wet river valley. Bones don't last under those conditions unless they petrify."

"Is the stone of the tokens the same as the stone of the colossus?"

"We're pretty sure it is," she answered. "It's not local stone."

"I wonder if I might have one," Amundson said apologetically. "I can use it to adjust my projector before I set it into place."

"I don't see why not; we've got dozens. Everyone's got one. Give me a minute."

She stood and left the tent. Amundson continued his meal. In a few minutes she resumed her seat and with a smile pressed something cold and hard into his hand. He studied it.

The black stone was surprisingly heavy and not quite circular, he noticed, but ovoid, some two inches across on its longest dimension and half an inch thick. Its edges were rounded like those of a beach stone. Into one face a simple geometric figure had been deeply carved. It was a kind of spiral with four arms. Amundson realized that it was a primitive form of sun wheel or swastika.

"Thank you," he told Luce Henders. "This will be very useful."

One of the grads, a red-haired Irishman from Boston

College named Jimmy Dolan, noticed the black stone and pointed at it across the table with his fork.

"I see you've joined the cult of Oko-boko," he said. Several other students laughed, including Luce.

"When we first started finding these stones, we noticed that they were going missing," she explained to the engineer. "Professor Laski was upset because he thought we had a thief in the camp. He and Gani started to question everybody, and it turned out that the Mongolian diggers were taking them for good luck charms. This valley is supposed to be real bad luck or something, according to local superstition, and the Mongolians believed that the stones would protect them from the evil whatever-it-is. They got upset when the Professor tried to take the stones back, so he realized he'd better let them keep them or he'd have a mutiny on his hands and we would never get any work done. Anyway, Gani made all the local diggers promise to give the stones back when the dig is finished. You'll have to give yours back, too."

Amundson dropped the black stone into the vest pocket of his shirt and laid his hand across it.

"I do solemnly swear to return it," he said.

Luce laughed, her blue eyes sparkling with something a little brighter than the table wine. Things are looking up, Amundson thought to himself, things are definitely looking up.

3.

HE ENGINEERING PROBLEM WAS SIMPLE. THE IMAGER had to be positioned directly above the face of the colossus, and no more than three feet away. Since the statue could not be moved, it was necessary to build a superstructure above it to support the machine.

When Amundson mentioned the problem to Sikes, the little Englishman said he had just what was needed, and came back with two aluminum ladders. The ladders easily spanned the sides of the trench in which the colossus lay. It was necessary to support them from below with diagonal bracing so that they would bear the weight of Baby Huey without buckling, but this was not difficult.

Within an hour the framework was ready and the squat yellow machine in position beside the hole. Amundson had already spent the previous evening setting its sensors for the density of the black stone, which appeared identical in every respect to the stone of the statue. It was surprisingly easy to skid the imager along the ladders, and only a bit more taxing to get it positioned precisely above the face using the built-in camera as a guide.

Laski had been right, Amundson thought as he looked at the camera image of the blank face on his monitor. The statue was oriented with its head in the west, and the beams of the morning sun slanting along its body highlighted the marks of the chisels that had been used to cut away its features. He wondered idly what strange compulsion had caused a primitive people to cast down the statue and mutilate it. Perhaps they were some warring tribe and thought they were defeating the god of their enemies. He shrugged. He was an engineer, not an archaeologist. There was no need to bother his mind with such questions, which were probably unanswerable.

Amundson found himself less nervous than he expected, considering that his future career at MIT was riding on the performance of the imager. He smiled to himself. Not all of last night had been spent on work. The latter part of the evening he had devoted to the relaxing task of exploring Luce Henders. She was interested in him only because he was the first unfamiliar male to walk into the camp in months—that much was obvious—but it had not diminished his pleasure.

Why make life complicated when it could be simple? That was his personal motto. It had served him well enough through the first half of his life, and he saw no reason why it should not serve equally well through the second half.

This morning, Luce was away from the camp with Laski and his wife, Gani, and most of the others, excavating an artificial passage that had been found amid the graves. The discovery had been made by chance, while digging exploratory holes. When first found, the passage had been completely choked with rubble and its entrance covered with dirt. Laski was removing the rubble slowly so as not to miss any objects that might lie in it. He had the students screening the dirt and gravel as it was taken out of the passage by the diggers.

Amundson noticed Luther White across the trench. When he looked at the black grad student, White turned his head away. He had worn the same sullen expression all morning and had failed to respond when Amundson greeted him at breakfast. Apparently it was impossible to keep anything secret in so small a camp. He wondered if Luce had even tried to conceal her late-night visit to his tent? Or had she taken some perverse pleasure in relating the details to Luther?

After a few minutes dithering around, White found his way around the hole and approached Amundson. All the cheerfulness of the previous day had vanished.

"Stay away from Luce," he said in a low voice.

"What?" The engineer smiled disarmingly. "What did you say?"

"You heard me," White snarled. "I'm not going to tell you again. Luce is mine, not yours."

He backed away before Amundson could think of a response. Sikes, working nearby on the wires that connected the imager to the data processing unit, gave no sign that he had heard the exchange, although he must have heard every word.

"I'm ready to switch on," Amundson told the Englishman in a neutral tone.

Sikes nodded. He started the generator with its pull cord. It fired on the second pull and ran smoothly. With his laptop computer across his knees, Amundson put Baby Huey through its paces. The scanner hummed and stopped at the end of each pass, moving slowly back and forth like a farmer ploughing a field. Its beam was invisible, but a red laser cast a spot on the stone below it to act as a guide.

Sikes approached behind him and peered over his shoulder. "You mind telling me 'ow this works?" he asked.

Amundson didn't mind. He had the time. The scan of the machine was largely automatic, once its parameters were programmed in.

"You know how it's possible to recover a serial number on a gun, when the number has been completely filed off?"

Sikes nodded. "They use acid. The metal is 'arder under the place where the numbers are stamped in, so the acid eats the surrounding metal quicker, and the 'arder numbers show up in what they call bas-relief."

Amundson nodded.

"It's the same with stone. When stone is carved using a chisel, the repeated impact of the blade aligns the molecules in the stone. The harder the impact, the greater the alignment; or the more frequent the impact, the greater the alignment—same thing, it's the total impact on the stone that determines the degree of stress."

"You mean a few hard 'its is the same as a lot of little 'its," Sikes said.

"You've got it. What this machine does is project energy down into the stone, and then read the resonance that energy produces in the aligned molecules. The greater the alignment, the stronger the resonance. A computer assembles the data into an image."

"It's sort of like ground-penetrating radar," Sikes said.

"It uses a completely different band of projected energy, but the overall idea is similar."

"So you can use this 'ere machine to recover any image that was ever impressed on any stone surface, even after it gets worn away by erosion?"

"In theory," Amundson said. "In practice, it's not so simple. Some images are carved using regular pressure instead of struck using hammers. Some types of stone work better than others— usually the denser stone yields a better result."

"Why won't the impacts of the chisel when the face was cut away spoil the image?"

Amundson raised his eyebrows and glanced over his shoulder at Sikes. The little man was no fool.

"Because they were all uniform, more or less. They will be picked up by the scanner, but they will be like a curtain of background noise. The computer will be able—should be able— to strip away that curtain and reveal what lies beneath it."

"Won't that be a sight," Sikes said, staring at the little red dot of the laser as it scanned back and forth across the face. "We'll be the first people for thousands of years to see what it looked like."

Amundson shrugged. The excitement for him was in the technical challenge of recovering a clear image. A face was a face. Undoubtedly the image on the colossus would be strange and uncouth, like most primitive art, but what would it signify in the scheme of things? The world was littered with old statues, each bearing unique features. What was one more such image, more or less? He only hoped it would be grotesque enough to catch the eye when printed in the newspapers.

"How long is it going to take?" Sikes asked.

"About two hours to scan. Then the computer will need another four hours or so to process the data into a coherent image. It should be ready by late afternoon."

"I can 'ardly wait," Sikes said with sincerity.

You and me both, Amundson thought. Everything in his life was riding on the outcome of this test. If it failed, he could always run it a few more times, but he knew that the imager would either yield a result on the first scan, or it would never yield a good result. Conditions were perfect.

4.

"E'LL KNOW IN A SECOND," AMUNDSON SAID.

He had moved his processing computer into the main tent and set it up on the cleared dining table. Almost everyone in the camp was waiting to see the image when it finally formed on the monitor screen. Laski stood behind him, with his wife and Gani close on either side. The grads milled behind them, and the Mongolians clustered on the other side of the long table, their faces curiously apprehensive. Many of them fingered the small stone disks as though they really were protective talismans. Amundson got the impression that, were it up to the superstitious diggers, he would never be permitted to display the image of the face.

"It will be in black and white," he said to those behind his chair.

A buzzer sounded in the bowels of the computer.

"Here it comes," he said, unable to prevent his voice from rising in pitch.

The image began to appear on the monitor in horizontal

strips, painting itself across the screen from top to bottom. When it was about a fifth of the way down, Amundson released the breath he had been holding unconsciously and relaxed the knotted muscles in his abdomen. It was going to be all right. He couldn't see what the image was yet, but he could see that it was a clear, coherent image, and for him that was all that mattered. The test was a success. It was not quite as sharp as a photograph, but he had never expected that degree of clarity.

They waited in silence as the gray bands continued to paint themselves onto the screen.

"It's human," Gani said.

"So it is," Laski said with excitement. "I was expecting something monstrous, but it's human."

"It looks female," Anna Laski murmured.

"No, it's male," Sikes said.

"It looks female to me," Luce told him.

Amundson wondered what she was seeing. The face, which by now was more than half visible on the screen, was clearly the face of a man. It was startling in its sheer ordinariness. It might as well have been a contemporary snapshot of anyone in the tent. Indeed, the more he looked at it, the more it seemed familiar to him. He wondered where he had seen the face before.

Luce laughed nervously.

"This is a joke," she said.

Amundson turned in his chair to look at her.

"What do you mean?" Laski asked.

"Well, look at it. It's a joke, that's all. You got me, Professor Amundson. You got me good, guys, you really had me going. I thought this was a real test."

"What are you talking about?" Amundson demanded.

She stared at him with wide blue eyes, the half-smirk frozen in place on her lips. She looked at the others.

"Come on, guys, funny is fun, but this is enough."

They all stared at her. She pointed at the screen.

"You used a picture of my face. Good one, you got me. Now turn it off."

Laski glanced at the computer screen, then back at the blonde grad student.

"Are you feeling quite well, Luce? Perhaps you had better go to your tent to lie down."

"It's my face," she said loudly. "Do you think I don't recognize my own face?"

"My God," Anna Laski said. Her fingers rose to her lips. "My God."

Amundson looked back at the screen. The face had almost completely formed itself in grayscale. It was a lifelike representation of a middle-aged man with short hair.

"My God," Anna Laski said more loudly, backing away from the screen.

"Jesus, I see it now," Sikes said.

"See what?" Laski demanded. He turned to his wife. "Anna, what do you see?"

"It's my face," she said. "I didn't recognize it at first, but it's my face."

Her husband looked at the image.

"It is a man's face, my dear. If nothing else, the beard should tell you that."

"Look again," Sikes told him in a faint voice. "Look 'arder."

Amundson wondered if they had all suddenly gone mad. There was no question about the gender of the face. It was definitely male, but clean-shaven. There was something maddeningly familiar about it.

"You say you see a beard, Professor?" Sikes asked him.

"Yes, a short beard much like my own."

"I see no beard," Sikes said.

"That's absurd," Laski said. "It's right there. You see it, don't you, Gani?"

The Mongolian shook his head. He was strangely silent, but there was fear in his eyes. The same fear was mirrored in the faces of his countrymen on the other side of the table. The tent had fallen still.

"It's my face," Joseph Laski said in a leaden voice.

"It is all our faces," Gani said.

Amundson stared at the screen. Recognition leapt out at him. How could he have missed it? The image on the screen was his own face, its eyes staring impassively back into his. It was like looking into a mirror—or better to say, like looking at a black-and-white photograph of himself. A mirror reversed his face from left to right, and he had become accustomed to seeing it that way. That was why he had failed to recognize himself instantly.

"It can't be all our faces," he said, his voice lifeless in his own ears. "I never scanned any of our faces. In any case, it's only one image—it can't be all our faces at the same time."

"But it is," Sikes said.

One of the Mongolian diggers began to jabber in his own language at Gani, who responded in a soothing tone, but the man was in no mood to be placated. Gathering his courage, he walked quickly around the table and stared at the image on the monitor. For a few seconds he did not react. Then he screamed and began to babble at the other diggers. Gani put a hand on his shoulders, and the man flinched as though burned with hot iron. He backed away from the monitor, unable to take his eyes from it until his back pressed against the side of the tent. The touch of canvas on his shoulders galvanized him. With a cry he ran from the tent. The other Mongolian diggers quickly followed, leaving only the archaeologists beside the table.

"There has to be a scientific explanation," Amundson said, his eyes captivated by the image on the monitor.

"Mass hallucination," Luce said.

"I've been on LSD, I know what it feels like," Dolan said with a shake of his red head. "This is no hallucination."

"But how is the image being formed?" Amundson asked. "How can it be different for each of us?"

"Maybe it isn't an image at all," Sikes suggested. "Maybe it's something that makes an image in our minds when we look at it."

Amundson bent over one of the machines on the table.

"What are you doing?" Sikes asked.

"I'm printing out a hard copy," the engineer murmured. "I want to see if it has the same effect as the image on the monitor."

The printer generated the black-and-white copy in a matter of seconds. Amundson took it from the rack and held it up for the others to view. They unconsciously backed away a step when he extended it toward them.

"It's the same, still my face," Luce said.

"And mine," Anna agreed.

"Mine, too," Sikes said.

Amundson stared at them, barely able to contain his excitement.

"Do you know what this means?" he demanded.

They gave him blank stares.

"It means we're all going to be famous."

5.

HE SOUND OF BANGING FROM OUTSIDE THE TENT DREW their attention away from the sheet of paper.

"I'll go see," Gani told Laski.

He left the tent. After a minute or so they heard excited shouting in Mongolian, followed by the sound of a single gunshot. When they rushed to the door, they were in time to see the three camp trucks speed away across the desert, leaving fantails of dust in their wakes.

"They've taken all the trucks," Luce said in bewilderment.

Gani staggered from the communications tent. There was a patch of redness on his left thigh.

"Those bastards shot him," Sikes said. He hurried over to support the archaeologist beneath the arm.

"They smashed the radio," Gani told Laski, pain in his voice. "I couldn't stop them."

"Well, they're gone," Laski said.

The reality of their situation slowly sank home. Without a radio there was no way to call Mandalgovi and report the incident, and without the trucks there was no way to leave the camp. It might be days before anyone in the town sent a truck to investigate the radio silence. On the plus side of things, there was no shortage of food and water in the camp. The main concern was for Gani. They managed to stop the bleeding from the bullet wound, but it was a serious injury. He needed a hospital.

Anna Laski moved the injured man onto the bed in her tent, which was larger than the camp cots. She appointed one of the grads, a quiet girl in glasses named Maria Striva, as his nurse. He had collapsed almost immediately after leaving the communications tent, and continued to lapse in and out of consciousness, but whether from pain, shock, or loss of blood, none of them was qualified to tell.

As dusk gathered, the others returned to the main tent and sat around the table with Laski at its head. Sikes silently served them coffee while they talked.

"We might as well go on with our work," the archaeologist told the students. "This dig is too important to abandon over one incident. In any case, there's not much else that we can do."

"It will be difficult without the diggers," White pointed out. Laski nodded.

"Which is why we will go slowly. We don't want to miss anything or, God forbid, have an accident. As you all know, we've almost finished clearing the tunnel of rubble. The echo gear indicates a sizeable chamber beyond. We should be able to break through to it tomorrow, even without the diggers."

White nodded and looked around at the other grads to gauge their mood.

"We're game," he said.

"Good." Laski turned to Amundson, who sat with the printout of the scanner image face down on the table in front of him.

"Run another scan," he said.

"The result will be the same," Amundson told him.

"Run another scan anyway. We need to be absolutely certain this isn't some kind of chance artifact of the machine itself."

Amundson did not argue. The order made sense. In any case, what else was he going to do with his time? He was not a trained archaeologist and therefore could not help with the excavation, even had he felt inclined to offer his services as a digger.

"You'll have to work alone tomorrow, I'm afraid," Laski told him. "I need every person at the tunnel."

"Now that the imager is in place, that won't be a problem."

He was rechecking his test results at the desk in his tent an hour later when Luce entered, wearing only a yellow silk robe tied at her waist. Her short blonde hair was immaculate, but the powder on her cheek could not completely hide the bruise beneath.

Amundson stared at her from his chair without rising. He had not expected a return visit, given the tense circumstances. Sex was not high on his list of priorities tonight.

"He hit you?"

She touched her cheek gently and winced.

"What does it matter? I do what I want, when I want."

She approached the desk and took up the printout, turning it over to stare at the image with fascination as though mesmerized by a serpent.

"What does it mean?" she asked in a low tone that was barely audible.

"It means we are all going to be famous, and quite possibly rich. No discovery like this has ever been made before."

She shook her head with annoyance.

"But what does it mean? Why our own faces?"

"I have no idea," Amundson said, wishing she would just turn around and walk out of the tent so that he could get his work done. "That's something you archaeologists will have to determine. I'm an engineer."

"Do you suppose the original face of the colossus, before it was chiseled off, had the same effect? Did everyone who looked at the statue see themselves?"

"Yes, I think so," Amundson told her. "What my imager generated is an accurate reproduction of whatever was on the original face of the statue. I don't see why the effect would be any different."

"That's why they cut it off," she murmured with conviction. "They couldn't stand seeing themselves, so they toppled the statue and struck off its face before burying it."

"I expect you are right," Amundson said, shuffling the printouts of readings from the machine. "Look, Luce, I'm really quite busy now—"

She sat across his thighs, her arms around his shoulders, and forced her tongue into his mouth before he could finish the sentence. Her robe fell open, and the erect nipples of her firm young breasts pressed against his shirtfront. She arched her back to raise herself and slide her breasts from side to side over his face. With a moan of desire, she dug her hand between his legs.

Amundson found himself thrusting into her as she lay diagonally across his cot. With part of his mind he realized she was naked, and that he wore only his open shirt. He had no memory of moving across the tent, or of taking off his pants. He shrugged out of the shirt with annoyance, relishing the freedom from its encumbrance. He felt wholly alive, like some powerful beast awakened from long sleep. When she bit his shoulder, he slapped her across the face, back and forth, until her upper lip split and blood marked her bared white teeth.

Only when he had exhausted his lust and lay panting across her did she push him off and leave the cot. Her eyes held a restless look, sliding over him as though he were of no further interest. Neither spoke. Shame mingled with regret welled inside Amundson when he looked at the blood on her lip. He might be many things, but he had never hit a woman. She bent to pick up her silk robe and slid into it, then flipped it closed and tied it with a sharp tug of its sash. Without a backward glance she left the tent.

Amundson lay naked across the cot, listening to the sound of his own breathing. What the hell had just happened? In an instant he had gone from bored indifference to white-hot lust mingled with violence. The sight of blood on the girl's face had excited him. That had never happened before. Sex had always been good for him, but nobody would ever describe it as anything other than white bread. The outburst of passion had left him drained. Suddenly, it was all he could do to keep his eyes open. He shifted himself on the cot into a more comfortable posture and knew nothing more until the following morning.

6.

HEN HE LEFT HIS TENT, THE SUN WAS ALREADY WELL above the eastern horizon and the morning chill had been driven from the stones that lay scattered across the pebbly ground. He was almost glad to discover that he had overslept and that the rest of the camp, with the sole exception of Sikes, had already left for the passage excavation. In the main tent, Sikes gave him scrambled eggs and toast, with black coffee. He sipped the bitter liquid with gratitude. A headache throbbed between his temples, making it hard to focus his eyes.

Sikes must have had a rough night of his own. The little Englishman was uncommonly quiet and seemed to perform his housekeeping duties in a meditative daze. After he finished clearing away the breakfast dishes and silverware, he announced to Amundson that he was leaving to help with the excavation work.

The engineer nodded absently at him and did not turn his head to watch him go. His thoughts were preoccupied by the question Luce had asked the night before. Why their own faces? What did it mean to see oneself, to have one's essential pattern exposed?

He had brought the printout into the dining hall with him. It rested on the table beside his coffee cup, face down. Turning it over, he held it up and studied it. The face, which was most definitely his own, stared back at him. There was a trace of amusement at the corners of its lips—or was that only his imagination? The longer he stared into the eyes of the image, the more variable the expression of the face seemed to become. It shifted from wry amusement to arrogance to lip-curling contempt. Its mouth trembled as though it were trying to speak to him.

Amundson set the sheet of paper down and rubbed his eyelids with his thumb and index finger. Little wonder his mind was playing tricks, given the stress he had been under for the past few days.

He took up the paper and regarded it again, striving to separate himself from it. This could not be an image. It had to be some sort of symbolic code series designed to affect the human mind at the deepest level and provoke the same illusion in every person who looked at it. He was not seeing the code, he was seeing only the effect of the code, but the code itself must be printed on the paper in his hand, just as it had been impressed onto the stone face of the colossus so many thousand years in the past.

There was a popular name for a self-executing code that reproduced itself from one medium to another. Virus. What he was looking at on the paper, without actually being able to see it, must be some form of symbolic mind virus, transmitted through the visual sense.

He turned the paper face down, his fingers trembling. The sophistication required to produce such a code was terrifying in its implications. No ancient human culture could have designed it, or at least no culture recognized by science. Unless the code had been generated by some intuitive process, or channeled from some higher external source. Perhaps if he divided the code into parts, he could analyze it without being affected by it.

He slammed the flat of his hand against the table and pushed himself to his feet. It was pointless to speculate in the absence of data. He would run another scan, varying the parameters from the first scan to see if it achieved a different result. It would probably be best to do an entire series of scans under as many conditions as possible.

Bright spots of light danced before his eyes as he left the

main tent. He gathered up the processing computer and the laptop from his own tent and carried them toward the canvas enclosure around the colossus, where he busied himself connecting wires and preparing for the scan. His mind was not on his work.

If a copy of the face were published in major world newspapers and shown around the globe on the nightly television news, in a single day it would imprint itself on the minds of perhaps a billion human beings. That was a sobering thought. Before releasing it to the press he would have to assure himself that the coding of the image was not harmful.

Thus far, it had not caused any damage. His thinking was still clear. It was absurd even to consider withholding the results of the test from the media: once it became public, his fame and prosperity were assured. He would write a book and it would become a bestseller. He wondered why the idea of withholding the results had even crossed his mind and laughed to himself. The eerie chuckle startled him, until he realized that it had proceeded from his own mouth.

The desert was filled with strange sounds this morning. On the other side of the canvas barrier, he heard a distant barking. It was followed by a series of drawn-out howls, like those of a wolf. He wondered idly if there really were wolves in the Gobi. It would be a fine state of affairs if the archaeologists returned to camp at the end of the day and discovered his wolf-mauled corpse. He couldn't let that happen. Was there a weapon in the camp? He decided to look for a knife or a gun, even a good solid club.

The ghosts were waiting for him when he emerged from the enclosure. They stood silent and motionless all over the open ground, watching him with dead eyes. Their bodies were translucent and colorless, but they wore some kind of ancient apparel that resembled none he had ever seen before. There were soldiers, priests, merchants, slaves, maidens, matrons, whores. Some were even children, but they stood as impassively as the rest.

The weight of their dead eyes on Amundson was like a physical force, compelling him to do something, but he knew not what. It produced an unpleasant twisting sensation in his lower belly. Coupled with his headache, it made him irritable.

"I don't know what you want," he muttered to them. "You'll have to be clearer, I don't know what you want."

He walked through them on his way to Laski's tent. He needed to acquire a weapon before the wolves reached the camp and tore him apart. The touch of the dead against his skin was similar to the brush of cool silk. The ghosts made no attempt to stop him, but merely turned to regard him with mute accusation.

Inside Laski's tent, the sweet-sick smell of fresh blood struck him in the face. He blinked in the dimness. The Mongolian archaeologist lay on his back on the bed with his throat torn out. Damn wolves, Amundson thought. The shy grad student, Maria Striva, crouched on his chest, naked, her body streaked with blood. She glared at the engineer, blood and bits of flesh clotting her teeth, her nose, the corners of her mouth, and her chin. Her bloodshot eyes were so wide open that he could see their whites all the way around their brown irises. There was no sanity there.

With some part of his mind Amundson realized that she had become a wolf. The desert was filled with wolves. Why didn't the Mongolians kill the verminous creatures? If the wolves were permitted to roam free in this way, sooner or later everyone would be attacked.

The woman threw herself off the bed, her blood-covered fingers clawing for his throat, but her feet became tangled together and she fell heavily onto her face and breasts, knocking the wind from her lungs with a sharp yelp. Calmly, Amundson stepped across her body and picked up a short-handled pickaxe that rested on the floor next to a travel trunk. As the woman pressed herself up on her hands, he sank the point of the pickaxe into the top of her skull. She collapsed, dead.

One less wolf to deal with, he thought with satisfaction. He remembered why he had entered the tent and rummaged through the trunk. At the bottom he found a revolver. When he left the tent, the ghosts nodded their heads at him with satisfaction.

7.

S AN EXPERIMENT, HE SHOT ONE OF THE GHOSTS. THE report of the revolver rolled across the desert and lost itself on the dusty wind. As expected, the bullet did nothing. The ghost merely smiled at him, and its translucent head became a naked, grinning skull. That was to be expected, but he was a scientist after all, and of what use was surmise without verification? Thereafter, he ignored the ghosts, even though they followed him all the way to the entrance of the passage.

He recognized the two corpses that lay near a mound of tailings, not far from a black hole in the ground, bodies grotesquely twisted in their death-throes. One was the red-headed grad, Jimmy Dolan, and the other was Sikes. Amundson tilted his head as he studied the tableau. It appeared that Dolan had stabbed Sikes in the back with a tent spike, and that Sikes—plucky little man that he was— had managed to bash in Dolan's brains with a rock before he died. Two more wolves taken care of, the engineer thought with satisfaction.

He climbed down the aluminum ladder into the pit and

entered the mouth of the slanting passage, which descended into the solid bedrock at a downward angle of around twenty degrees. The light soon failed behind him, but he saw a tiny square of brightness at the end of the long, straight tunnel, and continued on, feeling his way along the wall with his left hand. The stone felt smooth beneath his fingertips, almost like polished marble.

At the end, Amundson had to pick his steps with care over uncleared rubble. An opening had been made that was large enough to crawl through. He emerged into a vaulted chamber of thick, square pillars. The portion of it near the tunnel entrance was illuminated by the glowing mantle of a propane lantern. From the corners of his eyes, Amundson saw carved statues resembling animals and manlike beasts. They nodded their heads at him in approval, but he paid scant attention.

On the open floor lay the bodies of Laski and his wife, horribly mutilated. Between them, a naked Luther White, his muscular dark body glistening with sweat in the light from the lantern, stretched across the corpse of Luce Henders. She also was naked and lay face down on a low platform of polished stone. With scientific detachment, Amundson noticed that her head was missing. He glanced around but failed to locate it.

White was busy thrusting his erect member into the dead girl's pale, blood-streaked backside, and did not notice the intrusion. With each thrust he grunted, "ugh-ugh-ugh," and the headless body jerked on the altar as though by some undead animation. From the darkness beyond the reach of the lantern, ghosts began to gather. Amundson threw back his head and howled.

"She's mine," White snarled at him. "You can't have her."

He thrust himself away from the corpse of the girl and

stood up, still impressively erect, his penis coated with blood. Between the buttocks of the headless corpse there was only a mass of chewed flesh that resembled raw beef. White looked around with quick jerks of his head from side to side. He lunged and grabbed up a shovel with a short D-handle. Holding it like an axe, he advanced with cautious steps toward the engineer.

Amundson shot the black man in the chest. White looked down at the hole until it began to ooze blood, then laughed.

"Bullets can't kill me," he cried through lips caked with dried blood.

Amundson howled again and shot White two more times. The second bullet found his heart. The black grad student dropped like a marionette with its strings cut. The ghosts clustered close and nodded, their translucent eyes shining in the lantern glow like pearls.

The engineer thrust the revolver into his belt. The sharp tang of gunpowder cut through the cloying scent of blood. He felt strong. More powerful and more potent than he had ever felt before. His mind was clear, his thoughts ordered and supremely rational. He realized that his sexual organ was engorged with blood and gazed down at the headless corpse with a speculative eye.

"No, mine," he murmured to himself, and began to giggle.

Something drew him more strongly than his lust. In the darkness beyond the circle of the lantern light he sensed a vast space that extended downward, like the inverted vault of starry heaven. That was what the ghosts were trying to tell him. He must explore that space. It was his destiny, the only thing for which he had been born into this world. He listened, and now he could almost hear the whispers of the ghosts. If he remained in the darkness with them, it would not be long before they could talk to him and teach him. He could remain here a long time. There was ample food. Was that his own thought, or the thought of the ghosts?

As he started forward, his boot slipped in White's blood, and he fell heavily to the floor, the back of his head striking and rebounding from the polished stone. Something rolled beneath his hand when he struggled to get up. He blinked and held it to the light. Recognition entered his thoughts—the oval black stone he had put into his shirt pocket and then forgotten about.

As he held up the stone, a kind of sigh arose from the throng of the dead. Acting on some impulse below the level of thought, Amundson extended the stone toward the ghosts. The pallid forms withdrew like mist from flame. He blinked heavily and shook his head. What was he doing here in this dark cavern? The vague memory of leaving the camp and climbing down into the passage came into his mind. He tried again to stand, then cursed and began to crawl toward the lantern with the stone clutched firmly in his left hand.

Awareness came to him in flashes, between which there was oblivion. He was in the tunnel. He stumbled across the loose stones of the desert. He pushed through the resistless ghosts in the camp. Then he was sitting at the table in the main tent. Everything looked completely normal. He picked up his half-emptied coffee mug and felt a faint trace of warmth, or perhaps it was only his imagination. The printout of the face lay beside him on the table. He turned it over and looked at it. Fame. Fortune. Prestige. Success. Acclaim.

He let it drop from his hand. It drifted under the table. He realized with surprise that he still held the oval talisman clutched in his left fist and laid it with care on the table. He sat staring at the doorway of the tent. Through the opening he could see the ancient ghosts walking to and fro in their eternal procession of the damned.

With quick, economical motions he drew the revolver, cocked the hammer, put the muzzle into his mouth, and pulled the trigger.

8.

ENERAL GOPPIK SURVEYED THE CORPSE OF THE American with distaste. Blood and brains had splattered the wall of the tent around the hole left by the departing bullet. The man's pale eyes stared sightlessly, already starting to shrivel in the dry desert air. He picked up the black stone that lay on the table and regarded its carved surface with curiosity before putting it into his pocket. A keepsake for his young son, he thought.

There were corpses everywhere. The more his soldiers searched, the more bodies they found. Evidently the entire party of foreigners had gone mad and murdered one another with extreme violence—all except this one, who had taken his own life. It was a propaganda nightmare. The Western press would never stop talking about it. The archaeological dig at Kel-tepu would have to be closed down, naturally. There was no other course of action to follow. The entire site would have to be sanitized, and some story invented to account for the massacre. Terrorists, perhaps. Yes, terrorists were always useful.

Noticing a sheet of paper on the floor beneath the table, he bent and retrieved it. The paper bore some sort of computer printout of a black-and-white photograph, not a very clear one at that, showing a Mongolian man. He frowned and squinted at the image. There was something familiar about this face. He had seen it before, perhaps in some rogue's gallery of wanted criminals.

Grunting in dismissal, he started to crumple the paper in his hand, then thought better of it and smoothed it out on the table before folding it and putting it into his inner vest pocket. More than likely it held no importance, but it was evidence at a crime scene. He would take it back with him when he returned to Ulaanbaatar. If the face were publicized in the newspapers, perhaps someone would recognize it.

The History of a Letter

~~~ ⚜ ~~~

AS RELATED BY JASON V BROCK

Jason V Brock's writing and art have been published in Butcher Knives & Body Counts, Animal Magnetism, Calliope, Like Water for Quarks, Ethereal Tales, Dark Universe *(comic),* Logan's Run: Last Day *(comic),* San Diego Comic-Con's Souvenir Book, Fangoria, *and many other venues. He is Art Director/Managing Editor for* Dark Discoveries *magazine and coeditor (with William F. Nolan) of* The Bleeding Edge *(Cycatrix Press, 2010). His films include the documentaries* Charles Beaumont: The Short Life of Twilight Zone's Magic Man, The AckerMonster Chronicles, *and* Image, Reflection, Shadow: Artists of the Fantastic. *He lives in the Portland, Oregon, area and loves his wife, Sunni, reptiles/amphibians, and vegan/vegetarianism.*

INTRODUCTION

HEN THE EDITOR ASKED ME FOR A CONTRIBUTION TO this anthology (the very one in your hands), I knew I had my work cut out for me. A flurry of correspondence ensued: When was the book coming out? Who was the publisher? Was there a theme? What were the restrictions on length and so on?

As usual, the editor was courteous, prompt, and succinct. Did I mention thorough? At any rate, I went off to consider all this information and came to a stark realization—I had nothing to contribute! This was a quandary; I *wanted* to be part of the book, yet I had no idea what to write.

Weeks of vexation, false starts, irritable moods, and agitation followed. As the deadline loomed, I went through my normal course of actions, as is my coping strategy at such times:

1. I searched through my files and notebooks, hoping to stumble across that gem of an idea waiting to be fleshed out (always a dubious gamble, I might add).
2. I castigated myself as a procrastinator (though I had been quite involved in another task, which I will address in a moment).
3. I played loud music (a normal, albeit damaging, habit for me).
4. I stayed up very late, unable to sleep (another habit I cannot seem to rid myself of).

Finally, several months later and just a few weeks before the piece was due, I asked the (patient) editor if a nonfiction submission was acceptable, and the reply was "Of course! But I need it quickly." I felt better then, as I had been working on something that had haunted me for some time, but was unsure where it might lead. I hoped that the article would be of use, as I felt no small amount of guilt that I had been spending hours fiddling with it and trolling around various libraries, bookstores, and online venues doing research in lieu of writing a story for the anthology I had committed to those many months previous.

A brief explanation: While conducting an investigation for an unrelated project, I stumbled across an old copy of the Georges Bataille[1] classic *Histoire de l'oeil*[2] at Powell's City of Books[3] in Portland, Oregon. As I was leafing through the crumbling pages of this book, something fell out and fluttered to the ground—a letter. It was tightly folded, ragged, stained, and yellow with age. I picked it up, and what I read filled me with a peculiar disquiet; as I deciphered the cramped, spidery handwriting, I lost all interest in the Bataille volume and, though I knew it was wrong, I could not resist the impulse to take the dispatch.

What follows are the contents of that strange missive; the notes are my own, based on investigations that have distracted me, as I stated, for the better part of a year and sidetracked my other ambitions, consuming more and more of my time and attention.

---

[1] Bataille was a prolific and important French author whose works frequently dealt with surrealism, as well as the entanglements of human sexuality and mortality; other notable works of his include *The Solar Anus*; *The Tears of Eros*; *Erotism*; and *The Trial of Gilles de Rais*.

[2] *Story of the Eye* in English, as by Lord Auch (a pseudonym that Bataille employed because of the pornographic nature of the work).

[3] A venerated and excellent resource for bibliophiles in the Pacific Northwest.

THE LETTER

Dearest—[4]

Y THE TIME YOU READ THIS, I[5] WILL BE NO MORE, AND most likely your time will be limited as well.[6] Thus, as a final testament, I have decided to address a question that you posed long ago, and I never answered…

Do you recall when you asked what single event in my life had most disturbed me? I had scoffed at the notion, stating that I had no use for such banality, but the truth is—I was loath to revisit the moment. I'm ahead of myself: allow me to "begin at the beginning," as it were…

It was yet another melancholy fall afternoon about eight years ago,[7] and I was walking through the Olde Jewish Shopping District[8] when I saw it. Just the recollection sets my teeth on edge! At any rate, I was crossing the street when I glanced up and there the hideous object was, on display—obscene display—in an antiquarian book and curio dealer's window.[9]

Though I had been feeling febrile and ill for many months,[10]

---

[4] The addressee is not identified, but appears to have been a love interest.

[5] The writer is never revealed, but references suggest a male.

[6] The author does not elaborate on why both parties appear to be in danger.

[7] The letter is not dated, but the condition, and the parchment-like material of the paper, appears to be from the early 1900s, or perhaps even older.

[8] I could find no record of any such place in the United States; there are several so-called ethnic areas like this in Europe, however, notably in Prague (unfortunately, most of the others were destroyed during World War II). Some of the notations in the margins of the document appear to be either Cyrillic or Czech characters; also, there are several words and references in French in the letter, so it is possible that the writer was in Europe, or was European.

[9] Unnamed.

[10] It is possible that the author had tuberculosis, a common malady of the apparent era in which the letter was written.

and had been warned against undue excitement by my attending physician, I rushed back across the boulevard, pressing my hands against the cold glass of the display. I was horrorstruck that the rest of the world continued unabated as though this was the most natural thing in the world. My focus was now reduced—to this moment in time, to this instant of revulsion and comprehension brought on by the relic. The sky darkened for a moment and I felt nauseous, my stomach aflutter. As I extricated myself from the window, the Earth seemed somehow robbed of all colour, and the chilly air had the stale quality of a giant's exhalation. A man bumped into me, and his cursing brought me back to the external present. Dabbing perspiration from my face, I straightened my tie and decided to enter the shoppe.

An archaic bell, too loud in my sensitive state, jangled atop the door as I stepped through the ornate threshold. The musty atmosphere was frigid—colder even than the late fall day outside. A chill swept my bones and the crisp air inside felt alive; in every direction I looked, I could not escape the unspeakably ghoulish contents of the room. Sinister etchings and shadowed portraits peered from the corners of the weirdly expansive shoppe, and the dimly lit parlour seemed scarcely able to contain all the *objets d'art* that the owner had accumulated over the years. The place reeked with the mould of old furniture and older books, causing my nose to tickle as I observed the bottles of freak fetuses preserved in clouded green fluid, the rough-skinned shrunken heads with empty-eyed stares, the colorful voodoo effigies of the Caribbean, the strange skin-bound tomes of an apparently Arab[11] origin, their spines decorated in Sanskrit letters...

I glanced to the window that I had leered through only a moment before; the heavy door closed behind me with dreadful

---

[11] This term was used in reference to much of the Middle East in previous times.

finality, and I felt my throat constrict. I should have stayed away; in that moment, I had decided to turn, to leave, to try to forget the madness in the window, but was interrupted…

"*Mon Dieu!* I see you've returned," the shopkeeper said from the back of the cramped space. Lately, I had been experiencing disturbing bouts of *déjà vu*; as the wizened, stoop-shouldered proprietor shuffled toward me, the sensation reasserted itself in a forcefully disorienting fashion.

"*Au contraire, Monsieur*—I'm quite sure I've never had the pleasure of visiting your fine establishment before…. Perhaps I have a twin?" My clumsy attempt at humour was met with stoicism by the keeper, who was now in front of me, leaning on a gnarled wooden cane capped by a silver skull. Squinting, he studied me with piercing blue eyes from behind thick, wire-rimmed spectacles, thoughtfully stroking his white beard; after a long moment, he straightened his shawl-covered frame and flashed a brief smile.

"*Oui* quite a *remarkable* doppelgänger. How may I assist you?" He paused, then bent forward, conspiratorially peering over his glasses: "Let me guess—the display in the window, correct?" His voice was quiet, his enunciation precise.

The world seemed to spin for an instant. I glanced again around the claustrophobic showroom, with its dust-enrobed grotesqueries and curios from across the planet; its masks out of darkest Africa; its fetishes from the cannibal tribes of Papua New Guinea; its arcane trinkets from the savages of South America and the madmen of Asia.

"Yes," I managed at last. "The window." Our gaze locked, and I realised that I could no longer hear the bustle of the street outside, just the creak of wooden shelves, the wheeze of the shopkeeper's ragged breath. I dabbed my forehead again, though the dark room was chilly to the point of my breath fogging. Perhaps my fever had returned. Perhaps it was something else.

The owner nodded. "I thought so, just like yesterday, and all the days prior to that…"

Before I could rouse another protest, he turned his icy stare away, breaking our connection.

Here I must insert an aside: Though the aged retailer insisted that we'd met before, I know that this is not the case. His innuendo of "yesterday" would have been an impossibility, for example, as I had been in the next town over, acting as a pallbearer with Ernst, Alistair, and Isaac for my poor brother, Stefan,[12] who had finally succumbed to his injuries.[13] Given the great distance and my ill health, there was no way I could have been at the funeral service and then to his establishment in the same [*illegible*].

"*Oui, oui*—you've never been here before; I recall," he said, lightly tapping the side of his head as he moved to the front of the store. I followed, navigating around the jammed shelves, the queer items suspended from the ceiling. In the swirl of dust motes kicked up by our trespass, I continued to be plagued by the peculiar nag of *déjà vu*; the whole strange episode had the quaint aspect of a fever dream.

The old bay windows of the storefront rattled from a sudden gust. A dull ache began to throb in my temple as I felt the barometric pressure drop; such is the normal course of events in coastal towns when a storm gathers on the sea. The waning orange glow of evening glinted off the chop in the harbour across the bay,[14] clearly visible from the dirt-gauzed panes. The antiquarian dealer's battered shingle squealed as it

---

[12] Possibly the author is German or Jewish?

[13] This might be a reference to World War I (either a civilian or a military casualty). It could also be related to work or an accident; it is noteworthy that the object of the letter seemed unaware of the brother's fate or not involved with the author at this point in time.

[14] Interesting geographic clues, but still quite vague.

was buffeted by the wind. No one was outside; the cobblestones on the street glistened with rain, puddles reflecting the baleful flicker of the gaslights.[15] A cloud of dread enveloped me as I watched twilight cloak the city. It was rare that I frequented this aspect of the port, even more rare that I would be out this late in the day, especially at this time of the year, when the light and the darkness changed places so much earlier. My salivary glands tightened, making my mouth dry, my jaw twinge, adding to my headache.

"Storm's on the way," the proprietor said, staring at the water. The harbormaster's warning horn sounded. By this point, the scene had grown unbearably tense, and I knew I should take my leave—[*illegible*] just forget this horrible place and its contents for good.

"[*Illegible*]," the shopkeeper said at last; then he crept over to the display and reached in. I wiped the sweat from my forehead again, my stomach in turmoil and competing with the pain in my head.

"Perhaps it is too much effort—" I said. My voice was hoarse, a whisper.

"No, no: just one moment; it always takes a moment to [*illegible*]…"

Another odd statement from the owner; I was beginning to wonder if the old man was losing his grip on reality.[16] The wind kicked up again; it was now completely dark outside. A stroke of lightning split the night, followed by a low roll of thunder. As I watched, several denizens staggered against the mounting gale—they seemed unnatural, pained, ensconced in tattered overcoats and filthy gloves that obscured their features. They

---

[15] A reference to a pre-electric time. Combined with the geographic descriptions, the locale could be England (or perhaps the writer is British, as a few of the spellings seem to indicate), Paris, or even America (especially New England).

[16] An interesting point in light of the next few paragraphs.

determinedly made their way in the wind toward the opening night of the Ceremony,[17] no doubt driven by the long tradition of the Rituals;[18] indeed, I had forgotten that this was the return of that savage and disturbing five-year spectacle.[19] Backward hamlets such as this are places so entombed in their traditions, so ossified by their histories that they appear to have lost all [*illegible*] and rational thought when it comes to these "historic" defences of orchestrated mayhem. Rotting leaves plaster the windows, whipped onto the loose panes by the tempest, and the lights in the store, already dim, lower. Finally I look away, awash once more in the anxious sensation of inhabiting a nightmare, but knowing this could not be the case. At that moment the keeper was at my side, brandishing the foul item from the window.[20]

"This is what you seek?" he stated more than asked, thrusting the obscenity into my hands, his thin flesh clammy and vaguely scaly to the touch. I was horrified to behold the object up close, and for a moment just stared into the cold, rheumy eyes of the proprietor. "Go on," he commanded, his voice clotted, distant, as he pushed the artifact toward me. "Take it—there's not another on Earth."

As I held it in my hands, unsure if it were real or imagined, living or dead, I felt its dark energy course through my fingers… so much pain… so much filth… so much strength and cosmic wisdom… so much *power*. It appeared alive somehow, even *conscious*. Once again, the world started to tumble…

---

[17] No documentation.

[18] No documentation.

[19] A good clue: there are several "festivals" such as this throughout Europe and America, usually related to historic events or the harvest. It is possible that the one referred to here is related to a military victory over the local indigenous peoples.

[20] The references here are never fully explained: it is unclear exactly what the "object" actually is.

"How—how did you come to possess—*this*?" I asked, fingering the smooth, hard curves and planes, studying the bizarre runes and glyphs adorning the dreadful object. My impulses were divided as I hefted the thing: part of me wanted to destroy it, smash it into pieces, while another part of me longed to fall down in worship, inwardly cringing at its simultaneous beauty and loathsomeness.

"*Mon Dieu*—now that is a good question," he said, his smile dark, macabre, like a bruise on the face of a bride. It seemed starkly out of place. I glanced down—my hands were covered in what appeared to be blood: the thing was oozing a sticky red fluid; its rigidity was lessened and it now felt prickly, malleable. "Sadly," the shopkeeper said, "there is no answer: it comes from yesterday and tomorrow. It came to me long ago in a dream…"

A gust howled against the windows, and the light failed: suddenly a revolting, deformed face pressed against the iced glass of the storefront. A mewling din surged over the wind, and an ominous crowd began to gather outside the shoppe.

The proprietor laughed behind me, [*illegible*] I felt frozen, unable to move. As everything vanished from view, I thought about how this was the strangest thing in all the world… the most dreadful thing…. And then the idol was twitching in my hands… birthing…

Darkness: I awoke in darkness on the windswept street, my hands stained crimson, my palms singed and painful, though I have no memory of how I got there. I could not find the store, and the relic was gone…

SINCE THAT TIME, I HAVE BEEN TROUBLED BY A PECULIAR dream.

In the reverie, I am approaching a decrepit house on a devastated plain. The moon hangs low, bloated and blue in the sky. Fog snakes the ground. As I get nearer, a sickly yellow light winks on in an upstairs window, and a shadow passes in front of it. The wind blows, and a low rumble grows in the distance. The air is frosty, biting.

Closer now, the door opens: its hinges groan and the inside is darker than the outside; the smell of wet earth is robust, sickly.

In the foyer, on a table, there is a bundle of unbound, mildewed papers, tied together with a string. I untie it, and as I leaf through the stained manuscript, I notice that nearly every inch of the yellowed parchment is covered in weird symbols, incomprehensible diagrams, and crude illustrations.

And then, a few pages into the document, there it is: a hasty pen-and-ink sketch of the thing in the window!

I hurl the stack of papers to the ground and sense that I am not alone. Every time I have the dream, I am able to peruse more of the leaves in the bundle before I reach the drawing, and more of the presence reveals itself. Turning around, I can barely make out a ramshackle spiral staircase near the back of the room, which ascends to the ceiling, but not an ordinary one: it is instead a galactic canopy of stars and swirling celestial bodies, and the stairs climb into the face of a terrible midnight sun, its merciless solar flares blinding me, scorching my skin...

Then it appears: the idol from the shoppe. But not as some hand-held miniature, no. Instead it is a massive, jabbering horror, rending the fabric of my sanity with its tormented shrilling, its ultra-human sonorities.... It reaches to me across the aeons, the gulfs of eternity, and holds my broken body in its awful clutches—now I am the miniature!

I always awake screaming, and, more recently, I have had... injuries. Burns. Scratches. [*Illegible*] I feel that I must be hurting myself in my sleep, but, even though I take precautions against unintentional self-mutilation, the injuries are becoming more serious...

SUSPECT THAT THE DREAM HAS SIGNIFICANCE; THAT IT means I am destined to find the ghastly relic again. Since that horrible day all those years ago, I have been obsessed: searching for, but unable to find, the mysterious antiquarian dealer's shoppe. I still look for it daily amidst the new and unknown alleyways and shuttered businesses littering the darkened ends of the port. Every face I encounter I study, looking for the old merchant, to no avail. The place and its owner seem to have vanished from the Earth.

[*Illegible*] I recall the [*illegible*] shoppe to be has in its stead a mapmaker's facility; they claim that the establishment I look for was there once—but more than a hundred years previous. I have moved away several times, trying to forget what I saw that fateful evening, but the strange pull of the place compels me back. There must be a reason for this; I hold it as a sign.

I have carried this with me for so long now, Dearest One. The dreams are becoming more intense, more frequent, more vivid... I sense that I am on the verge... I know that am at the cusp of some great insight, some stupefying revelation... I *must* get to the bottom of it before I draw my last breath, but the way things are proceeding, I am not confident that this will happen. [*Illegible*]

If I ever find the infernal object again, I know what I must do... and I will do it.[21]

Heaven help me, Dearest, I have[22]

---

[21] An ominous statement.

[22] The letter ends here, in the middle of the page; the only other marks on the page are a series of dark brown spatters.

FINAL THOUGHTS

HIS LETTER IS AN INTERESTING DOCUMENT: IT RAISES more questions than it answers.

My hope is that I will one day be able to sort out where the port is located, what happened to the author, perhaps even understand the strange information seemingly "encoded" in the note. The vagueness of the memo and the obscured identity of its author are puzzling, tantalizing. Colleagues have even suggested that it is some elaborate hoax, but the content and the delivery make me wonder. Besides, to what end? So that, one day years later, someone would try to sort out the conundrum after the involved parties are (one would presume) all deceased?

Buddhists have a saying: "When the student is ready, the Master will appear." Perhaps this is one of those times: I have a theory that the phenomenon of *déjà vu* (touched upon in the letter several times) is related to the process of dreaming.

It might be a way for the unconscious or the subconscious to process the reliving of events from multiple lifetimes, or of the same life lived multiple times. Another religious group, the Hindus, have long held that life is a cyclic, recurring event (reincarnation), and that there might even be different physical selves, but with the same soul (read: consciousness) over vast spans of time. Who is to say that there could not be the same consciousness relived repeatedly in the *same* physical self in some other, parallel universe?

Since finding this letter, my life has changed: I have had increasing incidents of lucid dreaming, and have even envisioned myself in the same terrible house that the writer describes so richly in the note. Lately, too, I have had bouts of amnesia: I find myself scribbling—unconsciously—in my notebooks, and always in a strange script, in alien characters; later, fully cognizant, I cannot decipher the cryptic symbols, the bizarre drawings I have scrawled.

Perhaps these notations are a key?

Only time will tell.

Appointed

CHET WILLIAMSON

Chet Williamson is the author of over twenty novels and a hundred short stories, which have appeared in the New Yorker, Playboy, Esquire, and many other magazines and anthologies. His fiction has been nominated for the MWA's Edgar Award, the World Fantasy Award, and the Bram Stoker Award, and his short story collection Figures in Rain (Ash-Tree Press, 2002) received the International Horror Guild Award. Many of his e-books and audiobooks are now available from Crossroad Press.

"CHRIST, HE LOOKS OLDER EVERY YEAR."

"He *is* older every year. So are we."

"Well, hell yeah, but you know what I mean. At least we try to stave it off. I don't think he even cares any more. Look at him."

Sybil Meadows took a good look and thought that what she saw was not only sad, it was what could be her own future, which was sadder still. It was shitty enough that here she was, in her early sixties, behind a table at HellCon 4, for Christ's sake, about to peddle her photos for twenty bucks each. What was shittier was that Glenda Garrison was right next to her.

Glenda was friendly enough, but she could be a bitch on wheels. Her claim to fame had been a series of B-movies she'd made in her twenties and thirties, before her boobs had drooped to where she couldn't do the nude scenes that had made her such wet dream bait for teenage boys. She'd lucked out with a supporting role as the hero's mom on one of Joss Whedon's series that had run for less than a year, but that was enough to let her make a decent living doing the con circuit.

Unlike Sybil, who was happy both to sell and to sign her eight-by-tens from her years in the British series, *Donna Darkness*, for twenty bucks each, Glenda was a gouger. She charged twenty for the photo and another twenty to sign it or whatever piece of memorabilia anybody dragged in. She sold issues of *Playboy* with her photo spread (and spread it was) for thirty dollars, and signed it right across her breasts on the first page, for an extra twenty, of course.

Wesley Cranford, whom Sybil now observed as he slowly and methodically set out his various photos and DVDs, marketed similarly to Sybil, selling both photo and signature for a reasonable sum. Of course he, like Sybil, had never made a career out of displaying himself naked, the way Glenda had. On the contrary, the fame of her fellow Briton, such as it was and as far as Sybil knew, was based on only one film, but one that had made an impression on several generations of horror fans.

In 1963, he had played a character named Robert Blake in a low budget version of H. P. Lovecraft's "The Haunter of the Dark." The film had done next to no business when it had opened, but over the years had become a cult favorite and had overshadowed Cranford's subsequent career, which had consisted primarily of poverty row leads, B-movie supporting roles, and TV one-off appearances. Sybil saw him at various cons on the blood 'n' gore circuit, and he had been at the three previous HellCons. Two years before, he had even hit on her, discreetly enough for her to pretend not to recognize his intentions, thus letting him down gently. Always a gentleman, he had never tried again.

What Glenda had said was true, though. There was something sad and slightly seedy about Wesley Cranford, a few hairs out of place, an area on his jawline that had escaped the ministrations of his razor, a grease spot on the carefully knotted necktie, the shoes scuffed beyond polishing. He appeared a poor man who dreamed himself rich, or at least carried himself so as to project the illusion of richness to others. He certainly seemed gentlemanly, though Sybil suspected that he drank more than he should.

As if sensing she was looking at him, he looked up from his table, smiled, and gave a small wave. She waved back, then turned her attention to straightening her stacks of photos for the coming mob.

ESLEY CRANFORD LOOKED DOWN AT THE VARIOUS images of his younger self staring back at him and thought that if Sybil Meadows had only known him thirty years ago, even twenty, she would surely have found him worthy of more than a quick wave. That man with the dark hair and full moustache who stared up so coolly from the studio portrait was the same person who now sat down with a sigh, easing himself into the plastic chair on which he would spend the next six hours, except for bathroom breaks and the frequent standing up for fans who wanted to have their pictures taken with "Robert Blake."

Cranford patted the left side of his spindly chest to assure himself that his small flask was still there, filled with the bracing single malt scotch that was his sole luxury. A nip or two when no one was looking would help to sustain him through the weekend ahead. He made himself remember that this was the *celebrity room* and he was a *celebrity*, no matter how depressed and foolish he felt.

It was whorish, he felt, to peddle images of himself and his signature when he should have been making his money by doing what he had done ever since he was seventeen— acting. None of these fans, who asked him the same questions over and over about *Haunter of the Dark*, ever asked about his Hotspur and Romeo with the RSC or his Henry V and Coriolanus for the Stratford Festival, about the times he had shared a stage with Olivier and Richardson and Gielgud. But it was no wonder. Whatever took place on the stage was fleeting, transient, while film...

Film went on forever, didn't it? Cranford pursed his lips as he looked at the piles of *Haunter* DVDs he was offering for sale: barebones single disc, two-disc special edition with the commentary track he had recorded six years earlier, and now the Blu-Ray, priced at fifteen dollars more. A nearly fifty-year-old film and people still bought them at his inflated prices, just to have him sign the paper inserts tucked into the plastic sleeves, and so that he could smile with their hand on his shoulder as the red lights of the little digital cameras blinked and blinked again and captured fan and star.

His reverie was interrupted by the opening of the main doors into the hotel ballroom and the swift entrance of the fans, most of them in black T-shirts with the blood-drenched logos of current horror movies emblazoned on the fronts. For a moment, flight seemed the most attractive option, but Cranford steeled himself. These people were nothing like him. They had completely different tastes and concerns, yet they were the ones upon whom his survival depended. Were they not to buy his wares, there would be no money for rent or food or single malt.

And now it was time to smile and look approachable and friendly. He felt no dislike for the fans. Truth to tell, he was appreciative of those who remembered his work in *Haunter* or any of his other, even more obscure films. What was discouraging were those cretins, most often dressed in the height of punk goth "fashion," and sometimes in horrific makeup and even costumes, who would ask, "So, who *are* you?"

It seemed an unnecessary question, since the standing placard on his table stated in large print Cranford's name, and beneath it: "'Robert Blake' in *HAUNTER OF THE DARK*, and star of many other films!" Still, Cranford was always polite and told them the otherwise readily available information, had they had the patience to read it.

The first hour of the con, however, was gratifying for Cranford. He actually had a line of sorts, not as long as Glenda Garrison's, which he knew would be fairly constant throughout the weekend, and nowhere near that of George Romero, on the other side of the large room. Still, there were two or three people always waiting that first hour, and Cranford smiled and evinced graciousness and gratitude and posed with his arm around their shoulders and collected the twenties as he signed the DVDs and photos.

At last there was a lull when no one was waiting for or talking to him, and he leaned back in his uncomfortable chair, took a quick look around, then had a surreptitious swig of the scotch, savoring the taste of it in his mouth before allowing it to trickle down his throat, smoothly shining its way into his stomach, where it nestled like a warm living creature. And it was as he was sitting there, feeling the scotch inside him, feeling relatively happy with the day to the point where he could forget that there would be hours ahead of sitting there unnoticed and unloved, that he noticed the person in the costume with the silken mask.

A costume in and of itself was nothing in this exhibitionistic crowd. There would be a costume contest Saturday evening, and many of those who would enter were already stalking the halls and ballrooms of the hotel. Some were the more traditional creatures of horror, such as Death with a skull face, cowl, and scythe, or zombies with gruesome makeup effects of chewed flesh and severed stumps of limbs. Others were more fantastical in nature. A tall and slender young Asian woman was costumed as some vampire/demon hybrid whose main purpose in her undead life seemed to be to show as much tanned flesh as possible. A pair of five-foot-long, brilliantly realized leathern wings extended from her exquisitely curved back, and she had held Cranford's attention for some time when she had walked past his table and chatted with several admirers.

But the attention he had given her was only perfunctory in comparison to that which he gave the person in the yellow mask. There was more to the costume than just a mask, of course. The masquer wore a long robe of pale yellow, nearly the same color as the mask, embroidered simply but richly with stitching of various shades of brown and tan. A red sash contrasted starkly with the gentler colors.

The hands, Cranford thought, had been skillfully made up. At first he assumed they were rubber gloves, like the large monster hands he had seen children wear at Halloween, but the naturalness of the fingers' movements told him there was more to it than that. They seemed hideously thin, like spiders' legs rather than fingers, and Cranford wondered if they were purely prosthetic, their motion operated by hands hidden inside the costume.

The feet were equally well constructed, broad appendages covered with a coarse, thick hair that looked as if it had come off a burly animal rather than being made from some rayon fake fur. The claws that thrust themselves from the mass of hair were the shade of old ivory and had an iridescent realism that even extended to blood vessels visible just beneath their surface. Only, Cranford observed, the blood was a sickly green in color. Nice touch.

But what set off the whole ensemble was the mask. It glowed with a faint luminescence, and the eyeholes were pure black—the result, Cranford assumed, of using sheer black material, possibly cut from women's hosiery. The true novelty was the shape of the imagined head beneath the mask. The many folds were draped in such a way as to give the suggestion of the head of a non-human entity beneath, with features that bulged where human features would have receded, and showed hollows where a normal face would have boasted a nose, a jaw, a forehead. It was, Cranford thought, quite hideous through suggestibility alone.

The hooded person walked slowly through the aisles, seemingly unjostled by the teeming fans, none of whom, Cranford was surprised to see, seemed to pay much if any attention to him. Perhaps, Cranford thought, the costume was too subtle for those whose tastes ran generally toward the gory.

The person continued to walk until he or she stood directly in front of Cranford's table, then turned toward him.

The misshapen head tilted down until whatever eyes were behind the black pits of darkness in the mask were looking at the seated Cranford. Cranford started to give an appreciative chuckle, but it caught in his throat. The friendly smile he had planned likewise departed before arrival. The eyes, or the absence of them, discomfited Cranford, especially when he realized the eyeholes were not on the same horizontal level. The one on the left was an inch below the other, and neither was in the place where one would expect the eyes to be.

Another clever conceit, he thought, intended to bring a further alien touch to the whole. He forced the original smile back onto his face and said, as jovially as he could, "Well, that's *quite* a costume!"

The person said nothing. Only the long spidery fingers twitched.

"Are you planning to enter the contest?" No reply. "You should, you know."

Still there was no response from the masked figure. Cranford made himself look away, out over the throng.

"A lot of excellent costumes here this year, really. Were you here last year?" Cranford didn't look back at the person. Instead he looked down at his tabletop and adjusted the position of some of the stacks of pictures and DVDs, neatly aligning them and aligning again, as though he were trying to find the perfect marketing feng shui. He kept his head tipped down so that he couldn't even see the figure of the standing person.

He was planning to say, *Well, I'm sure you'll want to see some of the makeup tables in the other room* when he looked back up again, but when he did the masked figure was gone. Cranford's gaze darted about the room, but the yellow-robed countenance was nowhere to be seen. Cranford was relieved, yet puzzled.

How could the man have gotten away so quickly and silently?

Practice, he wryly told himself. Yellow alien stealth ninjas must practice a great deal. Cranford shook off the feeling of unease and made himself grin, but took another large sip from the flask just the same and felt better as a result.

Six o'clock finally arrived, and Cranford tallied his take. It was nearly fourteen hundred dollars, which meant that he'd sold an average of a photo or a DVD every five minutes. Not bad. Saturday morning, with its new influx of fans, might be even better.

He pocketed his stash and thought about dinner. Sybil, God bless her, invited him to dine with her and Glenda Garrison. He could have done without Glenda, but he wanted the company, so they walked outside and crossed the plaza to the Italian restaurant in the suburban hotel complex where the convention was held.

The walk was cold, and he was glad he'd worn his coat. Overhead the sky was bright with stars, jutting out like pinpricks on black velvet. Inside, the food was acceptable (though the menu offered only a few Italian items) and the conversation could have been worse. Sybil was always lovely to be with, though Glenda's coarseness dismayed Cranford. Still, the shots of scotch he'd had that afternoon, another double in his room before dinner, and two glasses of Chianti with his meal loosened him up until he could chuckle at Glenda's crude jokes.

He did discover one thing he had never known before, and that was that Glenda had actually been in *Haunter of the Dark*, in the small role of the girl on the altar, the sacrifice that the villain was making to bring back the Old Ones. Cranford had never met her because her scenes were shot separately and then edited in.

"I was underage," Glenda recalled as she sipped her fourth glass of wine, "so my Mom hadda be there and there weren't any guys allowed except the director and the crew. I had as little on as they could get away with, but it was colder'n hell—we shot it outside—and my nips were stickin' up like crazy, and it was before the ratings system, so the director... who was it?"

"Tom Newton," Cranford said.

"Yeah, him... he put this gauzy stuff over the lens. You couldn't even tell who it was in the finished shot, so I don't put it in my whatsit, my *filmography*..." She slurred the word.

"Weren't you in the credits?" Sybil asked.

"Yeah, as Felicia Freeman. 'S before I decided on Glenda Garrison. One letter away, y'know? Eff-Eff, Gee-Gee? So anyway, nobody knows, and I'll jes' keep it that way."

They were finishing their coffee when Gary Busey, who had been to a number of cons Cranford had attended, noisily entered with several cronies and went directly to the bar, only a short distance from their table. "Well, ladies," Cranford said, throwing down enough cash to cover his meal and the entire tip, "I suggest we depart before the situation grows... *abuse*yive."

"I dunno," Glenda said, "I think he's still pretty hot."

"Glenda dear," Sybil sighed, "you think Paul Lynde is hot. And he's dead *and* gay."

Nevertheless, Glenda remained behind to chat up Busey, while Sybil and Cranford left the restaurant. Back at the hotel, Cranford suggested that Sybil might want to join him for a nightcap in the hotel bar, but she smiled sweetly, he thought, and pleaded tiredness.

"It's a longer day tomorrow," she said, "and I'm not in my... *twenties* anymore."

He smiled. "I suppose you're right. Nor I. Well, goodnight. Maybe breakfast tomorrow?"

"Lovely. Around nine? I'll knock on your door when I'm ready."

Her tone was friendly, nothing more, but Cranford's step was a bit lighter as he walked down the hall toward his minisuite. Once inside, he threw off his coat, jacket, and tie, put the cash he'd made that day into the room safe, and poured himself a libation of single malt. Then, drink in hand, he sat down in the easy chair, put his feet on the hassock, and looked around the spacious room.

The hotel was one of the Wyndham chain, a new, modern building that appeared as a giant curved slab when viewed from the outside. Now, for the first time, Cranford was surprised to see that the interior of his room was curved as well. The wall with windows had a definite arc to it, and for some reason it seemed a bit disorienting.

Maybe it was just the scotch, he thought, as he looked away from the wall and sought the TV remote. He flicked it on, found the on-screen directory, and saw that Turner Classic Movies, his favorite, was available.

And there, miracle of miracles, coincidence of coincidences, was *Haunter of the Dark*, in gorgeous murky black and white. And there was Wesley Cranford in his early thirties, the moustache as dark as the tuft of chest hair that protruded from the V of "Robert Blake's" opened shirtfront. Those days were gone all right. Hairless chests for men were *de rigueur*, and what they called *manscaping* was the norm. Thank God he'd missed *that*. He turned off the room lights, took another sip, and raised the volume so his ears could catch the dialogue.

"...seemed to be alien geometries, not of this world," Blake was telling his friend Howard Carter, who had been written into the script as a bow to Howard Lovecraft, the story's creator, to provide a human villain, and to avoid Blake's having to convey most of the exposition in monologues. "Curved lines where straight lines should be, curving up into a hideous darkness, Howard! And down again into a primordial slime..."

The camera moved slowly in as Blake continued his story, and Cranford remembered having to project in words alone what the special effects of 1963 could not—and could not *afford*—to show. The film had been made on a minuscule budget, the producer/director Tom Newton refusing to even pay rights to the publisher who claimed to own the original story. "Public domain!" Newton had insisted. "I did my homework! Public domain!"

After the film was in the can, the publisher had threatened to take Newton to court, so Newton had made a token payment "just to shut 'em up," as he told Cranford at the time. When it came to promotion, Newton had made William Castle look like a piker, and they had pushed the hell out of the movie, but to no avail. It barely made back the original pitifully small investment in its first two years, but started showing up on television in the '70s, and as H. P. Lovecraft grew more and more popular, *Haunter* grew its own healthy fan base. With the advent of VHS tape and then DVD technology, the film had made a small fortune, not for Newton, who had died of a stroke in 1978, but instead for the studio to which he had sold it lock, stock, and barrel years before his death.

Wesley Cranford didn't own the slightest piece of the film that had brought him what little fame he had, so he had to profit from it the best he could, in an associational manner, buying copies in bulk and getting a small discount, then selling them signed for more than retail price at the cons. It was a living.

He tried to forget the business angle and let himself become involved in what was taking place on the TV screen. Blake was talking to the frightened Italian girl now, asking her about the deserted church and the dead bodies that were found on its grounds over the years. Italian, my ass, Cranford thought. She was Jewish, her name was Sheila Feldstein (not Amanda Paris, as it read in the credits), and she had almost become the second Mrs. Cranford, had he not caught her behind a set fellating a key grip the last day of the shoot.

Cranford became lost for a moment in erotic memories

of the woman, but popped back into the story when he saw himself opening the box with what had been called the Shining Trapezohedron in the story and original screenplay, but which Newton had changed. "A trapawhozis?" he had asked the screenwriter. "Nobody knows what the hell that is—call it the Sorcerer's Stone, f'crissake…"

"It's simple, Robert…" he heard Kelvin French, who had played Howard, say. "When the stars are right, at certain places on the earth, the gate can be opened by certain sounds, timbres of certain voices crying out the words that will call the Old Ones. I have tried, but in vain. It may be *you* they want… you they need. *You* may be the appointed one! Take the stone…"

Then came the scene of Howard teaching him the chant, one he hadn't forgotten, even after all those years. It was a mishmash of words from different Lovecraft stories, the same kind of mashup the screenplay had been, and he and Kelvin French had memorized it together during drinking bouts and repeated it jokingly for years afterward whenever they ran into each other. The whole thing went:

Iä-R'lyeh! Cthulhu fhtagn! Iä! Iä! Shub-Niggurath! Tekeli-li! Ngah'ng ai'y Zhro! Yog-Sothoth! Iä! Iä!

Cranston closed his eyes and repeated it back to himself perfectly. Damn, he still had it. Still sharp as a tack. If only his face and body were what they used to be…

He thought some more about Sybil, watching with only half an eye the boring scene with the police talking about the kidnapped girl. He perked up at the scene that followed, with a pubescent Glenda Garrison seemingly clothed only in strips of cloth on the altar, but try as he might, he could neither recognize her face nor detect a trace of erect nipple. He chuckled as he heard Kelvin chant the old words, and just as the darkness rose to engulf the horrified Howard Carter, betrayed by those he sought to free and worship, there was a knock on the door.

It startled Cranford, as he expected no visitors. He considered ignoring it and continuing to watch the film, since his big scene was coming up, the one where Robert Blake is tempted with eternal life if he takes Howard Carter's place and uses the Sorcerer's Stone to open the gate for the Old Ones.

But the knock came again, a single but inexorable rap, and the unlikely but appealing idea crossed Cranford's mind that it might be Sybil, looking for company, a drink, or even, dare he imagine, more. He set down his scotch, pushed himself erect, and walked slowly to the door, the large-screen television providing enough light for him to easily make his way.

When Cranford put his eye to the peephole, he felt his heart give a slight hop, for there, on the other side of the door, he saw Sybil Meadows, smiling and giving the same little wave she had given him when she'd seen him earlier that day, as though she knew he was watching her. He threw back the security latch and opened the door.

It was not Sybil Meadows who faced him in the hall, but the person with the yellow mask, still in costume, hands at its side, spider fingers twitching ever so lightly. The dark eyes seemed to observe Cranford, and for a second he felt as though he had fallen into those offset pools of ebony, that his head had been strapped to a board, his skullcap removed, and that his every thought and dream and fear was visible to the creature that now stood before him.

Then he shook himself both outside and in, and took a deep breath. This was absurd, ridiculous, and downright *rude*. How had this man, if man he was, gotten his room number in the first place? Was he with the convention? Whoever he was, he had no right to come knocking on Cranford's door at night.

"Now look," Cranford said, and his voice sounded small to him, as though the cloth-draped figure sucked in the words as they were spoken. "That's quite a splendid costume, as I said earlier today, but I've no time to play dress-up and go boo, all right? I don't know how on earth you got my…"

Cranford's words trailed away as the misshapen head of the creature (for such he had come to think of it) *shifted* beneath the mask, the protuberances and hollows ebbing and flowing as though a hand was randomly squeezing a rubber bag filled with rocks and gel. Cranford backed away into his room, and the creature followed. It did not occur to him to try to slam the door against it. He had the feeling that would do no good.

"The darkness has come. It is time…"

At first Cranford thought the echoing voice came from the creature that followed him, the door closing behind it in spite of the fact that he hadn't seen either of the spidery hands push it shut. No, the voice was coming from the TV, where Robert Blake was standing on a studio precipice, looking at a huge black screen on which was being projected swirling planets and stars.

"You are the appointed one. Speak the words," the voice commanded. "Bring back the Old Ones…"

The voice itself was that of Richard Shepherd, a voiceover specialist whose deep baritone had sold everything from used cars to feminine hygiene products in the '50s and '60s. Cranford recalled Tom Newton saying he had paid him fifty bucks to come in and record the three minutes of dialogue, as if that had been munificent beyond belief.

All those details flooded back into Cranford's mind, as if in an attempt to keep him from coming to the obvious conclusion that this was no horror fan following him into his room, but something else, something not even human.

"The stars are right… and this is one of the places on this world where, if the words are said by the appointed one, chaos will be unleashed. You are the one! Behold the stars in the darkness of night!"

The right arm of the thing in the mask slowly rose, and behind him Cranford heard the ratcheting sound of the curtains being drawn open. The creature made an imperious gesture just as Richard Shepherd's echo saturated voice ordered, "*Behold*, I say!"

Cranford turned, unable to resist, and through the wide curved window he saw not a parking lot where bright lights shone down on parked cars, but a cosmic vista of Kubrickian proportions, in which suns, stars, planets seemed bound together by a feathery chain of stardust, wan and sickly tendrils of green-gold light. Then he heard his own voice, decades younger…

"No! No, I *won't!*"

And again, Shepherd saying, "You must! And look at what you gain!"

But instead of the shoddily filmed insert of Robert Blake wearing a cheap crown and sitting on a throne with plastic planet models orbiting him on strings, Cranford saw the wisps of star stuff transform into a bas-relief of his own face, only young again, young and handsome, his flesh firm and clear, with not a trace of the broken veins that decades of drink had caused.

Wesley Cranford young. Young, oh young…

"*Speak the words!*"

Cranford heard them inside his head and knew he could recite them easily. What would be the harm? This wasn't real, was it? It had to be a dream, just a foolish dream, the result of exhaustion and too much to drink and seeing a boy in a silly costume. He began to speak…

"*Iä-R'lyeh… Cthulhu fhtagn…*"

And when he finished, perhaps the logic of the dream would make him young…

"*Iä, Iä… Shub-Niggurath…*"

And in his dream, maybe Sybil would come to him…

"*Tekeli-li… Ngah'ng ai'y Zhro…*"

And maybe then, maybe…

"*Yog-Sothoth… Iä, Iä…*"

The chant was finished. Cranford could feel his heart pounding in his chest, beating harder and faster than ever before. The cosmic landscape through his window blurred, softened, faded until he saw lights, cars, trees beyond the parking lot, and he wondered, was the dream over?

Then he felt the thin, wiry fingers of the creature in the mask close upon his shoulder, gently, lovingly, and the tempo of his heart quickened until muscle and bone could no longer contain it.

YBIL MEADOWS FINISHED ARRANGING HER PHOTOS and looked around the room. It was dismal. There were fewer than half the number of tables set up this year than there had been for HellCon 4. She supposed she should have been surprised that there were that many.

What with the new wars in Iraq and Pakistan causing the reinstatement of the draft for everyone under thirty-five, the devastatingly fatal Muslim flu pandemic, the Dow falling below 2000, and the new government dedicating all its dwindling resources to impeachment and internal prosecutions, horror didn't have much of an appeal anymore. Still, there were those diehards who had *some* discretionary income left, though Sybil had dropped her price for photos to fifteen dollars this year and planned to go to ten, depending on the response.

She half smiled, half grimaced as she saw Glenda Garrison enter the ballroom, dragging her luggage cart filled with cases of photos, DVDs, and *Playboys* behind her. No gofers for HellCon 5. "Hey, honey!" Glenda called as she came up to the table next to Sybil's. "Partners again, huh?"

Sybil nodded. "A bit different atmosphere from last year, though."

"You got that right. It's like somebody opened up a can of whupass on the world. Jesus, honey, it's *insane* out there. But how you doin'? God, I haven't seen you since you blew outta here early last year. You were the one who, uh...?"

"Yes. I found him."

"So like what happened? I mean..."

"It was Saturday morning. I was supposed to get him for breakfast. He didn't answer, but his door was ajar, so I went in, and... there he was."

"Heart attack, huh?"

"Yes. I don't think he had any pain. He looked very much at peace."

"Aw..." Glenda looked over at the ballroom door through which the few actors and writers were slowly trickling. "Ohmigod, not to change the subject, but there he *is*."

"Who?" Sybil asked, seeing a young man with three people around him, carrying what she assumed to be cases of his items for sale. The man seemed to be in his mid-twenties and was extremely handsome and stylishly dressed. A black moustache accented his perfectly straight, blindingly white teeth. Sybil recognized him then. "Blake Dexter," she said.

"Uh-*huh*," Glenda murmured. "God, is he hot. And *huge*. Kid comes out of nowhere—complete unknown—and gets a role in the biggest horror movie in years? Like a fairytale." She gave a twisted little smile. "Wonder if the prince has a princess yet..."

As if he'd heard her, Blake Dexter stopped talking to his entourage and looked in their direction. He smiled and gave a short wave.

Glenda grinned broadly and waved back. "Didya see that?" she said to Sybil. "He *waved* at me!" But Sybil wasn't sure which of them the young man had waved at. It didn't really matter. They were both far too old for him.

But as she looked at him more closely, she wondered. His

skin and body were young, but even from a distance his eyes were old, as though he harbored a guilty sadness with which he was unable to cope.

"I'm going up to my room, freshen up a little," Glenda said, still eyeing Blake Dexter across the large room. "Never know when you might meet somebody, right? Hey, what room you in?"

"324," Sybil said. "You?"

"349," Glenda replied. Sybil flinched, just a little. "What?" Glenda asked.

"Nothing." There was no point in telling her that 349 had been Wesley Cranford's suite the previous year.

While Glenda was gone, Blake Dexter looked over toward Sybil several times, but never came closer. At last Glenda returned, her lipstick redder, eye liner blacker, makeup base thicker. Even so, she looked shaken, almost pallid. "You okay?" Sybil asked her.

"Fine. Just ran into one of those costume creeps. Made my skin crawl."

"Another zombie?"

"Nah, just a newbie in a yellow hood—never saw him before. Couldn't see his eyes, but he was acting like he wanted to… oh I dunno, just creeped me out a little…" Glenda stopped talking, opened her cases, and started lining up her goodies on her table.

Sybil could hear the crowd of fans chattering outside the ballroom door now. Though smaller in number than the year before, they sounded excited and enthusiastic. One of the volunteers opened the door partway to let the mob get a look inside before allowing them to enter.

Sybil glanced at her watch. One minute till opening. She sat behind her table, took several deep breaths, and waited for the door to open wider and the chaos to be unleashed.

ABOUT THE EDITOR

S. T. Joshi is the author of *The Weird Tale* (University of Texas Press, 1990), *The Modern Weird Tale* (McFarland, 2001), *Unutterable Horror: A History of Supernatural Fiction* (PS Publishing, 2012), and other critical and biographical studies. His award-winning biography, *H. P. Lovecraft: A Life* (Necronomicon Press, 1996), has been expanded and updated as *I Am Providence: The Life and Times of H. P. Lovecraft* (Hippocampus Press, 2010). He has edited Lovecraft's stories, essays, letters, and revisions, as well as works by Ambrose Bierce, Arthur Machen, Lord Dunsany, Algernon Blackwood, and other writers.